"Sylvana was dancing for you," Della said softly. She had to know what he was thinking. "Aren't you tempted even a little bit?"

"Hell, no. Sylvana can pick your pocket so skillfully you won't even know it. And you wouldn't believe how many valuables she can hide in the folds of her skirt. She wouldn't be a good choice for a lawman, now would she?" He smiled. "And you're wrong about who she danced for. Any man fool enough to go off with Sylvana is likely to get Raul's knife in his back. That's what the dance was about. Making Raul jealous."

And me, Della thought, startled by the strong possessiveness she felt for him. She hadn't realized it.

They had moved close to see each other in the dim glow of the fire's embers, close enough that Della smelled the soap he favored, and woodsmoke and the scent of gypsy wine. She swayed lightly on her feet. "I still hear the music." Wild and sweet and seductive. "It curls through the blood . . ."

He ran his fingertips down her cheek and a shudder of pleasure raced through her body. She could have stepped away—she should have. But she gazed up at him, and her breath quickened.

Cameron's eyes held hers, then his arms went around her, pulling her into his body. It wasn't too late to step away, to pretend there had been a misunderstanding, no harm done. But the blood tingled in Della's veins and she pressed against him, feeling his arousal, hearing her reaction in a soft gasp that lifted her breasts.

Also by Maggie Osborne

I DO, I DO, I DO
SILVER LINING
THE BRIDE OF WILLOW CREEK

PRAIRIE MOON

MAGGIE OSBORNE

IVY BOOKS • NEW YORK

An Ivy Book
Published by The Ballantine Publishing Group
Copyright © 2002 by Maggie Osborne

www.ballantinebooks.com

ISBN 0-8041-1990-2

Manufactured in the United States of America

First Edition: November 2002

OPM   10 9 8 7 6 5 4 3 2 1

To Zane and Stephanie,
with all my love

Chapter 1

Della didn't recognize the stranger riding through the twilight toward her house, but she understood who he was by a sharp, intuitive tingling across her scalp. She had been expecting this man, or someone like him, for ten years. Finally he'd come. Standing slowly, she stepped away from her porch chair, then smoothed down her apron and waited as she'd been waiting for so long.

The man rode like a soldier, tall and straight in the saddle, alert to his surroundings, tension bunched along his shoulders and tightening the slope of his sun-darkened jaw. The war hadn't ended for men like this one.

Long before he reached the porch, Della felt his swift assessment of her, her small house, and the deteriorating outbuildings. She would have bet the earth that hard won experience told him what a soldier would need to know. How many cows and chickens she owned, the number of rooms in her house, where a person could hide on her property. By now he'd be reasonably confident that she was alone and posed no danger. As if to confirm her conclusions, he reined in front of the porch steps and flexed his arms, relaxing the tight squared line of his shoulders.

"Mrs. Ward?"

A low voice with no particular accent. Neutral. Not warm or cold. He was a stranger with a rifle and pommel holsters riding up to a woman alone, yet he made no effort to put her at ease by smiling or immediately announcing his name and business.

"I've been waiting for you," she said, knowing in her bones why he was there, watching as he swung to the ground and tipped his hat. He was as tall as she'd guessed, dark haired, and wearing a gun belt beneath his duster. Despite the weapons on his horse and at his waist, he didn't frighten her. She doubted anything could frighten her anymore.

"I've come about your husband."

"Yes."

Immediately after the war, she would have burst into tears and run down the steps, begging for whatever information he could give. But now she'd lived with guilt and regret and hopelessness for so long that she wasn't sure if she still wanted to know what this man had come to tell her. She did, and she didn't.

"Who are you?"

"The name's Cameron," he said, halting at the foot of the porch steps.

Della swallowed back an odd, shivery thrill that lay somewhere between alarm and attraction. The attraction was easy to explain. Cameron was a handsome, commanding figure of a man. She also understood the frisson of alarm curling like smoke in her stomach. This man didn't give a damn about anything or anyone, she saw that in his cool eyes. Such men were dangerous, possessed of a capability for violence and ruthlessness that showed in the way they moved and carried themselves. Della guessed that other men would take care what they said to Mr. Cameron, and how they said it. Certain women would be irresistibly challenged by the hard indifference flattening his gaze.

Suddenly conscious of her frizzy unkempt hair and her faded dress and soiled apron, Della nodded once, then gestured toward the door. "I have coffee in the house."

"Thank you."

Inside, she passed him on the way to the stove. He'd stopped to look around. There wasn't much to see; one fair-sized room that served as kitchen, parlor, laundry room, sewing room, whatever was needed. Her bedroom opened off the back, and above was a loft area that she used for storage. Once he had the layout in mind, he removed his hat and duster and placed them on the floor next to his chair. But he didn't ask if she'd rather he removed his gun belt as most men would have.

"I made a raisin pie. Fresh baked this morning," she offered, reaching for cups on the shelf above the stove.

"No, thank you."

"I guess you had supper in town."

Disappointment twitched the corner of her mouth. Company didn't come her way very often, and she didn't want him to leave immediately. Also, she wanted to delay his news by plying him with food and small talk. That was dumb. Mr. Cameron impressed her as a man who engaged in small talk about as often as she did. She placed a coffee cup before him and took the facing chair, surprised to discover him studying her as if he knew her, like he was looking for changes since he'd seen her last.

"Have we met?" Or was he just a rude bastard? She

remembered Clarence's friends as possessing refined manners. But the war changed people. Look at her. She didn't put much stock in manners anymore, either.

"I came through here years ago. You were working at the Silver Garter."

She almost dropped her coffee cup. "Wait." Yes, there was something familiar about him. But why on earth would she remember this man out of the hundreds who had passed through the Garter? But something about him ... And then she remembered. "It was cold that night. You stood beside the stove. You said, 'I didn't expect to find someone like you working in a saloon.' "

"And you said, 'You don't know me, so don't judge me.' "

How odd that both of them remembered so brief an exchange. Heat flooded Della's cheeks and she turned her face toward the window above the sink. She hated to be reminded of that year, hated that she was face-to-face with someone who had seen her wearing a skimpy costume and a feather in her hair.

Holding his long-ago image in her mind, she slid a look across the table. He'd filled out, and deeper lines etched his forehead and the corners of his eyes. He was more of a presence now, harder, edgier. In place of the fire and fury she'd seen in him all those years ago, she now saw a weariness that extended beyond a need for rest. The shivery mix of attraction and warning swirled in her throat, then settled in the pit of her stomach.

"Wait a minute." Comprehension came suddenly, followed by anger. She gripped the edge of the table. "You came here years ago looking for me, didn't you?" Cameron didn't answer and his expression didn't change. "So why didn't you tell me about Clarence back then?"

"I should have." He blew on his coffee before he tasted it.

Clarence would have given a dozen reasons, would have talked for twenty minutes to reach the same statement. And it wasn't acceptable. Pushing to her feet, she went to the window and stared outside, waiting for the storm in her chest to subside.

This was the wettest July that North Texas had enjoyed in years. Consequently, the prairie and low hills were green and thick with grass. On a hot evening like this, Della might have braved the mosquitos and walked down to the cottonwoods and dangled bare feet in the creek. Or maybe she would have donned the shapeless man's hat she wore and weeded her kitchen garden until it got too dark to see. Maybe she would have considered the heavy clouds blotting the sunset and stayed inside.

"Yes, you should have," she said finally. Anger was a waste of energy. He was here now and that's what mattered. "I always knew there had to be more than the letter Clarence's father received," she said in a quieter tone. "Something more than an official notification. There had to be a message for me."

The shadow of the barn stretched toward the house, reaching for the road. Not once had she imagined that news about Clarence would come in the evening. She had always pictured a messenger arriving in the morning. And she'd pictured him wearing a dress uniform, a foolish notion considering how long ago the war had ended.

Turning from the window, she returned to the table. "I'm sorry." Della wasn't sure if she'd snapped at him, but she'd wanted to. "I just wish you'd told me about Clarence when you were here before." He kept his gaze fixed on the front door. If his jaw hadn't tightened, she could have believed that he wasn't listening. The subject was closed. Drawing a breath, she pushed aside her irritation and stepped into a conversation she had imagined a hundred times. "Did you know my husband well, Mr. Cameron?"

"I was with him when he died."

"And Clarence gave you a message for me?"

Reaching into his jacket, he withdrew a packet carefully wrapped in oilcloth. It occurred to her that he had carried whatever was inside for almost ten years. She didn't know what to make of that. In a way it was touching, endearing even. But it was also puzzling, frustrating, and she felt a fresh burst of anger. He'd had no right to withhold this information. Swinging between resentment and dread, she watched him open the oilcloth and slide the thin packet across the table.

Her mouth went dry and she pressed her hands together. "It's a letter. From Clarence?" She sounded like an idiot. Of course the letter was from Clarence.

"Mrs. Ward? I'll just step outside."

"What?" Blinking, she raised her head, abruptly aware that she hadn't moved or spoken for several minutes. "No. That's not necessary." Mr. Cameron would have read the letter, of course. It wasn't in an envelope, wasn't sealed.

"If the stain is what's upsetting you, it is blood, but it's mine, not your husband's."

She'd been looking at a stain on the exposed portion of the letter, but the significance hadn't penetrated. Dropping her hands, she pushed back into her chair. She had imagined a verbal message. Never had she considered that Clarence might have had time to respond to her last terrible letter.

"Are you a drinking man, Mr. Cameron?"

"On occasion."

"This is an occasion."

Until the year she'd worked in the saloon, Della wouldn't have dreamed of pouring herself a glass of whisky. Ladies sipped mild sherry or perhaps a glass of rum punch.

"This isn't good whisky," she said, taking the bottle from under the sink. "It's cheap. But it does what whisky is supposed to do." She poured two fingers of liquor into thick glasses and slid one across the table.

She glanced at Cameron, then looked at the folds of oilcloth. "The last thing I said to him was 'I hate you.'" The whisky burned like raw flame against the back of her throat.

In ten years, not a day had passed that she didn't plead with God to turn back the clock and let her write a different letter. At least let her erase that final terrible line. But time didn't flow backward. Clarence had died believing that she hated him. Maybe if Clarence had believed she loved him, maybe he would have fought harder to survive.

Mr. Cameron didn't recoil in disgust as she'd half expected, and he didn't ask the question she deserved. So Della asked it for him. "What kind of woman would send her soldier husband a letter that ended with 'I hate you'?"

Standing, she gripped the whisky glass in both hands and returned to the window, keeping her back to the man at her table. By the time she spoke again, she'd forgotten him entirely.

"I was seventeen and pregnant, and I'd just received word that Mama had died. The slaves had run off weeks earlier, and Mrs. Ward and I were trying to keep the house up. What a joke that was. Neither of us knew how to do much of anything." The whisky flamed in her stomach. "Everyone said the Yankees were coming, burning everything in their path. But we couldn't leave because Mr. Ward was ill and Mrs. Ward was slowly losing her mind."

The years fell away and she was there again. Terrified and helpless. Listening to the boom of artillery in the distance. Smelling the slop bucket in Mr. Ward's sickroom, watching Clarence's mother scratch her arms and cry. There was no one to assist with the birthing, and her time was near. No one to turn to, no one to tell her what to do.

"I just wanted my husband to come home." Clarence would rescue her. Clarence would make the world right again. "I needed him to come home. Everyone knew the damned war was lost. There was no reason for Clarence to go on fighting, to continue putting his life at risk. There was no reason! We needed him at home."

Right now it seemed impossible that she'd ever been so young, or so helpless and completely overwhelmed. So pregnant and far from home and living with people who couldn't forgive her for being a Northerner. And every minute was overlaid by the nightmarish fear of Clarence being captured by the Yankees, or wounded, or coming home in pieces.

"I just wanted him to come home," she whispered.

"And for one hour of one dismal, hopeless day, I hated him for putting his obligation to the Confederacy above his obligation to me." Her hands curled around the whisky glass. "I prayed that Clarence didn't receive that letter. But of course he did."

Weeks after Clarence's death, she'd encountered Colonel George. Believing he offered comfort, he'd assured her that he had placed her letter in Clarence's hands.

When she turned from the window, the room had grown dark, and it startled her to see that Cameron was still there. He sat tilted back in his chair, one hand on his glass, watching her.

"I would give the rest of my life not to have written that last letter." Stiff with bitterness, she lit a candle stub near the pump handle, then lit the lamp on the table before she sat down. "You were there," she said finally, glancing at him, then touching the edge of the oilcloth packet with her fingertip. "What would you have said to your wife if she'd written that she hated you?"

"I've never had a wife."

"You have an imagination, don't you?" Anger flashed in her breast like a grease fire, hot and crackling. At the back of her mind she remembered the old adage about not shooting the messenger, but she didn't care. "Imagine you're in the thick of a war that's already lost, getting shot at and bombed for reasons you can't adequately explain. But it's your goddamned duty and you're doing it. You can imagine that, can't you? Wasn't that what it was like?" Cameron stared back at her. "Then here comes a self-pitying letter from your wife, doing her best to shame you or worry you into deserting, and the letter ends with 'I hate you.' She knows you could die, knows those could be the last words you'll ever hear from her. But she writes them anyway. Are you so dull witted, Mr. Cameron, that you can't imagine how you'd feel or how you'd respond?"

Holding his gaze on hers, Cameron stood and put on his hat, dropped the duster over his arm. "The answer you're looking for is there," he said, nodding toward the packet. "Or maybe it isn't. I'm going to water my horse. I'll check back before I leave."

The screen door banged softly behind him.

Della dropped her head in her hands. He'd come from God-knew-where to deliver a packet he could have mailed. He might be ten years late, but he had paid her the courtesy and respect of a personal call. Moreover, Cameron had been her husband's friend and had been with Clarence when Clarence died. Despite all that, she wanted to scream and pound him into bloody bits because—because he was here. That's all. Wearily, she pushed up from the table and carried a lantern to the porch.

"Mr. Cameron?" He stood beside his horse in the shadows, just beyond the reach of the light. "I apologize. I know it doesn't sound like it, but I'm grateful that you brought Clarence's letter." She chewed her lip, thinking about hospitality and how her manners had deteriorated and how Clarence would have expected her to treat his friend. "If you want, you can put your horse in the corral." The scent of rain lay heavy on the night air, and fast moving clouds blotted the stars to the northwest. "You could sleep in the barn if you don't want to risk a wet ride back to town." He'd probably still get wet. The barn roof was more like a sieve than a lid.

She waited, then added, "I'll give you breakfast." When he still didn't respond, she bit her tongue then appealed to whatever had brought him here. "There are questions I'd like to ask, but I can't do it now. I'm too wrought up. It would mean a lot if you'd stay until morning and give me a chance to settle my thoughts before we talk again."

Finally his voice floated out of the darkness. "I'd be obliged for the use of your barn." A creak of leather told her he'd swung into his saddle. For a long moment nothing more happened, sharpening her awareness that he could see her standing on the porch in the light, but the shadows concealed him.

"Shall I fetch you some soap?" she asked.

"I have my own. Good night, Mrs. Ward."

"There's a lamp hanging next to the side door," she added as she heard the horse moving toward the corner of the house. Cameron didn't answer.

Clarence's friends had been men of aristocratic breeding and background, and Mr. Cameron would be no different. By virtue of his friendship with Clarence, Della could confidently make definite assumptions.

Mr. Cameron would be well educated, had probably attended a Northern or European university. He would read voraciously and enjoy a spirited debate. He would have grown up in privileged circumstances and, before the war, mothers of marriageable daughters undoubtedly viewed him as a man with brilliant prospects.

The war had changed Mr. Cameron.

That thought led her to wonder if Clarence would have dramatically changed had he survived the conflict.

Would he have turned inward and become distant? Frowning, she peered toward the barn. Would Clarence have come home so damaged that she no longer knew him? That was as hard to imagine as it was to conceive of Mr. Cameron once being a laughing, carefree young man who liked to dance and race fast horses and sing in the moonlight.

Della blew out the lantern, but she didn't immediately go inside. Instead she strained to hear any sounds coming from the barn. Who was this man? Why did he carry a small arsenal of firearms? What had happened to him during the war, and where had he been in the years since? These were questions she knew she wouldn't ask. She wasn't sure that she'd even ask the questions that did concern her.

Listening to the rain songs of crickets and frogs, she closed her eyes and rubbed her fingertips across her forehead. She could stand in the darkness until the storm came, chewing on questions about a man she would never see again after tomorrow morning. Or she could go inside and face the past.

Tilting her head, she looked south at the few stars not yet smothered by clouds. Hope was a feeling she'd stamped out years ago, so at first she didn't recognize the tightness in her throat.

Maybe Clarence had understood about her letter. Maybe he'd known she was terrified and exhausted and feeling alone. Maybe he'd forgiven her rash, thoughtless, hateful words. Absolution could be in his letter.

Hope was such a terrible thing. A tease, a seduction, a trap.

After taking a deep breath, she gathered her courage

and straightened her shoulders. Then she marched inside and slowly slipped his letter out of the oilcloth.

Della,

Not Dearest, not Darling Delly, not Mine Own. Just her name, stark and bare. Angry. Impatient.

What would you have me do? Turn coward and desert the cause and my comrades? Is that how you see me, Della, as a man without honor or sense of duty?

Surely he knew that wasn't true. She'd always seen him as brave and honorable, a man of integrity.

I know you need me and my parents need me. How can you suggest that I don't care what's happening at home? I think of you all every day. I worry about the crops dying in the fields, about the house crumbling or being burned. I worry that Daddy will die or be disabled, or that Mama will injure herself trying to accomplish tasks she has no training or skills to attempt. I worry about so much responsibility falling on your shoulders, and if you can make the decisions that you must make. I worry about your health and well-being. With all my heart, I wish I could be with you when your time comes.

But, Della, I cannot. I don't know what I can say to make you understand. Even if I could do as you demand and go home, I couldn't fix the things that overwhelm you. I'd fail as apparently I have failed you in so many ways.

*You're angry. Marriage isn't what you hoped and
dreamed it would be. But, Della, you knew I was serving the Confederacy when you married me. You knew
we were in the midst of war. And you agreed when we
decided you would go to my parents during your preg-
nancy. It pains me deeply that your love has turned to
hate. My heart aches with*

The letter ended mid sentence, the final words smeared
by blood. After sitting very still, she swallowed the last
of the whisky and let the flames burn away any linger-
ing hope.

Clarence had died believing that she hated him and regretted their marriage. He died believing he had failed
her and his parents. She had done that to him. She didn't
deserve forgiveness.

After wiping the backs of her hands across her eyes,
she started to replace Clarence's letter within the folds of
the oilcloth, but stopped when she realized there were
two more items. With a sinking heart, she recognized her
last letter and a duplicate of their wedding photograph.

She didn't need to read her letter. Every hateful word
was engraved on her heart. Pushing the pages aside, she
rubbed her palms on her sleeves, then lifted the wedding
photograph toward the lamp.

Clarence stood tall and broad shouldered, solemn
and handsome. He wore his dress uniform, every detail
tailored to perfection. One gloved hand held his hat next
to his chest, the other hand rested on Della's shoulder.
She sat in front of him, her gown artfully arranged to
display a waterfall of lace and ribbons. Now, why wasn't
she wearing gloves? There must have been a reason that

she had removed her gloves, but she could no longer recall.

The lamplight and the sepia tint of the photograph made her look so young, so impossibly, innocently, heartachingly young. How old had she been on her wedding day? Barely sixteen. Young enough to gaze at the camera with a confident half-smile, sublimely certain that her happiness would endure forever and could withstand any test. There was not a smidgeon of reality in her shining eyes.

But Clarence stared gravely into the lens. Della remembered teasing him about looking funereal instead of festive. Now she realized he'd known the road ahead would be difficult. Their wartime marriage would not be the pleasant, romantic fantasy that Della had envisioned.

What a fool she had been.

She had imagined scenes of welcoming Clarence home on leave with dozens of kisses before she led him into a parlor filled with gaily gowned ladies and dashing officers in immaculate uniforms. Or she'd seen herself traveling in a racing coach to meet him at some point near his regiment for a hurried but romantic rendezvous. During those rare moments when she chided herself for being too idealistic, she had envisioned herself sitting in a circle of brave young wives, sewing bandages, valiantly aiding the war effort.

A week after the photograph was taken, Clarence had returned to his regiment. She had seen him three times during the following year. There were no rendezvous, no gay parties. One by one, her pretty fantasies died and sank beneath the reality of duty and fear and the deprivation and devastation of war.

Della stared at the fading photograph for several minutes. Lord, what was this? Tears? She hadn't wept in years and years. But she put her head on the table and cried for the solemn young man and the happy young girl who were gone forever.

Chapter 2

Della awoke gasping, her chest tight and her face wet with tears. Usually the dream stayed with her all day, an echo of slumbering grief and pain. Dreading the oppressive hours ahead, she wished she could remain curled in bed, but the animals needed to be fed, her garden tended, the ironing finished. Some days she cursed the drudgery that her life had become. Other days she blessed the chores for giving her a reason to get out of bed.

Sitting up, she tossed her braid over her shoulder, then swung her feet to the floor. Only then did she become aware of the noise of hammering—a homey, good sound that she hadn't heard in a long while. And suddenly she remembered Mr. Cameron.

Curious, she went to the window and peered toward the barn. He was up on the roof, sleeves rolled to his elbows, nails in his mouth. His hat brim shaded his face from the morning sun, but she didn't need to see his frown of concentration. The forceful swing of the hammer and the way he spit nails into his palm told her he was focused on the task. She also noticed he wore his gun belt even to repair her old barn roof.

Were the guns a holdover from the war? Or something

else? It was none of her business, but the question teased her while she dressed, then brushed out her hair and twisted the heavy mass into a knot on her neck, taking a tad more time and care than she ordinarily did.

Ignoring why she wanted her hair to be especially tidy this morning, she turned her thoughts to breakfast. Her habit was to have a quick cup of coffee and sometimes a bite of leftover supper, but that wouldn't do for Mr. Cameron. He impressed her as a breakfast sort of man. Oddly, the notion pleased her. Cooking for one person was hardly worth the bother, but the novelty of cooking for two made her eager to stoke up the old black stove.

The scent of frying ham and eggs sizzling in butter brought him down off the roof. Della heard him washing at the rain barrel beneath her kitchen window, and she set a cup of black coffee on the table for him.

" 'Morning," he said, stepping through the door. After removing his hat, he looked around for a place to put it, and Della remembered that he'd placed his hat and duster on the floor last night. She'd been too overwrought to think about it at the time, but now she flushed at her breach of manners. He would expect better from Clarence Ward's wife.

"You can hang your hat on the pegs behind the door." She watched him scan a child's sunbonnet and apron hanging beside her shawl and old work hat before she turned back to the stove. *Don't ask,* she pleaded silently. *Not yet.* "You could hang up your pistols, too."

"I'll wear them." His voice was pleasant, but an undertone announced this wasn't a subject for discussion.

Della pushed the ham slices to the side of the skillet and fried thick slices of bread in the grease. Men didn't wear side arms at the table, it simply wasn't done. She supposed he had his reasons. And she decided she didn't care. The pleasant singularity of sharing a meal far outweighed etiquette, which hadn't mattered for years anyway.

She placed a heaping plate before him, then sat down. "Did you get rained on last night?"

"I found a dry spot."

"I hope you like your eggs hard fried."

"Yes, ma'am, this is a fine breakfast and I thank you for it."

"Least I could do, considering what you've done for me." When he looked up with an odd glance, she added, "Bringing me Clarence's letter, and then patching the barn roof."

"You could use a hired hand," he said after a moment.

"I had one for a while, several years ago. But he died, and I didn't replace him." She had a monthly income, but the sum didn't allow for extravagance, and she'd discovered that a hired man ate enough to be an extravagance.

"How did he die?"

What a strange man. He seemed genuinely interested. "Doc Tally guessed it was a heart problem. Frank wasn't a young man. When he didn't come up to the house for breakfast, I went looking for him and found him dead in his bed."

"Lucky man," Cameron commented, finishing his eggs.

"Really? Dying isn't my idea of good luck."

"I meant dying in his bed."

"Oh." She thought about the pistols resting against

his thighs. Cameron wasn't a man who expected to die in his bed.

The dream flashed through her mind, images of a hearse seen through a heavy veil. To her surprise, the echo faded, not strong enough to withstand the presence of another person. Today she had someone to think about other than herself and dreams that were more than just dreams. And Lord, that was so good.

The fact was, she hadn't made an impressive start when she first came to Two Creeks, Texas. The exorbitant post-war prices had necessitated finding work, and the only female job in town had been at the Silver Garter. In the beginning, the townsfolk had shunned her for working to put food in her mouth, but over the years, attitudes had relaxed somewhat.

Still, some people would always believe that she had sold more than drinks at the Silver Garter. But now a few women returned her nods, and a few men tipped their hats to her. Even so, she didn't have a real friend. No one to talk to when the silence became unbearable. No one who cared about the small details of her life.

As if they'd had the idea at the same time, she and Cameron stood and carried fresh cups of coffee out to the front porch and sat in the wicker chairs facing the road. Away from the smells of cooking, she caught the scent of him. Shaving soap, sunshine, and that peculiar, indefinable male scent that always made her think of horses and sabers, cigars and brandy.

She sensed the solid heat of him close to her, and her stomach ached with gratitude. The simple pleasure of sitting on her porch sharing coffee with another person drove home the deep loneliness that she'd ignored for so long that she seldom noticed it anymore. But now, having Cameron beside her, the loneliness slammed against her ribs. She'd been by herself for so long, starving for another presence, for someone just to be there.

She glanced at him, then ducked her head in embarrassment. How transparent was she? Did he sense what it meant to her to sit beside him? To inhale the scent of a man? To speak if she wished and know that someone listened?

"Did the letter answer your questions?"

"No." But he already knew that. She drew a breath and gripped her coffee cup. The moment of silent companionship had passed. Frowning, she turned her thoughts to the questions she pondered every day of her life. "Did . . . Clarence speak of me before he died?"

"No, ma'am. Your husband died quickly."

So there was only the letter. Nothing further. She fixed her gaze on a hawk circling above the prairie and waited while the last vestiges of hope crumbled away. "Did he die bravely?"

"Yes."

"He didn't suffer."

"Not that I saw."

She'd always imagined she would have dozens of questions for whomever finally came to her. Yet she couldn't think of anything to ask, now that she knew Cameron couldn't tell her the one thing she needed to hear—that Clarence had forgiven her. The pain would continue.

"I always knew someone would come about Clarence," she said softly. The hawk dived toward the short grass, then swooped again toward the sky, its talons empty. "I prayed that would be the end of it. I told God if Clarence had forgiven me, I'd never do another wrong thing in my whole life. I'd never miss another Sunday sermon. I'd never look back at the life I used to have. I told God, if he sent word that Clarence had forgiven me, I'd accept any hardship he wanted to add to the pile." She looked down at her rough hands clasped around the cup. "Only a fool tries to bargain with God."

"Your husband didn't finish writing that letter."

"You read what he said. He was tired, impatient, angry. But even if Clarence had written that he forgave me for saying such hateful words to a man facing a battlefield, that doesn't change the fact that a good, decent man died believing he was unloved. Clarence Ward deserved better than that."

Cameron didn't look at her, he kept his gaze on the town road. Maybe he feared she would cry, but there were no tears in her eyes. She'd cried last night, and she always awoke from the dream with her eyes wet, but years ago she'd exhausted her lifetime allotment of tears. She figured she didn't have many left.

"You know one of the worst things? I can't remember what Clarence looked like." Seeing him in their wedding photograph had been a shock. She would have sworn he was taller and that his face was square instead of round. Had his eyes crinkled when he smiled? What had his voice sounded like? For the life of her, she could no longer remember. The shame of it made her turn her face away.

"It's been a long time," Cameron said after a while.

"Some days it feels like yesterday." She guessed it was the same for him. The war was still with Mr. Cameron, there in his wary gaze and hard, tight mouth, in the manner in which he sat his horse, in the way he seemed always to be listening and watching.

"Two men are riding this direction," he said abruptly, standing and narrowing his eyes toward town.

There it was, proof of what she'd been thinking. Shading her eyes from the morning glare, she squinted, finally spotting a distant plume of dust. It would have been another five or ten minutes before she might have noticed if he hadn't pointed it out. "How can you possibly know it's two men?"

"Are you expecting anyone?"

The question made her smile. "No one comes out here. Why would they?"

He nodded, then went inside for his hat, returning with the old shotgun she kept behind the door. "Do you know how to use this?"

"Yes." She frowned at the weapon, trying to remember how many years had passed since she had last fired it. She lifted her head. "Who are *you* expecting?"

A great weariness settled in his eyes and deepened the lines across his forehead. "No one. But they come anyway." He shrugged and touched the butts of the pistols at his hips. "Stay on the porch," he said over his shoulder, heading down the steps, "while I see if this is trouble."

Not knowing what to expect, Della stood at the porch rail, cradling the shotgun. A sigh of relief dropped her shoulders when she recognized the two men riding down her driveway. "It's just Hank Marley and Bill Weston," she called. "About as threatening as prairie dogs." Who had Cameron thought it was?

Cameron nodded, keeping his gaze on the men as they

reined and swung to the ground. "Stop right there. Place your weapons on the ground."

"It's really him! That's James Cameron!"

"We don't have no weapons, Mr. Cameron."

Hank Marley bobbed his head. "We heard you were in town, asking where Miz Ward lived. We came out to meet you so's someday we can tell our children that we shook your hand."

"Turn around slowly." Cameron kept his palm on the butt of his right pistol and narrowed his eyes into slits, staring hard as they turned for his inspection.

Curious, Della set aside the shotgun and walked into the yard. Hank Marley and Bill Weston glanced at her and nodded, but she held no more interest for them than if she'd been a scarecrow. They studied Cameron as if memorizing his face, his expression, the way he stood with his boots braced and his hands near his guns.

"Is it true what that book said about the shoot-out in Dodge City?"

"Did you really bring down Kid Krider with one shot?"

Excitement raised their voices and the questions tumbled one after another. "Did you catch the Martin gang in Deadwood before you started bounty hunting, or was that after?" "What's your preference, sheriffing or bounty hunting?" "Was you nervous at all when you faced down the Colt brothers in Laramie?"

Della stared, flabbergasted, as it dawned on her that James Cameron was famous. And apparently not comfortable with fame. He stood stiffly through the barrage of questions, silent, his face tight and his eyes chilly and distant. When Hank Marley and Bill Weston ran out of questions that weren't receiving answers, Cameron thrust his hand forward, gripped their palms, then turned without a word and strode toward the barn.

"Goddamn," Hank Marley said, looking down at his hand. "We just shook with James Cameron!"

"Nobody's gonna believe this. We stood right here and shook his hand!" They grinned at each other.

"Excuse me," Della said as they walked toward their horses. "I . . . you say someone wrote a book about Mr. Cameron?"

They stared at her in disbelief. "Don't you know who that is?" They saw her bewilderment. "James Cameron is about the most famous lawman in the West, that's all."

"He's cleaned up a dozen towns, brought in more outlaws than you can count. Damned right there's a book about him. A couple of 'em. Wish I'd had the nerve to bring mine and ask for an autograph."

Eagerly they told her about vicious outlaws either imprisoned or dead by Cameron's hand. Related notorious shoot-outs and acts of foolhardy courage, until it began to look as if they'd still be standing there talking a week from Sunday. Della raised a hand to stop the stories, her head reeling.

"James Cameron don't care if he lives or dies," Hank Marley said, marveling, "and that makes him invincible."

Bill Weston nodded. "Them who fear dying hesitate just a fraction when the fear bites down. Cameron, now, he don't ever hesitate."

They stared toward the barn roof, watching the sun glint off Cameron's side arms as he spit a nail into his palm and swung the hammer.

The two men looked at each other, then Weston urged

in a low voice, "If he's staying a piece, you best warn him about Joe Hasker."

Della listened, then watched the men ride out of her yard. When they were out of sight, she turned toward the barn, studying Cameron's profile against the sky and considering what she'd learned. His name was James. And he was a legend. A man whose hand other men wanted to clasp so they could say they had.

Shaking her head, she returned to her kitchen to clean up breakfast and continue her chores.

Now she knew what he'd been doing since the war. James Cameron had been a sheriff and a bounty hunter. Very likely he was one of those things now, for all she knew.

In the West, people glorified the gunslingers and killers on both sides of the law. Journalists heaped notoriety on the thugs who rampaged across the territories, wreaking mayhem and murder, and they created heroes out of the hardened men who gunned them down.

She was still trying to sort it out when Cameron walked toward the house for his noon meal, wiping sweat from his forehead. He paused beside her kitchen garden, glancing at her faded work dress and the old saw-toothed man's hat she wore.

"Pumpkins?"

Della pushed her garden knife into the ground and came to her feet beside a pile of weeds. "I don't have much use for pumpkins. But growing anything in this soil is hard work, so I like to grow something where you have a big thing to show for it when the season ends."

For the first time, he smiled, and Della went still with surprise. He looked like a different man, so handsome that her heart tripped over itself. Until now, she hadn't imagined that his mouth ever relaxed or that the chill could leave his eyes.

"What do you do with all those pumpkins?" The number of blossoms on the vines promised a bumper crop this year.

She shrugged. "I give them to the school, and to the church ladies. I guess they make pies, or bread. I've never asked. Whatever's left, I feed to my old sow, Betsy. But she's not too fond of pumpkins, either." Her tomatoes, corn, potatoes, onions, peas, carrots, and beans kept her through the winter. But it was the damned pumpkins that she sweated over most and took the greatest pleasure in growing. "I had one last year that weighed over forty pounds," she said, walking toward the rain barrel.

She washed her face and hands, then stepped aside for Cameron. "I didn't know you were famous." She mentioned two of the stories Marley and Weston had told her. "Are those exploits true?"

He took the towel she handed him and dried his face. "The basic facts are true. The details are mostly embellishments to sell books."

"Do you make money from the books?" Realizing she'd asked a rude question, she hastily backed away. "I apologize. I shouldn't have asked that." Maybe it was a blessing that she seldom had visitors. She wasn't fit for polite company.

"The publisher sends a bank draft a couple of times a year," he said, looking at the pink on her cheeks. "I never asked for those books to be written, didn't want it, and never spoke to the lying son of a bitch who wrote them."

It was the most heated speech he'd made since he'd

ridden into her yard. Maybe some of the West's notorious gunslingers welcomed fame, but James Cameron clearly was not among them.

Silently they entered the house, and Della dished up the ham and beans she'd been simmering since breakfast, watching him from the corner of her eye. He wandered into the sitting area and examined a doll's dress in her sewing bag, then picked up one of the school primers on top of a small bookcase.

"Your dinner's ready," she said, putting a plate in front of what she already thought of as his seat. After he flicked the napkin across his lap, she told him about Joe Hasker. "He's a troublemaker, Mr. Cameron. He's been in and out of jail since he was no bigger than a tadpole. Everyone knows Joe Hasker will wind up in prison or swinging from the end of a rope." Cameron didn't seem to be paying much attention. "Marley and Weston asked me to warn you that Hasker's talking about how he'd like to be the man who outdrew James Cameron."

He nodded and buttered a second square of cornbread.

"Mr. Cameron, I know about Joe Hasker. This isn't an idle warning." His indifference upset her. "Marley and Weston think Joe Hasker intends to kill you!"

His smile stopped the words in her throat. "Every town has a Joe Hasker, Mrs. Ward."

Flustered by his smile, she frowned down at her plate. "That doesn't worry you? Believe me, Mr. Cameron. Joe Hasker is a problem."

"A problem would be if Monk Sly rode into Two Creeks."

"Who is Monk Sly?" Della gave up on the beans and ham. Unlike the man sitting across from her, she couldn't talk about gunfights and dying and continue to eat as if they were discussing something as bland as chickens.

"Monk Sly murdered two men and a woman in Fort Worth. Sly swore he'd kill me before I could take him back to be hanged."

Della threw out her hands, staring at him. "So there are two men out there right now who want to kill you?" No wonder he wore his pistols at the table. It wouldn't surprise her to hear that he wore them to bed.

Cameron shook his head. "I caught Sly. He's in jail in Fort Worth. I'd hate to see that one escape." A shrug lifted his shoulders, and he turned his attention back to his dinner.

Della couldn't believe it. Marley and Weston were correct. James Cameron didn't care if he lived or died. Men like him didn't expect to see old age.

The realization shocked her until a second thought crept unwanted into her head. Did she care if she lived or died? What did the future offer but loneliness and hard work? Looking ahead, she saw years of sweating in the hot sun to raise pumpkins she didn't want. Saw herself growing older as she sat alone on her porch and watched the empty road. There was no future for her, only the past. Maybe she understood Cameron better than she'd imagined.

"Will you be leaving Two Creeks soon?"

"Not immediately. I still have some unfinished business," he said uncomfortably, as if he expected her to pry into what his business might be. "As soon as I finish patching the roof over the hay, I'll leave for town."

Picking up their plates, she carried them to the sink

and scraped hers into the slop bucket, disappointed that he hadn't come to North Texas solely to find her.

"You can stay here if you want," she said, keeping her voice light, as if it made no never-mind to her where he decided to stay. "No one can ride out here without being seen and heard. You wouldn't have to worry that Joe Hasker or someone like him is coming up behind you." If, indeed, he did worry about being ambushed. She suspected he didn't. More likely he relied on instinct and skill and left the rest to fate.

"That's a generous offer, Mrs. Ward," he said after a period of silence. "I'm obliged."

"I'm sure a bed would be more comfortable than a haystack in a leaky barn. But I've eaten at the hotel, and unless things have improved, I can promise you better cooking."

She heard the scrape of his chair behind her and felt him watching her. "I never thought of you as being a cook."

It surprised her greatly that he'd thought of her at all. Then she remembered her wedding photograph. "When that photograph was taken," she said, pumping water into the dishpan, "I didn't know how to make a pot of coffee. After the slaves ran off, I learned fast; it was that or starve, which we almost did anyway."

Raising her head, she looked out the window. "There was an old man named Dough who didn't run off, bless him. He helped with Mr. Ward, who we thought was dying, and he brought meat every few days. God only knows what kind of meat. I never asked. Didn't want to know. He found wild onions, too. Dough taught me how to make stew, and we stayed alive."

"Put in enough salt and almost anything becomes edible."

Della nodded. "After the war, we moved to town and Mrs. Ward hired a maid. The maid wasn't much good at anything except cooking. That woman could cook. By then I knew that cooking was a good skill to have." She shook her head and plunged her hands into the soapy water. "Turned out that I like to cook."

But cooking for one was like an actor reciting to an empty theater. "So you'll do me a kindness if you stay. I can practice dishes I haven't tried in a while."

He said something about her place needing work and excused himself. And no wonder. She was babbling. He'd made a simple comment and she'd responded by going on about how and where she'd learned to cook. Another few minutes and she would have started quoting recipes. Disgusted with herself, she washed and dried the dishes and then put a roast in the oven for supper. Later this afternoon, she'd make a pecan cake with vanilla frosting.

But right now she needed to assure herself that she wasn't dreaming. Hurrying to the bedroom, she eased back the curtain and peeked toward the barn, hoping he didn't see her. He was back on the roof, making those good sounds with the hammer. And he wasn't leaving.

Lowering her head, she whispered a prayer of gratitude, absurdly pleased that he'd stay a few more days. She had expected him to ride away after answering her miserably few questions. Heaven hadn't given her the answer she craved, that Clarence had forgiven her, but heaven had granted her a visitor as a brief token of consolation.

Chapter 3

Artillery bombarded the grassy field, tearing up the earth and pinning him in the adjacent trees and brush. Separated from his men, frustrated, he scanned the exploding dirt and stones and considered making a run for the north end of the field, estimating his chances for surviving the hail of explosives. Not good, he decided.

He didn't know which side was firing on the clearing, but the decision was ill conceived. Some overzealous officer had directed his men to destroy an empty field.

All right, attempting to dodge the artillery was suicide. He'd wait out the bombardment, and try to second guess which direction the battle had swung and where his unit might be.

Cursing, he moved deeper into the trees, looking for a ditch or gully where he might pass a few hours in relative safety and comfort. Once settled with his back against a mossy embankment, he set his rifle aside and rummaged in his jacket, looking for the stub of a cigar that he'd poached off the company cook.

Before he lit the stub, he rose carefully and scanned the trees, searching for figures darting through the brush. For all he knew, the battle had shifted and he could be

*sitting behind enemy lines. A tree splintered and fell near
the edge of the field, but he didn't spot any movement in
the undergrowth.*

*He lit the cigar and leaned his head back against the
embankment, listening to the explosions erupting behind
him. Everyone said the war would end soon and this
would fade to just a memory. They'd all be going home.
He planned to sit in a hot tub for a day, then sleep for a
month.*

*The ground shook beneath him as artillery brought
down another large tree. What irony it would be if he got
killed or maimed when it was almost over, after having
survived this long with nothing worse than minor flesh
wounds. Those were the deaths hardest for families to
bear, those that occurred when the end was near. That
was a misery his family would not have to bear as he was
the last surviving member of the Boston Camerons. His
parents were gone. Last year his sister Celia had died in
childbirth.*

*He was remembering Celia when he caught a flash of
movement from the corner of his eye.*

Over the years, Cameron had spent countless hours
studying Clarence and Della Ward's wedding photograph.
Della Ward had occupied his thoughts as he rode across
miles of empty prairie or sat before a solitary campfire.
He'd propped her photograph on a succession of bureaus
in a succession of boarding houses in the succession of
rough and rowdy towns where he'd worn a badge. Occasionally during his long drift through the West, in the
later years, he had sometimes fantasized that she was his
and waiting for him to come home.

He knew every nuance of the girl in that photograph, both real and fancied. The curve of her cheek and breast were as familiar as his own palm. He knew exactly where her hair had caught the photographer's light, could describe her gown in every detail.

At various times he had read innocence or idealism in her gaze; confidence, apprehension, or vulnerability. The shape of her lips suggested sensuality waiting to be awakened, spoke of sweetness and tender smiles. Other times he saw dreaminess in the shape of her mouth and chin.

The way she leaned slightly toward Clarence told him that she was dependent and in need of protection, a malleable woman-child eager to please and be cared for. A woman raised to be cherished, to bring gentleness into a man's life.

Her letter to her husband had seemed to confirm his judgement of her character. He'd grasped her bewilderment and desperation in every pen stroke. Had seen the young bride floundering beneath demands and fears and responsibilities that nothing in her experience had prepared her to cope with. Even on his first reading, Cameron had understood the impulsiveness of her plea for help and her momentary flash of resentment and hatred for the man who had abandoned her to an overwhelming situation. He'd guessed that she had regretted the letter almost at once.

The sound of the dinner bell interrupted his reverie, and he drove in the last nail, then climbed down from the barn roof. It had taken three days, but the job was finished. Surprisingly he'd enjoyed the physical labor and sweating under the Texas sun. It occurred to him that he might like a place of his own someday.

The thought made him smile as he walked toward the rain barrel at the side of the house. Men like him didn't settle down. If he needed a reminder, all he had to recall was the steady trickle of men riding out here to take a look at him or shake his hand. So far, the calls had been harmless. But he was aware that the next man who rode into Della Ward's yard could be the one who lusted for a footnote in history stating that he was the quick shot who had killed James Cameron.

"It's hot in here," Della called through the kitchen window. "Must have reached close to a hundred degrees today, plus I've had the stove going all afternoon."

The water from the rain barrel felt cool on his face and neck. "Whatever you're cooking, it smells good."

"Turtle soup and a shepherd's pie. Baked apples for dessert. I thought we'd eat on the porch. It's cooler outside than in here."

She smiled at him through the window, her expression uncertain, as if she didn't smile often. A lock of damp hair lay pasted to her cheek, her face was flushed with heat.

Only hints remained of the girl in the photograph.

The rounded plumpness had vanished, leaving behind interesting angles and sharper definitions. He doubted her dark hair had felt the crimp of a curling iron in years; she wore her hair simply now, coiled in a knot on her neck. Sun and weather had drawn faint lines beside her mouth and across her brow. Soft pampered hands had become rough, reddened, and calloused.

Her lips still impressed him as sensual and hinting of

mystery, but sharp words could fall from her mouth. This was no longer a dependent girl seeking to please and be protected. The most noticeable change, however, lay in her hazel eyes. Sadness had matured her gaze, as deep as the earth.

The young beauty in the photograph had stepped into the fire and vanished. A handsome woman forged by the flames of war and loss had emerged capable, independent, and no longer malleable. She'd become a sad, angry woman.

More deeply than he could ever express, Cameron regretted that she had lost the life she had expected to live. She had been destined for balls and musicales, for silk gowns and cashmere shawls. She had expected to reign over a household of servants, and spend idle days tinkling on a piano, painting delicate patterns on china cups, reading frivolous novels, paying and receiving calls, being the heart and center of a husband and family.

Instead, she lived alone on the edge of nowhere, working dawn to dusk on a property that was deteriorating around her. She raised pumpkins that were useless to her. And her eyes were filled with pain.

The war had done this to her. The war, and James Cameron.

"Supper will be ready in just a minute," she called as he came up the porch steps.

She'd spread a cloth across the porch table, and she'd made time to gather and then arrange a clutch of willow branches in a vase.

Stepping inside, Cameron hung his hat on one of the pegs, then leaned in the doorway, watching her move from stove to sink. When he realized he was staring, he shifted his glance and saw something that he'd failed to notice before.

There were marks on the doorjamb. Bending forward, he read a series of penciled notations above the rising lines. Three years. Five years. Eight years. Nine years. Frowning, he glanced toward the bookcase and the school primer atop it.

"Would you give me a hand with the soup bowls?" She untied her apron and dropped it on the sideboard. "I already dished up the plates. I'll carry those."

There were signs of a child everywhere. The items in the house. A pair of small gloves in the barn. A swing hanging from a thick cottonwood branch. But where was the child? He kept expecting her to mention the child's whereabouts, but she didn't.

"It looks like you finished patching the barn roof," she said, tasting her soup.

Was she relieved, thinking he'd leave now? Or was she disappointed? She appeared to enjoy having company.

Pushing aside his soup bowl, he frowned down at the plate of shepherd's pie. He should finish his business here and ride away. Every minute that he delayed saying what he'd come to say, was another minute that he deceived and wronged her.

Damn it to hell. He'd performed one cowardly act in his life. That was coming to Two Creeks and finding her years ago, then riding away without telling her the truth.

This time he would tell her. Tomorrow.

But tonight, he would warm himself in the light of her rare smiles. Would let the sound of her voice ease the tightness in his chest. When he looked at her, he didn't feel like someone who had killed more men than he could remember. When he looked at her and inhaled her scent, he glimpsed what his life might have been.

"You don't talk much," she said when they'd finished the baked apples.

"I guess I'm out of practice."

"I would have said that myself, but listen to me go on." She made a face and lifted a hand. "It's like I've stored up all these words. Dull words about Daisy's milk going sour last year, and silly words about seeing pictures in fallen leaves. I'm talking you half to death."

He waited until she'd fetched the coffeepot and filled their cups. "I wonder if I might have permission to ask a few questions." Her eyebrows lifted in surprise, and he felt himself flush beneath his sunburn. "All these years . . . there are things I've wondered . . ."

"Like what?"

"Like why are you living in North Texas? I spent a year after the war looking for you in Georgia."

"A year?"

"Off and on. You know how chaotic it was in the aftermath. Or maybe you don't, maybe you were here by then. No one knew what had happened to neighbors and friends. People died, moved, were relocated."

"It's a long story," she said finally, stirring her coffee.

"I found what was left of the Ward plantation. Months later I located a woman who said she thought the Wards had taken a house in Atlanta. It took a while, but I found the place on Peachside. Weeks later I tracked down the people who had lived across the street. A family named Beecher. Mrs. Beecher said the Wards had moved again, to a grander place, but she felt certain that you had gone west to Texas."

"You read my letter to Clarence," she said, turning her face to the shadows stretching toward the road. "There were difficulties between myself and Mr. and Mrs. Ward."

"Because you were a Yankee?"

"I guess they saw it that way, but I wasn't much of a Yankee. Not in my mind." She made a sound of dismissal. "Mama sent me to Atlanta to visit a cousin when I was thirteen. Six months later, when I was due to go home, there was talk of war. Already it was becoming dangerous to travel. My cousin advised me to stay in Atlanta until things were resolved, and Mama agreed." She tasted her coffee. "Those were impressionable years. By the time I married Clarence, I was sixteen. All the young men I knew were Southerners. All the *people* I knew were Southerners. My loyalty lay firmly with the South. That's where I saw my future."

"The trouble with the Wards . . . did they oppose your marriage to Clarence?"

She clasped her hands in her lap. "Clarence never told me straight out, but it was clear later that his parents were horrified by his choice. I imagine they did what they could to change his mind. To them, I was and would always be a Yankee. It was especially hard on Mrs. Ward to have her son married to a Northerner. After the war, I came here, as far from Atlanta as I could get on the money I had."

"If these questions are upsetting you . . ."

Standing, she moved to the porch rail, where he couldn't see her expression. Her slim back was stiff and as straight as the barrel of his rifle.

"My courtship and my wedding day were the happiest

days of my life, Mr. Cameron. War raged across the South and it was all anyone could talk about. We rationed provisions, gave our horses to the army, sold our jewelry to buy uniforms for the soldiers. We read about slave revolts and cities burning. But it was all a dream to me, not real or even important. What mattered to me was that I was in love and loved in return."

She turned to face him. "Others talked about battles that later became famous. I talked about wedding plans. Others read newspapers and learned the names of the generals on both sides. I read romantic poetry. All around me, people saw blood on the moon. I looked at the same moon and smiled because it shown down on my beloved. Does it upset me to talk about the war years? No, Mr. Cameron. I floated happily through the conflagration without ever looking at the flames around me. Not until near the end."

She made herself sound shallow and superficial.

"Clarence and I had a week together, then he returned to his regiment and I moved to the Ward's plantation. That's when the war became real, and yes, that part is upsetting to remember. Before the slaves ran off, we worried that they'd murder us in our beds. If the slaves didn't kill us, we were certain the Yankees would. Except for me, of course. Mrs. Ward believed the Yankees would spare me and take me to safety. If the slaves or the Yankees didn't murder us, we feared illness would. Dysentery and fever and malnutrition killed people by the hundreds. If illness spared us, then starvation would surely get us."

He'd known what it was like in the towns and

countryside. But he hadn't heard it described like this, in a flat voice and without expression.

He cleared his throat and tried to think of something to say. "I believe I'll start on the corral tomorrow. The poles are rotting, and many of the rails are splintered."

"Mrs. Ward lost her home and all her belongings to the Yankees, Mr. Cameron. The Yankees killed her only son, the son she adored. And there I was. A Yankee. In her home, under her nose. If she hadn't needed my help so desperately, I believe she would have figured out how to use Mr. Ward's hunting rifle, and she would have shot me. I was an abomination in her eyes."

Standing, he set down his cup. "I thank you for a fine supper."

Her hands trembled and waves of heat radiated from her rigid body. "The Wards didn't invite me to accompany them to their new home. Mr. Ward gave me the deed to this place and enough money to get here. That's how I ended up in North Texas."

"I apologize for intruding into areas where I have no right to be."

She stared at him, then the air rushed out of her body and her shoulders slumped. She shoved back a lock of heat-damp hair.

"No," she said, shaking her head. "You asked a straightforward question. It was me who strayed into areas I haven't examined for a while. Please. Sit down and finish your coffee."

Uncertain, he took his chair and didn't protest when she refilled his cup. "It's hot tonight." The triviality of what he'd just said disgusted him.

"Do you talk about the war, Mr. Cameron?"

"No."

"I guess most of us don't." She added sugar to her coffee as if to sweeten a bad taste in her mouth. "But it's always there. The war changed everything."

They sat in the twilight silence, watching shadows lengthen and occasionally waving away a mosquito or gnat. At some point Della entered the house and returned with an old palm fan which she waved in front of her face. He noticed damp patches beneath her arms and breasts, felt his shirt sticking to his back.

"If I were alone, I'd probably go down to the creek on a night like this," she said after a while, "and dangle my feet in the water."

The image made him smile. "I haven't done something like that since I was a boy."

"I guessed. Going barefoot would damage your heroic image as a gunslinging sheriff and a legendary bounty hunter."

Narrowing his eyes, he turned to look at her, then realized she was teasing. No one teased James Cameron. After an instant of astonishment, he laughed. That surprised him, too.

"All right, fetch a lantern and we'll go dangle our feet in the water."

"Truly? Give me a couple of minutes. I need to take off my stockings and tie up my skirt."

While he waited, he yanked off his boots and socks and rolled up his pant legs. When she emerged, carrying the lantern, they looked at each other's bare feet and laughed.

The creek wasn't far from the house, maybe fifty yards. Della placed the lantern on the weedy grass at the top of a short embankment, then she walked into the shallow creek with a sigh of pleasure. "In the daytime, it's cooler under the cottonwoods, but at night it's nice to see the stars."

It wasn't full dark yet, but a few bright stars pierced the fringes of the sunset residue. Cameron stepped into the cool water and let it swirl around his ankles. Bending, he scooped water into his hands and splashed his face and throat while Della did the same.

"This was a good idea."

"If you want to kick and splash around, I promise not to tell a soul." Tiny droplets caught the fading light and sparkled on her face and long throat. Her feet were pale beneath the water.

What did she see in him that others didn't? The question intrigued him. Of all the people in the world, why did this one particular woman feel comfortable joshing with him? Absurdly, he wanted her to do it again.

Instead she sat on the embankment, keeping her feet in the water, and unwrapped leftover biscuits that she'd brought in her pocket.

"What would you have done with your life if the war hadn't intervened?" She handed him a biscuit. "Would you still have come west?"

He made it a point not to speak of the past and never to explain himself. But after his questions on the porch, he owed her more than evasiveness or silence.

"Shortly after the war began, I sat for the bar," he said finally. "If I hadn't put on a uniform, I probably would have entered the family law practice back east."

Leaning forward, she splashed water farther up a shapely leg. "Is your father an attorney?"

"He was a judge."

"Was. He's dead, then?"

"Both my parents died years ago."

"Do you have any brothers or sisters?"

"I had a sister. Celia died in childbirth."

"I'm prying, aren't I?"

"Yes."

She clasped her hands in her lap and tilted her head back to look at the stars. "So why did you decide to come west?"

He turned his head to stare. "You just admitted that you're prying into personal affairs."

"I know. I'm still doing it. Why did you come west?"

Cameron thought a minute, then let his frown dissolve into a smile. He was seeing flashes of the woman-child's barefoot charm, and understanding why Clarence Ward had defied his parents to marry her.

"I came west because that's where the outlaws are," he said.

A moment passed as she considered his statement and worked out the meaning. "You learned to kill during the war," she said softly, not looking at him. "You've gone on killing."

Ordinarily he would have left it at that. But she had trusted him with part of her story.

He crumbled the biscuit between his fingers. "Until the end of the war, I never thought much about killing. When we went into battle, I only saw the enemy. I didn't see the men under the uniforms." He supposed it was the same for everyone. Otherwise no soldier could do his duty or fire his weapon.

"Cameron?" she said gently, touching his sleeve.

"Then something happened. And abruptly I understood the enemy was just an ordinary man. He wasn't evil. He was tired and hungry and he wanted to go home, just like me. He had parents and family who cared about him. He was decent and honorable. The enemy was simply a man doing his duty. The only difference between him and me was a point of philosophy and the color of our uniforms."

"What was the thing that happened?"

Here was the moment. There would never be a better opportunity to tell her the truth.

But he felt the warmth of her shoulder and her foot almost touching his beneath the water. An intoxicating scent clung to her skin and hair, the fragrance of apples, raisins, and woman sweat. At any moment she might tease him again. He wanted this interlude of closeness to last. Needed this brief experience of intimacy at a depth that shook him.

Right now he couldn't think about her hating him. Not yet, not tonight.

"I intend to tell you what happened," he said slowly, marking the second incidence of cowardice in his life, "but not now."

If she had pressed, he would have told her, but she didn't push, she merely nodded.

"I don't know how many good, decent men I killed during the war," he said, finishing his answer. He had detested those who kept count of fallen enemy soldiers. "I came west to even the score, to kill those who deserve to be killed for a better reason than the color of a uniform."

It was dark enough now that he couldn't see her expression or judge her reaction. The woman-child in the photograph was too young to understand what he was saying, but he sensed the woman she had become did know.

"The war will never end for you and me, will it," she murmured. She gazed up at the stars and touched her throat. "I'll go on hating myself for a letter that shouldn't have been written. You'll go on trying to atone for doing your duty. We can't change the past, and we can't let it go."

The night was never silent. Bullfrogs and crickets thrummed in the undergrowth, mosquitoes vibrated near their faces. Something splashed through the creek downstream and a cat screamed out on the prairie.

"How badly were you wounded?" she inquired, standing. When he asked which time she meant, she reminded him, "You said the blood on Clarence's letter was yours."

"That wound was superficial." He shrugged and stood. "None of the wounds I received were especially serious. I was lucky."

And he'd been lucky since the war. Dozens of times he'd faced men known to be deadly accurate killers, but the worst that had occurred had been one shot in his side and a couple of knife cuts.

One day his luck would run out. He accepted that inevitability as a natural consequence of the path he'd chosen.

It didn't matter.

Chapter 4

~⟡~

Upon awakening each day, the first thing Della did was hurry to the window. She doubted James Cameron was the kind of man to ride away without a fare-thee-well, but still, it reassured her to see him.

This morning she peeked through her bedroom curtains and watched him thumb back his hat, then frown at one of the warped rails he'd pulled from the decaying corral posts. Next he unfolded a long ruler and measured the board. Seeing him at work—his sleeves rolled to the elbows, his collar opened to the early morning sunshine—she wouldn't have guessed that he was a famous gunslinger. If she ignored the gun belt at his waist, he looked like an ordinary man fixing up his place.

Well, not ordinary, she decided. Ordinary men didn't have James Cameron's bearing or steely blue eyes. Most men weren't as tall. And even now, focused on the job before him, something in his posture and attitude told Della that he was keenly aware of his surroundings, alert to the morning rhythms. If an unusual sound or movement occurred, he would know at once.

His constant vigilance was a legacy from the war, of course, a habit he had carried into his present occupation.

She suspected that what Cameron referred to as luck was more a highly developed instinct for survival. He might not care if he died, but neither did he intend to let carelessness hasten the event.

She took great pleasure in knowing this about him, and in knowing what she suspected few others did, why he had come west. She loved observing the small details about him. That he was right-handed, that he shaved every morning, that he placed his knife and fork across the top of the plate when he finished eating. He drank his coffee black, he salted his food before he tasted it. He had a habit of lightly touching his palms to the butt of his guns before he dropped his arms to his sides. His horse's name was Bold, and he talked to Bold in a low voice while grooming him and when giving him grain in the evenings.

This was what she had hungered for, the sharing of those small details that made up a life. Without fully realizing it, she'd longed to look into another person, even if she couldn't see far, and she'd wanted someone to look into her, even if there wasn't much to see.

But there was one thing; not a secret but something she didn't want to talk about, either. Pressing her lips together, she gazed into the mirror and lowered her hair brush.

Cameron had surprised her last night. His first question wasn't what she had dreaded it would be. But as surely as she was standing here in her second-best dress, that question would come.

"You look fine this morning," he said when he came inside for breakfast.

He wasn't a man accustomed to giving compliments,

and she wasn't a woman accustomed to receiving them. Della blushed violently and splattered bacon grease on the floor. Cameron cleared his throat and took a sudden interest in the items hanging on the clothes pegs.

"The reason I'm not wearing a work dress ... I thought I mentioned this last night ... I'm going into town today to replenish staples." Irritated, she told herself he'd only made a polite comment, for heaven's sake. Once upon a time she'd received compliments as a matter of course, it was nothing to get flustered about. "The bank receives my money at the middle of the month, so that's when I go to town," she added, babbling and definitely flustered. "I remember you said something about unfinished business ... would you like to accompany me?"

She preferred to believe that his primary purpose in coming to Two Creeks had been to see her. That irritated her, too. She had no claim on this man, and no interest in him beyond the fact that he'd been Clarence's friend and had been with Clarence when he died.

"If you don't mind some company," he said, pulling out his chair and sitting, "I believe I will."

"I can't tell you how much I appreciate the work you've done around here, it's a nice tribute to Clarence, but I'd say you deserve a day off." She noticed him looking at her with a quizzical expression. "I guess you're wondering about the money."

"I don't want to pry into your affairs."

"Unlike someone else we know," she said, almost smiling. If she let a silence develop, she knew she'd think about him saying she looked fine, so she kept talking. "I have a monthly income. It isn't much, but I couldn't manage without it."

"I'm glad you have it then."

Apparently he wasn't comfortable talking financial matters with a woman, because he didn't look up from his plate.

"Clarence's father sends me the money."

Now he did look up. "Mr. Ward?"

"Mr. Ward transferred most of his fortune to Europe at the start of the war. He didn't lose everything like so many people did." She reached for the salt. "Actually, Mr. Speers—that's my banker—won't reveal who sends the money, but who else could it be? I figure Mrs. Ward would object, so Mr. Ward sends the money anonymously, and without her knowing."

Cameron finished his breakfast before he spoke again. "I didn't think of this before, but Ward ought to send you an income. He owes you." Anger chilled his eyes. "If I understand your letter to Clarence, you were responsible for keeping Mr. Ward alive during a serious illness. Plus, you're his son's widow."

"Those are the reasons I think he sends the money." She didn't understand his apparent anger. "If it wasn't for Mr. Ward, I'd still be working at the Silver Garter." The thought made her skin crawl.

"Instead of living in luxury." He sent a pointed glance around her one-room kitchen, parlor, living room.

"I'm grateful to have anything at all," she said stiffly, regretting that she'd mentioned finances.

"I'll hitch up the buckboard."

After he left for the barn, she stood beside the table,

holding their plates and looking around her small house, seeing it through his eyes.

She couldn't invite Cameron to sit inside in the evenings because she owned only one parlor chair. She'd positioned the chair near the bookcase and a side table, with a colorful braid rug to keep the winter chill off her feet. Right now none of her sparse furnishings seemed as cozy or comforting as she usually told herself they were. The room just looked cramped and shabby.

The plates she held were old and chipped. She didn't have three glasses that matched. Her curtains were sun-bleached, the pattern faded almost to white.

Heat flared in her cheeks. Whirling, she strode to the sink and slammed the plates into the dishpan. She didn't care what he thought of her house. It suited her needs, and that's all that mattered. And what right did he have to turn up his nose anyway? From the sound of it he didn't own property, he drifted from place to place, sleeping on the ground or in a hotel or a boarding house, or in someone's barn. If what she had to offer wasn't good enough for him, then he could just . . .

What was she thinking?

Cameron had done nothing but display a flash of anger that her financial situation kept her at poverty level. Very likely it shocked him to see his friend's widow living in such reduced circumstances. Certainly he could see how far she'd fallen from her previous life. All he had intended was to make the point that Mr. Ward should be helping her financially, and should be helping to a larger extent.

Raising a hand to her forehead, Della chastised herself for behaving so erratically. First she veered this way, then that. She didn't have to look far to guess the reason. She wasn't accustomed to having a man around the place, and James Cameron wasn't just any man. He was virile and handsome, silent and strong, and he was a living link to a past that hadn't felt this immediate in years. Sooner or later, he would ask the question she didn't want to answer, but today he'd paid her a compliment. Everything considered, it was no wonder she was swinging on an emotional pendulum.

By the time she'd donned her bonnet and composed her list of provisions, Cameron had brought the buckboard to the front of the house and was waiting to assist her up to the seat. After a brief hesitation, she placed her gloved hand in his and felt his palm against the center of her waist. It had been a long time since she'd experienced a man's touch, and she responded with an embarrassing rush of heat to her cheeks.

"Thank you." Actually, she'd missed the small niceties of polite company. And it was a pleasure not to hitch up the buckboard herself or stain her gloves with the reins.

But it was disconcerting to see her skirt partially draped over his knee, and to feel his solid presence so close that her shoulder bumped his along the uneven road to town.

"There's something I've been meaning to ask."

Della turned her head toward the prairie. Because of the rains, there were more wildflowers this year, splashes of color against pale green grass. Surely this wasn't the moment to ask the question she dreaded. Don't let it come now.

"Ask whatever you like," she said, not meaning it.

"Is my staying at your place causing you a difficulty?"

A breath of relief dropped her shoulders. "I've lived

like a saint for eight years, Mr. Cameron, but it hasn't re-instated my reputation. The folks in Two Creeks have long memories, and they see me as a saloon girl." She shrugged. "Having a man at my place isn't going to blacken my name any more than it is already."

"Is that why you never remarried?" He glanced at her and raised an eyebrow. "I apologize for making a personal inquiry, but you did give your permission the other night."

"I don't object to the nature of your questions." The opposite was true. It was wildly flattering that someone was interested enough to be curious about her. "You were Clarence's friend, and that makes you my friend, too. Sometimes it feels as if I've known you for years." Other times he was a fascinating enigma. A man who didn't talk about himself, but who seemed to want to know everything about her.

"About five years ago, there was a man came calling," she said, looking down at her gloves and feeling her cheeks go hot again. "He said he was lonely and he figured I was lonely, too. Said he could see I needed a man around the place, and he needed a woman. He said he didn't care what people whispered about me, didn't care that I was sharp tongued, he wouldn't mind marrying me anyway."

Cameron kept his gaze on the approaching town and didn't comment.

"I decided I didn't want to double the laundry and cooking to accommodate an irritating man who thought he was doing me a favor. I've learned to enjoy my independence, Mr. Cameron, such as it is. And most of the time, the loneliness is tolerable. I have no desire or any intention to marry again." She decided turnabout was fair play. "Have you ever been tempted to marry?"

"Me?" He made a snorting sound and smiled. "Hell, no."

"You're not interested in having a family?"

His smile vanished and suddenly Della sensed that his loneliness cut as deep as her own.

"I don't stay in one place long enough to think about settling down."

She knew he could have added that he didn't expect to survive his reputation. A family and a short life didn't mesh for a man who took his responsibilities seriously.

"It's not much of a town, is it?" Della said as they turned onto Main Street.

Two Creeks, Texas, had begun as a trading post situated at the confluence of two year-round creeks. A town had grown around the post, and now Two Creeks survived as a stopover point midway between Fort Worth and Santa Fe. Two hotels, three saloons, and a hodgepodge of businesses fronted Main Street's dusty road. Saturday nights could be lively, when the ranch hands came into town, but on a weekday morning, there weren't more than forty or fifty people along the entire length of the boardwalks.

"One thing in its favor," Della said, alighting after Cameron set the brake on the wagon, "the trees along the creeks make a pretty background." Cameron offered his arm, and she suppressed a sigh of pleasure mixed with reluctance, then took it. "The bank's on the corner, then I'll come back to Mr. Yarrow's to stock up my pantry. I suppose you have business."

"My business isn't in town."

It frustrated her that his answers went to the point without embellishment. When he asked a question, she gave him the full whys and wherefores. She wished he'd do the same.

"If your business isn't in town," she said testily, "then where . . ."

Joe Hasker rose from a bench in front of the barber-and-bath shop and stepped directly in front of Della. In the last year, Joe had shot up four inches. He was tall, gangly, turning mean, and wore an expression that said he was looking for trouble.

Della pressed Cameron's arm, signaling they should walk around Hasker's rude display.

Cameron halted. "Step aside for the lady."

"I don't move for no bar girl." Joe's eyes narrowed above a crooked smile, but Della understood this wasn't about her. Joe was pressing a confrontation that addressed legends and guns and history.

She had time to form that thought before she was aware of being pushed to one side and everything became a blur. An eye blink later Joe Hasker was lying on his back in the street, disarmed, and Cameron was standing over him, his pistol aimed down at Hasker's wide eyes. It had happened so fast, Della wasn't sure if she'd even seen it.

"I imagine you want to get up and apologize to the lady," Cameron said in a tone as icy as his gaze.

Hasker rolled his eyes back, trying to see who all was watching.

Cameron drew back the hammer. "You have two seconds to think it over."

Della stared. Cameron's stony face did not betray any

hint that he might scruple to pull the trigger or that he would regret killing Joe Hasker.

Hasker jumped to his feet, his eyes wild, his face as red as a cherry. "I'm sorry, ma'am. My mistake." He slid a glance toward Cameron. "Can I have my gun back, Mr. Cameron?"

"You can pick it up at the sheriff's office." Cameron stuck Hasker's gun into the waist of his trousers, then offered his arm to Della.

Trembling, she drew a breath and gripped his sleeve. When her heart stopped pounding and she could speak, she said, "That boy wanted an excuse to kill you."

"Turns out he was disappointed."

"And you would have killed him." Her heart was still thumping and her mouth was dry. She had almost witnessed a killing. "You know, don't you, that he'll go somewhere and sulk for a few days, then he'll come after you."

Cameron looked down at her and shrugged. "Or maybe the sheriff will convince him to stay out of my way and stay alive."

Silently they entered the bank and Della conducted her business. When they emerged, she was aware there appeared to be more people on the street, and it seemed they all took an interest in her and James Cameron.

Now she understood why he dismissed the idea of a wife so easily. What woman could accept that her husband was a target for every outlaw and hothead in the West?

But then, what wife could accept that her husband was a target for every Yankee soldier in the Union army? A shudder passed along her spine. Never again did she want to live with the fear that every time she saw a man she loved, it might be the last.

She told herself to remember this revelation and keep it before her to balance knowing how much she would miss Cameron when he rode away. And she would. Having him with her this week had been the best thing to happen in years. But this was a man with no long-term future, a man she wouldn't want to become entangled with. She couldn't go through it again, worrying every minute that someone would kill the man she loved. She could not do that to herself.

Well damn all if she wasn't doing it again, letting her imagination take a kernel of a thought and grow it into something fantastical.

Standing in the back aisle of Mr. Yarrow's General Store, she looked down at the potato in her hand and laughed out loud. She had just decided not to marry a man who hadn't a thought of romance in his hard head. To James Cameron, she was simply a loose end, the widow of a man he'd known long ago. If he could read her mind, he would be shocked and mortified, and he'd hightail it out of Texas this afternoon.

"Was that you laughing back here all by yourself?"

"It was," she said, smiling up at him. Lord, he was a handsome specimen. The only man to stir something inside her since Clarence. What a pity they were so ill suited. When he raised a quizzical eyebrow, she shook her head. "It's nothing. I was just laughing at what a foolish woman I am. Give me an imaginary thread, and I'll spin a carpet."

He took her shopping net and filled it with the potatoes she handed him. "My sister had an imagination."

"Well, my heavens." She slapped a hand on her bosom and staggered backward a step. "James Cameron volunteered a smidgeon of personal information. I think I'm going to faint."

A lopsided smile tugged his mouth and his eyes. "By God, you're right. I apologize and I'll try not to do it again."

They both laughed, and Della told herself to remember this moment, standing in the back aisle surrounded by the good scents of pickle brine, earthy potatoes, and strings of onions. Long after he was gone, she would hold this memory to the light and enjoy it anew.

If only . . . but no, she wouldn't let her thoughts wander down that path.

"That was about the best meal I've ever eaten," Cameron said, meaning it. She'd fried him a steak the size of a plate, and garnished it with potato salad and fresh corn on the cob, followed by peach cobbler and coffee.

"It wasn't anything fancy," she said, but her cheeks warmed with pleasure.

The trip to town had pushed back the chores, and consequently they'd eaten later than usual. It was dark now and cooler on the porch than it had been last night.

"Tell me about Clarence," he said, watching the play of candlelight on her face. Now that he no longer had her photograph, he would have to remember the arch of her brows and the shape of her mouth.

"You were his friend, you knew him," she said with a puzzled expression.

"Imagine that I didn't. Tell me about Clarence from your perspective."

"Well," she tasted her coffee, then added more sugar. "He was a devoted son and loyal to his friends, but you already know that." She thought a minute. "He played the piano. He liked to hunt." A teasing smile curved her lips. "Clarence was a talker. Lord how that man could talk. If you asked him the time, he'd be telling you the history of timepieces twenty minutes later."

"What would Clarence have done if he'd survived the war?" It was a question he'd asked himself again and again. What would Clarence Ward have done with his life if he'd had the chance?

"If the South had won, Clarence had plans to buy more acreage and experiment with different crops." She tilted her head to one side, and her gaze looked into the past. "He stopped talking about the future when it became apparent the South would lose. To be honest, I'm not sure what he would have done. As I mentioned, Mr. Ward protected a large portion of his wealth . . . maybe Clarence would have entered business. Or maybe not. He always said he didn't have much of a head for figures."

"Was he a spiritual man?"

"The Wards had a pew at the Old Standard Church, and when Clarence was home he accompanied the family to services." She paused. "How odd. I don't really know if he attended services to please his mother or to please himself."

"Would it be too personal to ask why you married Clarence instead of another suitor?" He didn't doubt that she'd had many beaus.

She ducked her head, then gazed toward the road. "I was very young, Mr. Cameron. I married Clarence for the wrong reasons. I think I fell in love because he was nice looking, a wonderful dancer, and he came from a good family. He was easy to talk to and his manners were flawless."

Cameron leaned back in his chair and studied her expression. "What am I hearing in your voice?"

"I'm surprised by how difficult these questions are," she admitted finally. "It's shocking me to realize I didn't know Clarence well. I'm describing the surface, not the substance of the man." She frowned and briefly touched her tongue to her upper lip. "I saw Clarence as a mentor and protector. He would teach me and take care of me," she said slowly. "Maybe if we'd had the chance, we would have matured into a more balanced give-and-take. I don't know." She looked at him across the table. "How did you see Clarence?"

Here was another opportunity to say what he'd come to tell her. And once again, he couldn't bring himself to speak the words.

"We'll save that for another time if you don't mind." He took his watch from his waistcoat pocket and opened the lid. "It's getting late."

Standing, he gazed down at her, enjoying how the candlelight softened her mouth and raised a shine to her eyes and hair. Unlike her shapeless work dresses, her town dress molded her body, revealing a full bosom and narrow waist, and when he'd assisted her from the wagon he'd caught a glimpse of trim ankles. She was a fine figure of a woman. If she'd lived in a town where she had no history, he figured every man within a hundred miles would have come courting.

"Good night, Mrs. Ward."

"Good night, Mr. Cameron."

They looked at each other for a moment, as if there were more to say, then Cameron nodded and walked down the porch steps into darkness.

At the barn, he checked all the animals, then sat outside on a tree stump and lit one of the short, thin cigars he'd purchased in town.

Damn his hide. He had to tell her. He had to stop playing with the notion that he could ride out of here and leave things as they were. Honor demanded the truth. She had a right to know who she'd been feeding and opening her heart to. She had a right to hate him.

And he couldn't delay much longer. Della hadn't asked how long he planned to stay, but she had to be wondering. He'd already stayed long past anything reasonable. He could have—should have told her everything that first night. That's what he had intended. But a weakness in him had wanted to know the woman whose photograph he had carried for ten years. Who had she been, who was she now? He'd discovered that she was so much more than he'd imagined.

Smoking, gazing up at the canopy of stars, he briefly wondered what it would be like to be loved by a woman like Della Ward. Clarence had been a lucky man. Had he known it?

After a time, he ground his boot heel on the cigar, then stood and stretched, glancing toward the house. She'd carried the lantern into her bedroom, and he saw her silhouette pass the curtains. Did she braid her hair for sleeping, or did she wear it loose?

Turning, he slammed his fist against the side of the

barn. He was being a damned fool, and it was time he left.

But first, there was one more question he needed to ask. Since she hadn't volunteered the information, he knew the subject would pain her.

Chapter 5

Artillery fire shook the ground and showered clods of earth and ragged leaves on the Reb who appeared at the top of the embankment. The man ducked his head, then jerked when he saw Cameron crouched in the gully. A lifetime passed during the second they stared at each other, before each of them fired. Cameron rolled to the side and shot his rifle from the hip. A burning sensation sliced through the fleshy part of his forearm but he hardly noticed, his attention intent on the red blossom unfurling on the Reb's uniform jacket.

The Reb dropped his weapon and clasped his chest as he sank to his knees. He stared at Cameron until his eyes closed and he toppled down the embankment, rolling to a stop a few feet from Cameron's boots.

Cameron held the rifle on him until he was certain the man was dead, then he cocked his head and listened to the explosions cracking trees and throwing up dirt around him.

Damn all. He was pinned in the gully with a dead Rebel. And there might be more Rebs in the forest. Scanning the top of the embankment, searching for movement, he removed his jacket and peeled back his bloody shirt to examine his wound. The ball had passed through without hitting bone. His luck had held.

After tearing a strip off his shirt, he bound the wound as best he could, then considered his options. Make a run for it? Instinct told him that he'd exhausted his luck for the day. Trying to dodge the hail of artillery would end in death. Which gave him no choice but to stay in the gully with the dead Reb until the bombardment ended.

Pressing his back into the mossy ferns, he gripped his weapon and stared at the opposing bank.

He'd seen the Reb's face.

Throughout the whole miserable war, he'd deliberately avoided looking at the face of the enemy. He'd fought in close combat, but the enemy's faces had blurred, and that's how he'd preferred it. The enemy was a single monstrous entity, different and alien, to be feared and hated.

But he saw the Reb in his mind standing at the top of the embankment, shoulders slumped in fatigue, eyes reddened and sore from the smoke and exploding earth. The man's uniform was soiled and patched, as shabby and threadbare as Cameron's own. He was of medium height, sandy haired, his eyes were blue gray. For an instant, he had reminded Cameron of Howard Ellison, a childhood friend. That's what his mind recoiled from, the recognition that the Reb could be an ordinary man like Howard Ellison, like himself.

He relit the cigar stub, smoked, and felt the ground shake when the artillery fell nearby. How the hell long was he going to be trapped here?

After a time, he couldn't restrain his curiosity. He looked down at the dead Reb. He'd seen countless dead *men. Had seen men torn by canon and ball, had stood outside the operating tents and stared at hills of amputated limbs. Likely, the man at his feet had seen the same horrors.*

How different were they? Aside from philosophical differences, were they more alike than not? The question disturbed him.

Acting on impulse, he slid down next to the man, hesitated, then went through his pockets, driven to know who he was. Something inside warned that he'd never be the same if he put a name to the Reb or learned anything about him, but he searched anyway.

He found a pipe and a nearly empty pouch of first-rate tobacco. Matches in a tin box. A pocket knife with an ivory handle, and a gold watch on a heavy chain. And then a packet tucked in the Reb's inside jacket pocket, protected by an oilcloth wrapping.

Aware that he was about to invade the man's privacy, but driven to know who he had killed, he looked down at the Reb, then moved away from him.

His hands shook slightly as he opened the packet and a photograph fluttered to his lap. For a long time he studied the young woman and man in what was obviously a wedding picture. Damn it. Then he read the wife's letter and a half-written response.

He read the letters again, dropped his head, and covered his eyes. The man's name was Clarence Ward. He had a pregnant wife, an ill father, and a distraught mother. His home was in shambles, in the path of the Union army, and his young wife was terrified and nearing the end of her rope.

James Cameron had killed a decent man with family

who loved him and wanted him home. He had killed a good man because the color of their uniforms was different. That's what soldiers did.

He turned his head to look at Clarence Ward. In different circumstances, they might have enjoyed each other's company. Maybe they could have been friends.

The full wrongness and horror of war seeped into him like poison. How many good men had he killed? Ordinary men like himself who were just doing their duty and hoping to stay alive until the madness ended and they could go home to their families.

He'd been able to perform his duty because the enemy didn't have the reality of faces or names. Until now it had been simple. The gray uniforms were the enemy, and his duty was to kill the enemy. The enemy didn't have a young, pregnant wife or parents who needed him. He was just the faceless, nameless foe.

Christ. He'd put a face and a name to the soldier at his feet. He knew something about Clarence Ward and his family. Nothing could be the same.

He'd killed too many ordinary men in different colored uniforms. He had widowed too many young wives. He had killed men who had not wronged him or anyone else. How did a man live with this knowledge?

Standing, he studied Clarence Ward's face. It wasn't fair that Ward, who had a family, was dead. But Cameron, who had no family, would survive. Bending, he laid his rifle beside Mr. Ward's body, then climbed up the embankment.

He started walking north. The war had ended for James Cameron.

*   *   *

He spent the morning checking Della's animals. The old sow was healthy. Any chicken that looked poorly would show up in the Sunday stew, so he didn't concern himself there. He trimmed the manes, tails, and hooves of her horses. Doctored a cut on the ear of her milk cow.

It hadn't rained since the night he arrived, so he filled the stock tanks from the creek. Decided he'd carry a couple of buckets up to her garden.

That's when he noticed the laundry flapping on the line. Halting, he narrowed his gaze on three of his muslin shirts, two pairs of trousers, and two sets of long johns. She'd even washed his socks.

Angry, he set down the buckets and went to the house, entering the open door without rapping first. She was standing near the stove, whistling an old lullaby and ironing another of his shirts.

"I didn't give permission to wash and iron my things, and I don't want you doing it."

Her lips had curved when she saw him, but the tentative smile faded quickly. "Why on earth not?"

"It's not right."

"It's no trouble. I was doing wash anyway. Truly, I don't mind."

"I mind."

She set down the iron and tilted her head, studying him with a puzzled expression. "It seems the least I can do is include your wash. Washing and ironing a few pieces doesn't begin to balance out the work you've done, but it makes me feel like I'm giving something back."

God almighty. Turning, he stood in the doorway, scowling at the road. He understood what she was saying, and in a different situation he would have been pleased and grateful.

Tell her, he ordered himself. Tell her right now that she's standing in a hot kitchen ironing the shirts of the man who killed her husband.

"Mr. Cameron?"

"You weren't reared to iron." Her life had collapsed that day when Clarence Ward had rolled down the embankment. If it were true that Mr. Ward had protected his fortune, then Clarence would have come home to a changed life, but one of comfort. Della Ward sure as hell wouldn't have been putting up a wash and sweating over an iron on a hot August day.

"Is that what's bothering you?" She made a sound midway between dismissal and a laugh. "I'll tell you something, Mr. Cameron." He heard her place the iron on the stove top and pick up another that was hot. "I wasn't reared to do much of anything useful. But I've learned there's satisfaction in doing for myself. I like knowing how to cook and put up a wash. Most of the time, I like tending my garden and caring for my animals. It feels good to put my hands in a dishpan full of warm, sudsy water. At the end of the day, I like knowing that I kept body and soul together, and I did it myself."

When he turned around she wore a peculiar expression, as if she'd said things she hadn't considered before.

"I have to tell you something."

"I figured as much. It has to do with that unfinished business of yours, doesn't it?" She arched an eyebrow, certain that she'd guessed correctly.

Right now she was as beautiful as any woman he had ever seen. The collar of her work dress was open and her skin was dewy from the heat, her throat and face were flushed. A few tendrils of rich brown hair floated around her cheeks. Her mouth was slightly open and he could see the tips of her teeth.

He wished he could walk over to her, take the iron out of her hand, then pick her up and carry her into the bedroom. The image was so vivid that he could picture himself removing her faded dress and her shimmy and drawers. He could see her standing before him in a light sheen of summer sweat, her magnificent body trembling in anticipation of his touch.

He ground his teeth together and clenched his fists. Is this how he respected the man he'd killed? By lusting after the man's wife? Cursing beneath his breath, he ran a hand across his eyes and down his face.

He shouldn't have come here. He should have posted the packet to Two Creeks. He could have told her the story of Clarence's death in a letter.

Could'ves and should'ves were a waste of time. Honor demanded that he face her, and here he was. So why in the hell couldn't he speak the words? What difference did it make if Della hated him? Once he rode out of Two Creeks, he'd never see her again. They shared a common point in the past, but even at his most fanciful he'd never imagined he would establish anything ongoing with the girl in the photograph, or the woman she'd become. The outcome had always been inevitable.

He looked at her, trusting and pink with heat, and his resolve shattered. Tomorrow. He would tell her tomorrow. One more day wouldn't make any difference. He'd have one more day of conversation and perhaps a smile, one more day of looking at her and being near her.

And there was one more question he had to ask.

"I'll be leaving before you do another wash," he stated abruptly. He couldn't change that she'd already washed his clothing and would iron it, but he could by God make sure that she didn't spend any more of her labor on him.

Her lips twitched with a hint of disappointment. That he was leaving? Or that he hadn't yet explained his unfinished business?

"I suppose you need to get on with the business of hunting outlaws." She ran her fingers over the collar of his shirt, then smoothed the iron along the curve of muslin. "Are you searching for anyone special?"

Cameron shrugged, watching the back-and-forth movement of the iron. "There are a couple of bank robbers reported to be between here and Santa Fe. If I don't catch them, some other bounty hunter will."

"Would that bother you?"

"Hell, no."

Turning his shirt, she ironed the yoke, then glanced at him quizzically. "Do you care about anything? Does anything matter to you?"

She asked the damnedest questions, questions no one else would dare put to him. And he felt obligated to answer because she'd been so open with him. And because she was who she was.

"I care about evening the score," he said finally. Before she could insist that wasn't possible, he added, "And a few other things. Right now I care about filling the rain barrel and greasing the buckboard's axle."

He left the house as riled inside as he'd been in a long time. Seeing her ironing his shirts had shocked him, had brought him face-to-face with the one weakness in his life—Della Ward.

Once he told her, she'd think back to washing and ironing his clothes, and she'd detest him for letting her do it. Well, she couldn't hate him any more than he hated himself for not noticing earlier and stopping her.

He had to tell her before she did him any further kindnesses.

Since the night they'd dangled their feet in the creek, Della had sensed that Cameron held back something he wanted to say to her. Initially, she'd guessed it must have something to do with Clarence, but they had discussed Clarence often, and she'd offered him ample opportunity to speak. Perhaps he wanted to tell her about his mysterious unfinished business. She wished he would. Curiosity was getting the better of her.

Most of all she wished she'd known James Cameron before the war did its damage. Had his blue eyes sparkled and twinkled as they did so rarely now? Had he laughed easily? Had words come quickly, or had he always been a reticent, solitary man?

"You're quiet tonight," he said, placing his fork and knife across the top of his plate.

"I guess I still don't understand why you were so angry about me doing your laundry."

Anyone else would have taken her comment as an invitation to explain, but he just nodded. There were things about James Cameron that could drive a woman crazy.

And there were things about him that would make

a woman forgive just about anything. He always wet down and combed his hair before he came to the table, for example. And his hair dried in soft loose curls just above his collar. He had strong, sure hands that didn't waste a movement that wasn't necessary.

But the thing that gave her a fluttery feeling inside was the way he looked at her. As if he really saw her, as if he saw all she had been and all she might ever be. No one before had looked at her in that way.

"I'd rather you hadn't done it, but thank you."

"It was my pleasure," she said, meaning it. The novelty of doing up a man's wash had made an onerous chore speed by.

"You were whistling when I came inside . . ."

His comment made her smile. "See how far my manners have deteriorated? Would you like more coffee?"

"Please. Where did you learn to whistle?"

"A neighbor boy taught me. My mother was appalled." Lord, she'd smiled more since Cameron arrived than she had in a decade. "I've never regretted learning. It's nice to have music whenever I like."

"Mrs. Ward, I'll be leaving soon . . ."

The words hung between them, spoiling a pleasant mood. Della turned toward the pool of darkness gathering in the yard beyond the reach of the porch lamp.

She would miss him. It shocked her to realize how quickly they had established habits and routines. After he left, she wouldn't dress the table on the porch. She'd eat her meals standing at the sink. She'd return to not speaking for days on end. The dream would return to haunt her. And the loneliness would seem worse for having been interrupted.

"Before I go, there's a question . . . something I've wondered about for years."

Here it came. The question she had expected and dreaded. Dropping her head, she looked at her hands twisting across her lap. "I know what you want to ask."

"What happened to your child?"

All the pleasure of the evening vanished with her next breath as if a tight band squeezed her chest. As always when she thought of Claire, her eyes felt hot and scratchy and the back of her throat went dry as if she'd swallowed sand.

Cameron must have seen the color drain from her face because his voice was gentle when he spoke again. "I figure the child died. If you can bear to confirm it, we'll leave it at that."

"Her name is Claire. After my mother."

He hesitated. "Did she die recently?"

"I guess by now you know I can't answer without explaining." She drank the last of her coffee to moisten her throat. "After my last letter to Clarence, Clarence died, we fled to Atlanta after the plantation was burned, and I gave birth to my daughter."

She couldn't sit still while she told the story. Standing, she moved to the rail and walked back and forth across the porch. "Mrs. Ward lost her home, all her belongings, and her servants. Then she lost her son. The Yankees did this to her. The Yankees destroyed everything she valued. And there I was, every time she turned around. After Clarence was killed, Mrs. Ward started attacking me verbally. This wasn't new, but it got a lot worse. When I didn't go away, she shut herself in the bedroom of the Peachside house rather than look at me or talk to me. She didn't come out of her room until the night Claire was born."

Della hadn't seen her mother-in-law during her long difficult labor, but she'd heard Mrs. Ward in the hallway issuing orders to the midwife. And Mrs. Ward had taken charge of the nursery after Claire's birth.

"This part is hard," she said, drawing a deep breath. She gripped the railing and stared blindly into the darkness.

"A week or so after Claire's birth, I went to fetch her to feed her. She wasn't in the nursery. I looked everywhere. Finally I ran into the parlor where Mr. Ward liked to sit in the mornings and read the day's news."

Nothing in her voice conveyed how frantic she had been, how terrified that something unthinkable had happened. Her voice was flat, unemotional, the words tumbling out in a rush to reach the end of the story.

"I told him that Claire was missing. And Mr. Ward said no she was not. He had a speech prepared. It was a long speech, which said, in essence, that Claire was all the Wards had left of their son, and the Wards would raise her. But I had to leave at once. Mrs. Ward would never recover her health as long as I was present."

The words scraped her throat and the hot evening air choked her.

"The Wards had money and I didn't. The Wards could give Claire a comfortable life while I couldn't. Leaving her with the Wards was the best course for everyone." She drew a long breath and pressed her fingertips to her lips. "I took the deed that Mr. Ward gave me, and enough money to get here."

Cameron cleared his throat. "The bonnet on the hook? And the primer and the growth marks on the door-jamb?"

"Only pretend things. I imagine she's here, just out of sight. Sometimes I call her for supper and wait for her to come running up the porch steps." She couldn't believe she was telling him of her private madness. "I picture her in my mind. How tall she'd be now. What she would be learning in school and what Mrs. Ward is teaching her about managing a household. I'd like to think she knows how to whistle."

She hadn't heard Cameron stand, but suddenly his arms came around her waist. For an instant she stiffened, then sagged against the warm hard length of him, hoping to absorb his strength as memories flooded her mind and she thought her knees would buckle.

"She smelled so good," she whispered. "Her hair was like corn silk. And her little mouth reminded me of a rosebud."

"I'm sorry," Cameron murmured against her hair.

"What hurts the most, what I can't stand to think about, is that they've probably told her I'm dead." Now her voice broke and she turned to bury her face against his chest. She didn't cry, but her eyes burned and her hands trembled. "She's so real and alive to me, but to her, I must be . . ."

Cameron held her, inhaling the lemon scent of her hair. He'd guessed that her daughter was dead, but the truth was worse. Because of him, Della had lost her husband, a way of life, and her baby. Because of him, a little girl was growing up without either of her parents.

He could continue killing outlaws and cleaning up corrupt towns for the rest of his life, and it would never atone for what he had done to this woman and her child.

Chapter 6

Cameron tilted his chair against the back wall of the Silver Garter. From this position he could observe the room and who entered and exited the saloon doors. Placing one's back to the wall had become a cliché in the West, but necessary for men like him.

Sheriff Cowdry refilled their glasses from the whisky bottle on the table. "Joe Hasker won't be a problem. After I finished with him, his daddy took over. I heard yesterday that Hasker Senior is sending young Joe to a military school back east."

It took Cameron a second to recall who Joe Hasker was, then he nodded.

The sheriff turned the shot glass between his thick fingers. "For the most part this is a quiet town. But young Hasker has friends who are as hotheaded as he is."

"I'll be leaving in a few days."

"You know how it is; you've worn the badge. A name comes to town and everyone wants to shake his hand and buy him a drink. Then the speculation starts. How fast is he? Sooner or later some misguided pup decides to find out, and people get killed."

The sheriff continued talking, but Cameron let the

words flow over him, only half listening. His gaze followed one of the bar girls, watching her deftly fend off hands that reached for places they shouldn't. On her return to the bar, she leaned in and said something in the piano player's ear. The piano man shook his head and shrugged as if to say that's how things were.

Years ago Cameron had sat in this same chair and watched Della slip away from grasping hands and murmur something to a piano man. He'd made the right decision that day in not telling her why he'd come, but he hadn't taken his decision far enough. Earlier today he'd corrected his mistake by sending his banker a telegram, worded so his instructions would be clear but meaningless to the Two Creek's telegraph operator.

His attention sharpened and refocused when he heard the sheriff mention names he recognized.

"I'd have taken those boys myself, except I didn't learn they were in town until after they'd gone," the sheriff said uncomfortably. "They only stayed the one night."

The sheriff was talking about the bank robbers that Cameron Fort Worth?"

"Looked that way."

If he lived to be a hundred, Cameron would never understand the criminal mind. The bank robbers were heading exactly where he expected them to go.

"What are the chances that someone mentioned I was nearby?"

Sheriff Cowdry shrugged. "Pretty good, I'd say. You're about the only thing folks have been talking about for two weeks. How many people have been out to the Ward place to shake your hand? A hundred?" The sheriff gave him a long look. "You're going after them, right?"

"Not this time." Cameron's priorities had changed yesterday evening. Even so, he hadn't realized until now that he'd already made the decision, probably before Della finished telling him about her daughter.

"Well," Cowdry said eventually, "I suppose you can't go after them all." Clearly he wanted to ask what could be more important than capturing a pair of notorious robbers, but he glanced at Cameron's face and remained silent.

"It's time I headed back to the Ward place." He brought the chair legs to the floor and stood. "Thank you for the drinks."

Cowdry also wanted to satisfy his curiosity about Cameron's connection to Della Ward and why he was staying out at her place, but he didn't ask that question, either. A prudent man.

As Cameron was also prudent, he chose to ride across the range. He doubted an ambush waited by the roadside, but a man couldn't be too careful. And he had things he wanted to ponder aside from shadows along a road.

It was late when he arrived at the barn, but he suspected Della hadn't been sleeping any better than he was. After he turned Bold in to the corral, he walked up to the house and stood beside her bedroom window, listening for sounds inside.

"Are you awake?" he called softly when he thought he heard a rustle of movement.

"Mr. Cameron?" She didn't sound as if she'd been asleep. "What time is it?"

The moon was waning, but the stars were still bright. "I don't know. Late."

The curtains twitched and he inhaled a faint lemon scent, but she stood in the shadows and he couldn't make out more than a silhouette. "What's wrong? Did something happen in town?"

"I've thought about everything, and I've decided to go to Atlanta and fetch your daughter. You can come with me or wait here."

A gasp came from deep in her throat, then she stepped directly in front of the open window and stared at him. He still couldn't see her face, only a pale starlit oval.

"What . . . I . . ."

"This is the right thing to do."

"Mr. Cameron." Her hands fluttered near her breast. "I don't know what to say. This goes far beyond . . ."

"Can you be ready to leave by the day after tomorrow?"

She was silent for so long, he peered in the window to see if she was still there. "Mrs. Ward?"

"It appears neither of us is going to sleep tonight, so you might as well come inside. I'll heat up the coffee."

By the time he'd walked around the house, she'd lit a lantern in the kitchen and fired up the stove beneath the coffeepot. One of his questions was answered—she didn't wear her hair loose for sleeping. A long, dark braid swung down the back of a light wrapper.

"I suppose this could have waited until tomorrow," he said uncomfortably. It wasn't proper or seemly for him to see her in her nightclothes. He hadn't considered that, before calling at her window. And he hadn't anticipated the powerful effect of seeing her in a state of undress.

Men didn't see women with their hair down and wearing a wrapper unless the women were wives or intimate relations. If someone were to discover them in this state, Della Ward would be irretrievably ruined.

Cameron backed toward the door. "I apologize, Mrs. Ward. We'll talk in the morning."

"No, Mr. Cameron," she said firmly. "We'll talk now. No one is going to come to the door at this hour. At least I hope not." Gathering the collar of the wrapper at her throat, she glanced at the coffeepot. "Sit down." They didn't speak again until the coffee was brewed and poured. "Now. Tell me why you want to fetch Claire." Her shock was wearing off, but her reaction wasn't what he'd expected.

"Your husband wouldn't have wanted Claire to grow up without her mother."

"Given the circumstances, I'm not sure that I agree," she said, speaking slowly and thinking about it. Cradling her cup between her hands, she studied a pair of moths batting against the lantern glass. "The reasons I agreed to leave Claire with the Wards still apply." Finally she met his gaze. "Look around you, Mr. Cameron. Is this any life for a little girl? I can't give her the things the Wards can."

He returned her steady look and said nothing, trying to figure her out.

"There's no second bedroom here, but I imagine Claire has her own room where she is. I doubt she has a list of chores to accomplish before she goes to school or when she returns. Undoubtedly there are servants to do her laundry, prepare her meals, clean her room. I assume she has friends and goes calling with Mrs. Ward. I take as a given that she has an armoire filled with dresses and cloaks and trimmed bonnets. Do you really believe Clarence would want his daughter to exchange that life for . . . this?" She spread her hands.

"You're her mother. She should be with you."

"Most of the people in Two Creeks don't have that high an opinion of me. Maybe they don't believe I'm an outright whore, but they don't consider me respectable, either. Would Clarence want that taint to fall on his daughter, as well? I don't think so. Would he want his daughter to grow up with no friends and no place to wear a pretty party dress? With none of the refinements, like piano lessons, and dance and singing lessons, or time to learn how to embroider? Would Clarence want his daughter to go to bed lonely and exhausted from chores? Do you really believe that's what Clarence would have wanted?"

"You don't have to stay here, Della. You and Claire could make a fresh start somewhere else."

She looked at him as if he'd lost his senses. "If I could afford to leave and start over anywhere else, don't you suppose I would have done so?" She shook her head. "Claire is better off where she is than she ever would be with me."

She was so hard on herself, never flinching from hard truths. "None of your arguments stand against the fact that a daughter should be with her mother."

"Living on a crumbling farm on the edge of a crude little Texas town? Doing without things she takes for granted now?" Her eyes were tired and defeated, dark with pain. "I love my daughter. I want her to have nice things and a comfortable childhood. I like to think of her laughing with friends and going to parties wearing pretty dresses."

"You said you pretended that Claire lived here with you." God help him, did any man understand a woman's mind? He had believed she would burst into tears and embarrass him with gratitude. Instead he was beginning to grasp that she didn't want him to fetch Claire home to her. He didn't understand it.

"I'm not crazy," she said sharply. "I know the difference between pretending and what's real. When I call Claire to supper, I know damned well that she isn't going to appear in the doorway. That's when I imagine her sitting down to real silver and real china and real damask. That steadies me, Mr. Cameron."

"You can drop the mister."

"I like knowing she's learning good manners and living with people who use them. I'm glad she has the opportunities she has. I'd give up everything I have, if it meant she could keep the life she has now."

Frustrated, he reached out and grabbed the moths, crushed them in his fist. Three more appeared, and he ground his teeth. "Let me ask you something. Are you in regular contact with the Wards?"

"No." Her eyes narrowed suspiciously. "Why would I be?"

"Then you don't really know what kind of life Claire is living. Do you?"

She stared. "What are you saying?"

He leaned forward. "Do you know for certain that Mr. Ward's fortune survived the war?"

"Well . . . he sends me money every month . . ."

"Or are you making assumptions that might not be

true? About servants and lessons and expensive dresses. All of it. Do you know that Claire is hale and hearty? Do you know if she's even alive?"

Della started violently and spilled coffee across her wrapper. "Of course she's hale and of course she's alive!"

"But you don't know it for a fact."

"All right, damn it. I don't know it for a fact! Is that what you want to hear?" Upset, she went to the door and kept her back to him. "If something terrible had happened, the Wards would have informed me."

"Would they?"

"Why are you doing this? Why are you putting these terrible images in my mind?"

He wasn't ready to tell her that he needed to put together two lives that he'd torn apart. "Reuniting you and Claire is right, and it's important."

"Did Clarence ask you to look after us? Did you make him some kind of promise?"

"Della, what are you afraid of?"

Her braid twitched as a ripple traveled down her spine. Finally she returned to the table, her face expressionless. "This is a moot discussion because I can't afford a trip back east."

"I can."

"That goes beyond friendship. You don't owe this to Clarence, he wouldn't expect it. Mr. Cameron . . . I appreciate what you want to do, truly. But it's too much. I couldn't possibly repay you for the expenses of the journey you suggest."

"My reward would be knowing you and Claire are together."

For a long time she sat silently, gripping her coffee cup and studying him with a skeptical expression.

"I want to do this," he said stubbornly.

When she finally spoke, he had to lean forward to hear. "What if Claire refuses to see me?"

Cameron had no answer. But now he grasped an inkling of why she was so resistant to the notion of fetching her daughter. "That's a bridge to cross when you reach it," he said eventually, knowing the comment was no help.

"She's only nine years old. A child. She'll never understand why I left her. Very likely she's been told that I'm dead. It would be a shock to discover that I'm alive."

His instinct was to take her into his arms and comfort her. Before he weakened, he stood and reached for his hat. "Think about it."

She gazed up at him, her eyes golden and confused in the lamplight. "You're turning my life upside down."

Never in all his days had he wanted to hold a woman this badly. Just to fold his arms around her and inhale the scent of her and move mountains to make her happy. "We'll talk again tomorrow."

She glanced toward the band of pale color rimming the eastern horizon. "Tomorrow is rushing toward us," she said quietly. She didn't sound happy like he'd thought she would be.

There was no point going back to bed. Della knew she wouldn't sleep, her mind was spinning like a tornado.

Because it was easier than thinking about Claire, she asked herself again and again, why had James Cameron made this astonishing offer? What was in it for him?

The question was cynical and made her feel ashamed of herself. But nothing in life came free. There had to be a cost that she wasn't seeing. And surely Cameron's motivation had to be something stronger than uniting a mother and daughter whom he didn't know.

Or was that fair? She and Cameron were no longer strangers. Last night she had leaned back in his arms and found comfort in his scent and the hard strength of his body. Later she'd spent a restless night battling thoughts she had certainly never directed toward a stranger. They knew each other's habits. But still . . . to interrupt his life to help her—and pay for the inconvenience—she didn't understand why he would do that.

As the sun popped above the horizon, she drank yet another cup of coffee and forced her mind to Claire. Her darling, sweet-smelling baby. Not a day passed that she didn't think about her daughter and wonder how tall she was and what color her hair had become. Had her eyes remained blue? Did she resemble Clarence or Della's side of the family? How did she spend her days? What was her favorite color and flower and holiday and song and, and, and.

These thoughts hurt. But it eased her some to imagine Claire safe and protected and living in comfort.

Now Cameron had shaken that image. Maybe Claire was a sickly child. Maybe she'd been felled by a childhood disease. Or maybe Mrs. Ward was still queer in the head, maybe she treated Claire badly. Maybe money was scarce and Claire lived in penury.

She didn't know.

That was the thought digging at her mind as she went

about her morning chores. She didn't know what Claire's life was like. And now she had doubts about her previous assumptions.

When Cameron came to the house for breakfast, she slammed a plate in front of him and sat down hard.

"Aren't you eating?" he asked.

"I'm too angry to have an appetite."

"All right." He put down his knife and fork. "Why are you angry?"

"I'm glad you asked," she said, speaking between her teeth. "I can't figure out if you're some kind of fairy Godfather sent here to work magic, or if you're a devil in disguise, here to destroy any peace of mind I might have had."

"I'm just a man who's spent a third of his life trying to do right."

"Right by whom, Mr. Cameron? Maybe your idea of right isn't the same as my idea of right. Have you ever thought about that when you're making decisions about other people's lives?"

"Why in the hell are you so upset about this?" The flat look in his eyes stated that her reaction was a far cry from what he had expected and had hoped to receive.

She shoved back a wave of hair and glared at him with flashing eyes. "How dare you just announce that you're going to fetch my daughter! What gives you the right to disrupt her life and mine? Exactly what is your plan, anyway? You kidnap her from her grandparents—you, a stranger—and then drag a frightened little girl a thousand miles west, and set her on my doorstep before you wave good-bye?"

The more she talked, the angrier she got. The gall of him. Jumping from her seat at the table, she paced in front of the stove, waving her hands.

"And then what happens, Mr. Cameron? Do you imagine that Claire and I will fall on each other with joy and happiness? Or do you picture a woman who knows nothing about children, and a shocked child who believed her mother was dead? Do you picture a child missing the people who have raised her, and her own room and belongings, and her friends? Do you picture a woman bowed with guilt because she can't give that child a comfortable life?"

"If the problem is money, I'm willing to . . ."

She threw up her hands, appalled. "Stop right there. Don't insult me by implying that I'm trying to pry money out of you!"

"Good Lord." He stood and threw down his napkin. "I never met a woman who was so damned hard to help."

"And I never met a man who was so eager to interrupt his own life to help a woman he didn't know until two weeks ago!" She faced him across the table, hands on hips, her hair flying around her face. "If your friendship with Clarence was so strong that you feel this much obligation . . . then why didn't you give me his letter ten years ago? Why did you wait until now?"

When he didn't answer, she threw up her hands and stormed out to the front porch and down the steps. Stopping at the cottonwood, she pressed her forehead against the rough bark.

"I'll do whatever you want," Cameron said from behind her. "If you want your daughter, I'll move the earth to get her here. If you don't want that, I'll saddle up right now and ride out. You can forget I was ever here."

She hit the tree trunk with her fist. "No matter what I decide, I'll regret the choice for the rest of my life. If we bring Claire here, I'll hate myself for depriving her of comfort and a very different future. If I don't see her, I'll hate myself for missing an opportunity that won't come again."

"What do you want me to say?"

"Nothing, damn it, don't say anything."

In her heart she knew he was a decent man trying to do a good thing. He'd expected gratitude and excitement. Maybe a flood of tears. And she'd surprised them both with a gale of anger.

"I'm sorry," she whispered, pressing against the tree bark until her forehead hurt. "What if she hates me?"

There it was, the monster question that dwarfed everything else. She couldn't have said it aloud if she'd been facing him.

"You're her mother," Cameron said in a low voice.

"I left her. I got on a train and left her behind."

"You had no choice, Della."

"Of course I had a choice. I could have stolen her from them and run away. Or I could have found work in Atlanta and stayed near her. Maybe if I'd begged hard enough, the Wards would have let me stay with them. I could have done *something* instead of getting on that goddamned train."

His big hands closed gently on her shoulders. "Where would you have run to with no money? How would you have supported yourself and your daughter? There was no work in Atlanta after the war. It was chaos. And staying with the Wards? That was never an option, Della. You know that. You did the only thing you could."

She turned and fell against him, her forehead burning. "She'll never forgive me. Never. Once she sees me, she'll know that I left her. The reasons won't matter, not to her and not to me. I left her!" She hit his chest with her fists. "I let them steal her. I left my baby."

He stood as solid and unyielding as the tree until her arms fell to her sides and she collapsed against him, her face wet with silent, choking tears. Scooping her into his arms, Cameron carried her away from the house.

Worn out, she lay against his chest trying to sort things through and failing miserably. She opened her eyes when he placed her on the grass beside the creek and handed her a wet handkerchief.

"Thank you." Gratefully, she pressed the hankie against her hot face. "What are you doing?"

"I'm taking off your shoes so you can put your feet in the water."

"All right," she said after a minute. It was as good an idea as any. Maybe better than anything she would have thought of. "Never mind the stockings," she said when she saw him eyeing her hem uncertainly. She pushed her feet into the creek and let the cool water flow over her workday stockings. Amazingly, she felt better almost immediately. When he didn't say anything, just sat beside her chewing on a blade of grass, she looked up through the branches of the cottonwood. "I wish it would rain again."

The sky was a vast empty canopy, not a cloud in sight to sail on the hot wind. Her garden was suffering and the range grasses were turning August brown. Everyone went a little crazy this time of year.

"Tell me what to do," she said quietly.

"So you can blame me when you're hating the result?"

She grimaced. "I hadn't thought of that, but it strikes me as reasonable."

"No one can make this decision for you, Della."

When had he started calling her Della? This wasn't the first time, she realized, but she hadn't really noticed until now. She guessed a man who had held her in his arms twice could call her by her first name. To hide the sudden color in her cheeks, she pressed his damp hankie to her eyes.

"I really do appreciate what you're trying to do," she said, the words coming hard. "I never dreamed an opportunity like this could happen. Now that it has, I feel— I don't know—all confused and upset and wrong inside." She had believed that nothing could frighten her anymore, but she'd been wrong.

"That's not what I intended."

"I know." She touched his sleeve with the tips of her fingers, then moved her hand away. "I'm all stirred up, thinking about things I thought I'd buried so deep I couldn't find them again."

Before Cameron rode into her life, she would have said that she thought about Clarence and Claire every day, and that would be true. But she saw now that she'd thought of them both by skimming the surface. She'd kept a barrier between herself and the pain of how she had failed them.

"The thing is, I long to see her. Just see her. That would

be enough. See for myself that she's healthy and happy. See what she looks like."

"We could do that," Cameron said after thinking about it.

She stared at him. "Go to all that expense and travel all that distance, just to look at someone? That doesn't make sense." He had to be suffering the August crazies.

"Let's settle this money issue. I have plenty of money. No, let me finish. I've earned large sums since the war, and I've banked most all of it. What is there to spend it on?" A shrug lifted his shoulders. "Believe me, this trip won't make a dent in my circumstances." He slid a glance in her direction. "I can afford to do this, and I'd like to."

"We'd just look at her, that's all."

"If that's what you want."

"Oh Lord." A wave of electricity raced through her body. "Maybe this is possible." She could see Claire. She could fill her mind with memories. She wouldn't disrupt Claire's life, wouldn't alter her future. Claire wouldn't have to leave anything behind or live in reduced circumstances. And she would never have to know anything about Della. Della could ease her heart by just looking.

Claire wouldn't hate her. Claire would never have to know.

She wanted to scream and shout and run spinning out on the range, wanted to throw her arms around James Cameron and find the words to make him understand the miracle he'd offered her.

She clenched her hands and stepped out of the creek, drying her feet on the prairie grass. "What do you want in exchange?" she asked softly.

Stiff with offense, he stared at her, then walked toward the barn without a backward glance.

Damn it. Dropping her head, she pushed the heels of her palms against her eyelids. But it was such a large gift of time and money . . . how could she understand?

"I'm sorry," she shouted at his retreating figure. He didn't look back, but if today was the day an outlaw took a shot at him, she didn't want her last words to him to be an insult.

Chapter 7

The air is heavy and moist. Spring turning into summer has filled yards with colorful flowers for weddings, or funerals.

Della inhales the fragrance of roses, thick enough to penetrate the heavy folds of her veil, and knows she will hate the scent forevermore.

Mr. and Mrs. Ward walk slightly behind her. Their faces are deeply shadowed, though sunlight gleams on the black lacquer of the hearse, bright enough to hurt Della's eyes.

She blinks hard, watching iron wheels roll across the cobblestones. The stones are uneven and some are missing in the aftermath of war. Her heart stops each time the hearse dips or lurches over a broken stone.

Gold leaves etch the glass in the hearse's back window. There are forty-two leaves twining from a continuous vine. She doesn't look beyond the glass.

Sometimes there is music, which confuses her and makes her head ache. Usually the silence is profound, broken only by the clip clop of the horse's hooves against the cobblestones. The rhythm of the hooves matches her heartbeat, which becomes louder until finally her pulse is the only thing she hears.

She stumbles, catches herself and walks on, so exhausted that she's falling behind. Anxious, she reaches beneath the veil and blots tears with her gloves, struggling to keep the hearse in sight.

"Don't leave me!"

But the hearse has pulled ahead, suddenly a black dot in the distance. Lifting her skirts, she tries to run, but the hollowness inside has made her lighter than the air, which pushes against her and holds her back.

"Wait for me. Please! Wait!"

Della woke in a panic, her heart slamming wildly against her ribs, her ears ringing. Sitting up in bed, she pressed the sheet to her wet face and gulped deep breaths of air that didn't smell like roses, thank God. There were no roses on her property and never would be.

When her pulse settled, she sank back to the pillow and stared up at the ceiling, thinking about Clarence. Cameron had made assumptions about what Clarence would want, and so had she.

"Tell me what to do," she whispered. "Send me a sign."

By the time she'd climbed into bed, doubts had diminished her euphoria. Would seeing Claire make her life easier or harder? Would she return to Two Creeks with memories to sustain her for the rest of her life, or with a hole in her heart? And what if she couldn't resist the temptation to speak to her daughter? What was the right thing to do?

And then there was Cameron. Last night it had occurred to her that the trip to Atlanta was a lengthy journey.

They were committing to spending weeks in each other's company. On the one hand, the realization was exciting, even a little dangerous given the stirrings he roused in her. On the other hand, this trip would change her life, and she wasn't sure how she felt about that. It wasn't much of a life, granted, but she knew the demons here: guilt, regret, loneliness, anger, emptiness. What new demons would awaken if she confronted the past?

And there was something that Cameron wasn't telling her. Frustrated, she sensed it in the measured manner in which he occasionally studied her, in the way he tightened his jaw and turned aside.

But he was right, she thought later in the day, pausing in the midst of making a list of the things she had to do before she could leave. In her heart she longed to see Claire. Now that such a miracle was possible, she let herself feel the need so deeply that she swayed on her chair and thought she might faint.

"Are you all right?"

When she loosened her grip on the table, she discovered Cameron watching from the doorway. "I truly regret what I said yesterday. Down by the creek. I guess I don't have to know why you're making this generous offer."

"I've told you why." He passed her and poured a cup of coffee from the pot on the stove. "Have you decided what to do with the animals?"

He drank more coffee than anyone she had ever met. "I've made a list of people I can talk to." She hesitated. "Should I offer to pay for the care of my animals? Or would that be an insult? What do you think? I can't pay much, but I could manage a little."

"You know your neighbors," he said with a shrug. "I don't."

Since he seemed to thrive on coffee, she decided another cup would suit her, too. "Can you really afford the time for this journey? Shouldn't you go after those bank robbers?"

"If we run across an outlaw between here and Santa Fe, we'll take him in." He carried his coffee to the window over the sink and gazed out like he was impatient to leave.

"We?" She blinked.

"It could happen, but I doubt we'll see any outlaws."

Working in the afternoon sun had dampened the dark curls on his neck and added to the mahogany tan darkening his forearms. Mentally Della traced the line of his shoulders and the muscles running down his back.

She loved to look at him. Ever since he'd arrived, she'd been finding chores outside so she could snatch glimpses of him when he didn't know she was watching. At first she'd peeked at him to enjoy the novelty of having a man on the place. But now she watched because it was Cameron. And sometimes, embarrassingly, her mouth went dry at the sight of him.

When she realized she was staring at how he stood with his legs apart, his boots planted, she pressed her lips together and bent her head over her cup.

Remember this, she admonished herself: There is no future with a damaged man who's a target for every criminal drifting around the West. There's nothing but pain for a woman who loses her heart to a man who doesn't care if he lives or dies. She needed to keep these thoughts at the front of her mind.

"Cameron?" He didn't say anything, but he tilted his head the way he did when he was listening. "It's not easy for me to accept what this trip will cost and . . . I guess I've never met anyone like you, so I just . . ." She shook her head and twisted her hands together. "I don't know how to tell you what this means to me, or how to thank you."

"You don't have to say anything."

"This is strange, and I never thought I'd say such a thing, but it's a little frightening to leave here. I know every square inch of this old place. I have my routine and it doesn't vary much. There are no surprises. While out there,"—she waved toward the door—"everything will be new and different."

Now he turned from the window. "Maybe you'll like those new and different things."

"That's what frightens me the most," she whispered. After a minute she cleared her throat and straightened her shoulders. "Now, about the animals. We can't leave tomorrow. I'll need the entire day to call on these people and make arrangements." She tapped a finger against her list.

"I'll take care of provisions."

"Provisions. Aren't we taking the stage?"

"I thought I explained," he said with a frown. "We'll ride to Santa Fe, then take the train from there."

"Ride? Like, horses?"

"You do ride, don't you?"

Oh Lord. "I haven't been on a horse in years." And she would have preferred to keep it that way.

"I took your bay out this morning. I don't think he'll give you any trouble."

"That would be Bob." The last time he'd been ridden was . . . when?

"We'll also take the mule, and board them in Santa Fe."

Of course they had to ride. Otherwise, he'd have to come back here to fetch his horse. "How far is it to Santa Fe?"

He shrugged. "Three hundred miles. Maybe a little more."

Shock darkened her eyes. Over three hundred miles on a horse? "Are there towns along the way?"

"We'll camp out mostly."

Camp out.

What on earth had she gotten herself into?

Upset without knowing why, Della changed her mind a dozen times regarding which items to pack. Cameron had explained, several times, that she could take only what would fit into the saddlebags. Rebecca the mule, he insisted, would carry camping supplies, no personal items.

In the end she packed her Sunday suit for the train ride, along with proper undergarments and shoes and gloves. She took as many shirtwaists as she could cram into the bags, and an extra riding skirt and stockings. Into the crannies she tucked a comb and brush and various toiletries. She took her wedding photo and Clarence's last letter, plus a small pouch containing the few dollars she had saved, and her jet earrings.

Cameron eyed the bulging saddlebags before he swung them across Bob's haunches and tied them down, but he didn't say anything until he'd finished. "Ready?"

Della turned her face into the hot August wind and gazed at the small farm that had been her home for ten years. Without the noise of the animals, she heard the windmill creaking, a lonely sound that she didn't usually notice. And she didn't ordinarily let herself see how weathered and shabby the house and barn had become. The harsh Texas sun and the winter cold were hard on buildings. And women.

Pushing back her hair, she pulled her old work hat down to her ears and nodded. "I'm ready."

If she never returned, there wasn't a thing here that she would miss, a sad admission because she would return. This was her life and her future.

Cameron boosted her into Bob's saddle, waited until she was settled, then he mounted and caught the mule's lead rope. After running an eye over Della's stirrups and reins, he rode down the driveway.

Della followed without a backward look.

He kept the pace slow and easy, stopping to rest whenever they came to a water hole. Even so, by midday he could see that Della's early enthusiasm had slid toward grim-lipped endurance and determination.

When he helped her off Bob near the thin shade beneath a patch of low oak, she groaned and hobbled toward a tree stump.

"Lordy. You said three hundred miles?"

"Maybe a little farther." He handed her a canteen.

She wet her handkerchief and pressed it to her face. Long ago she'd removed her jacket. Her shirtwaist was sweat-plastered to her back, and long damp ovals extended beneath her arms. In an hour the ragged brim of her hat would no longer protect her face, they'd be riding directly into the sun.

"Are you hungry?"

If he'd been traveling alone, he would have eaten some jerky or cold biscuits atop his horse. In a week or so, when Della was trail-seasoned, he'd suggest not stopping at midday, unless the temperature continued to soar.

"I honestly don't know," she said, her voice muffled behind the handkerchief. Already the handkerchief was drying in the heat. "The thought of walking over to Bob and fetching the sack and bringing it over here seems overwhelming. Give me a minute."

She'd fried chicken at dawn and boiled a dozen eggs. Had packed raw carrots and onions, and wrapped thick slices of raisin cake to see them through the first day.

"I'll get the food."

The handkerchief dropped and her eyes narrowed. "I don't want you serving me. I've made up my mind that food is my chore. I don't want to be a bother on this trip."

"Suit yourself. I'll get some coffee going."

"How can you drink coffee in this heat?"

Instead of watching her struggle to stand and then hobble toward the horses, Cameron went in search of firewood. But he heard her muttering "lordy, lordy" every few steps.

He'd seen enough greenhorns to know that she was stiff and sore, and her back and shoulders ached. If her inner thighs weren't red and chapped, they would be by tonight. On the positive side, sleeping on the ground wouldn't bother her as much as she probably thought it would. She'd fall into an exhausted sleep the instant she closed her eyes.

"How far do you think we've traveled?" she asked after

they'd eaten. In the end, she'd accepted a cup of coffee but claimed she didn't want sugar. Cameron suspected she couldn't force herself to walk back to the mule and search for the sugar sack.

"Maybe ten miles." With all the rest stops, he figured it was closer to eight than ten. Alone, he could cover thirty miles a day. Today, he'd be pleased if they completed twenty miles.

"That doesn't sound like much," she said, letting a handful of sandy soil trickle through her fist. "You know, I was thinking. I suppose there's lots of snakes out here."

Her effort to sound unconcerned made him smile. "Snakes don't like us any more than we like them. We could make this whole journey and never see one."

"I had a rattler in my barn last August." She made a face. "I shot him. Scared me half to death. I haven't fired a gun all that often. Not at something living." After glancing at the guns on his hips, she tossed out the coffee left in her cup.

"Had you fired at something before the snake?"

Everything she did fascinated him and fell into one of two categories. Something that seemed like his impression of the girl in the photograph, or something that seemed like a different person, the woman she had become.

"A couple of years back, two red wolves killed a few of my chickens. It took a while, but eventually I got them."

"Wolves won't be a problem much longer. Not many left."

"And there was another time shortly after I moved to

the farm." She frowned, remembering. "I kept hearing noises in the yard after I'd gone to bed. So one night I sat beside my window with the shotgun in my lap. Along about midnight, I thought I saw a shadow coming toward the house. It might have been a man or it might have been something else, I don't know. But I fired in his direction." A note of pride crept into her voice. "I haven't had that kind of trouble since."

He could imagine the girl in the photograph shooting at shadows, but not at a shadow that might have been a man. While he packed up their utensils and kicked sand over the fire, and she pretended not to notice what he was doing, he asked where she'd learned to shoot.

"It was a long time ago."

"Did the boy who taught you to whistle also teach you to shoot?"

"Actually, it was Clarence." Unconsciously, she touched her skirt pocket and he realized she must be carrying something of Clarence's. He'd hoped . . . well, that didn't bear thinking about. "The hunt club Clarence belonged to had a target range."

In a previous life, he too had belonged to a hunt club. Now the concept seemed so ludicrous that he could no longer recall why he had joined the society. Different times. A different James Cameron.

After he handed her back in the saddle, he gave her a pair of sunglasses. "You'll need these."

She turned them between her gloves. "Do you have a pair?"

He patted his vest. "The sun's going to be in our eyes."

"I read about blue lens. Very fashionable."

Maybe she was teasing him, maybe not. He couldn't

always be sure. "I prefer dark lens, but blue was what they had at the general store."

She put them on and peered around her. "Very strange. Oh my, look at the sky."

Perhaps the novelty of a blue world would take her mind off her aches and pains during the next five hours. Or for the next twenty minutes. Smiling, Cameron checked his horse and mule then swung into the saddle.

It was a slow but good beginning, he thought. She was stronger and tougher than he'd imagined.

His decision to reunite Della and her daughter had been impulsive, but it had felt right three days ago and it felt right now. On some level, knowing she was on the horse behind him fulfilled a longtime fantasy. But he didn't examine that thought too closely. He did let himself realize that he had extended his time with her, a gift that tightened his chest, and felt a sense of relief that he didn't have to tell her about Clarence yet. Telling her now would only make an arduous journey harder. He could wait a few more weeks.

He chose to make camp early when he spotted an old campsite nestled in a circle of twisted mesquite. A nearby riverbed was dry but not a concern, as he carried enough water for necessities.

"Is this when you would usually stop for the day?" She looked down at him from atop Bob, speaking through her teeth.

"You're willing to continue?"

"If that's what you usually do."

"I'm usually not trailing with a greenhorn about to fall off her horse." He lifted his arms. "You've had enough for one day."

When he set her on her feet, she fell down.

"Della?"

She slapped his hands away, embarrassed and blinking hard. "Damn it!" After a minute she sighed, then extended her hand and he pulled her up. Immediately she doubled over. "I haven't been this sore in . . . I've never been this sore. Damn. I'm sorry, but . . . damn." She wasn't crying; however, he suspected she wanted to.

"Let me fetch some liniment." He looked around then cleared his throat. "You could have some privacy over there behind that big clump of mesquite. To rub on the liniment."

He promised himself that he would not think of her pulling up her skirts and stroking liniment on her thighs. Naturally he could think of nothing else.

By the time she returned, he'd set up camp, had the last of her fried chicken on plates, a pot of coffee over the fire, and he'd laid out their bedrolls, placing hers on one side of the fire and his on the other. Whoever had first selected the campsite had chosen well. There were rocks to sit on beside the fire. And yes, he had thought about pale thighs. He was still thinking about pale thighs.

She sat down with a small sound, which she immediately bit off. "And I thought the saddle was hard," she said, arranging her skirt over the rock.

She'd brushed the dust off her clothing and tidied her hair. The odor of liniment reached him every time she moved.

"The liniment isn't helping much."

"Give it time," he said, irritated that from now on every time he inhaled the odor of liniment, he would think about her rubbing her thighs. "Here. Smooth this on your face." Her cheeks and forehead were sunburned, getting redder by the minute.

"What is it?" Lifting the bowl he gave her, she sniffed and frowned.

"It's egg white and castor oil." They were lucky to have the ingredients. He'd overlooked sunburn as a problem.

She hesitated, then removed the sunglasses he'd given her. White rings were appearing around her eyes as her skin turned redder. Silently she smeared the concoction on her face.

"This journey is going to get easier, isn't it?"

"Yes."

Nodding, she glanced at the sun sinking toward the horizon like a huge red ball. "I'm sorry I wasn't any help setting things up. I swear I'll get better at this."

"It's fine the way things are. I have my own routine."

Her gaze narrowed. "I meant what I said earlier. If I see something I can do, I'm going to do it. Gradually we'll work out a new routine."

At times like this, she irritated him. A stubborn expression tightened her mouth and made her eyes squinty. A sure signal that arguing would only make the situation worse.

He wasn't accustomed to dealing with women, that was the problem. The women he'd encountered were whores who were generally straightforward and uninterested in changing a man's routine, or respectable ladies of brief acquaintance who either feared him and said little or who gushed over him and sent him looking for an escape.

Even before the war, he'd been shy around women.

The fair sex inhabited a world that impressed him as trivial. Therefore, it was difficult to talk to them. What did he know about embroidery, menus, china painting, piano pieces? And what did they know about law books, racing four-in-hands, stocks and bonds, or good whisky?

Granted, women in the West could surprise him. He'd met women out here who knew horseflesh as well as he did. Many respectable women had no time for trivial pursuits, but worked as hard as their husbands. He'd even met one or two females who could discuss politics as astutely as any man.

But he'd never spent as much day-to-day time with a woman as he had with Della Ward. She was proving to be as mysterious, puzzling, and irritating as he'd always thought women were. But he also saw her charm and beauty, as well as qualities he hadn't expected. Courage, determination, and a quiet sense of honor and duty.

And opinions. She had opinions about things and expected him to accommodate those opinions, even if it meant changing routines that had worked well for ten years. He wondered if a more experienced man would know how to get around a woman's opinions and her need to change things.

"Cameron?"

"Sorry. I was thinking about something."

She waited a minute as if she expected him to explain what he was thinking. When he didn't, she made an impatient gesture, then smothered a yawn.

A man shouldn't feel guilty because he didn't care to explain himself.

"Do we have plenty of water?"

Leaning forward, he poked the fire, thinking about the horses, coffee, the canteens. "I'd say so."

"Good. I want to wash out some things."

He glanced up at her. "You mean like laundry?"

"Yes." She averted her gaze and images of stockings and undergarments flashed through his mind. First thighs, now undergarments. He, too, looked aside, cursing under his breath.

"We don't have enough water to do laundry."

"I was afraid of that," she said unhappily. "Well. When will we come to a town? And will we stay there overnight?"

"The next town is about a week's distance. We could stay overnight. If you insist." And if the town had a hotel. He couldn't recall.

But he did recognize another change in his routine. On his own, he didn't travel from hotel room to hotel room. He camped on the plains until he smelled ripe and every item in his saddlebags needed a wash. Obviously that wasn't how it would be on this trip.

Resentment began in the center of his chest, but receded when he glanced at her. Della stared into the fire with a morose expression that suggested she wasn't happy about how the journey was shaping up, either. Plus she was aching in every muscle and bone, and her face was taut and shiny with egg white and oil. Clearly she was utterly miserable.

Just when he thought he'd figured out one small thing about her, she proved him wrong, this time by suddenly lifting her head with a radiant smile.

"We're really doing this," she said softly. "We're going

to find Claire. I'll get to see my baby. Oh, Cameron, I'm so happy."

Happy? She was so stiff and sore she could hardly move, and her sunburned skin had to be hurting. But he gazed into her eyes and believed her. The sadness seemed lessened tonight.

When she could no longer restrain her yawns, she excused herself as politely as if they were sitting in a drawing room, and she left the fire to examine the bedroll.

Cameron had no idea what the protocol might be for traveling with a woman. Did he walk into the darkness and stay there while she did whatever women did to prepare for sleeping? Did he just avert his eyes? Pretend there was nothing out of the ordinary about sleeping a few feet from a woman he'd fantasized about for ten years?

Uncharacteristically indecisive, he waited to see what she would do, still considering a walk out on the range.

Keeping her back to him, she tugged off her boots, hesitated a moment, then crawled into the bedroll wearing her clothing. Thank God for that, he told himself, trying not to feel disappointed. Then she took down her hair and produced a brush out of thin air. Fascinated, he watched her brush a cascade of waist-length brown hair before she turned her face to the darkness and nimble fingers plaited a braid quicker than he would have believed possible.

While he was thinking about the brief glimpse of a silken waterfall tumbling to her waist, she wiggled down between the blankets. "Good night," she called over her shoulder.

"Good night," he said in a scratchy sounding voice.

Yes sir, this was going to be a very different kind of journey.

He poured another cup of coffee and did some flame gazing himself. There was no hope that he'd be going to sleep anytime soon.

Chapter 8

There wasn't much to look at on the open range. With no shade and no rain, the sparse wildflowers browned in the heat, tucked amidst grass turned dry and tough. Occasional dust eddies spun funnels of whirling red sand across the horizon.

Cameron had explained that the ground rose to the west, and Della tried to see the lift but couldn't. The plain looked flat as toast to her untrained eye.

By the third day she realized there was more definition than she'd first imagined. Gullies appeared, too wide and deep to cross, which necessitated going around and that often meant traveling an extra mile or two. Gradually she began to notice small hills and clumps of oak or wild pecan, began to realize that the lay of the land changed from hour to hour. Once she saw a small herd of pronghorns kicking up a plume of dust. She spotted enough rabbits that she stopped worrying about fresh meat.

But there wasn't much to occupy her thoughts once she'd observed what little there was to see and had mentally checked how hot and uncomfortable she was. On that count, yesterday had been the worst.

For a full minute, Della had believed she could not get

out of the bedroll. Muscles she'd forgotten she possessed ached and protested every small movement. Climbing back on Bob for a day's ride had required every ounce of will power, and the first hours in the saddle had been agony.

Today was marginally better, which encouraged her to believe that Cameron was correct. Surely every day would get a little easier.

As it didn't improve her spirits to think about hard saddles and chaffing thighs, she focused on Cameron.

He rode tall and easy in the saddle, scanning the open country in front of him. Every now and then he looked back, but not often. It pleased her that he assumed she was keeping up, but it also peeved her because sometimes she wondered if he'd forgotten that she was behind him.

Such thoughts were irksome. It was fine, just fine, that Cameron did not spend as much time thinking about her as she wasted thinking about him. But how could she push him out of her mind when there was little else to look at but his straight spine and the tanned back of his neck?

She could think about Clarence. Since Cameron's arrival she'd spent less time remembering Clarence than she had in years. So, yesterday, feeling guilty that she'd neglected her miseries, she'd read his letter again and again, and felt her spirits sink below ground level. Finally she told herself that if he'd had time to finish writing his letter, he would have forgiven her. But she didn't believe it. She told herself that he would never have posted this letter. He would have reconsidered, then would have written an understanding and forgiving response. But she didn't believe that, either.

Staring at Cameron's back, watching the dampness between his shoulder blades soak through his shirt, she understood that his coming hadn't changed the essentials no matter how it sometimes felt. She was still a woman whose last words to her husband had been "I hate you." Clarence had not forgiven her. And she was a woman who had left her baby behind when she came west.

Head bowed with familiar pain, she didn't hear Cameron call until he circled back and rode up beside her. Then she glanced up with surprise.

"Is it time to stop?" It looked to her as if sunset were still a couple of hours distant.

"We'll make camp early. Do you see that elm about a quarter of a mile ahead?"

"I see it." Elms weren't common on the open range. Their leafy shade extended an invitation as welcome as a parasol.

"If I remember correctly, there's a water hole a few yards from that tree."

Della couldn't see his eyes behind the blue lenses, but his expression suggested he was trying to gauge her mood. "How are you faring?"

"Well enough that we don't have to stop early on my account." That wasn't true. Relief had eased the stiffness in her shoulders the instant he mentioned they could stop now. But she would have continued despite her aching back and bottom, rather than raise a bump in his all-important routine. He was, after all, making this journey for her.

By now she didn't expect Cameron to offer an explanation without some prodding. "So . . . are we stopping on my account?"

He scanned the horizon. "I have a hunch that something is going to happen, and I want to set up camp before it does."

"What's going to . . . ?"

But he'd given Rebecca's lead rope a tug and set off for the elm, Rebecca trotting along behind him.

Annoyed, Della sighed, then urged Bob forward. To her way of thinking, Cameron had been easier to get along with back at the farm. There he'd been less terse and more accommodating. Out here he seemed tense and distracted.

Maybe his edginess was a result of being responsible for a greenhorn like herself. Or perhaps it strained his nature to travel with another person. Maybe he regretted his offer to take her to Claire. The last possibility loomed large in her mind.

"Cameron, we need to talk," she said after dismounting. Lord, the shade under the elm felt good. Three days of traveling into the sun had set her face on fire. The egg white and castor oil helped, she supposed, but she knew her skin must be turning the color of a tomato. She didn't have the energy or the courage to find her small mirror and have a look.

"Later," he said. Moving faster than he usually did, he dug a firepit and filled it with twigs and small dry branches. When the flames were jumping, he added thicker branches, then strode toward Rebecca to fetch utensils and the bedrolls.

Della picked up the coffeepot where he'd dropped it

beside the fire. "I'll find the water hole and fill the pot." Apparently a serious discussion would have to wait.

"No. Stay right here." When she lifted a puzzled eyebrow, he glanced over his shoulder away from the shade. "I'll fill the pot. If you want to help, you can pick a spot for the bedrolls."

"Heaven forbid I should actually roll them out, but I'm allowed to pick a spot." She was tired, hot, and worried that he'd changed his mind about taking her to Atlanta.

He gave her a long look, then walked toward a small clump of willows, the coffeepot dangling from his fingers.

She moved away from the fire, wishing they had lemonade and ice instead of coffee. Every summer she longed for ice, and tried to remember the sensation of it melting on her tongue. Not once had she ever longed for a cup of hot coffee in August. Coffee wasn't going to improve her mood or make her feel cooler.

When Cameron returned, he glanced at the bedrolls that she'd opened, and noticed the tree stumps she had rolled up to the fire for seats. The last thing Della wanted to do was sit beside a fire, but once the sun set, the flame's warmth would be welcome.

Tight-lipped, she watched him prepare the coffee and set the pot over the fire. It appeared to her as if he made a pot of coffee exactly as she did, so why was he so possessive of the chore?

"Where are you going?"

She held up a bundle of items that she'd pulled out of her saddlebags. "I'm going to the water hole to wash out a few things. Do you mind?"

He took off his blue glasses for a moment and rubbed his eyes, a clear sign of exasperation. "I want you to stay here."

"And I want a bucket of ice." She stared at him, then pushed through the underbrush in the direction he'd gone earlier.

"You're a stubborn woman, Della," he said from directly behind her.

She shoved through the willows, letting the thin branches snap back on him. "There was a time when I was accustomed to sitting idle while people waited on me, but those days are long past." Stepping into the clearing around the water hole, she examined the animal tracks at the edges, then turned to him, her eyes narrow behind the blue lenses. "It's hard enough that you're paying for everything. I need to contribute something along the way. I'm certainly capable of making a pot of coffee."

He leaned over her, so close that she felt the heat rolling off his body, inhaled the strong male scent of him. "I've been roaming the plains for years. It's faster and easier for me to set up camp. Besides," he added, speaking through clenched teeth, "I like taking care of you."

The shape of his mouth always surprised her. His lips could go thin and tight with strangers or when he was irritated, but the lines were sharp and firmly defined. An exciting mouth with no softness or yield.

But she didn't believe what those lips were saying. No man took a shine to waiting on a woman unless courtship or illness were involved, and neither situation applied here.

She lifted up on tiptoe until she was almost nose to

nose with him. "I intend to do my share of the work on this journey. Now that's how it's going to be or you can take me home right now."

"Damn it." Stepping away from her, he swept off his hat and slapped it against his thigh. "All right," he said finally, turning to her. "Can you lay a campfire? Can you cook over an open fire?"

"I can learn." She lifted her chin.

"Do you know how to pack a mule? Are you strong enough to saddle the horses?"

"Have you changed your mind about us going to Atlanta?"

"What?"

"Is that why you're so obstinate and strange out here? You hope I'll suggest that we go back?"

To give him credit, he stared as if she'd lost her mind. "Are you saying you want to go back?"

"No, damn it." She stamped her foot in frustration, something she hadn't done since she was a young belle. "I'm just trying to figure you out!"

Needing to do something, she knelt beside the water hole and dipped water into a bucket, then pushed her stockings and drawers inside, along with a sliver of soap. Then it occurred to her that she was washing unmentionables in front of a man.

"Why did you follow me here? Isn't there something you should be doing back at the campsite?"

He studied the bucket, then turned aside. "You never know what might be hiding a few yards from camp. I doubt you'll get hurt, but accidents happen."

The only thing that truly worried her were snakes, and

she made a point of making plenty of noise when she needed a moment of privacy. "There's nothing here except you and me."

"Possibly. Nevertheless, I'll wait."

For heaven's sake. Rushing the job, she washed her things, wrung them, threw out the water, then silently marched back the way she'd come. If he hadn't been standing over her, she would have had a wash herself.

"Are you coming with me while I hang these things on the bushes to dry?" Her expression warned against it.

"You go ahead. I need to rebuild the fire."

"Good."

When she returned, he was leaning against the trunk of the elm, cradling a cup of coffee between his hands, his hat tilted back on his head. If the tension hadn't quivered between them, the sight of him would have taken her breath away. He was tall and lean and powerfully built. Smooth cheeked and tan. A dangerous man with cool eyes and pistols on his hips. And they were alone in the middle of nowhere.

Della drew a long, slow breath and poured herself a cup of coffee that she didn't want. The sun was lower in the sky, but it would be at least an hour and a half before it would be dark enough to go to bed.

"At your farm, we ate and worked and slept by your routines. I didn't request that you change anything to accommodate me. Out here, I ask you to respect my routines."

"Is it so hard to understand that I want to do my share of the work? Isn't that why you fixed my barn roof and mended the fences? Because you couldn't accept shelter and board without giving something back?"

"It's not the same thing. Out here, a man has to be alert for every sound, for everything that doesn't feel right."

She threw out her hands, spilling half of her coffee. "Cameron, there isn't another living person within thirty miles!"

"You're wrong about that."

She wished he'd take off the blue lenses so she could see his eyes. In fairness, maybe he found her blue lenses irritating, too.

"What I'm saying," he continued, "is that a routine doesn't require any thought. When the routine is disturbed, thoughts aren't as focused."

Finally his resistance made a little bit of sense. "Traveling with me is a change in your routine," she said after a minute. "Are you less focused?"

"We're going to find out."

Della tossed out the rest of her coffee and gave her skirts an impatient twitch. "What do you think is going to happen?"

"The important things for you to remember are to stay out of the way, and that you are in no danger." As he spoke, he removed his gun belt, which astonished her. He ate and probably slept wearing his gun belt. But he was removing it now?

"What do you keep looking at?" she said, waving toward the range. She was exasperated enough to almost regret the journey. "There's nothing out there!"

And he must know it, too, because he dropped his gun belt at the base of the elm and rolled up his sleeves.

Skirts billowing, she strode toward the fire, frustrated

by his small mysteries. If he thought being mysterious was appealing then he had . . .

A growling scream shattered the silence. Della spun and froze as a creature leapt out of the sandy soil on all fours, dirt and twigs streaming off his body. A shocked second elapsed before she recognized the creature was a man.

His hair was wild and bushy, coated with sand. Soiled buckskins were part of what made her think he was some kind of animal. In fact, what she was looking at was worse than an animal. As he sprang to his feet, Della saw a tomahawk in one hand and a knife flashing in the other.

Screaming, she dropped to her knees, unable to breathe and certain that she was about to be killed, until she remembered Cameron. But he didn't fire as she expected. Oh God. He'd removed his gun belt. The one time he needed his pistols, they weren't within reach.

Shaking with fear, she watched Cameron charge toward the crazy man, armed with nothing but his bare hands. Lord, Lord. Why had he taken off his guns, now of all times?

There wasn't time to think. The two men came together in a clash of shouts and blows. Della didn't see how it was possible that Cameron could survive the knife and the tomahawk, and she covered her eyes. But when she dared to look again, Cameron wasn't dead as she'd half expected. The two rolled on the ground in a billow of dust.

What was she thinking of, to sit there and do nothing? Pushing to her feet, she frantically looked around and then remembered Cameron's guns. But the men were fighting between her and the gun belt. Lifting her skirts, she edged around them, unable to see through the dust well enough to judge if Cameron was holding his own. Then she spotted the tomahawk, the blade deep in the ground, well away from where they were fighting. Thank God. But there was still the knife.

When she reached the gun belt she was gasping and shaking and swore at the difficulty of jerking a pistol out of the holster. Immediately she suspected she couldn't hold it steadily enough to hit anything.

And what if she shot Cameron? Blinking hard, she peered through the dust and tried to identify which man was on top. The attempt proved futile as they kept rolling around, their positions changing. Swallowing, she adjusted the pistol in her hand and tried to decide what to do. She would let them roll up near her, then lower the pistol next to the wild man's head and pull the trigger. That would work.

But the men were on their feet again, flailing at each other, feet and fists flying. Della tried to follow the wild man with the barrel of the pistol, but the dust made her eyes water. On the positive side, she no longer saw his knife, they were fighting with bloodied fists.

"Good Lord. That's a woman!"

Through swirls of dust, she returned the wild man's surprised stare. His fist had halted in midair on a path toward Cameron's face.

There wouldn't be a better chance. She pointed the shaking pistol at him and pulled the trigger.

She would have shot him square in the chest if Cameron hadn't knocked her hand aside. The bullet chunked into the trunk of the elm.

"For the love of God, Della! I told you not to interfere."

Dust whirled around them, as thick as morning mist. But she spotted blood on his lip and chin. Blood seeped through a slash on his shoulder.

Blood ran freely from the wild man's nose. One eye was swelling rapidly. Blood leaked from a cut on his thigh.

"Give me the gun. What were you thinking of?"

"I was trying to save your life, you ungrateful bastard." She looked back and forth between them, her heart still pounding, her nostrils pinched by the stink of gunpowder and dust. "What's going on here?"

"This is Luke Apple. Luke, this is Mrs. Ward."

"I'm pleased to meet you." He wiped his bloodied knuckles across his buckskins before he narrowed his eyes on Cameron. "Another minute and I would have killed you."

"Like hell. But I figure this round is finished. Agreed?"

Mr. Apple inspected Della with frank interest. "Considering there's a lady present . . . agreed. There'll be another time."

"I'd be obliged if you'd fetch our doctoring kit," Cameron said to Della. "It should be in one of Rebecca's saddlebags." He examined the blood seeping from Luke Apple's thigh. "Tell me where your horse is tied, and I'll go get him."

Now Della noticed that Luke Apple was not a young man. What she'd mistaken for dust in his hair was gray, and his sun-darkened face was seamed with lines. His hands and wrists reminded her of gnarled branches.

"I'm not moving until I know what this was all about."

The whole thing was bewildering. A minute ago, they'd been trying like hell to kill each other. Then abruptly they'd agreed to stop fighting, and now it appeared they knew each other well enough to be friendly in spite of trying to kill each other.

Luke Apple lowered himself to the ground beneath the elm and touched his swelling eye. "James Cameron killed my wife's nephew. I've sworn to kill him back. It was the only way to keep peace in the family."

Cameron pressed his lip, then inspected his bloody fingers. "His wife's nephew burned the home and barn of a Kansas farmer. When I shot him, he'd just raped the farmer's thirteen-year-old daughter."

"My God." Della's eyes widened on the old man.

"I'm not saying the bastard didn't deserve what he got. But he was family. And a man can't let a family killing go with a never-mind. There has to be retribution."

"When did this happen?"

"Seven years ago?" Cameron asked Mr. Apple.

"Mighta been eight."

"You've been trying to kill Cameron for eight years?"

"Lord, if she don't sound just like Green Feather." He considered Della out of his one good eye. The other was nearly swollen shut. "These things take time. You can't rush revenge."

They both looked at her as if they didn't expect a woman to understand. And she didn't.

"How many times have you tried to kill him?" she asked the old man.

"I don't know. Once or twice a year." He looked up at Cameron. "You don't move as fast as you used to, and this is the third year in a row that I caught you without your guns. You're getting careless. Next time I'll get you."

"Next time I'll bury you and ride away without a backward glance. You aren't as good as you used to be. I knew you were here."

Disgusted with both of them, Della went looking for the doctoring kit. Cameron's saddlebags were neatly packed, which she expected, but she took her time locating and then checking the kit. Figuring things out.

She couldn't guess how Cameron had known that Luke Apple was in the vicinity, but he had. And while Mr. Apple might—or might not—have seriously intended to kill Cameron, Cameron had removed his gun belt. She thought about that. And when she returned to the men, she wasn't as grim-lipped.

Cameron had stripped off his shirt and helped the old man out of his buckskin trousers.

"Green Feather will flay me alive when she sees these pants cut up."

"How is she?"

"Fat and mean and crazy. Just like always, God love her."

Cameron grinned. "Tell her I send my regards."

"Like hell I will." He glanced up at Della. "Do you intend to douse these wounds with whisky?"

"That's my plan, since I didn't see anything else in the kit." A quick look told her that both had long slashes, but the major wounds didn't appear deep enough to require stitches. Good. Even the thought of stitching skin made her feel queasy. "I brought the bottle of whisky from your saddlebags," she said to Cameron.

"Where's your hospitality, James Cameron?" Luke demanded. He jerked his head toward the bottle in Della's hand. "If you were bleeding at my place, I'd offer you a drink."

Cameron started to get up, but Della waived him down. She poured herself a cup of whisky first and took a long, fiery swallow. An armadillo was easier to understand than a man. Men simply did not live in the same world that women did.

She washed their wounds, doused the cuts with whisky, applied ground charcoal to draw out poisons, and bandaged them.

"There's nothing I can do for your eye, Mr. Apple."

"I know it. This ain't the first time I had a shiner."

"And you're going to crack open your lip every time you talk. It'll take a while to heal," she said to Cameron. The cut was small but ill placed.

"Nothing to be done about it." Pushing to his feet, he flexed his shoulders and tested his body for aches and bruises. "I'll fetch your horse."

"It's the same old paint I always ride. Over yonder."

"I'll start some supper," Della said. Apparently Mr. Apple, their revenge-crazed guest, would be staying. She eyed him uncertainly. "You're finished attacking us?"

He jerked back with offense. "I got nothing against you, just him. I don't attack women. What kind of a man do you think I am?"

"I'm trying to figure that out." She worked while she talked, keeping a wary eye on Mr. Apple, and reminding herself that Cameron wouldn't have left her alone if he thought she was in danger. On the other hand, he hadn't let her go to the water hole alone, so Mr. Apple wasn't harmless by any means. "What kind of man are you?"

"Well, now. Been a long time since anyone asked me that." Mollified, he considered. "I admire Indians, for one thing, like 'em fine, which I guess makes me different from most folks. I liked 'em better before they ended up confined. They ain't taking to it well. But who would? I got me an Indian wife; third one, in fact. That would be Green Feather. The other two up and died on me."

"Is she really mean and crazy?" Supper would be simple. Beans, bacon, and biscuits. A 3-B supper, Cameron called it.

"Crazy people are interesting," Mr. Apple said at length, as if he'd given it considerable thought. "It's the crazy that makes her mean."

"I knew a crazy woman," Della said, remembering Clarence's mother. "She was mean spirited before she went queer in the head. Getting crazy just made her worse."

"Did your crazy woman try to kill you?"

Her head jerked and she looked up at him. "Possibly." She cleared her throat. "Once she threw a pan of boiling water at me. It was lucky that I was wearing several petticoats."

"That's what makes a crazy woman interesting. You never know what they'll do. Once Green Feather staked me out on the range and left me to die. An old man like me." He shook his head and swallowed half his cup of whisky. "When I finally came home, she said she didn't remember doing it. But she asked if I still planned to take a second wife." He laughed. "Where's your husband, missus?"

"He died at the end of the war." The beans and bacon were coming along nicely, but her biscuits looked too skimpy. She powdered them with more flour.

"That's a long time to be a widow lady."

As she couldn't think of anything to say, she busied herself seasoning the beans. Lots of salt, a little pepper. She didn't find any other spices.

"A woman could do worse than to cast her eye on James Cameron," Mr. Apple said after a minute. "That's a good man."

She raised an eyebrow, resisting the urge to smile. "But one with a short life span." In a more serious voice, she asked, "Were you truly trying to kill him?"

The old man's good eye sharpened. "Did you really try to kill me?"

Silence answered the questions for both of them.

"I admire James Cameron, I truly do," Mr. Apple said. "There's many a time I've wished some other lawman had killed Green Feather's nephew. There ain't going to be much celebrating when I finally get my revenge."

"That's kind of you," Della said, not sure if she meant it sarcastically or sincerely.

"I know it," he said cheerfully. "But back to what we were talking about . . . it ain't natural for a woman not to be married. A woman needs a husband."

Cameron appeared then, leading a swayback, spotted horse carrying spare saddlebags. Every now and then he made a sound and touched his bandaged shoulder, but he didn't ask for help unsaddling the paint and settling it for the night.

After they'd eaten, he thanked Della for the meal. "The biscuits were especially fine."

"Best biscuits I had in a while," Mr. Apple agreed.

The biscuits had been flat and too browned on the bottom, but Della didn't point out the difficulties of camp cooking. She scrubbed the plates and pot with loose sand while Cameron and Mr. Apple exchanged news and talked over cups of coffee mixed with whisky. Cameron dabbed at his lip occasionally when a drop of blood leaked past the salve Della had provided as treatment.

Occasionally she looked at him across the fire, thinking about what Mr. Apple had said regarding a woman's need to be married. Certain things went hand in hand with marriage, things she hadn't thought about in a long time. Suddenly her stomach felt hot.

"If you'll excuse me, I believe I'll just . . ." She waved a hand toward her bedroll. Then she looked at the two of them. "It is safe to sleep, isn't it?"

Mr. Apple rolled his eyes and looked disgusted. "You disappoint me, missus."

Cameron smiled, and Della's stomach burned a little hotter. "Luke's finished for today. He's too tired to assault a gnat. Between the fight and the whisky, he can hardly keep his old eyes open."

"Now that is a damned lie!"

"You're safe," Cameron said in a serious tone, his gaze meeting hers.

In fact, she'd never felt safer than she did in the company of James Cameron. The realization surprised her a little, but she supposed it shouldn't have. The man was a legend.

He was also a wee bit of a fraud, she thought before she fell asleep. He'd known the old man was hiding nearby. But he'd set down his guns.

There were layers to James Cameron that she hadn't suspected.

And there was that strange hot weakness in her stomach . . .

Chapter 9

"So, what kind of a woman are you, missus?"

"Today, a cold and wet one."

A steady drizzle had fallen since morning, running down the neck of Della's oilskin duster, leaking between her wrists and gloves, and finding entry into her boots. By the time she realized that her hat must have a hole, the knot of hair coiled atop her head was soaked and dripping rainwater down her cheeks.

"The temperature's dropped thirty degrees since midday," she said, shivering. Using her saddle as a backrest, she leaned against the damp leather and blew on her fingers to warm them.

She and Luke Apple sat on blankets spread over wet buffalo grass, listening to the hum of raindrops singing on the canvas roof of their lean-to. They looked out into the rain, watching Cameron moving around the campsite.

"How did he manage to get a fire going?" Della couldn't see the fire from the lean-to's opening, but she could smell hot coffee, and for once she was eager to have it.

"If a man can't start a fire, he should live in a town and stay there."

"I don't remember it ever being this cold in the middle of August."

"Huh. This ain't nothing. Out here on the range, it can snow one day and bake your hide the next. Especially late in the season, with fall coming on."

She wondered if it was worthwhile to try to dry her hair or if the air was too damp. Wondered if it was worth the energy needed to rummage through her saddlebags and find her towel. "Why does it take more out of a person to ride in wet weather than when it's dry?"

"Now *that* I don't know."

"And why does he," she nodded toward the rain falling past the opening, "have to be so stubborn?"

Cameron had helped Luke erect the lean-to, then he'd insisted that he didn't need an old man and a female getting in his way. Della had mentioned that the work would go three times as quickly if she and Luke helped set up camp, and besides they were already soaked.

"Which is a worry," he'd said. "I don't need either one of you getting sick on me."

As if he were immune to ague and chilblains, but they were ripe for illness. She had argued that they didn't need him coming down ill, either, but he'd dismissed the comment as if he'd never had a sick day in his life.

"When I was younger, I'da done the same thing," Luke Apple said, adjusting a stiff horse blanket around his shoulders. "I didn't cotton to folks messing with my camp. A man likes things a certain way."

"Women prefer to share chores."

"Even in your kitchen?"

"Well, not in my kitchen," she admitted with a thin smile.

She wasn't sure why it made her angry that Cameron didn't want her help. Over the last two days he'd surrendered a couple of small tasks, yielding them up like treasure, but also making his reluctance clear.

Filling the coffeepot and opening the bedrolls didn't satisfy her need to contribute. Nor did it fulfill her secret image of the two of them working side by side in productive harmony. She blinked. Now where had that thought come from?

Needing a distraction, she found her towel, then set her hat aside and removed her hairpins, carefully catching them all and tucking them in her pocket. Vigorously she toweled her hair, showering drips down the front and back of her oilskin duster.

"You didn't answer my question." The old man was a talker. He listened well, too.

"I guess you could say that I'm a woman who doesn't amount to much," she said at length, glancing past her towel into the rain. "I've been a wife and a mother, but I wasn't good at either. I didn't do right by my husband or by my baby girl." Riding alone in the rain had opened her mind to a deluge of bitter memories.

"Go on."

"That makes me angry. Deep down, gut-hurting angry." The minute she spoke the words, she understood they were true. Lowering the towel, she stared into the gray, wet landscape. "I didn't do right, and I let myself get stepped on," she whispered. How could she have failed to understand that sorrow was not her defining characteristic, anger was.

"There must be something good about you," Luke said after a minute.

"Well, there is," she snapped. "I'm generally capable, can stretch a dollar; I grow the biggest damned pumpkins in Two Creeks, Texas; and I can whistle."

"I never did learn to whistle. And I don't stay in towns."

Either he'd lost interest or he found her as dull as dishwater. "I guessed that was why we didn't stop." They'd glimpsed a town yesterday but had given it wide berth. Later Cameron had inquired if she minded much, and she'd just shrugged. But right now she would have given everything she owned to be sitting in a dry, warm hotel looking forward to a hot meal and a fluffy mattress.

"Here's coffee," Cameron said, ducking into the lean-to. He sounded irritatingly cheerful. Sinking to the ground, he folded his long legs Indian fashion, then inspected the wet hair dropping to Della's waist. "A hole in your hat?"

"Now how did you guess?"

"She's an angry woman," Luke explained. He still wore his own wide-brimmed hat trimmed with a green feather tucked into a snakeskin band. Cameron's hatband was plain, fashioned of braided rope.

"Are you angry at anything particular or just in general?"

"Sounds like she's mad at everything, but mostly she's mad at herself."

"I can speak for myself," she said to Luke. Then she threw down her towel and gripped the hot coffee between her hands. "I don't know why I'm angry." The two men exchanged a glance, which made her grind her teeth. "I'm mad at the rain, I'm mad at you because I feel useless and dependent," she said to Cameron. "And I'm mad at you for scaring me and trying to kill him," she added, narrowing her eyes at Luke.

"I guess that's fair," Luke decided. He studied the canvas overhead. "I'm mad because I have to go home and tell Green Feather that once again I failed to kill James Cameron." He looked at Cameron as if to say, your turn.

"All right, I'm mad, too. I'm mad because my lip keeps splitting and because the rain slows us down." They both turned to Della.

"I'm getting madder by the minute because I suspect you're teasing me," she said slowly, searching for a betraying twitch in their expressions.

"I ain't teasing about being called squaw-man for forty years. That pisses me off something fierce."

"I guarantee that I'm damned mad that some two-bit bastard wrote a sensational book that painted a target on my back."

Luke sat up straight, indignant. "By God, we should go shoot somebody! Who do you want to shoot, missus?"

"What I'm really mad about is that Clarence had the mother he had."

"You want to shoot your mother-in-law?"

Della considered the suggestion. "She said and did hurtful things. She held herself above gratitude and forgiveness. She had a cruel streak a mile wide."

"That was a long time ago," Cameron offered quietly.

But the time with the Wards had been so intense, so terrible, that it had burned as deep as a brand. She couldn't seem to shake free of them.

"Time stopped when Mrs. Ward stole my baby and Mr. Ward let her do it." A bubble of fury expanded in her chest. Not the pain and sadness she usually felt, but acid rage, erupting against her insides as hot as lava. "And *I* let her do it."

There was no place to put the rage, no way to handle it and crush it. Burning inside, she shoved to her feet and stumbled past Cameron, needing to run and scream, to rend and tear.

"Della, wait."

Skirts sweeping the mud, she spun and pointed a shaking finger at him. "I swear if you come out here, I'll rip you apart with my teeth and nails!" She ran into the rain.

"What in the hell just happened here?"

Luke shrugged and adjusted his blanket. "Damned if I know. Traveling ain't easy for white women."

"Did you say something that upset her?"

"Not that I know."

At the farm, Cameron had felt her sadness, but out here on the range her sadness had hardened into anger. He'd decided a little anger was beneficial, it erected a barrier between them, and that wasn't such a bad thing. But what was the cause? At first he'd wondered if it was him. Now the answer seemed obvious. Knowing she would see her daughter had triggered powerful memories and emotions.

Reaching for her towel, he blotted the rainwater on his face and throat, then swallowed the last of the coffee she'd left behind.

"You're a married man. You must know about women," he said to Luke. "What would you advise?

Should I find her and try to offer comfort? Or did she mean what she said?"

Luke puckered his lips and considered. "Well . . . usually when a woman says she'll tear you apart with her teeth, she's mad enough to mean it."

"She could get lost out there."

"She's been lost for a long time, son."

He stared at Luke, remembering why he cared about this old man, then he pulled down the brim of his hat and stood.

The rain had settled into a steady downpour with no indication of ending. He could see about ten feet before the slant formed a gray wall.

Where would she have gone? He checked the fire first, and discovered the flames had gone out. The grass was too thick to hold prints. He couldn't tell if she'd come here. There was no sign of her anywhere near the lean-to. Water poured off his hat brim as he faced the range, wondering how far she'd gotten.

Ducking his head, he walked toward the horses. If it took all night, he'd find her.

"I told you not to come after me!"

She was leaning against Rebecca, rain running off her oilskin in sheets, wet hair streaming down her back. As he came closer, he saw that her eyes were wet, but that might be only rain. She'd bitten her lips. Her bare hands were red with cold.

Christ. He had no idea what to say to a wet, angry woman. "If you want to make the coffee and take over the cooking, I have no objection." She turned away and leaned against Rebecca's flank. "In fact, I'd be obliged."

"Just go away."

"The truth is, I don't much like to cook, but you're good at it."

"I don't know anything about cooking over an open fire."

"I'll teach you."

She stood away from Rebecca and shook her head. "I know you mean well, and I'm sorry I said I'd tear you apart if you came out here. But please. I need to be alone."

He moved closer, running his hand along Rebecca's back. "I'm not good at this. Tell me how I can help you."

"No one can help me." She pushed away from Rebecca and dug her fists against her eyes. "I should have stood up to her. I should have said this, I should have said that. I talk to the Wards in my head. Most of the time I don't even realize I'm doing it." She dropped her hands. "I replay the scenes and make them come out differently. I'm strong and in control, and they can't do or say anything to hurt me." Anguish hunched her shoulders. "And you know the worst of it? Even if I could go back and live that time again, I'd do it the same way. I wouldn't stand up to her." She struck her thighs with her fists. "Because they were Clarence's parents! So I didn't talk back, I wasn't rude, I let them use me and say hurtful things, and finally I let them take Claire!"

He brushed his fingertips across her cold cheek. "It's over. You can't change what happened."

She drew back as if he'd slapped her. "You have no right to tell me to forget the past. Not when you live there, too! Not when you've spent ten years trying to atone for an imagined wrong."

"You think I imagined killing good men?"

"When you killed a Yankee, Cameron, he wasn't a good man. Not at that moment. He was a man who was trying to kill you."

"I didn't come out here to talk about me."

She wiped at the rain on her face. "It's the same thing, isn't it? You? Me? We're both trapped in the past like flies in a spider web."

He stared at her hair, black in the rain and gathering darkness. She hadn't said anything that he hadn't pondered before, but hearing it aloud drove home a truth he didn't like to examine.

"Listen to me," he said, cupping her shoulders between his hands. "We're going to fix your past. We can't turn back the clock and change what happened with Claire, but we can change what happens in the future. Della? This time you can make that scene end differently."

She shuddered beneath his hands. "Don't ask that of me. All I want to do is look at her. I just want to see her. Please." She gazed up at him with panicked, pleading eyes. "It's done. I wish to God that I hadn't left her behind, but I did and I'll never forgive myself for that. But, Cameron, if she's happy, if she's safe and comfortable and happy, then I can't punish her by taking her away from the only life she's known. I won't."

Now was not the time to argue. They were a long way from Atlanta. There would be other chances.

"Come back to the lean-to and get out of the rain."

"I know how crazy I sound." She gripped his arms, wanting him to understand. "I'm wild and raging because she stole my baby, but I want to leave everything as it is and let her continue to have Claire."

It wasn't so hard to grasp. Bitterness choked him when he let himself realize that he could never settle down like an ordinary man. Yet he was proud of what he'd accomplished in the last ten years.

Dropping an arm around her shoulders, he gently led her back to the lean-to. The instant they ducked inside, Cameron felt the warmth.

Luke's saddle and blanket were gone, but he'd dug a fire pit inside the lean-to and started a pot of beans and fresh coffee. Cameron peered into the rain, but he saw no sign of the old man, didn't sense his presence.

"Should we look for him?" Della asked. Worry deepened her gaze. "Where would he go?"

"He's gone home."

"At night? In the rain?"

"Luke's lived his life on the range. He'll make camp if he feels like it."

The rain muffled sound, but it annoyed him that he hadn't heard Luke ride out. That would have pleased the old man.

"I didn't say good-bye! I didn't tell him that I like him more than I was mad at him."

"I suspect he knows." Now he noticed that Luke had brought in Cameron's saddle and bags, had laid out the towels. The sly old devil. He almost smiled, guessing what the old man had imagined.

With the fire pit inside the shelter, it was warm enough that Della removed her duster and shook off the rain near the lean-to's opening. She hesitated, then wrapped her long hair in one of the towels.

"I don't know what came over me," she said, sinking to the ground next to her saddle. She didn't look at him.

"I feel like a fool. We were just talking, and suddenly I was furious for no good reason. Just . . . so angry I couldn't hold it in."

After removing his oilskin and hat, he poured them coffee and added sugar to hers.

"I wasn't like this at the farm." She sipped the coffee, closed her eyes and murmured a word of thanks. "At least, not often. Do you get angry?"

"Sometimes I want to shoot some vicious son of a bitch instead of taking him in to stand trial."

"Have you ever done it?"

"Came close a couple of times. Are you hungry?"

They ate Luke's beans, then placed the bowls outside to be washed by the rain. The beans were a bit too salty, and some biscuits would have sat right, but all in all Luke had done well by them.

Now what?

He and Della were alone, listening to the rain on the canvas of a small lean-to. They would sleep not three feet apart. Conversation died in his throat. Luke had provided a buffer between them, had made conversation easy and natural. He wished the old man were still there.

Uneasy, he glanced at Della. She'd loosened the towel around her head and was drying her hair. Firelight softened her expression and for a moment he saw the girl in the photograph.

Never had he let himself imagine that he would be alone with her like this. Close enough to smell her rain-fresh scent, to reach out and touch her if he'd had that right.

And now he understood that the girl in the photograph had been ephemeral, a construction of his imagination. In truth, the girl was the seed which had produced the rose in front of him, a complex combination of beauty and thorns.

"Talk to me," she said when their silence became uncomfortable. She reached for her comb. "Talk about something not connected to the past."

Not since childhood had he seen a woman comb wet hair, hadn't guessed at the patience required to unravel tangles left from toweling. The intimacy of watching her perform a private toilette made his stomach tighten.

"Would you like whisky in your coffee?" He needed a task that required him to look away from her. "It'll help you sleep." More likely, he was the one who would need help sleeping. "What would you like to talk about?"

"I don't know, anything. What do you do for pleasure?"

"Read, mostly. When I'm staying in town, I attend lectures, lyceums, and community events. I don't mind working with my hands when there's an opportunity. I enjoy chess."

"What do you read?"

"Law books, usually. Sometimes fiction." Now the comb slid smoothly through her hair. The shorter strands around her face were drying in soft curls. "I like Mark Twain. I enjoyed *Through the Looking-Glass* by Lewis Carroll." A fact he would have admitted to very few people.

She looked up with one of her rare smiles. "I read that. It wasn't really a children's tale, was it?"

"What do you do for pleasure?" Fascinated, he watched her tilt her head and nimbly plait her hair into a long, glossy braid.

"About five years ago, Mrs. Linsey turned her old

chicken coop into a library. Everyone donated books. The books I like best are those where someone has underlined passages. I try to imagine why that passage was important to someone. Sometimes I think I can guess, other times I can't."

"Do you underline passages?"

"Never," she said, smiling again. "And I'll wager that you don't, either."

"What else do you enjoy?"

She tied off the braid with a twist of twine. "My garden is a chore, except I like growing the stupid pumpkins. Cooking is a pleasure when there's someone to cook for." She lowered her gaze and brushed the end of the braid across her palm. "I used to enjoy playing the piano, although I wasn't particularly talented at it. Do you like to dance?"

He pulled his legs up and rested his wrists on his knees. If the journalist who'd written *James Cameron, An American Hero* had overheard this conversation, he might have written a very different book. The thought made him smile.

"As a matter of fact, I did enjoy dancing. Can't say I've done much of it in recent years, though."

"I used to love to dance." Her eyes shone in the firelight. "I loved the music and the big ballrooms. The ladies in beautiful gowns whirling around the room like pale, fragrant flowers. And the men all in black with their hair slicked down. Remember how it smelled? The candles and the perfume and the scent of the powder on the floor?"

She would have worn her hair up with a jeweled ornament in her curls. He imagined her with sparkling eyes, flirting with a silk fan and tapping her foot beneath a satin hem.

"That's a nice memory." Raising a hand, she covered a yawn, then tossed her braid over her shoulder. "I think I'm dry enough to try to sleep. You were right about the whisky. I can hardly keep my eyes open."

"It's been a long day."

"Are you going to sleep now?" A rush of color brightened her cheeks and she busied herself opening her bedroll and plumping up a thin pillow.

"I'll sit up a while. Wait until the fire burns down."

She looked relieved. Interested, he watched her climb into the bedroll, amazed that she managed to do it gracefully and without exposing a flash of ankle. Her boots were neatly placed beside her saddle, although he hadn't seen her remove them.

"I made a spectacle of myself. I'm sorry."

"I've done the same."

"I doubt that." She smiled and held his gaze until they both looked away. "Well. Good night, then."

"Good night, Della."

Turning inside the bedroll, she arranged herself on her stomach and cradled the pillow in her arms. How could she breathe with her face in the pillow?

"You're certain we don't need to worry about Mr. Apple?"

"Luke's fine."

"Mmm. I like the sound of the rain."

There was a finger of whisky left in the bottle, and he poured it into his cup, then faced the dark opening. If Luke had stayed, they would have had a problem with the sleeping arrangements. Cameron couldn't visualize himself agreeing to put Della between them, not in close quarters like these, where it would be easy to offend by accidently brushing against her. Neither could he visualize placing himself in the middle, where it would be awkward to rise swiftly if the necessity arose.

Despite the drumming of rain on the canvas, he imagined he could hear the steady rise and fall of Della's breath. Damn it. And long after the fire had settled into dimly glowing embers, he saw her braid in his mind's eye and wanted to slide the luxuriant weight of it through his hands.

He tossed back the whisky and let the scald burn down his throat. He had no right to these thoughts. No right at all.

Chapter 10

Morning sun lit the range, transforming a sea of grass into glistening golden waves. Rabbits swam in the undercurrents, and a herd of antelope bounded across the surface. Brilliant blue curved overhead, washed clean of haze and clouds.

As the day warmed, the knots dissolved between Della's shoulders. She deliberately anchored her mind in the present, pleased to discover that finally she could ride all day without aching, could enjoy a day as bright and sunny as yesterday had been cold and damp.

In late afternoon, Cameron circled around and rode up beside her. "Did I hear you whistling?"

"It's a barroom song called 'Mary Avaline.'" In the end, she was who she was. A former bargirl who whistled. She wouldn't apologize for enjoying a pursuit that was not considered feminine. But she did sound a little defensive.

"I know that song." Cameron tilted his head and whistled a few bars. "Can you sing it?"

"Heavens, no. I can't carry a tune in a bucket. But for some reason I can hit the notes true if I whistle."

"Start again. I'll come in on harmony."

She stared at him through her blue lenses. What a surprising man this was, a study in contrasts. Rigid in so many ways, but tolerant in others.

After wetting her lips, she whistled the first notes of the song, waiting for him to join. He tracked perfectly, whistling alto to her soprano.

When the last notes faded, Della twisted on her saddle and blinked in astonishment. "That was wonderful. We created real music!"

He grinned. James Cameron actually grinned. Her heart soared.

"I loved it," she said enthusiastically. "Let's do it again. Do you know 'The Girl I Left at Home'?" The song was slow and melancholy, but well suited to harmony.

"That's amazing." A stranger would have believed they had practiced together for years.

"The horses enjoyed the performance." Leaning, he stroked Bold's neck. "Bold's been restless all day. I think the songs calmed him a little."

"If you want to run him, I'll take Rebecca's lead rope." When he hesitated, she arched an eyebrow. "Yes, it's a ploy. First, I take over the cooking, then I start leading Rebecca. Next, caring for the animals will be my job. Then, I'll start digging the fire pit and setting up camp. I figure in a week or two you won't have anything to do except twiddle your thumbs."

He pursed his lips as if he half believed her, then he suddenly laughed. "You'll still need me to carry the saddles and bags."

"Only until I grow eight inches and put on some weight and muscle. Give me Rebecca's rope."

As he galloped ahead, she thought about how good it

made her feel when she said something that made him laugh. Since she doubted he laughed easily or often, his laughter made her feel special.

But he'd made her feel special from the beginning by listening and by seeming to genuinely want to know and understand her. At first she had attributed his interest to a natural curiosity about his friend's wife. However, recently she'd begun to suspect Cameron might be interested in her for her own sake.

The possibility was flattering but also disturbing.

In all these years, she had never seriously considered remarriage. One or two men had let their interest be known, but she'd made it clear their attentions were unwanted. First, the past tied her to Clarence. Second, she'd proven she made a selfish and unworthy wife.

Now Cameron's attentions confused her thinking. It wasn't that she looked at him wondering about marriage, she hastily assured herself. He would be the worst possible choice, another husband who placed himself in harm's way. She couldn't bear that.

But spending so much time with Cameron reminded her that men and women were meant to be together. Luke Apple had practically said the same thing. Her sense that Luke could be correct warred with her ties to Clarence and her unworthiness.

And there was something else. Having decided she would spend her life alone, she had shut the door on sex. And she had sealed away sexual thoughts and feelings so completely that, until James Cameron rode up her driveway, she could have truthfully said that she seldom, if ever, thought about sex.

That was no longer the case. It was like vowing never

to eat another piece of cake, and finding the vow easy to uphold because there was never cake in the house. Then the most tempting, most delectable cake imaginable appeared and suddenly she had a raging hunger for cake. Cake was all she thought about. Imagining the taste and texture, the look and size of it on her plate.

Della swallowed hard and turned her gaze away from the figure far out on the range.

The odd thing about her recent thoughts was that sex had never played an important role. She hadn't disliked sex, she thought loyally, remembering Clarence, but she hadn't particularly liked it, either. Sex was an awkward duty one performed to appease one's husband and to conceive a child. It was neither pleasant nor unpleasant.

But lately, lying in her bedroll, shocking thoughts had crept into her mind. Was sex the same with every man? What would it be like with Cameron? That question and the images provoked by the topic flooded her body with damp heat.

"Your face is pink. Are you all right?" Cameron asked, reining hard beside her in a spiral of dust.

"It's just the sun. It's hot today. Hard to believe, isn't it, that it could be so cold yesterday and hot today?" She was babbling, trying not to look at his muscled thighs or the tanned sureness of his hands.

Feeling the heat in her cheeks and stomach, she turned her head. He was totally unsuitable. She was unworthy. And that was the end of it.

"There's a place about a mile ahead that would make a good camp."

Nodding, she glanced at the sinking sun. Every day, as she grew more accustomed to riding, Cameron extended their time in the saddle. Oddly, the hours passed more quickly now than when the days had been shorter.

"If you're all right by yourself, I'll go on ahead and bag a rabbit for supper."

"I'm fine. Rebecca is no trouble."

When she reached the campsite, Cameron had dug the fire pit and skinned two rabbits, enough for tonight and tomorrow's supper. He came forward and pulled the saddlebags off Bob's rump.

"I'll get you set up, but the cooking is your job."

"Look. If it truly makes you uncomfortable . . ."

"I've thought about it. I'll establish a new routine."

There were many things she could have said, but she restrained herself. "What an excellent idea." And then she busied herself untying her bedroll and dropping it to the ground. Even the smartest men occasionally had skulls as thick as posts.

She reminded herself of this as Cameron hung over her shoulder while she set up the coffee.

"I like to start with a few of the leftover grounds. Gives the coffee a stronger flavor," he said.

"I did that." She'd never known a man to be so damned particular about his coffee.

"Did you find the bag of egg shells? A few egg shells give the coffee . . ."

Straightening, she placed her fists on her hips and narrowed her eyes. "Do you want to do this?"

Raising his palms, he stepped back. "No. You're doing fine."

"Here. Fill the stew pot with water. Please."

It felt good to have chores of her own. Her mother would have been pleased. One of her mother's concerns about sending her to Atlanta at an impressionable age had been that becoming part of a household with servants and slaves would spoil her. And it had.

She paused in peeling potatoes and thought about the years she had missed with her mother. When she departed for Atlanta, she'd been at the age when she was just beginning to see her mother as a person.

"The rain brought up the water level. There's plenty of water if you need to wash out anything." Cameron put the pot next to the coffeepot. "You look pensive."

"I was thinking about my mother."

"Tell me about her," he said after they'd finished setting up camp and were drinking coffee while they waited for the stew.

"My mother? She was widowed when I was four. I don't remember much about my father." He'd been a tall man with an accountant's hands who smelled like peppermint drops. "What I remember about my mother is that she was always busy. Cleaning, sewing, polishing. It wouldn't have occurred to her to while away an afternoon reading, like my cousin in Atlanta, or to spend an entire day at the park with me." Frowning, she tried to remember. "Proper behavior was important to her. I never saw her cry or raise her voice. I had a feeling that she didn't care much for children, that she and I would get on better when I was an adult."

"Did you?"

"I didn't see her again after I left for Atlanta. By the time Clarence and I married, travel was out of the question as the war was underway, and then she died shortly before Clarence did. So I never knew her on a woman-to-woman basis. I wish I had. What about your family?"

"I think I mentioned that my father was a judge. My mother was involved with temperance societies and groups lobbying for women's rights. My sister and I were expected to read the newspapers and be prepared to discuss the headlines at dinner."

"I think I might have enjoyed a family like that."

"The judge held high expectations for everyone around him. Both Celia and I were a disappointment. He wanted Celia to attend the university and pulled strings to make it happen, but she married instead. He strongly objected to me going to war."

"How did your parents die?" she asked curiously, keeping an eye on the stew.

"The judge was shot by the wife of a man he sentenced to prison. A year earlier, my mother had been exposed to measles at a temperance meeting. She died within a week."

"And Celia died in childbirth?" she asked softly.

"Yes."

Like herself, Cameron had suffered much loss and was the last of his family. "Well," she said after a minute. "I believe supper is ready."

The hours after supper were the hardest of the day. That's when Della became acutely aware of being alone with him. On a night like this, when distant stars spangled an inky sky and the range seemed empty and silent, she could almost believe they were the only two people left in the universe.

What did the last two people in the universe say to each other? Especially when one of those people was increasingly consumed by secret speculation and thoughts that dared not be spoken aloud.

This was the time when firelight defined his lips and the hard angle of his jaw. When she wanted to comb her fingers through his hair and smooth out the unruly tangles of the day. These were the oddly tense moments when she wondered if one man's kiss was the same as another's. And when she remembered the hard muscle of his chest and the way his arms had come around her that evening on the porch.

Della cleared her throat and made herself stop twisting her hands in her lap. "Would you like to whistle?" Anything to chase away the embarrassing questions circling her mind.

"If you like."

Shy at first, then with greater confidence, they alternated choosing songs to try, stopping with laughter when one of them missed a note.

"We're good at this," Della said, when they finally halted because her lips were tired of puckering. Tilting her head, she gave him a teasing glance. "If the legend business doesn't work out for you, we could join a theatrical company."

For a moment he looked startled, then he laughed. "You can be a saucy creature."

The comment pleased her, mostly because it had been years since she'd considered herself saucy. Or flirtatious, which, perhaps, was another word for the same thing. That possibility shocked her and she stood abruptly, making a gesture toward her bedroll.

"It's gotten late. I'll just . . ." This part of the journey wasn't easy, either. Saying the word "bed" in front of a man would have scandalized her mother, her mother-in-law, and just about every woman she'd ever known. She liked to think that she'd become a no-nonsense woman who was above such silliness, but in this instance she wasn't.

"Thank you for an enjoyable evening."

"I enjoyed it, too." And she'd learned something, watching him. The pucker for whistling was not the same as a pucker for kissing. A whistle pucker could be amusing, but she didn't recall ever thinking a kissing pucker was funny.

She didn't know if Cameron observed her crawling into her bedroll, but it felt as if he did, which made her awkward and clumsy. The difficulties with hair followed.

It felt unseemly to brush out her hair with a man watching, but if she didn't plait it, her hair would be a mass of tangles in the morning, plus loose hair got in the way of sleeping comfortably.

When she glanced toward the fire, sure enough Cameron quickly turned his head. Knowing she'd guessed correctly, and that he had been watching, made her feel strange inside, and oddly pleased. Which wouldn't do.

The solution to the hair problem was to braid her hair and leave it in a braid all day. There was no one to see her out here on the range.

That settled, she started by turning her back to him. Then, after counting to one hundred, she turned as if asleep and peeked at him through her lashes.

He sat hunched forward, staring into the dying fire, his coffee cup clasped between his calloused palms. What was he thinking? About tomorrow's ride? About a new routine? About the incidents that had made him a legend and a target?

About her?

Groaning slightly, she turned over on her stomach and pushed her face into the thin pillow. She had to stop letting him dominate her thoughts. Think about Clarence and Claire, she commanded herself, squeezing her eyes shut.

The pumpkin patch stretched as far as she could see in any direction, flowing toward a shimmering silver horizon in a lacy tangle of vines and blossoms.

The blossoms should have delighted her, but instead produced a growing sense of alarm and anxiety. The flowers were long and slender, a greenish gold tube with a fringe of orange ruffling the opening.

Della knelt between the rows, distantly aware that she was barefoot and wearing her nightgown. Afraid, she reached a quivering hand toward one of the blossoms, dreading what she would discover but driven to see inside the petals.

Heart racing, she peeled back one of the long petals to reveal a baby inside the blossom, cradled by the curve of the flower and wrapped in a silken petal.

The baby waved a tiny angry fist at her and she jerked back, feeling her throat close.

Choking and panicked, she ran down the dirt row, halting to look inside another blossom and another. The babies recognized her and cried out. "Don't leave me." "Take me with you." "Mama, Mama, Mama."

Pressing her hands to her ears, she spun in a circle, despairing at the sight of miles and miles of baby blossoms, at the vines that seemed to stretch toward her.

"I can't take care of you all. I can't."

Did they hear her? Did they understand? She could see their faces peering out of the blossoms, anxious and angry, betrayed, frightened, and needing her.

Stumbling, she ran down another row. "Forgive me. Please listen, I can't take care of you. There are too many . . ."

What would happen to them? Maybe if she picked a few of the blossoms, but there were miles and miles of them.

"Della?" Gently, Cameron shook her shoulder, his fingers inches from her braid. "Wake up. You're having a bad dream."

She bolted to a sitting position, gripping his arms and shaking. Tears welled in her eyes.

"I can't," she whispered. Anguish cracked her voice. "I can't take care of them." Her gaze slowly cleared and she frowned. "Cameron?"

"It's a dream."

"Oh Lord." Releasing his arms, she raised trembling fingers to her lips. "It wasn't like the other dreams, but it was terrible."

"I'll bring you some coffee."

Food and drink were the cure-alls for everything. If a man was wounded, someone handed him a whisky bottle. If a family lost a loved one, the neighbors brought food to their door. A new baby elicited punch and desserts. Unexpected company called for lemonade and cake or cornbread. New neighbors received baskets of baked goods. The only thing Cameron could think of for a nightmare was to fetch coffee.

"What did you dream?" he asked, sitting on the ground

beside her bedroll. She had a warm, sleepy scent that he could have inhaled for the rest of his life.

"It's almost gone, but it was something about an enormous pumpkin patch. Acres and acres of pumpkins. And babies, but I can't remember . . ." A shudder passed across her shoulders and for an instant her gaze went flat. "Pumpkins and babies don't sound frightening or upsetting, but somehow they were."

"Dreams are odd things," he said.

She lifted her cup and he noticed her fingers weren't shaking as badly. The dream had left her. "Do you have nightmares?"

"Occasionally." Lord help him, he was admitting to nightmares like a child. "I suppose everyone does," he added, hoping that was the end of the subject.

"Do you ever have a nightmare that you've had before?"

How could she know that? He stared at her. As usual, she'd introduced a topic he preferred not to discuss but felt he had to, since now they were into it and she'd shared a personal observance. Damn it. Now she was waiting, looking at him with wide, expectant eyes.

He hated this kind of thing. "Sometimes I dream I'm in a town. Walking down Main Street."

"Are there other people in the dream? Or are you alone?"

"I'm always alone. But there are people on the boardwalks, families mostly, going about their business. They don't see me."

"Go on."

"I'm looking for my family, then I remember that I

don't have a family. At the same moment, I see my reflection in a store window. I'm old. I have gray hair."

"And this upsets you."

"Yes," he admitted reluctantly. He guessed that she'd expected his nightmare to involve a gang of outlaws and himself outnumbered, something like that. Certainly she hadn't anticipated his worst nightmare would be that he was alone in the middle of a bustling little town. "I don't understand it, either."

Irritated, he went back to the fire and cracked eggs into the skillet. Never mind that he'd told her that fixing breakfast was now her chore. He needed the ease of routine.

What was it about Della Ward that made him tell her things he wouldn't tell another soul? Why did he feel a need to explain himself to her, when he made a point of never explaining himself to anyone else? And why did her good opinion matter so much?

That was the crux of his annoyance now. How could she admire a man who had nightmares about not having a family? He should have said he preferred not to talk about nightmares. That's what he would have done with anyone else.

"I know what you're thinking," she said, walking up to the fire. She'd washed her face and tidied her hair but left it in a braid.

"No you don't."

She studied the eggs bubbling in hot butter. "You're thinking a nightmare should be more horrifying than walking down the middle of a street. You're uncomfortable that this dream is a nightmare for you."

Damned if she hadn't guessed right; she did know

what he was thinking. He sure as hell didn't know what to make of that, so he frowned and said nothing.

"I think dreams send us a message, but not directly."

"That's pure nonsense." He didn't believe in hocus-pocus.

"Then what are dreams?" She elbowed him aside and slid three eggs onto a plate, then handed him the plate. Using her fingers, she dropped several strips of bacon beside his eggs. "Some of my nightmares seem more like memories, but distorted, disturbing memories. Mostly my dreams are incidents that never happened, that couldn't happen. Sometimes it feels as if they should mean something, but I can't figure out the message. And you know what else?" She looked at him over her own plate. "I never dream about Clarence or Claire or my mother. I'd love to see them, but they don't appear in my dreams."

Now that was an odd observation. He had dreamed about Della when all she was to him was an image in a photograph. But he hadn't dreamed of her since she'd become real.

"Seriously, what do you think dreams are?"

"I don't know." A glance at the sky told him they were getting a late start this morning.

"Don't you have an opinion?"

"I'll have to think about it." He'd never discussed dreams. Couldn't imagine that he ever would again. A sudden thought made him smile. "The judge would have enjoyed you."

She looked startled, then pleased.

"The judge had an opinion about everything, and liked nothing better than to debate someone with differing thoughts."

"You think I'm opinionated?" She arched an eyebrow and waited, conveying the impression that she might be testing him.

He was tempted to say no and avoid hurting her feelings or making her angry. But maybe he was in a testing mood, too.

"Of course I do. Aren't you?"

They studied each other across the campfire, measuring things that couldn't be seen, then her face lit in a smile.

"Absolutely. When you're alone as much as I am, you have all the time in the world to form opinions about everything. If you ask me about shadows, I have an opinion. If you ask me about turnips, I have an opinion." She laughed. "I guess I would have enjoyed the judge, too." Now she tilted her head the way she did when something puzzled her. "You've spent a lot of time alone, why don't you have opinions about everything?"

"Because I don't feel a need to share opinions doesn't mean I don't have any. Differing opinions can erupt in a shoot-out. And if opinions align, it makes for dull conversation."

"I don't agree with your last statement. It can be delightful to discover another person of like mind."

All day he thought about her ideas, arguing one side in his mind and then the opposite side. The only conclusion he reached was that she made an interesting traveling companion.

"All right," he said after supper, girding himself for a discussion he would not have had with any other living person. "Let's suppose you're right and dreams are a message sent to the dreamer . . . who or what is the guiding force behind the dream? And if the message is important, why doesn't the guiding force simply state it plainly? And why do dreams fade so quickly that you can't remember them for more than a few minutes? You tell me your opinions on these questions, and I'll tell you why you're wrong."

She smiled, then leaned forward, eager for the discussion.

Lord, he loved the look of her. Beneath the castor oil her face had begun to take on a golden tan, but still showed a becoming sweep of sun-pink. And he liked that she'd worn her hair down, wished he could run her thick braid through his hands. Most of all, he enjoyed the way her face became animated and alive when a topic interested her. Her eyes sparkled and danced, and he could guess her thoughts by the expressions her mouth assumed. And she talked with her whole body, leaning forward earnestly, then pulling back in skepticism. Tilting her head, lifting her chin, gesturing with capable hands that were rough and reddened by work. There was nothing about the look of her that he didn't like.

"That was a good conversation," she said after they'd exhausted every idea either of them could conjure regarding the mystery of dreams. She covered a yawn. "I guess I'll just . . ."

This was the day's most awkward moment. She never said "go to bed." But the instant she began groping for another expression, the image of a bed popped into his mind.

"Good night," he said. Standing abruptly, he walked out on the range away from the fire and her bedroll. Last night she had caught him watching her brush her hair and he'd felt embarrassed over invading her privacy. Tonight he was determined to not let that happen.

Thrusting his hands into his pockets, he kicked a small stone, sending it skittering into the darkness. He'd never traveled with a woman before. Strictly speaking, that wasn't true. He'd shared a stage or a seat on a train with women, but he hadn't traveled the plains or spent this much time alone with a woman. He hadn't known what to expect, but if he'd thought about it, he would have supposed there would be long periods of silence where each struggled to find bits of conversation that might interest the other.

That wasn't the case with Della. There were no uncomfortable silences between them. When a period of silence did occur, it felt right, and he didn't notice except in retrospect. She didn't complain about sleeping on the ground as he would have expected from a woman. Far from resenting any campsite tasks, she demanded to have her own chores. She was interested in weather changes, but didn't grouse about the heat or a sudden chill.

Instead of presenting a difficulty, Della amused, engaged, and stimulated his mind. Sometimes he relaxed enough to realize how much he enjoyed her company. In fact, he preferred her company to that of anyone else he could think of. Usually he left it at that. But sometimes a warning sounded deep in his thoughts. Nothing good could come from his admiration of Della Ward's qualities or the pleasure he took in her company. Or from his growing desire.

When he returned to the campsite, she was settled in her bedroll, her face buried in her pillow. Quietly, he poured the last of the coffee and seated himself where he could watch the firelight shining in the curves of her braid.

"Are you still mad?" he asked in a voice low enough that he wouldn't wake her if she were already asleep.

"Yes."

The anger went deep, with tendrils rooted in the past.

"I'm not mad at you, though."

That's what he'd wanted to hear. "Good night, then."

He could remember each time she had touched him or that he had touched her. A man didn't forget an electric shock that branded every nerve ending.

When the embers burned low and the night was dark enough to hide an ox, he let himself explore the memory of holding her in his arms and carrying her down to the creek. It had seemed the right thing to do, and she hadn't resisted.

But what he thought about tonight was the firm yet soft curve of her body against his chest, the scent of her skin and hair, the weight of her in his arms. He remembered wanting her then as much as he wanted her now.

Grinding his teeth, he raked a hand through his hair and cursed the trick of fate that attracted a man to absolutely the wrong woman.

If there was anything to Della's theory about dreams being messages, he hoped his dreams would tell him how to cope with futile emotions and with the firestorm that would erupt when he told her the truth.

Chapter 11

"We've passed several towns," Cameron commented, riding up beside her. Bold wanted to dance today, picking up his front feet, prancing sideways.

"I've noticed."

Della had glimpsed clusters of trees and buildings in the distance. Even from miles away, the breeze occasionally brought scents of civilization—cooking smells, stable odors, the fruity pungence of burning rubbish.

"I promised you a hotel room whenever you wanted it."

She hadn't forgotten. Whenever she spotted a town or noticed the small cotton farms in outlying areas, she asked herself if she was ready to disrupt the routines they'd established. Unexpectedly the answer was no. She actually enjoyed the long days in the saddle and she didn't mind sleeping on the ground. It was pleasant working side by side with Cameron to set up their camp, nice to wear her hair swinging in a braid and not to care that her riding skirt and shirtwaist were wrinkled and soiled.

"We're running low on a few perishables. If you're ready for a soft mattress and a real bath, we could put in

163

for the night at Rocas. I've stayed there before. The hotel is better than most out here on the plains."

"Rocas. That means rocks in Spanish, doesn't it?" The eastern edge of the Rocky Mountains had appeared on the western horizon, and they were seeing occasional rock outcroppings among the scrub and grasses. "You know, Cameron, it occurs to me that you were wildly optimistic about the time required to reach Santa Fe. You predicted three weeks."

"Or more."

"A lot more." They'd been on the trail for over two weeks and hadn't yet reached the mountains that would certainly slow them further. "I don't mind," Della decided, thinking about it. "I wasn't doing anything anyway. And traveling on the plains, living outside, this is an adventure I never thought I'd have."

She liked to think about telling Claire of this experience and wished she had brought paper and pen. A trip journal would help her remember the amazing nights when the stars curved down to the horizon as if they were pasted inside a black bowl. She didn't want to forget the smell of the horses and a campfire and bacon crackling and popping in the skillet. And she wanted to remember the wind in the grass, and whirling eddies of sand.

Of course she didn't intend to have a conversation with Claire. All she wanted to do was look at her daughter. Nevertheless, it was pleasant to think about describing the trip, a nice daydream to imagine Claire listening with rapt admiration.

"All right, let's stay the night at Rocas. I'd like to purchase writing materials when we buy supplies." Della had never kept a journal before because she'd had nothing interesting to write. Now she did, thanks to Cameron. When they rode into Rocas, she cast a sharp eye around the town, considering what to describe and what to leave out of her new journal.

Hot, dusty, and small, those were the words that came to mind. The Grande Hotel was by far the largest building fronting the reddish dirt road that served as Main Street. The other stores and cantinas featured false fronts that had weathered in the sun and wind to the point that it was difficult to determine if the buildings had ever been painted.

Cameron led them down the center of Main, nodding here and there to folks who came to doorways to see who rode past. At the stables he shook hands with a man he introduced as Robert Allen.

"Pleased to make your acquaintance, ma'am."

Now Della wished she'd taken a moment to pin up her braid and put on the clean shirtwaist she'd been holding in reserve. While Cameron talked to Mr. Allen, she followed the scent of frying tortillas to the door of the stables and looked down the street. The hotel had a shaded porch and three stories with lace curtains at the windows.

Suddenly she longed for a bath as powerfully as she had ever longed for anything. She wanted the dust and grime off her skin and out of her hair. Wanted to smell of lemon or lavender instead of horse and sweat. And she desperately wanted to slide between crisp, clean sheets on a bed as soft as down.

"You want your usual room, Mr. Cameron?" The hotel clerk eyed Della over the wire rims of his glasses.

"I do. Put Mrs. Ward in the room next to mine."

The clerk licked the end of his pencil then laboriously wrote Della's name in his register. "Will you want a tub in the room or will you be going to the barber-and-bath?"

When Cameron raised an eyebrow, Della whispered, "A tub in the room." She hadn't stayed in a hotel since her honeymoon, a lifetime ago. It didn't feel decent to be standing in the lobby with a man, renting a bedroom for the night.

"Take a tub to the lady's room," Cameron instructed, "and bring her coffee with sugar and some of Sophia's pastries. We'll both be sending out laundry. And we'll have supper in the hotel dining room at six o'clock."

Della didn't know much about hotels, but she knew hotels generally accommodated a class of people accustomed to polite society. The knowledge made her acutely aware of her disheveled appearance and embarrassed by it. She should have thought ahead and freshened herself before riding into town.

Leaning to Cameron, she said in a low voice, "Six o'clock is scandalously early."

"That's when you and I usually eat."

She wondered what the clerk made of that comment and felt the heat rush to her cheeks. "We're in town now. Eight o'clock would be a more acceptable hour to dine."

Cameron gazed down at her with an amused expression. "Acceptable to whom?"

Who was there in this small, dusty town whose opinion mattered enough that she was willing to wait an additional two hours and listen to her stomach growl? She, who hadn't followed fashion since the Yankees marched on Atlanta? Who was traveling alone and un-chaperoned with a hard, virile man who could make her pulse race with a glance?

Sighing, she rubbed her forehead. "Sometimes I am a very foolish woman."

Cameron paid the clerk and flipped a coin to a boy to take their saddlebags to their rooms. He walked as far as the staircase with her. "If you want an eight o'clock dinner, I'll tell the clerk."

"An eight o'clock dinner is the past. A six o'clock supper is the here and now. It's odd how things you haven't thought about in years can jump out of nowhere and blindside you." She ran her palm along the bannister. "I'd be pleased to have supper at six."

"You're off the range and in the big city, ma'am. The hour may be early, but you'll be dining, not merely eating. So wear your going-out-to-dine dress."

"Cameron, I'm feeling foolish enough. A clean skirt and jacket should be adequate." She would have started up the staircase, but he caught her arm and led her to a set of double doors opening off the small lobby. Wordlessly he opened the doors.

Della stared inside and her mouth fell open. There were eight tables in the Grande Hotel dining room, all dressed in white linen and gleaming with heavy silver. A young girl who looked part Indian was placing wild asters in the vases on each table. A boy who might have been her brother paused in polishing silver candlesticks and looked up curiously.

Cameron closed the doors and consulted his pocket watch. "It's one o'clock now. I'll knock on your door at a quarter to six. That should give you time to do whatever you need and have a nap if you like."

"This isn't what I expected," Della said, tilting her head to look up at him. Usually Cameron shaved first thing, but this morning he hadn't. The beginnings of a dark beard shadowed his jaw. Just when she believed she had him figured out, he did or said something that surprised her.

Her comment must have pleased him because he smiled. "If you need anything, pull the rope by the door and the clerk will send someone upstairs."

James Cameron never fully relaxed, but he was more at ease on the range away from people. Now, as he turned toward the hotel's outside doors, Della watched the mask of vigilance descend. His eyes narrowed, his lips thinned. The lines deepened beside his mouth and eyes, and his palms brushed the butts of the pistols on his hips. A cold gaze and unyielding stride made him about as approachable as a cougar.

A shiver of apprehension and attraction tightened Della's stomach. There was something about a dangerous man that stirred secret longings in women, like the seduction of the fire for the moth.

Weak-kneed, she clasped the bannister and climbed the stairs.

Rocas was a familiar stopover. Those who wanted to shake the hand of a gunslinger had done so. Those who wanted to make a reputation killing a gunslinger hadn't yet worked up their nerve.

"But they will. You know that."

Cameron and Shot Markly sat in two of the tin tubs in

Gadd's Barber and Bath House. They wore their hats to stop sweat from rolling into their eyes. On the table between the tubs was a large ashtray for the cigars they enjoyed, and two glasses of whisky alongside the bottle Shot had purchased. A shotgun and a pistol lay within easy reach.

Cameron blew a smoke ring and watched it float toward the dark ceiling. "No one lives forever."

"I thought maybe you'd changed your attitude, seeing 's how you've taken up traveling with ladies. You going to tell me who she is? The way I hear it, your lady friend is going to clean up real nice."

"Have you heard how much your cattle fetched? Or has the drive ended yet?"

"Changing the subject, huh?" Shot grinned. "The boys are about a day out of Abilene, letting the beaves graze and fatten up a bit before they run them in to the railhead. The price per head is a little less than last year, but I think you'll be pleased with the return on your investment."

Eight years ago, Cameron had helped Shot Markly and his wife get their ranch started. At the time he was just giving a hand to a man he liked and believed in; he hadn't thought of the money as an investment. But every year a deposit appeared at Cameron's bank, marked "return on investment."

Money didn't matter much to a man with nothing and no one to spend it on. A decade had passed since he'd given any real thought to finances. But earlier this afternoon, when he'd checked into the Grande, Cameron had felt a spark of gratitude that he could afford to take Della Ward to Atlanta and bring her home again without

thinking about the cost. For the first time, he had someone to spend money on, and he liked that. He looked forward to Santa Fe, a town large enough to have shops
filled with foo-fa-raws that would interest a woman.

"Laura will kill me if I don't invite you and your mystery lady to the ranch for supper."

Cameron blew another smoke ring, then sipped the
whisky. "I already reserved a table at the hotel."

His lady. When had his name last been linked to that
of a woman? Must have been before the war. A Miss
Hamilton, if he recalled correctly. A laughing, dark-eyed
beauty with less brains than a cocker spaniel. The Union
army had provided him a natural escape and saved him
from an awkward situation with the very persistent Miss
Hamilton and her determined mother.

"Tell me about the new sheriff," he said, deflecting another question about Della. "I stopped by the jailhouse
before coming here. I have a sense that Sheriff Bannon is
still settling in."

"He's good at moving strangers out. I imagine his first
question to you was, When are you leaving? He's less
good keeping a rein on the local troublemakers." Shot
frowned. "Maybe he's still working out the pecking order, not sure of connections or who's protected under
whose wing. But he shows promise."

"Anybody I should know about?"

"Naw. There's a few hotheads. Nothing you haven't
handled before. You'll be gone before they know you
were here."

That wasn't likely. He'd been in town only a few hours,
yet word of his arrival had reached Shot, and Shot had
known about Della and that Cameron was still riding

Bold. It wouldn't surprise him to learn that Shot knew the brand of saddle soap he carried in his bags. News traveled fast in small towns.

When Arnie the barber came into the tub room to drape a hot towel around Cameron's face, Shot rolled his eyes toward the ceiling. "A bath, a shave, a haircut, and a private supper. So when's the wedding?"

"Go to hell, Markly."

Shot laughed and lolled back in the tub. "Just remember. If you don't invite us, Laura will find you and skin you alive."

"Damn it, there's not going to be any wedding."

He pulled the towel over his mouth and retreated into silence, his good mood soured.

It was irritating and silly to be so nervous about having supper with a man, especially a man she knew as well as she knew Cameron. Besides, they'd been eating supper together for well over a month. But tonight was the first time they'd dressed for the event, and the first time they'd gone out. These differences created a sense of excitement and anticipation.

Della glanced at the mantle clock, then frowned into the bureau mirror and tugged at her bangs. She'd held the crimping iron too long over the lamp chimney, and consequently had singed her bangs. She'd snipped off the singed ends and now her bangs were shorter than she would have liked. Damn.

But the rest of her hair was clean and shiny and piled in a looping arrangement atop her head. Rather elegant, she thought, wishing she had an ornament to tuck into the mass of curls. She'd tugged loose a strand or two to sort of waft near her cheeks in front of her good jet earrings. A nice softening touch.

Standing back, she studied the molded fit of the jacket to the suit she planned to wear on the train. She'd dressed up her train ensemble with her jet brooch and evening heels, but the suit was far from a fancy dine-out gown. She didn't own a dine-out gown. Her train suit would have to do.

When a knock sounded at her door, she pinched her cheeks and bit her lips for color. After her sunburn had peeled—and thank heaven the peeling had ended—her skin had turned light gold. Well, what did it matter? She hadn't worried about milk-white skin in years.

"Oh my." Her breath caught when she opened the door. Cameron stood before her in evening dress, freshly barbered and smelling of expensive bay rum. Her heart knocked against her rib cage and her nervousness increased. A few hours ago she couldn't have imagined him wearing anything other than his wrinkled duster and travel-worn riding clothes. Now he was a dangerous man wearing evening dress as if he'd never worn anything else. James Cameron was a man who could seduce a woman with a single glance. And break her heart with the second glance.

"You look beautiful," he said softly, his gaze traveling from her hair to her mouth.

They studied each other in uncomfortable silence, awkward with the formally dressed strangers they had become. Then they moved at the same time and bumped into each other.

"Excuse me."

"No, it was my fault." Stepping aside, he waved her into the corridor, then offered his arm.

"When I bumped into you . . ." She looked over her shoulder to be certain there was no one in the hallway to overhear. "Are you wearing a pistol under your jacket?"

"Of course."

Della didn't think she would ever get accustomed to the idea of wearing arms to the table. What seemed natural at a campfire impressed her as eccentric in a hotel as refined as the Grande.

"Do you really think you need a weapon in the hotel's dining room? Surely they don't serve meat so rare that you have to shoot it before you can eat it." Lifting her skirts, she descended the staircase on his arm, pleasantly aware that they made a handsome couple.

Smiling, Cameron led her into the dining room, and the maître d' guided them to a table at the back of the room, where he seated Della.

The candles were lit on every table, even though only one other table was occupied at this early hour. Mirrors artfully hung on flocked wallpaper reflected the soft glow of candlelight and the gleam of silver, crystal, and elegant bone china.

"We'll each have a whisky." When the maître d' departed, Cameron looked at Della across the vase of wild asters. "Should I have ordered tea or sherry for you?"

Once she would have pretended a faint rather than take a sip of whisky in public. But the incident about when to eat had reminded her who she was now. She lifted her head. "I suspect I'll like the whisky here better than the cheap bottle back home."

"Is your room adequate?"

"It's wonderful. Large, airy, and tonight I'll sleep on a cloud. Are you expecting someone?"

"No."

He sat with his back to the wall, giving him a full view of the room and entrance, which seemed to interest him more than anything Della said. His restless gaze scanned the room, rested briefly on Della, then returned to the entry doors and began the circuit again.

The soldier would always be part of him, she decided. Or perhaps the habit of vigilance had come with a sheriff's badge or the years of bounty hunting. She admired him for the good he had accomplished, for his courage and dedication. But it was disconcerting to talk to a man who appeared to be only half listening.

She sipped from the whisky glass and let smooth, liquid fire slip down the back of her throat. Very nice. And much better than anything else she might have ordered if she had wanted to be oh-so-proper. She had never liked sherry.

A revelation struck her in the midst of a sentence and her eyes widened.

Her sudden silence brought Cameron's gaze to her face. "Is something wrong? Della?"

"You don't care what I've done in the past," she whispered, staring at him. "And you don't care what rules I break. You like me anyway."

What a thing to say to a man. Her mother must be spinning in her grave.

Flustered, a blush of embarrassment tinting her cheeks and throat, she waved a hand. "I mean, I think you like me anyway. I didn't intend to put you in an awkward position, or—"

His full attention went into the smile he turned on her. "I do like you."

"I like you, too."

Good Lord. There must be something about expensive whisky that loosened one's tongue and trampled good sense. Next she'd be handing him her room key and suggesting they return upstairs. A violent wave of heat shot from her collarbone to her forehead. What was she thinking? She must be losing her mind.

Helplessly caught in the moment, her gaze locked to his and a shiver tingled up her spine. Cool blue eyes, narrowed in speculation, moved slowly to trace the shape of her lips, the angle of her jaw and throat. Swallowing hard, Della tried to look away but couldn't. Her breath quickened, and her stomach felt tight and hot.

"There are green flecks in your eyes," Cameron said, his voice rough.

"There's a tiny scar near your upper lip."

A commotion erupted at the entrance to the dining room, and Cameron's gaze swung toward the sound of raised voices. Instantly he jumped to his feet and reached inside his jacket for his pistol.

"Get away from the table. Now!"

"What?" Della looked over her shoulder in time to see a wild-eyed man strike the maître d' with the butt of a long-barreled pistol. The maître d' crumpled to the floor. Good Lord. She could hardly believe her eyes.

"Move, Della!"

In two seconds she was up and pressed against the wall, away from the line of fire. Oddly, time seemed to slow, giving her the leisure to notice details.

The other couple sat frozen in their chairs, horrified faces shifting from the man in the entry to Cameron.

The man appeared to be drunk, slurring words and stumbling a little. Della couldn't see him well in the candlelight, but she guessed him to be in his late twenties or early thirties. Aside from his wild expression, half frightened, half belligerent, he didn't look like the sort of man who would rush into a dining room waving a gun. Of course, she didn't know what such a man ought to look like.

"Are you James Cameron?" he shouted.

"I am." Cameron stood steady and relaxed, the pistol in his hand at his side.

The man waved the long-barreled gun. "I'm Harvey T. Morton. It's the last name you need to know." He lowered the long-barrel to his side. "Draw, Cameron."

"Go on home, Harvey Morton."

"On the count of three. One . . ."

"You've proved yourself. You're willing. Let that be the end of it."

"Two . . ."

"Damn it."

Della saw Harvey Morton say "three," but she didn't hear the word. Harvey's arm swung up and he fired. The mirror over Cameron's left shoulder exploded in a shower of glittering shards. A wall sconce not far from Della shattered and fell.

After what seemed a lifetime, Cameron raised his arm and fired. Surprised, Harvey T. Morton stared down at his chest before he fell to the floor hard enough that Della felt the impact beneath her evening slippers. Harvey Morton said something, maybe he swore, then he rolled onto his back.

Della's eyes were so wide they ached. Still pressed to the wall, she stared at Cameron. Not a hair was out of place. He didn't appear agitated, didn't seem upset or moved. After a moment he stepped forward, pistol in hand, and walked to the entrance.

A lot was going on there. One of the waiters was helping the maître d' to his feet. The desk clerk and several other people had crowded around the doorway. A man wearing a badge arrived, scanned the scene and Harvey Morton's body, then looked up at Cameron and swore. Della couldn't see everything, but it looked as if Cameron prodded Morton with his boot, then pushed his gun back inside his jacket.

"I mighta known this would happen." Sheriff Bannon stepped up to Cameron. "Killing follows men like you. Gunslingers." With a look of disgust, he spat on the floor.

"Hold on." The man who'd been sitting at the other table came forward. "That man," he pointed to Morton, "came in here while Mr. Cameron was doing nothing more provoking than having supper with his wife. He challenged Mr. Cameron to draw even through Mr. Cameron tried to talk him out of it. And then," he stared at Cameron, "Mr. Cameron let Morton draw first and fire a couple of shots before he fired himself. I'll swear to that in court if need be."

"I saw it, too," the waiter confirmed. "It was self-defense."

The sheriff nodded slowly, rocking back on his heels to look up at Cameron. "I want you out of here tonight."

"That isn't convenient." Cameron's voice was level

and expressionless, but there must have been something in his eyes, because the sheriff studied him a moment, then colored slightly.

"You can stay tonight, I'll bend that much. But you leave first thing in the morning."

"That's acceptable." Cameron turned to the waiter. "You may serve our entrées now."

"You have an appetite after everything that's happened?" Della said when he returned to the table. She couldn't believe it. "Cameron—you just killed a man."

He brushed slivers of broken mirror off their seats. "This must be your napkin." Holding out her chair, he waited for her to be seated.

Della sat down hard. She'd never been in a situation like this. She had no idea how a man was supposed to behave after he killed another man. Or how a witness should respond. She replaced her napkin across her lap with shaking fingers. "Do you regret killing that man?"

His eyes were cold, distant. "Perhaps you didn't notice the part where Harvey T. Morton fired at me. Twice."

Della glanced at the broken pieces of mirror sparkling on their table linen. "That's another thing. Why in God's name did you just stand there and let him shoot at you?" Remembering how she had almost collapsed in fear made her mouth go dry and her stomach cramp.

"The pistol Morton was carrying is notorious for not firing accurately; plus he'd been drinking. The odds were in my favor that any shots would go wild." He tossed back the rest of his whisky. "This kind of situation is unfortunate enough. It's easier on the sheriff, the witnesses, and the man's family if there is no question as to what happened. From my point of view, I don't want anyone thinking this was murder. I want everyone clear that it was self-defense. So I'm never going to fire first."

"But he could have gotten lucky and shot you."

"Yes."

Della considered the entrée the waiter placed before her. Bundled veal, rice and tomatoes, corn and beans, served with a basket of warm tortillas. She couldn't eat a bite. Instead, she asked the waiter to bring her coffee, which she drank while Cameron calmly ate his supper.

Sadly it seemed a lifetime ago since they had gazed into each other's eyes and whispered about green flecks and small scars. Were those the same two people who now sat in silence?

Near the end of the meal, Cameron looked across the candles and their eyes held.

He could have been killed. I cannot love this man. I cannot walk behind another hearse.

Even if I hadn't killed Clarence Ward, I couldn't give her the peace of mind she needs. This was never meant to be.

Chapter 12

Since it felt as if they needed a little distance, Cameron didn't ride beside Della as he'd taken to doing before their stay in Rocas. He rode out ahead for a few days, leading Rebecca, studying the mountains that rose against the sky as they entered the foothills.

Toward midday two men passed about a mile south, riding east. Later in the afternoon he exchanged nods with a half dozen cowhands heading for Fort Worth. He and Della didn't exchange more than a dozen words until they stopped for the night. Working smoothly together, they set up camp, then sat down to wait while a rabbit roasted over the fire pit.

"I always thought it would be empty and solitary out here," Della remarked, taking off her hat. She removed a few hairpins and let her braid fall down her back. "It surprises me how many people we've seen since this trip started." She started to rise. "I think the coffee's done."

"Stay put. This is a whisky-drinking occasion. I'll get the bottle and a couple of cups." Her eyebrows arched and she looked up with a question when he handed her a cup of whisky. "You've hardly said a word for three days. Let's talk about what happened in Rocas, then put it away."

"You're right. This is a whisky-drinking occasion."

"You asked if I regretted killing Morton and I didn't answer. Of course I regret it." He wished he could leave it at that, but Della had to talk things around from every angle. Maybe all women did. "I would have liked to enjoy our evening without some son of a bitch forcing a confrontation. What makes it worse is Harvey T. Morton didn't have to die that night. If he'd made a different choice, he'd be alive. I regret that he chose to fire at me. I regret that I had to kill him." He took a long swallow of whisky. "But Morton had a choice."

"And you didn't." Lowering her head, she inspected the whisky in her cup. "I've thought about it. There's nothing else you could have done. I guess you couldn't just wound him . . ."

"The bastard journalist who wrote about me—he said one true thing. He said, when a man is famous enough to become a target, his safety lies with every assailant knowing any challenge will result in life or death. There's no other outcome. Someone will die. It has to be that way."

"I don't know how you live like this." She lifted her chin, bewilderment darkening her hazel eyes. "You're either a hero or a target. Every man you meet wants to shake your hand or put a bullet in your heart. There doesn't seem to be anything in between."

She was in between. That's part of what made her special. She seemed to admire him, possibly respect him, but he didn't sense that she viewed him as heroic or larger than life. She didn't see him as a legend, or as unapproachable; she wasn't tongue-tied or awkward in his presence.

"Do you know anything about Harvey T. Morton?" she asked.

"I don't want to know who these men are."

"The woman who brought my breakfast told me that Morton made saddles. Nobody knew he even owned a gun."

She was going to tell him whether he wanted to hear or not. Cameron finished his whisky and refilled his cup.

"He and some friends started drinking around midday. As a joke, the friends dared him to challenge you to a shooting contest."

"A contest? Like setting up a row of bottles and we try to outshoot each other? Me . . . and a saddle maker?" He pulled a hand through his hair. "Christ."

"The friends figured you'd refuse and everyone would have a good laugh and buy Harvey Morton more drinks because he was brave enough to challenge you to the contest." She lifted a hand to her eyes. "But something went terribly wrong. You could have been killed because of a dare and a joke."

The odds were slim, but it could have happened. Knowing she understood released some of the tension in his shoulders.

"Instead, a joke and a dare killed Harvey Morton." She shook her head. "That's sad, and tragic."

He cradled his hands around the whisky cup. "It's never easy to kill a man, even when he's trying to kill you. If the killing is a mistake or for a stupid reason, then it's always sad and tragic."

"I've never seen anyone killed before, not even during the war." Rising, she went to the fire and turned the rabbit on the spit. "I don't know if I said the wrong things, or if I offended you. But it just didn't seem right to sit down and eat supper like nothing had happened."

"You've known from the beginning who I am and what I do."

"It's one thing to hear about a legendary gunfight, and another to see a killing before my eyes. Hearing and seeing are different things."

She'd been lovely the evening he took her to dinner in Rocas, the kind of woman a man was proud to display on his arm. But she was most beautiful, in his eyes, in everyday dress, doing everyday things. Watching her at the fire made his chest tighten and hardened the muscles in his thighs.

She knelt beside the rocks, adjusting the spit. Her face was rosy in the firelight, her long braid lay over her shoulder. In her photograph, he'd noticed that her hands were slender and now he knew that she kept her nails short.

He tried not to think about her body, but of course he'd noticed. In her wedding photograph she'd been tightly corseted, and she'd worn a corset that evening at the Grande Hotel. At her farm and here on the trail, she let herself be natural. In Cameron's opinion, she didn't need a corset. Her breasts were full against the white shirtwaists she wore. Her waist was small, flowing into a flare of hips made to receive a man.

Biting down on his back teeth, Cameron turned away from the fire and faced the moonlit shadows dappling the hillside. The day after tomorrow they'd be out of the foothills and into the mountains. The nights would turn cold.

"I'm not criticizing," Della said from behind him. "Society needs lawmen who are willing to pull the trigger. I'm just saying that witnessing it up close is new to me, and a little shocking, I guess."

He hadn't taken her feelings into account, hadn't thought that it might be the first time she'd seen a man killed. It was hard to imagine there was anyone in the West who hadn't witnessed a killing. That's how cynical he'd become, living in rough border towns and hunting outlaws. Della reminded him there was another world that he didn't often visit, where shoot-outs and killings were not everyday occurrences.

"Cameron?" When he turned, she was standing beside the fire, holding their supper plates. The sadness that he hadn't seen since the night it rained had returned to her eyes. "I couldn't live like you do. Not knowing if this is your last day. Wondering if the next man who comes in the door will shoot you." She drew a breath and met his eyes. "I couldn't live like that."

The way she spoke, slow and with reluctance, told him that she was saying more. She was saying, don't come closer. He nodded. It was best this way. He ought to feel relieved.

But the long, hot hours riding in the sun gave a man time to ponder. And sometimes an idea shimmered in front of him, as possible and real as a heat mirage, and just as deceptive and insubstantial.

Lately he'd had the idea that maybe he didn't have to tell Della that he was the man who killed Clarence. There were several arguments in favor of saying nothing. First, telling her wouldn't change anything. Clarence would still be dead. His last letter still wouldn't say what Della needed to hear. If Cameron kept his silence, then he and Della could remain friends. He could imagine himself stopping in to visit over the years, and her being glad to see him. He could even imagine more than that. He could imagine that maybe . . .

This was the place where his argument fell apart and an imperative for truth kicked in. Telling her the whole truth about her husband's death was the right thing to do. Because she deserved the truth was why he'd searched for her. If he didn't tell her the whole truth, his secret would wedge between them like a wall of dishonor.

But that night in Rocas . . . she had leaned toward him in the candlelight with her lips parted and her eyes soft and almost shy, and he'd realized that she was drawn to him.

How many times over the years had he gazed at her photograph and imagined her looking at him as she had that night? In that moment he had glimpsed a different world and a different life, and for a brief while that life had seemed solid and possible.

Now he understood that even if he never told her about Clarence, she couldn't accept his life. He understood. He'd never expected that any woman could. But for one fleeting moment at a candlelit table in Rocas, he'd let himself hope that he was wrong.

When he turned, she'd dished up the rabbit and rice and was holding his plate, biting her lip as if she had more to say but wouldn't let herself say it.

He took his plate and sat on the ground. "A man can't

retire from being a legend." He kept his voice flat, tried not to sound bitter. This was the life he'd chosen and created. He'd found it satisfactory until Della stepped out of the photograph and into his life.

"I figured that out," she said, sitting beside the fire. "Even if there was something different you wanted to do, your fame would always get in the way. You'd still be James Cameron. And there would always be men like Harvey Morton and Joe Hasker and Luke Apple."

After they scrubbed their plates and utensils, Cameron sat on one side of the fire, cleaning his pistols, and Della sat on the other side, doing some light mending. Once, he looked across the flames and found her watching him. They held their gazes for a beat longer than was comfortable, then they looked away.

Eventually he would tell her about Clarence, and she would hate him. Until then, he would enjoy her company and her friendship and not hope for anything more.

It wouldn't be easy to set his hope aside. Particularly now that he knew she had leanings in his direction. He didn't think he was wrong about that. And particularly since the sight and scent of her made him want to hold her in his arms and kiss her until she was wild with desire. Being with her but not touching her made him feel crazy inside.

Della mopped sweat from her throat and temples, her gaze on Cameron's back. As usual, he rode tall and easy as if he was unaware of the sun beating down on them. Earlier he'd pointed north, drawing her attention to a small herd of deer on the rocky hillside. She wouldn't have seen them, as they were almost the same color as the rocks and golden-leafed bushes.

She'd lost track of the days, but she suspected they were into September now. Autumn would be upon them soon. As they gained altitude, the nights were getting chillier, but so far the mountain sun was hot during the day.

What else could she think about that wasn't Cameron? She had considered every nuance of the weather. Had noted the change of terrain as they climbed higher up the foothills. She had berated herself for her last letter to Clarence. Had wondered about Claire until her head ached. She had planned her journal entry but knew she wouldn't write it. The journal wasn't working out. That left Cameron.

Squinting behind the blue lens of her glasses, she watched Cameron look over his shoulder to make sure she wasn't too far behind before he turned Bold and Rebecca into a narrow cut between two rock walls.

She had come so close to disaster. If Harvey Morton had not burst into the dining room, she didn't know how the evening at the Grande Hotel would have ended. However, she suspected that she might have awakened the next morning with much to regret.

But Harvey Morton had burst into the dining room, and everything had changed between her and Cameron. She had seen with brutal clarity that he could be gazing into her eyes one minute, and could be dead two minutes later. It hadn't happened that way, thank God, but it could have.

And what if she'd been in a different mood? What if

she'd said something angry or cold in the minute before
Harvey Morton burst through the double doors?

The horror of such a possibility made her shrink inside
her jacket. If she and Cameron ever became more than
friends, she would have to censure everything she said
to him. She couldn't behave normally, could never risk
getting angry. Because anything she said might be her
last words to him. Luke Apple and Harvey Morton had
demonstrated how quickly Cameron could face mortal
danger. There wasn't time to say, "I didn't mean what
I just said." Or, "Those words were spoken in anger,
please forgive me."

She couldn't live like that. Teasing herself with thoughts
that she could accept his life was a frivolous pursuit. He
was right—he couldn't decide to stop being a legend.

Della had known this from the beginning. But then, in
the beginning she hadn't known him. Hadn't slept a few
feet from a muscled body that she could visualize in
her mind. Or watched him shave in the morning. Hadn't
felt a thrill of electricity when fingertips accidently
brushed, or shoulders touched. Hadn't stood in the rain
and wished he'd come after her and felt her heart leap
with confusion when he did. They hadn't whistled together or shared a hundred meals.

"Stop this," she whispered, wiping the back of her
glove across her forehead.

Ahead of her, just out of sight, she thought she heard
angry voices. Worried, she urged Bob into a trot, following a faint trail through a tight opening that widened into
a shallow valley.

There she found Cameron sitting patiently atop Bold,
watching a dozen people engaged in a volatile argument

beside four brightly painted enclosed wagons. Men, women, and children talked at once, waving arms and shouting. Dogs chased under and around the wagons and Della spotted a goat.

"The Baldofinis," Cameron said as she reined up beside him. "They claim to be Romanian gypsies."

The tall wagons had Baldofini painted on the side in fancy crimson letters. On one of the wagons, someone had lettered an advertisement for Countess Blatski's miracle salve, guaranteed to cure scabies, rashes, female discomfort, insomnia, snoring, pox, and catarrh. On the second wagon was a sketch of a mysterious looking woman waving her fingers over a crystal ball. Beneath the drawing was a promise that one could learn the future for ten cents.

The gypsies paused to glare at her and Cameron, then returned to the argument. "Baldofini," Della said. "Is that a Romanian name?"

"I have no idea. I've never been able to work out the names or relationships. But it wouldn't surprise me if someone just made up the name thinking it sounded Romanian. Who knows if it really does?"

"You know them?"

"We've had two or three encounters."

She knew he wouldn't say more, and this wasn't the moment to pry. "What are they arguing about?" Della asked after a minute. "And why are we sitting here watching them?"

The gypsies were good-looking people. The dark-eyed men were smooth skinned, with chiseled profiles and slender hands. The women were beauties, even the old woman at the center of the group. They wore brilliantly colored skirts and scarves, gold earrings and tinkling bracelets.

Cameron glanced at Della over the rim of his blue glasses. "The gypsy king, that would be Bernard Martinez, insists that you and I must pay a toll to pass the gypsy wagons. The king believes we expect to pay since gypsies are notorious for extracting money when opportunity arises. He assumes we accept this."

Della stiffened in disbelief. "They don't own this trail. Let's ride past them right now. There's enough room."

"The king's supporters will pull the last wagon across the trail and block our passage if we attempt to avoid the toll."

The valley beyond the tight, rocky entrance could not be reached without passing the gypsies. "Are some of them arguing against charging us a toll?"

Cameron nodded. "Our supporters say if we're allowed to pass without paying the toll, then I'll owe them a favor. I won't arrest them the next time they come into a town where I'm wearing a badge."

Della stared. "Have you arrested the Baldofinis before?"

A thin smile touched his lips. "Once or twice."

A sultry black-eyed beauty stepped forward and placed her hands on her hips. "James Cameron. If you pass without a toll, you won't arrest us when we meet again, eh?"

"If you pilfer my town, I'll arrest you." He shrugged. "How much is the toll?"

"Wait." The beauty gave him a long, measuring stare before she tossed her long, black hair, then returned to the cluster of people beside the wagons. The argument resumed, but it was halfhearted now.

"It appears we've lost our supporters," Cameron said.

"Do you know the gypsy's spokeswoman?" Della tried to sound casual, but wasn't sure she did.

"That's Sylvana."

She tried to hear an opinion in his tone, but couldn't identify any nuance. Still, there was something provocative in the way the gypsy beauty had stood, and she'd given Cameron a look of challenge that had charged the air and had made Della shift in her saddle.

This time a handsome silver-haired man came forward and squinted at Cameron, then leaned on a wooden cane. He flicked his eyes at Della then back to Cameron.

"May I present Mrs. Ward. Mrs. Ward, this is King Bernard."

Della gave Cameron a startled look. "I'm pleased to make your acquaintance," she said.

"The pleasure is mine." The king had a Mexican accent. "You will have to pay a toll. I expect this. You expect this."

"And the amount?"

"There is disagreement as to whether you must pay twice, for two people, or three times because there are three animals."

Cameron rested his forearm on his saddle horn. "Has anyone mentioned that we don't need to pass you as we're all traveling in the same direction? We could avoid the toll by following you through the cut."

Della's eyebrows rose. She couldn't tell from Cameron's voice or from his profile if he was taking the situation seriously or merely enjoying himself.

"This observation was made and dismissed," the king said.

"I see. And what is the amount of the toll?"

"You may pass us," the old man said slyly. And thereby incur the toll. "And the amount will be decided later. Come to our fire tonight and you'll be informed of your debt."

Cameron nodded. "What shall I bring?"

"Coffee, whisky, sugar, and tobacco."

"We'll bring coffee and tobacco." He nodded to Della. "You go first."

That Cameron didn't ask her to lead Rebecca told her better than anything else that he didn't expect to need his pistols. Still, he'd moved his duster back, showing his holsters.

She clicked her tongue and urged Bob forward, past the gypsies and the brightly painted wagons. The men smiled, flashing white, white teeth and three or four children grinned up at her. Sylvana leaned against a wagon wheel, her breasts thrust against a thin white blouse, the fingers of one hand toying with a gold hoop in her ear. Her gaze was fixed behind Della.

"Mrs. Ward. Della Ward."

Reining, she looked around with a puzzled expression. The heavily pregnant woman who came to Bob's side looked familiar, but Della couldn't place her.

"It's Marie. Marie Santos from the Silver Garter. That was a long time ago, but—"

"Marie! Of course." They had both been younger then, tired and discouraged and dressed in embarrassingly low-cut, tight-fitting costumes. "You look wonderful. Is this your first?" She smiled at the rounded front of Marie's skirt.

"It's our third," Marie said with a laugh. "We'll talk tonight." She gave Della's leg a pat, then stepped back.

Della couldn't have imagined in a hundred years that she would meet someone she knew out here. "What a strange world this is," she said to Cameron as they finished setting up camp. They had ridden about a third of the way down the small valley before stopping for the evening. The gypsies had chosen a site on the same creek, but nearly a mile behind them. Della could see the wagons and hear the faint murmur of voices and laughter and argument.

"Your friend is married to Eduardo," Cameron said, feeding twigs into the fire. He told her that Eduardo played the violin, had a way with animals, and might be the nephew of King Bernard's sister's second daughter.

"Marie and I weren't true friends," Della said, sitting on top of her bedroll. "At the end of the evening, we went our separate ways. None of us were proud of how we were making a living. We didn't socialize." She wrapped her arms around her upraised knees. "But I remember one night. It was cold and blowing rain, and there was only a handful of customers at the bar. We talked about what we would do if dreams came true."

"What was your dream?"

"I wanted to bring my daughter home to live with me. Marie wanted to marry a rich rancher."

While she talked, Della unplaited her braid, brushed out her hair, and wound it into a knot on her neck. As he always did, Cameron found something to do and didn't look at her while she did up her hair. His consideration made her feel more comfortable about performing an intimate part of her toilette in front of him. She tried to return the courtesy by not staring when he shaved in the mornings.

Suddenly she realized Cameron hadn't set out any cooking utensils. "Are we eating with the gypsies?"

"We're taking coffee and tobacco, so we won't owe them anything for the meal."

"Thank you for this trip," Della said quietly, speaking from the heart. "Already I've seen and done more than I have in the last ten years. I'll never forget this." She shook her head in wonder. "I never dreamed that I'd ever spend an evening with gypsies." Or check into a hotel with a man not her husband. Or travel alone with him. Or any of a dozen other things. "What will the evening be like?"

"You'll enjoy yourself."

The gypsies had positioned their wagons in a U shape at the base of a rocky slope, enclosing a large bonfire. The days were shorter now—already, lanterns were lit and hanging from the wagons. The smell of incense and goulash permeated the camp, along with the odors of animals and woodsmoke.

Marie appeared, smiling and pushing two little girls in front of her. "This is Roma, and this is Alise." The girls dipped into a shy curtsy, then ran off giggling.

"They're beautiful. How old are they?" Younger than Claire. That made it easier to be genuinely happy for Marie.

"Five and three." Marie led her to one of the wagons and they sat on the steps leading up and inside. "Did you ever bring your daughter home?"

Della gazed across the campsite and spotted Cameron drinking with the men near the horses. Drawing a breath, she explained that she was going to Atlanta to resolve the situation with her daughter. Marie lifted an eyebrow at the wording Della had chosen, but she didn't press.

"And you, are you happy with the gypsies?"

Marie smiled and put a hand on her burgeoning stomach. "We'll turn south soon. We're going to Mexico. Eduardo's parents are there and they want us to take over their ranch. I'll miss the traveling, but it's time to settle in one place. Yes, I'm happy." She, too, looked toward the men. "Some here are wondering why you and James Cameron travel together . . ."

"Mr. Cameron was a friend of my husband. He's escorting me to Atlanta." Damn. She felt a blush rise from her throat and realized Marie had seen it.

Marie nodded slowly, then she stood and stretched out a hand. "Come. We'll eat, then Madam Blatski will read your cards, and afterward there will be music and dancing."

"Marie, is anyone here named Baldofini?"

Marie laughed. "I think King Bernard's grandmother might have married a Baldofini, but I'm not certain. It doesn't matter. Everyone who travels in the caravan considers themselves a Baldofini."

The gypsy women served the men, then ate with the children at separate tables across the camp. They absorbed Della as if visitors were not unusual, talking among themselves and shouting at the children. Occasionally they included Della in the jokes and conversation, but she was content just to listen and enjoy the food and the rhythm of their conversation.

Eventually she became aware that Sylvana stared at her, noting every detail of Della's hair and clothing with obvious disdain. "The gypsies know how to live free," Sylvana said to an older woman seated to her right. "We wear our hair loose. We aren't afraid of color."

The remarks were directed at her, Della suspected. Suddenly she was conscious of the bright scarves and skirts and glittering bangles and flowing black hair. And herself, pinned and corseted and colorless.

"It is said that once a man has lain in a gypsy's arms, no other woman will ever satisfy him."

"Really? Who says that?" The women at the table smiled at Tala, the woman who had challenged Sylvana.

Sylvana's black eyes glittered. "Are you sure of your man, Tala?"

"You stay away from Stefan, or I'll cut your heart out."

Marie placed a hand on Della's shoulder. "Are you finished eating? Madam Blatski waits for you." Once they moved away from the women's table, Marie said in a low voice, "Never mind Sylvana."

"Sylvana seems to have taken a dislike to me," Della said, stating the obvious.

"She's angry that you travel with James Cameron. There aren't many men who refuse Sylvana, but James Cameron is one of them. She would like to seduce him, then throw him aside to appease her pride and to make Raul jealous."

"Mr. Cameron and I are friends, nothing more. Sylvana is free to pursue him if she likes." And if Cameron were foolish enough to let himself be used to make another man jealous, well it was none of her business. But surely he wasn't that dumb.

Marie led her into one of the wagons, where a white-haired woman waited at a table lit by a single candle. Inhaling the scent of spiced incense, Della glanced around her, gathering an impression of richly woven wall and ceiling hangings. She guessed living quarters existed beyond the velvet curtain behind the old woman.

"You know, this really isn't necessary," she said uncomfortably. "I don't believe in fortune-telling."

Marie paused at the door. "Perhaps you will."

"Sit."

The woman's hair was white beneath a bright scarf she wore tied like a cap. But her face was unlined. She wasn't as old as Della had first assumed. Like all the gypsy women, she wore gold earrings and bracelets, but her clothing wasn't the rainbow of color preferred by the others. Her skirt, blouse, and shawl were unadorned white.

"First, you shuffle these cards, then I look at your palm."

For the first time, Della heard an accent that might actually be Romanian. Certainly it wasn't an accent she recognized. Accepting the well-worn cards, she sighed, then shuffled. After enjoying the gypsies' hospitality at supper, she didn't wish to insult the woman.

"Now, your hand."

The woman's fingers were surprisingly warm, almost hot. She tilted Della's hand toward the candlelight and ran her thumb over Della's palm.

"You go alone," the woman said finally. "Everyone close to you is gone. There is no family, no husband."

Della's mouth dried. How much of her background did Marie know, and how much had Marie told Madam Blatski? She resisted an urge to jerk her hand out of the gypsy woman's grasp.

"You are healthy and strong. No illness. Once you were compliant, now you are headstrong." The woman smiled. "There is much change from here to here. Now you are sensible, practical, no? You are a different woman, I think."

"I suppose."

"Money. Not to worry. You will be comfortable in your lifetime." The woman shrugged. "Children. Three, two of them spaced close together."

That was false, and Della smiled thinly as the gypsy woman laid out the cards that Della had shuffled.

She cleared her throat when a silence became uncomfortable.

"Very interesting. The past is everywhere in these cards." The gypsy woman waved a hand over the pattern she had laid out. "The past. It's all the past. The past wraps you like a cocoon. I've not seen this before. Even your future is your past."

Della peered down at the cards as if she could see what the gypsy saw. "That doesn't make sense," she said, frowning.

"There is anger and blame here." The woman tapped a card and frowned. "But misplaced. Blame long ago and blame very soon, all misplaced."

"The blame is not misplaced," Della stated firmly, thinking of Mr. and Mrs. Ward stealing Claire.

"Look." The woman tapped her fingernail on top of a

card. "Secrets surround you." She studied Della curiously. "Powerful secrets, do you understand?"

"No."

"But you sense things. Secrets that can destroy. You don't want to know."

Annoyed, Della told herself to get up and leave. But she couldn't resist hearing the rest. "Leave that, and go on."

The gypsy woman leaned over the cards. "The future circles to the past. Always the past. There is a death, but not a death. Another secret going into the future, but shared." She shook her head.

"Well, thank you for your time."

"Let me see your palm again." The gypsy woman jabbed Della's open hand. "Here, do you see it? A fork on the line. You can go this way or that." Frowning, she went back to the cards. "So much blame. Where there is blame, forgiveness must follow. To forgive or not will decide your direction."

Della stood abruptly, anger flooding her chest. "Some things can never be forgiven." She would never forgive the Wards. Never. And she couldn't forgive herself for letting them keep Claire.

"This is not for me to say. You will decide," the gypsy woman said, speaking softly.

Some of what the gypsy woman said seemed true. Della had become headstrong and practical. Some of the predictions were nonsense, like the number of children. And most were too vague to interpret. But the words about blame and forgiveness had given her a headache. She didn't need or want a stranger's advice when it came to her daughter and the Wards.

"Was it a good fortune?" Marie inquired when Della emerged from the wagon.

"I suppose," Della said. She didn't want to disappoint Marie. "According to Madam Blatski, I'll have more children, and I won't have to worry about money."

"Ah, that is a good fortune."

The tables had been pushed back and chairs set out. Two men stood to one side of the bonfire, playing a lively tune on violins. The children danced and frolicked to the music. Della found Roma and Alise in the group, and decided that Eduardo must be one of the handsome men playing the violins.

"I'm glad for you," she said to Marie, pressing her hand. What different paths their lives had taken. She'd wasted ten years alone on a dilapidated farm while Marie had spent the same years traveling with the gypsies, marrying her Eduardo and having babies. "I think I envy you."

"It's been good. I love being a Baldofini." Marie's eyes sparkled. "Of course, it's not so pleasant when someone like Sheriff Cameron arrests one of us."

"Have you—"

"No, but Eduardo . . . well, we've paid a few fines. At least Sheriff Cameron always treats us fairly. Some arrest us simply because we're gypsies."

Della looked at the men, talking and laughing. Apparently the gypsies didn't carry any grudges, they all seemed relaxed and at ease. Men operated by a code she didn't understand, she decided, remembering Luke Apple.

But Cameron had been correct. Della was thoroughly enjoying herself. After the children had been tucked into bed, she and Marie sat with the women and nibbled sugary pastries and sipped ruby-colored wine and clapped and cheered as various couples danced in front of the bonfire.

Violins and guitars played sad, sweet melodies that broke one's heart, then built to crescendos of wild whirling that matched the beat of one's pulse and coaxed it ever higher.

Sylvana spoke to the perspiring musicians, then moved before the bonfire, facing Cameron. The music began slowly, and she swayed to the sweet seduction of the violins, her eyes closed, her lips parted. Slowly, slowly, she untied the scarf on her head and drew it across her lips like a veil, opening her black eyes to smolder and flash at Cameron. Smiling, she signaled the musicians with a tambourine, and the music became wilder, the tempo faster.

She tossed her hair back and raised her arms above her head, shaking the tambourine in one hand, clicking castanets in the other, catching a heartbeat, then whirling past, waiting, spinning forward. Her skirts billowed, flashing a glimpse of strong brown legs, the glitter of gold around slim ankles.

Della's breath caught in her throat. Never in her life had she heard music like this, music that reached inside and heated the blood. Nor had she imagined anything as beautifully erotic as Sylvana with her throat arched, her black hair flying, the castanets coaxing, teasing, pulling heartbeats toward frenzy. The wildness of the music, coupled with Sylvana's sensuous body and provocative movements, were blatantly sexual, a public seduction performed for one man.

When Della looked at Cameron, her heart sank. He

watched Sylvana with narrowed eyes, his mouth tight and his face expressionless. To Della's eye, Cameron was male to Sylvana's female. Both were lost in the wild seduction of the music.

When the music ended, the silence seemed shocking. Sylvana whirled to a stop, her skirts wrapping around her legs. Her lips parted, her black eyes blazed. A trickle of perspiration ran from her throat to the panting slope of her breast. She stared at Cameron and arched an eyebrow. No invitation had ever been plainer.

Della waited in a torment of jealousy. She fully expected Cameron to rise and silently drag Sylvana into the darkness behind the wagons, and she couldn't bear it.

Instead, heaven help her, Cameron yawned. Then he turned toward Della, jerked his head slightly in the direction of their camp and mouthed the word "soon?"

"Now," she answered, stunned that he could appear so indifferent to Sylvana's wild, seductive performance. But her jealous heart leapt.

They both stood. While Cameron said good night and paid their respects, and the toll, to King Bernard, Della thanked the women for their hospitality. She felt Sylvana's fury like a tangible force.

Lifting her head, she walked to the bonfire and met Sylvana's black gaze. "It was a lovely dance." She made herself smile. "Quite entertaining."

"You won't keep a man like that," Sylvana snarled. Spinning away, she stormed toward one of the wagons.

"I think it's good that we're parting company," Marie said, moving up beside Della.

"It was wonderful to see you again. I wish you all good fortune on the ranch in Mexico."

"And I wish you what I think you already have," Marie said, her gaze sparkling on Cameron.

With the gypsy music still heating her blood, and feeling triumphant that Cameron left with her and not Sylvana, Della hardly noticed the walk back to their camp.

"The fire is almost out," Cameron remarked, standing over the embers. "Shall I build it up, or are you ready to turn in?"

"I think I'll turn in." She drew a breath, telling herself not to say more. "If you want to return to the gypsy camp, I'm sure I'll be safe here by myself."

Genuine puzzlement made him frown. "I'm tired. It's been a long day and it's going to be a long day tomorrow." He flexed his shoulders and rubbed his neck. "I'm ready to turn in, too."

"Sylvana was dancing for you," Della said softly. She had to know what he was thinking. "Aren't you tempted even a little bit?"

"Hell, no. Sylvana can pick your pocket so skillfully you won't even know it. And you wouldn't believe how many valuables she can hide in the folds of her skirt. She wouldn't be a good choice for a lawman, now would she?" He smiled. "And you're wrong about who she danced for. Any man fool enough to go off with Sylvana is likely to get Raul's knife in his back. That's what the dance was about. Making Raul jealous."

And me, Della thought, startled by the strong possessiveness she felt for him. She hadn't realized it.

They had moved close to see each other in the dim glow of the fire's embers, close enough that Della smelled the soap he favored, and woodsmoke and the scent of gypsy wine. She swayed lightly on her feet. "I still hear the music." Wild and sweet and seductive. "It curls through the blood . . ."

He ran his fingertips down her cheek and a shudder of pleasure raced through her body. She could have stepped away—she should have. But she gazed up at him, and her breath quickened.

Cameron's eyes held hers, then his arms went around her, pulling her into his body. It wasn't too late to step away, to pretend there had been a misunderstanding, no harm done. But the blood tingled in Della's veins and she pressed against him, feeling his arousal, hearing her reaction in a soft gasp that lifted her breasts.

Pressing her hands flat against his vest, she ran her palms up his chest and around his neck. His hair was thick and soft. She felt his wine-scented breath on her cheek, heard the low sound he made deep in his throat.

When his lips covered hers, another electric shudder sapped the strength from her knees. Finally, finally. It seemed as if she had waited for this kiss all of her life. In her fantasies, a kiss could ignite the mind and body, but it had never actually happened until now. Her hips had never moved on their own because a man kissed her and explored her mouth. Her mind had never felt adrift in tides of sensation when a man's tongue touched hers, and his large hands moved on her waist.

When Cameron pulled back to speak, his voice was hoarse. "Della—"

She placed a finger across his lips and gave her head a shake, hoping to clear the confusion. "Good night," she whispered. If she didn't step away right now, the wildness inside her would erupt in frantic urgent kisses and then surrender. She knew this as surely as she knew they had crossed a line that they both had been trying to avoid. She needed to think about what that meant.

Stumbling in the darkness, she found her bedroll and sank to the ground. She touched her fingertips to trembling lips. She'd learned one thing. Men didn't kiss alike. Kisses could be as different as a breeze and a tornado.

That night she dreamed of the hearse, and awoke with wet cheeks and shaking.

Chapter 13

The Texas–New Mexico trail joined the Pecos River northwest of Fort Sumner, and followed the river valley into the Sangre de Cristo Mountains.

"Staying by the river makes an easier ride than I expected," Della observed. "I feared we'd be riding up and down mountains." Pushing back the brim of her hat, she gazed up at the peaks rising beyond the valley walls then let her glance slide back to the river. "There's plenty of water and grass."

And stage posts and small adobe forts, all of which Cameron had avoided. None were fit places for a lady. "I figure another week and we'll be in Santa Fe."

"When we started, you predicted three weeks." She settled back in her saddle. "We've already been out here— what?—seven or eight weeks? Longer?"

"Would you have agreed to come if you'd known you'd be on a horse for two months or more?"

She considered. "Maybe not. It would have sounded too daunting."

Cameron had shaded the truth, but he hadn't lied. Men had made the trip in three weeks of hard riding. He'd done it once himself.

"On the other hand, this is the only chance I'll ever have to see my daughter." She turned her face toward the river. "My pumpkins will be ready to harvest soon. Assuming Mr. Hays watered them. He probably didn't. No reason to."

"Are you homesick?"

"Lord, no." Her braid swung when she turned back to him. "When I think about everyone I've met, and everything I've learned, I don't want this trip to end." Cameron watched her mouth curve into a smile. "I can't thank you enough."

It made him uncomfortable when she started with the thank yous. Nothing he said had convinced her that she'd covered the subject weeks ago. Touching his boot heels to Bold's flanks, he rode ahead, looking for a spot to camp. With the days short now, they stopped earlier. Some of the lost time could be made up by eating the midday meal in the saddle, but it was also true that he was in no hurry to reach Santa Fe and end his time alone with Della Ward.

There was always the possibility that she might permit him to kiss her again. As days turned into weeks, the possibility had dimmed. Nevertheless, he'd spent hours remembering that night and battling his desire and his feelings for her.

He'd expected Della to mention what had happened between them, but she didn't. Eventually he understood that she never would.

Instead of feeling relieved that he wouldn't have to discuss an awkward subject, it irritated him that she could just pretend that nothing had changed. That kiss hovered in the air between them no matter what they talked about or what they were doing. He looked at her, saw her mouth, and thought about kissing her. She spoke and he remembered her throaty voice when she'd said good night. She walked about the campsite and he could almost feel her hips fitting into his. And trying to sleep a few feet from her bedroll had become torture.

"You're quiet tonight," he said after they'd eaten supper and washed the plates in the river. That was another thing. Since the night of the kiss, the tension between them was as thick as a wall. They didn't talk as easily.

"There's something I've been thinking about since the night at the gypsy camp," she said. "I'd appreciate hearing your opinion."

Finally. It was time they cleared the air. When she started fiddling with the braid laying over her shoulder, he knew she was disturbed. Well, he was, too. He put down the bridle he'd been repairing. A man couldn't work and talk about kissing at the same time.

"I told you the nonsense Madam Blatski predicted. You know, about money and more children." Frowning, she met his gaze across the flames. "Since then, I've realized that I don't think about Clarence as often as I used to."

This was an odd approach to the matter at hand, but sometimes she came at things from a different direction than he would have guessed. "Go on," he said cautiously.

She twisted her hands together and worried her bottom lip. "Before you rode up my driveway, there wasn't a single day that I didn't think about Clarence and Claire. It was like picking at a scab, keeping the pain alive. And that's what I wanted, what I deserved."

Maybe this conversation wasn't going to end talking about the kiss.

"What the gypsy woman said about more children, well, that implies another husband." Her hands came up and she rubbed her cheeks. "And that thought made me realize that, now, several days can go by when I don't think about the husband I had." Guilt pinched her features and she frowned toward the river. "I don't think about writing 'I hate you' or about how Clarence died. That's never happened before and it feels wrong."

She wasn't going to confront the kiss. They would go on keeping a distance, avoiding eye contact, trying like hell to elude an accidental touch.

"I don't believe in fortune-telling. But suppose I did marry again. Someday, way in the future. It wouldn't be right to marry someone if I was thinking about Clarence every day, would it? So, is not thinking about him a good thing or a bad thing?"

"Is this what you want my opinion about?" She nodded earnestly. Damn it. "I thought you said you never intended to remarry."

"I did say that, and it's true. I'm not a good wife. But just for a minute, pretend the gypsy woman is right and someone wants to marry me, and maybe I'm considering it. You were Clarence's friend. What do you think Clarence would want me to do?"

Whenever she made a reference to Cameron and Clarence being friends, his chest tightened and he felt cold inside. "I don't know what Clarence would think. But it seems to me that ten years of grieving is enough."

"That's another thing I don't feel good about." After a minute she drew a breath and continued. "To be honest,

I think the grieving ended long ago. I don't think about Clarence because I'm still grieving. I don't know why I've kept him in the front of my mind. Regret, maybe. Remorse."

Cameron knew. "Ten years of punishment is also enough." A few months ago he would have laughed himself weak if someone had told him that he'd rather talk about a kiss than talk about Clarence Ward. "You can't change what you wrote in a letter long ago. It's time to stop blaming yourself and move on."

"How odd." She stared at him. "The gypsy said something about blame and forgiveness. But she meant Clarence's parents."

"Are you sure?" He picked up the bridle and turned it in his hands.

"I don't want to talk about this anymore."

"Is there anything else you'd like to talk about?" His gaze held hers across the campfire. The flames were too bright to tell if a rush of color spread up her cheeks, but he had the impression that she definitely understood his reference.

"There's nothing to be gained by talking about something that shouldn't have happened." Her voice was low and she didn't look at him. But she pulled on her braid.

She was right of course.

Why had he forced the issue? What did he want her to say? He didn't know. It just seemed that when something momentous occurred it should be acknowledged. And for him at least, kissing her had been momentous.

"I apologize." She'd know what he was apologizing for. Maybe that was enough of an acknowledgment.

She started twisting her hands again. "No one's to

blame. The thing is, it would be so easy to . . ." Even in the firelight there was no mistaking the scarlet burning on her cheeks. "And I can't deny that I . . . but—"

But he was a man who couldn't offer a woman a lasting future, and he was the man who had killed her husband and ruined her life. Holding her in his arms and kissing her had made him hope the obstacles could be overcome. Which demonstrated how love could make a fool of a man.

Love? He sat up straight and blinked. This was the first time he'd actually applied the word. Love?

But of course he loved her. He'd loved her for ten years. He loved the look of her in the photograph, had loved the angry, feisty young woman who wrote the letter demanding that her husband come home. And he loved the woman she had become. Still angry, still feisty, but seasoned by life. She'd lost the surface artifice that didn't matter and she'd found an honest center.

God help him, he loved her.

"Cameron?" Wetting her lips, she looked at him uncertainly. "Did I say too much?"

"No." He stared at her, knowing he could never have her. "I'm going down to the river to have a smoke." If he stayed with her another minute, he'd say something that would embarrass them both.

The next day they shared the evening meal with a family heading toward Texas. The Eliots' son looked to be about Claire's age, Della thought. Being a boy, he was probably a little taller, a little heavier. Fascinated, she watched his every movement, trying not to stare.

At the back of her mind, she'd been toying with the

idea of talking to Claire. She wouldn't identify herself, wouldn't upset Claire or cause any upheaval in her life. She'd just talk to her a while.

But watching the Eliots' boy made her aware of how little she knew about children. She couldn't think of a single thing to say to the boy—why would it be different with Claire? Knowing what interested a child was something a person grew into. A mother started learning about her child from the minute that child was placed in her arms, and she never stopped learning. A mother and her child kept pace with each other.

Was it possible to make up the missing years? Della considered the Eliot boy and swallowed a rush of panic. She had no idea what a ten-year-old child needed or wanted. No notion of what would make that child laugh or cry. The lost years could not be retrieved.

At the end of the evening, the Eliots returned to their own campsite, but not before shaking hands all around and wishing everyone a safe journey. The Eliots called Della "Mrs. Cameron," and neither Della nor Cameron corrected the error. There was no sense scandalizing a nice couple.

In the beginning, when Cameron first proposed this journey, no thought of impropriety had entered Della's mind. She'd been so dead to men/women tensions that a chaperone had seemed unnecessary. Moreover, she'd told herself that she didn't care what other people might think or assume.

But things had changed. She was starting to care what others thought, and she was no longer immune to desires she'd believed long dead.

Della stood in the shadows and listened to the Eliots'

receding voices. "It was a nice evening," she said. Having company around the fire gave her something to think about besides Cameron. Wondering what he was thinking. Wondering why it had become difficult to talk to him. Wishing they could still whistle together and be easy with each other.

Cameron didn't say anything. He'd been particularly quiet lately. They'd kept a distance between them since the night of the gypsy camp. Several weeks had passed since that night, but Della remembered every detail as vividly as if she had stepped into Cameron's arms only last night.

She gave her head a shake, scattering pieces of a memory that wouldn't leave her alone. "The Eliots didn't have an accent, did you notice? Living in the West tends to flatten regional accents. I don't hear the South when you speak, and I doubt you hear it in my voice."

Cameron still didn't say anything. He stood near the horses, listening to the night, facing the dark flow of the river.

"At least Harold Eliot didn't want to shoot you." Eliot had been the awed, handshaking type. If his son hadn't been present, he would have asked about outlaws and gunfights. "I liked having company for supper." Before the Eliots had arrived at their camp, Della had brushed out her hair and pinned it up, and had donned a clean white shirtwaist. Now she started removing the hairpins holding the knot atop her head.

Out of nowhere, a rush of anger enveloped her. Lowering her arms, she squeezed her fist around the hairpins and stared at nothing. She wasn't Mrs. Cameron, she would never be Mrs. Cameron. And she would never sit beside a fire and smile proudly as her child recited a poem for company. Clarence would never forgive her. She would never forgive the Wards for stealing her baby. She could never regain those lost years. If she'd had any tears left, she would have wept.

She would never again live in a fine house or have lace curtains at her windows. Wouldn't own a satin gown or a velvet cape, and had no need of such luxuries. Never again would she attend a grand ball or have an idle afternoon without a dozen chores waiting.

Drawing a deep breath, Della lifted her chin and tilted her head to gaze up at the stars. Did those things matter?

Never again would she listen to the horror of approaching artillery or look back to see flames consuming a house where she had lived. Never again would she stand on a corner and watch wagon after wagon of dead soldiers roll past her shocked eyes. She doubted she would ever be gut-wrenching hungry again. She would never stumble along behind another hearse, blinded by pain and anguish.

She had a lot to be grateful for.

At the top of her gratitude list was James Cameron. It seemed a hundred years ago that they had gazed into each other's eyes across the hotel's dining room table and said: I like you. Now a kiss had dried up easy conversation, and she couldn't tell him that she was grateful that he'd been Clarence's friend, and she was happy that he was her friend, too. Fortune had smiled the day James Cameron rode up her driveway. He was opening the world for her, and because of him, she would see her daughter.

And he had taught her that all men did not kiss alike.

As she brushed her hair and plaited it into a long braid, Della watched him moving between the horses, talking to them in a low voice. It would be so easy to love him. In her heart she believed that she could heal the dark places inside him. And she suspected that he could make her whole, too.

But for how long? A year? Three years? Five? How many years of waiting in fear for the day when he didn't come home?

No. She couldn't walk behind his hearse. And he wouldn't ask it of her. Sometimes she recognized a certain look in his eyes that made her turn away and swallow hard. But he never followed up on that look. He was a gentleman, and he was proud.

"Oh, Cameron."

With all her heart she wished things could have been different for them.

At least three major trails poured travelers and immigrants into Santa Fe, one of the oldest towns in the West. Covered wagons lined up along San Francisco Street, waiting to pay duty before they found space at one of the tent towns that had sprung up on the outskirts near the Rio Santa Fe. Stages raced along the narrow streets with no regard for pedestrians or other conveyances. Wagon drivers shouted and waved their fists.

"It's sheer chaos," Della said, her eyes sparkling with excitement.

That it was. They were stuck on the wrong side of a long line of prairie schooners, trying to reach the stables. From where he sat atop Bold, Cameron could see a Mexican cantina, a French bakery, and a rubbish dump.

To his left, two Indian men smoked and observed a half dozen German immigrants arguing over the backs of their oxen. Dogs barked, horses reared. The noise and odors made Cameron wish for the clean quiet of the plains.

The covered wagons moved forward a few feet then stalled again. He could see the stables between the wagons, but no one would yield an inch to let them through.

"I'm in no hurry." Della had to shout to be heard. "There's so much to see."

For their entry into Santa Fe, she had aired and brushed her riding skirt and jacket. A crisp white shirtwaist showed at the lapels. Last night Cameron had polished her boots while she mended her gloves. This morning for the first time in weeks, she had wrapped her hair in an elegant bun and teased out a few tendrils at the nape and before her ears. The blue-tinted sunglasses that he'd given her at the start of the journey were scratched and nicked now, but she still wore them. Looked good in them, too. But he should have insisted that she wear one of his dusters. The choking dust hanging over the street was worse than anything they'd encountered on the trail, and already fine particles were settling on Della's hat brim and shoulders.

"Son of a gun. I know you." A man came out of the cantina and peered up at Cameron. "That there is James Cameron," he said to everyone within hearing. Rocking back on his heels, he sized up the situation in the street.

Cameron didn't recognize the man. When they'd entered town, he'd eased back his duster and checked that his pistols were easy to reach. He placed a hand on the stock of his rifle, checked that it slid handily within the leather scabbard. And hoped there wouldn't be trouble now, on a street crowded with bystanders.

"Hey, you." The man walked into the snarl of traffic. "Turn them oxen aside and let this man and his lady get through. This here is James Cameron."

"Und who ist James Cameron?" The oxen's owner scowled up at Cameron and Della.

"He's about the most famous lawman in the West, that's who he is. He could draw those pistols and shoot you dead, mister, and you'd never even see his hand move."

Cameron didn't glance at Della. If she looked as if she agreed with his admirer, he'd be disappointed. If she looked as if she might laugh, he'd be irritated. It was better not to know what she was thinking.

The man from the cantina and the oxen's owner turned the oxen across the street, blocking traffic in both directions. The man from the cantina waved Cameron forward. "You come on through, Mr. Cameron."

"I'm obliged." He touched his hat brim and nodded. "Glad to do you a service."

He heard Della say, "Thank you very much, sir."

"My pleasure, ma'am."

If he'd been by himself, he would have turned over the animals to the stablemaster then slung the saddlebags over his shoulder and walked up to the Palace Hotel. But he couldn't expect Della to check into a hotel carrying saddlebags. He told the stablemaster to send their things to the hotel, then he offered his arm and escorted her past the plaza.

This time he left her in the ladies' saloon while he arranged for a room, returning to find her having tea and tiny rounds of toast with a half dozen other ladies. The moment she spotted him, Della came to the doorway.

"It's like turning back the clock to another time," she said in a low voice, her hazel eyes shining. "Each lady is trying to outdo the other with the quality of her refinements." She looked as if she was struggling not to laugh. "I'm afraid I've already disgraced myself at least a dozen times."

"Della, you saw how crowded the town is. The only room I could get is a suite." He examined her face, watching her expression. "It's the bridal suite. I'll leave you there, and I'll bunk in at the stables," he hastened to add.

She gave him a long, thoughtful look. "I'm not going to be silly about this," she said after a minute. "There must be a sofa in the suite. Sleep there. We'll be sleeping farther apart than we ordinarily do." Crimson stained her cheeks. "That is . . . well, you know what I mean. It's all right, really." She took his arm. "I suppose the hotel clerk thinks we're married . . ."

"I don't know what he thinks. I booked the suite in my name, mentioned that a lady would be staying in the rooms." Cameron tugged at his shirt collar and cleared his throat. "I don't mind putting a bedroll down at the stables."

"That's not necessary, really. You're paying for a suite, you should enjoy it. We'll manage."

Her hand on his arm felt hot and heavy. When she moved, he caught the scent of dust and lavender and boot polish. He couldn't tell if she was just putting a good face on things.

As if she'd read his mind, she pressed his arm and

looked up at him as they climbed the staircase. "Cameron. I worked in a saloon. Most of the folks in Two Creeks wouldn't be at all surprised that I'm sharing a hotel room with a man. I stopped caring about that sort of thing a long time ago."

"Really?"

"Well, most of the time." Lowering her head, she studied the flowered pattern twining across the carpet. "You and I know we're not engaged in any impropriety. It's the truth that matters, not what other people think."

She gave him too much credit. He spent hours speculating about improper behavior.

Cameron straightened his shoulders. "It's early. I'll take care of boarding the animals and arranging our train tickets. You can do some shopping, get some rest."

She dropped his arm when they reached the third floor. "I doubt I'll do any shopping."

"I'd like to buy you a go-out-to-dinner dress." He'd never said such a thing in his life, had never imagined that he would. To his irritation, he felt a flush under his tan. "As a birthday gift," he added when she stopped to stare.

"It's not my birthday."

"As a reward then, for making a long and difficult journey."

"It was lengthy, but not especially difficult."

"Damn it, Della, I want to buy you a nice dress to wear out to dinner." He wiggled his fingers near his hat brim. "And a bauble thing to wear in your hair like those other women wore at the hotel in Rocas."

She stiffened. "I don't want to owe you any more than

I already do. What did this suite cost? What will the train tickets cost? And what did it cost to feed me all these weeks?"

"What the hell does it matter? I don't care about the cost. I can afford it. If you want to thank me, then give me the pleasure of taking you shopping for a fancy dress." He could see by her expression that tying the dress to gratitude gave her pause.

He opened the door to the suite and stepped back so she could enter.

"Oh." She stopped and he almost stepped into her. "I haven't seen a room like this since I left Atlanta. Not since the Ward's plantation burned."

The suite's parlor faced large arched windows that opened to a balcony. That's what Cameron noticed first, but he suspected Della referred to the multitude of tables, desks, chairs, tasseled lamps. Some of the items appeared to be antiques, others were of more recent vintage. Everything was draped or swagged or trimmed or tasseled in the fashion of the day. He spotted the sofa where he would sleep and realized his feet would hang over the end.

"Look at these ferns. I tried to grow ferns at the farmhouse and never could. And the carpet! Oh my. It looks like a genuine Turkish carpet, not an imitation." She peeked inside the bedroom. "Our saddlebags are already here. I have things to send to the laundry, things to mend." Then she discovered the water closet and a claw-foot tub with brass fittings. "Oh my heavens." She clasped her hands on her breast. "A tub right here in the room!"

"I take it you like the accommodations," he said, pleased.

"You have to go now." Grabbing his hand, she tugged him toward the door.

"Go where?"

"I don't know, just go." Eyes shining, she smiled up at him. "I'm going to have a long, soaky tub bath, right here in the room. So, you have to go."

He laughed. He didn't recall seeing her this happy before, with her eyes glowing in anticipation and an easy smile on her lips. If he stayed another few minutes, he suspected she would spin around with sheer exuberance. He would have liked to see that.

"Out, out, out." Giving him a little push, she followed him to the suite's door. "Oh, Cameron, this is wonderful."

"Enjoy yourself." Her cheeks glowed and her eyes sparkled. "I'll go by the barber-and-bath shop, take care of some things and come back . . ." He pulled his watch out of his vest pocket. "About seven. In time for dinner."

"That's seven hours!"

"Plenty of time for you to do whatever you need to do. You can explore the town, go shopping, or you can spend the day here, resting. If you get hungry, order something—"

"I know. Good-bye." She closed the door.

This is what it felt like to have a woman of one's own. Absurdly happy when she was happy. Eager to put that shine in her eyes and that glow on her cheeks.

Feeling better than he'd felt within memory, Cameron settled his hat at a jaunty angle and set out to find the Santa Fe sheriff. It was a courtesy for men like him to let the sheriff know he was in town. But he wouldn't surrender his guns, even if that was a town rule.

As it turned out, the sheriff didn't raise an objection. Any other time, Cameron would have accepted the sheriff's invitation to come back after supper and drink and jaw a while. But this time he didn't have that restless, solitary hole behind his ribs. This time he had Della. For tonight, at least, he had a woman of his own.

Chapter 14

Cameron was only steps from the entrance to the barber-and-bath shop when a man he'd noticed in passing shouted his name in a tone that Cameron had heard to the point of weariness. There was nothing novel in what happened next. Both men drew and an instant later the man lay dead on the street, and Cameron's good feeling was gone.

"Makes me glad I'm not famous," Sheriff Rollins commented half an hour later. They stood in the shade of the awning jutting out from the barber-and-bath shop, watching the undertaker's men toss the body into the back of a black wagon.

"Don't let a journalist write a book about you. The lying bastard will paint a target on your back." He'd known Jed Rollins for years. They had discussed the price of fame a dozen times.

"Arnold Metzger, that's the man you just shot. If you hadn't killed him, eventually he would have ended up with a noose around his neck. Not a doubt in anyone's mind that Metzger's been involved in three robberies and at least two murders. I can prove it, but not solid enough to satisfy the law. You did me and the citizens of this town a favor." Sheriff Rollins pursed his lips. "You're lucky, Cameron. He could have shot your butt. Metzger was handy with a gun."

"I noticed."

"This story's going to get told and exaggerated, and that's too bad. Every time some idiot draws, that target on your back gets a little bigger." The sheriff pushed out his hand and they shook. "Damned shame."

One thing troubled Cameron about the shooting, and he thought about it while he drank a whisky and soaked off the trail dust in a deep, hot tub.

He had hesitated. Not by a lot, but in that fraction of a second he had thought Della's name and he had cared about dying. A man who hesitated in a shoot-out was a man who was going to get himself killed, sooner rather than later.

There was another thing. Ordinarily he prided himself on cool efficiency, but he'd been angry when he fired. Lately it seemed that he arrived someplace and, before he had time to get his boots shined, everyone knew James Cameron was in town and they wanted a piece of him. At least Arnold Metzger needed killing. As always, that fact offered consolation.

Leaning back against the rim of the tub, he scowled at the steam condensing on the ceiling. He was weary to the bone of the challenges, the gunfights, the life he was living. The peculiarity was that he hadn't let himself realize or admit it until this trip.

What else was there?

He couldn't visualize himself living a different life. But did he want to pin on another badge? Men who wore the badge were the loneliest men in the West. Bounty hunting? Riding the plains for weeks on end in search of human refuse?

His choices were limited and, no matter what he chose, it all came down to waiting for the man who was younger and faster on the trigger. That's how it would end, the only way it could.

Maybe he should head for one of the coasts. He'd considered this before, but not seriously, because eventually the legend would catch up to him.

Besides, his work was here. There was no shortage of killers who needed hanging or shooting, and that's what he wanted to do: balance his personal scales of justice.

Finally, what was the point of settling down and living forever? He had no family and that wouldn't change. No one cared if James Cameron lived or died, and that didn't figure to change, either.

If he hadn't met Della Ward, he wouldn't be having this back-and-forth discussion with himself.

That brought him to another question he'd been wrestling. When to tell her the truth. He'd decided to tell her once they reached Atlanta, but he didn't know if that was the right choice.

There was no guessing what might happen if he told her before they arrived. If he waited until Atlanta, at least he'd be certain about the reunion with her daughter. And if she refused to speak to him again or to return to the West in his company, she'd be in a place where he assumed she knew people who could assist her and help her get started again. These were his arguments when his conscience troubled him.

Meanwhile he would savor every minute with her. He'd store up a lifetime of memories that he could pull out and examine during the long, solitary treks across the Great Plains. And hope like hell that his discipline held until they reached Atlanta.

There was no honor in what he had to tell her or in delay. He didn't want to say or do anything to make a bad situation worse.

Yet that's all he thought about. Making it worse by taking her in his arms and adding to his guilt and to her reasons to hate him.

Della didn't know what Cameron did immediately after leaving her, but she could track his activities later in the day. First, he went to the Santa Fe Ladies Most Elegant Emporium. She knew this because a delivery man from the Santa Fe Ladies Most Elegant Emporium came to the door of the suite to deliver a gown and cape. The gown was cream-colored faille with emerald satin stripes and emerald crepe de chine, matched by a cape of a slightly deeper tone featuring a beautifully draped hood to cover her coiffure.

Which suggested that she should have a coiffure to cover. She was staring into the mirror, holding loops of hair this way and that when the next knock sounded. This delivery came from Edleston's Accoutrements. White mid-length gloves and a half dozen hair ornaments to choose from, plus a delicate fan made of parchment and point lace.

Mulvaney's Shoe Parlor arrived next, bringing green silk evening slippers with sparkles embedded in the heels. The sparkles made the slippers inappropriate and too vulgar for a lady. Or so she would have believed at one time. Now Della loved them. She would have worn the sparkly slippers even if they had pinched a whole lot more than they did. But Cameron had come very close to a good fit.

The next delivery arrived in a package with no store name on the wrapping or on the delivery man's uniform. When lingerie spilled out of the package, Della understood the discretion, and laughed aloud at the image of stern, aloof James Cameron buying lady's unmentionables. He hadn't done as well here as in the other areas. Most of his choices were too plain for a gown as elegant as the one he'd selected. But then he'd erred on the extravagant side with his choice of rose-colored stockings and garters fit for a courtesan.

Della told herself that she couldn't accept nonperishable gifts from a man. Flowers and sweets were acceptable, and that was about all. However, she kept touching the items laid across the coverlet and wondering if she was applying rules from another age and era, and did it matter in any case?

At this point, she was already beholden to James Cameron for more than she could ever hope to repay. But he'd said it would give him pleasure to buy her a dinner gown. And he'd purchased the items without her being present, so she couldn't protest. He didn't expect repayment or want it.

Holding the gown against her body, she studied herself in the mirror. James Cameron was Clarence's friend. He'd been with Clarence when Clarence died. James Cameron wouldn't give her a dinner ensemble if he thought for an instant that Clarence would have disapproved.

She really didn't feel that Clarence would object. Even though it suddenly occurred to her that Clarence had

never given her a gift. They'd been apart at gift-giving oc-
casions, and gifts hadn't been easy to come by during the
war. Besides, if Clarence had thought of a gift, at that
time in her life Della would rather have received a chunk
of beef than something to wear.

It occurred to her that she was seeking justifications to
accept this new ensemble because she lusted in her heart
to have it. And she did. Oh, she did. A very short while
ago she'd told herself that she'd never again own a gown
like this or have a place to wear it.

"Damn," she muttered, holding an ornament against
her hair and leaning to the mirror. "Just say thank you.
That's all he wants to hear."

Not since she was a young girl had she taken such
care preparing for a dinner engagement. She wanted
James Cameron to take a look at her and gasp. She
wanted his pulse to stop. She wanted to mow him down
at the knees.

When she realized what she was thinking, she laughed
then set about to make it happen.

Women believed they were at their most alluring when
all gussied up for a dressy evening. But in Cameron's
eyes, Della was most appealing in everyday garb while
performing the everyday chores that took her outside of
herself.

Nevertheless, when she opened the door and he saw
her dressed in the finery he'd sent to the suite, he made a
sound deep in his throat. She was beautiful. Lovely. His
riding and camping companion had undergone a magi-
cal transformation. She'd turned into a princess.

"That is exactly the expression I was hoping for," she

said, laughing. "Come inside. I assume you ordered whisky; a boy brought it about twenty minutes ago. I've already had a taste, and it's smoother and better than any whisky we've shared so far." She gave him a side-long glance. "You look wonderful yourself."

He'd had a shave and ordered his hair cut short to suit the fashion back east, and he'd bought himself some new dress clothes. He still remembered how to knot a formal tie, but he'd forgotten the stiffness of a dress collar.

Della accepted the whisky glass he handed her, then frowned at him as if trying to recall something. "I know," she said, snapping her fingers. "This is one of the few times I've seen you without your pistols."

He touched the pointed ends of his waistcoat. "I'm carrying a small waist pistol. It's almost a woman's gun," he said with a twist of disgust.

"Would you like me to carry it for you?"

She had that sparkle that told him she was teasing. He smiled, enjoying the moment. "The man who sold me these clothes insisted a gun belt would spoil the effect. A gun belt might look good on that dress, though."

"Thank you, Cameron. I didn't believe I'd ever again wear a gown like this." Careful not to disturb any bows or tassels, she ran her fingertips along a pleated drape of emerald crepe de chine. Cameron knew it was crepe de chine only because the saleslady had told him so. "This is lovely."

He would have commented that the dress fit her as if tailored to suit, but that would have sounded too personal, as if he were examining her bosom and waist. Naturally he'd noticed her bosom and waist, but he wouldn't go so far as to say he'd actually examined them. Though he would have liked to.

He cleared his throat. "If you're ready . . ."

"I'll just fetch my cape and gloves." She paused before the foyer mirror to arrange the cape's hood over an elaborate arrangement of curls pinned high on her crown and cascading to the nape of her neck.

These small womanly habits delighted him. When he observed her pinching her cheeks, then stepping back from the mirror to judge the effect, he felt as if he'd caught a glimpse of a mysterious world that many men never got to see. Until Della, he hadn't observed much of a woman's private world or guessed the intimacy those glimpses created between a man and a woman.

Outside the hotel, she slipped her gloved hand through his arm, and his muscles involuntarily tightened. "It isn't far, but I should have ordered a cab," he said, suddenly aware of her train. The stone walk beneath the bare-branched trees was cracked and dusty, not accommodating to a lady wearing a train and heels. Sparkling heels, he recalled, daring to hope for a glimpse of sparkles and ankles before the evening ended.

She looked up at him, her face framed by the drape of the cape's hood. "It's a lovely evening. Dry and not too cold. I don't mind walking."

Cameron stared at the dark sweep of her eyelashes and the inviting curve of a half smile. Was she flirting with him? The possibility knocked the air out of his chest. Immediately he told himself he was imagining things, opening himself to wishful thinking.

Or maybe he wasn't. Ordinarily Della Ward wore the expression of a no-nonsense, capable woman. But tonight she'd wrapped herself in the soft dreaminess he'd observed in her wedding photograph, that aura of mystery and fascination that sketched images in a man's mind.

Aware of her arm on his sleeve, and the light scent of her perfume, Cameron led her across the plaza toward The Cattle Baron, an opulent restaurant despite the name. During the day the plaza was crowded with vendors selling everything one could think of. At this hour the square became a thoroughfare leading to the cantinas, restaurants, and hotels surrounding the town center.

For at least ten years Cameron had stood alone, watching couples walk along various streets in dozens of towns. Occasionally he'd wondered what they said to each other. How had they found one another and what had drawn them together? Now he noticed a few glances cast his way. Pride squared his shoulders, and he pressed Della's arm possessively to his side.

"I chose The Cattle Baron because weapons have to be checked at the door," he explained, leading her inside. When she raised an eyebrow, he shook his head with a humorless smile. "No." And when asked, he didn't declare the small gun tucked at his waist, didn't surrender it. In Cameron's view, the management's rule didn't apply to him. As was his habit, he insisted on a table where he could sit with his back to the silk-papered wall.

"It's a beautiful room," Della said softly, her eyes shining. They'd been placed in a corner or she would have been seated facing the wall.

Silver, crystal, white linen, cream-colored candles, and hothouse roses graced each table, Cameron noted absently. Exactly as he recalled from a couple of years ago, when he had dined here with a task force from the governor's house. As far as he knew, there had never been a shooting at The Cattle Baron.

"Is this a celebration?" Della asked after he'd ordered champagne and oysters.

"In a way," he said finally. "Plus I figure I owe you a dinner after the fiasco at the hotel in Rocas."

"You don't owe me anything, Cameron."

"I suppose it is a celebration." The chandeliers were dim, but they cast enough light to capture the hints of red in her dark hair. Her eyes had turned to liquid in the glow of candlelight. "The journey is almost over."

Surprise lifted her brow. "It's a long way from New Mexico to Atlanta."

"By train it's only about ten days, depending on weather and mechanical problems." He shrugged. "The longest part of the trip is behind us."

"Ten days," she repeated.

"We'll stop in St. Louis for a night, then take a different line from there to Atlanta."

From here on, he wouldn't have much time alone with her. People would surround them on the train, in the dining car, and they would go to separate sleeping berths. They didn't often say anything to each other that couldn't be said before a church congregation, but he preferred being alone with her.

He knew he behaved differently with Della than with other people. Talk came easily, and he'd laughed more in the last weeks than he had in several years. In her company he was able to relax and do pleasant, silly things, like whistle or tell tall tales. He trusted her to the extent of revealing more of his past than he had to anyone else.

She brought light into his mind and spirit. Knowing he would leave her was a thought he couldn't yet examine too closely.

"To you and to your daughter," he said, touching his champagne glass to hers. Champagne wasn't a favorite, but ladies seemed to like it, or so he'd been told. "I hope the reunion is everything you want it to be."

Her breath caught. "I'm not going to talk to Claire. I'm only going to look. We agreed to that."

"You can take it as far as you like, Della. It's your choice. Whatever you decide to do will be the right thing."

Tonight her eyes were more green and gold than brown, her lips seemed wider and softer. Cameron wanted to walk around behind her and remove her hairpins, then catch the weight of her hair in his hands.

She drew her napkin through her fingers then looked up at him. "Only ten more days." A frown troubled her brow. "The closer we get, the more—I don't know— nervous and agitated I feel. Almost afraid."

"Afraid of what?"

"Everything. Afraid that Claire won't be there. Afraid that she will be there, but confined to a wheelchair or bedridden or terribly ill." She pressed her fingertips to her lips, her eyes pained. "I'm afraid that she'll be arrogant and spoiled and that I won't like her. Or that she won't like me, that she'll be annoyed if I attempt to speak to her, or politely indifferent. And I don't know how I would arrange to speak to her if I wanted to. I can't very well accost her on the street. I think about these things and my stomach gets tight and my mouth goes dry and I think I must have been crazy to do this."

"You don't have to do anything," he said after a minute. "If you truly—"

"No. I want to see her more than I've ever wanted anything. I just . . . I'm afraid seeing her won't be enough."

"You can—"

"No, Cameron. Tearing up her life isn't right. I'm self-ish, but not that selfish. I won't do that to her, but heaven help me, I might want to. And that will hurt."

Her eyes glistened and she blinked hard. If they hadn't been in a public place, Cameron would have reached for her hand, but they were in public and neither of them favored open displays.

"I'm sorry," she whispered while he was trying to think of what to do or say. "It shocked me to hear I'm only a week from seeing my baby."

And he was a week or ten days from turning the look in her eyes to loathing.

"We won't talk about it. Not tonight." She sipped the champagne then wrinkled her nose and managed a smile.

She was wearing rose-colored stockings. Cameron cleared his throat and touched his tie. And black garters trimmed with pink roses.

"What did you do after you left the hotel? Did you stop by the sheriff's office?"

Rose-colored stockings next to the milky white of her thighs. Damn, he shouldn't do this to himself. He touched his collar, wishing the maître d' would open a window. When she repeated her question, he looked at her.

"I've known Sheriff Rollins for years. He likes knowing who's in his town. He's a good chess player."

He didn't tell her about shooting Metzger and hoped no one else would. But when she raised an eyebrow and gave him a long, level look, he realized someone already had. He released a breath then admitted there had been some trouble.

"I'm glad I wasn't present," she said in a low voice. "I don't ever again want to see someone shoot at you."

"I'm lucky. Didn't I tell you?" He signaled a waiter and ordered supper.

"I'm glad," she murmured after an obvious struggle. He knew she wanted to tell him that one day his luck would run out.

"The nonsense will end once we get on the train. The farther east we go, the less likely it is that anyone will recognize me. If someone does, it's unlikely he'll think about a challenge." He shrugged. "In any case, once beyond St. Louis, we won't see many men wearing guns."

"But you will be, won't you." It wasn't a question. "Maybe you won't wear your gun belt, but you'll carry a weapon."

"Who told you about Metzger?"

"One of the delivery men." She tilted her head and studied him across the flowers and candles. "I thought about it afterward. It must feel good to know you rid the world of a man like that. The delivery man said Metzger had done terrible things."

"I defended myself, that's all. But, yes. There's one less criminal out there."

They talked about less weighty topics during supper, but she returned to his reputation over coffee.

"You could leave the West and live on either coast, where every other stranger isn't trying to kill you. It strikes me as an heroic act to stay here. And unnecessary."

He decided to treat the subject lightly. "And what would I do with myself back east or farther west?"

"For one thing, you wouldn't be watching the door as you've done all evening." Her smile removed any suggestion of criticism. She understood. "You could practice law, couldn't you?"

"I suppose so."

"You could continue bringing criminals to justice, you'd just be doing it in a courtroom instead of in the streets or out on the plains."

What she didn't realize was that it was easier to be lonely in an empty land than it was to be lonely in a city, surrounded by people. The West was filled with men like him—silent, solitary men who would never marry or have children or settle in one place. They drifted from town to town, sometimes visible, sometimes not, looking for the life their younger selves had hoped to have. Waiting for the man who was faster on the trigger.

"Maybe someday I'll do that." He said it to appease her on a night that he wanted her to be happy.

Della saw through his light answer. A long, lonely life with an ocean view wasn't more appealing than a short, violent life under open skies. What she didn't understand was why he assumed he would always be alone. He was handsome, a man of means, thoughtful, generous, and charming if a woman took the time to work past his reserve.

The problem was geographical. While Cameron stayed in the West, he had a limited future. All he could offer a woman was the inevitability of widow's weeds. But if he left the territories where his reputation made him a legend, it appeared to her that everything would change.

A rush of color tinted her cheeks as she thought about the old gypsy woman's prediction that she would have more children.

If Cameron decided to leave the West . . . then what now seemed unthinkable became thinkable. Maybe, just maybe, she and Cameron . . .

She slid a look at him as they left the restaurant. His profile was watchful and stony, his jaw set. His mind was open to everything around them, aware of people and things that Della didn't notice. One of the things he was aware of was her, she knew that from the way he pressed her arm close to his body.

She also sensed he wanted to tell her something, that frustrating feeling had not gone away. But he wasn't a man to speak his emotions, she knew that. From the way he looked at her, she suspected she could guess some of the things he might say if he could speak easily about feelings.

And possibly she could listen if he could speak.

Everything had changed because she saw a way they could reach each other, if he was willing to leave his legend here and walk away from it. Ducking her head, she hid a hot face, felt her hand tremble on his sleeve. And she stumbled as steam seemed to build in her stomach and behind her ribs.

Cameron steadied her. "Are we going too fast?"

He wasn't, but she was. Pausing, she touched her fingertips to her forehead and commanded herself to proceed slowly. Because Cameron could leave the West didn't mean that he would. And she was still guilty of being a thoughtless and bad wife. Guilty of leaving her baby behind, an unconscionable act.

Moreover, she was putting thoughts in his mind that perhaps he didn't have. Men could be attracted to women without wanting to marry them. And she didn't want to marry, either. At least she hadn't until the gypsy woman put the idea in her head.

"Damn." She glared at him, irritated by the confusion whirling in her mind. "Why can't things ever be simple?"

"What's complicated?"

"You. Me." She threw out her arm. "You want to say something to me, I know you do, but you can't. I want to listen, but I don't know if I'm ready."

Mostly she wanted to kiss him until she was dizzy with desire. She wanted the heat in her belly to ignite against the fire on his skin. She wanted to taste him, touch him, drag her fingernails down his naked chest and hear him groan her name. She longed for him to break down the walls of resistance and release the passion she'd driven deep into an almost forgotten corner. She wanted to offer herself to his hands and mouth, to his lips and tongue. She wanted to lose herself in the sweet oblivion of his body and touch.

She opened her eyes, shaken by the intensity of inappropriate thoughts, and discovered him staring down at her, his eyes a dark starlit blue.

"My God," he said softly. Slowly he raised a hand and touched his fingertips to her cheek, let his thumb drift across her lips. "Della." His gaze narrowed and she understood that he could read what she was thinking.

She touched her tongue to his thumb, tasted salt and soap, felt a jagged flash of electricity sear through her body. Sagging forward, she leaned against his chest, not caring if anyone saw them. She didn't move until she thought her legs would support her, until she felt his hands slip beneath the folds of her cape and circle her waist, steadying her.

Cameron looked deeply into her eyes, then without a word, he took her arm and quickly walked the short distance to the hotel entrance. Stealing looks at each other, but not speaking, they climbed the stairs, then turned, breathless, in front of the doors to the suite.

She could never remember who moved first, but suddenly she was in his arms, her hands framing his face, bringing his mouth down hard on hers.

His hands slipped beneath her cape, moved up her rib cage then back to her waist, pulling her into his body. When she felt the rigid urgency of his arousal, she gasped and pushed harder against him. Urgent kisses slid to her throat, back to her lips.

Della couldn't breathe, couldn't think. Instinct and desire overwhelmed her and she welcomed surrender. For weeks, she had known in her secret heart that this moment would come. Foolishly, she had imagined that she would have a choice when it did.

"Cameron." She whispered his name, her breath ragged and hot. "I . . . we . . ." They were in the hallway, for heaven's sake. "Open the door." She placed a hand on his chest and felt his heart racing beneath her palm.

Straightening, Cameron looked down at her. He touched her throat and she felt a tremor in his fingertips. He released a long, low breath then knots ran up his jaw. He stepped back from her and found the key to the suite.

The instant the door opened, Della reached for his

hand but he didn't move when she would have tugged him inside.

"Cameron?" Confused, she watched the struggle warring across his expression.

"I'll see you in the morning." His voice was rough with desire and the look in his eyes made her go weak with wanting him.

"I don't understand."

He started to say something, then swore and strode away from her. At the staircase he looked back, holding her gaze, then he moved down the stairs and out of sight.

Chapter 15

The dream came again, leaving Della with a guilty headache when she awoke. After wiping her eyes with the edge of the sheet, she experienced a burst of anger toward Clarence as intense as the anger she'd felt on the day she wrote her last letter to him.

Was she supposed to be celibate and lonely for the rest of her life? Is that what Clarence would have wanted? Finally a man had come who stirred her emotions and made her feel alive. In the past weeks she had whistled and laughed and talked more than she had in years. She felt herself awakening as if from a deep numbing slumber. Was that so terrible?

Sitting up, Della pushed a wave of hair out of her eyes then covered her face with her hands. She had done wrong by Clarence. If she could, she would turn back the clock and write a different letter. She would give anything, anything, to have let Clarence die believing he was loved. God could look into her heart and know the truth of her pain and remorse.

But as much as she longed to change the past, she couldn't do it. Pulling her fingers down her face, she thought about what the old gypsy had said, that everything in her life circled back to the past.

This morning the gypsy's comment appeared discouragingly true. Cameron had walked away from her when he remembered she was his friend's wife. She had figured that out late last night. And it was an example of the past overshadowing the present. As was the awful dream about following Clarence's hearse. And so was this journey, a deliberate confrontation with the past. Even behaviors from a bygone era had recently jumped up to surprise her.

It shouldn't be a wonder that the dream was coming more frequently, she thought while she dressed and packed her things in the small traveling trunk that one of the delivery men had brought to the suite yesterday. The dream reflected the confusing mix of emotions that grew stronger with every step toward Atlanta. Today she felt chilled by a consuming dread.

Part of the dread was caused by a reluctance to face Cameron after last night's feverish display in the hallway. A wave of crimson flowed up to her cheeks as she came down the staircase and saw him waiting in the hotel lobby. What on earth should she say?

I couldn't sleep for thinking about you and longing for you. I didn't want you to leave, you must have known that. I respect your honor and I'm grateful that you respect mine, but we are adults who need each other and we feel so right together. I ask nothing from you, I expect nothing. I just want . . .

"Good morning, Mrs. Ward."

"Good morning, Mr. Cameron."

They each formed awkward smiles then looked away.

Della smoothed the skirt of her dark blue traveling suit, adjusted the brim of her hat. A glance about the lobby confirmed that her trunk was now downstairs. Inside her purse was a clean handkerchief, a bit of rice powder and a tiny puff, and the ten dollars that she'd taken from the bank before they left Two Creeks. She also had some hard candy, extra hairpins, an emergency sewing kit.

A bearded man wearing soiled chaps and a heavy duster strode into the lobby. "The stage for the railhead leaves in ten minutes. Is that trunk going?"

Cameron saw to her trunk then returned. "It's a twenty-mile trip over rough roads, and the coach is crowded." He turned his hat between his hands. "About last night . . ."

"You don't have to say anything," she murmured, looking down at her purse. "I understand."

"I doubt it." He settled his hat and offered his arm. "It will take most of the day to reach the station. Once we arrive, we'll board immediately and have supper on the train."

It occurred to her that they wouldn't have much privacy from here on. "Cameron? I'm crazy inside, thinking about Claire and seeing the Wards again. All of it. One minute I'm elated and the next minute I'm frightened and want to run in the other direction." She raised her eyes to his. "But this is the most wonderful thing anyone has ever done for me. I'll never forget that you made it possible."

"Are you saying good-bye? It's not time yet." A strange, thin smile touched his lips.

Good-bye? The idea startled her. Cameron had become so much a part of her daily life that his absence would leave a hole. Her chest tightened and she bit her lip.

At some point, they needed to have an embarrassingly frank talk. Della needed to find a way to suggest that if Cameron would relocate to either of the coasts, they might have a future together. This, of course, assumed that she hadn't misread his emotions. And it assumed that he believed she could be a better wife than she had been to Clarence. And it assumed that he could overcome his strong resistance toward courting his friend's wife.

There were too many assumptions. Sighing, she took Cameron's arm and let him help her into the cramped stagecoach. She squeezed between two male passengers who stank of tobacco and sausages.

Cameron stared inside, his expression stony enough that conversation died among the other passengers. "I'll ride topside with the driver," he said, closing the stage door.

Della inhaled the sour smell of smoke and onions, and wished she could ride topside, too. She'd been spoiled by traveling in the open clean air.

Several hours later, she realized this was the longest time she'd spent apart from Cameron since he'd ridden up her driveway. She missed him with a sharpness that made her throat ache.

Dark clouds piled above the mountains to the northwest and turned the sky a leaden color. The temperature had dropped in the last hour. Occasionally the stage driver glanced at the sky then cracked his whip over the backs of the horses, hoping to reach the station before the weather did.

It wouldn't be the mountains' first snow this season. Cameron had noticed patches of white along the roadbed when they went hurtling over Kahoe Pass. Give it another six weeks and Kahoe would be impassable. Santa Fe would have to look west and south for supplies.

Eventually the Atchison, the Topeka, and the Santa Fe would raise the money to blast a rail bed through the mountains and take the railroad the rest of the way into Santa Fe. Cameron didn't doubt this for a moment. He had, in fact, invested in several railroads, including the Atchison, the Topeka, and the Santa Fe. Rail was coming to the mountains and plains from both coasts.

Things were changing, he thought, sitting beside the stage driver, hunched against a cold wind. There were still Indian uprisings to deal with, but for the most part the Indian wars had ended. Eventually all the territories would become states. Farms and ranches had spread across the Great Plains faster than a man could count. Men like himself were pinning on a badge and taming the frontier towns. When Cameron first came west, a man could ride for days without seeing another soul. Now it didn't matter where he went, it was an unusual day that he didn't encounter someone on the trail.

A few short years from now the West wouldn't be wild anymore; it would feel a lot like civilization. When that happened, a man might as well move to California, where he could be warm all year while he put up with civilized society. Cameron sniffed the cold air and smelled snow. California sounded tempting on a day when the wind drove cold needles against his face.

Della had said she understood why he walked away from her last night. He narrowed his eyes on the road and wondered what reason she'd come up with. At least she didn't seem angry. But he was.

It was goddamned unfair that he'd found the one person in all the world who made life seem worth living, and she turned out to be Clarence Ward's wife.

What sank this injustice to a tragedy was his suspicion that Della Ward could have been his. She had come into his arms willing and eager, he'd seen a softness when she looked at him.

If it meant he could have Della, he would have moved to California on the next train. Instead of catching or shooting outlaws as a sheriff or a bounty hunter, he would balance his personal scales in a courtroom. He'd send the bastards to prison or the gallows, and satisfy his need in that way. He could have made that life work, if he could have had Della.

He stared into the waning light and remembered whistling with her on the trail. Remembered dozens of good conversations, laughter, and teasing glances. Thinking about last night and rose-colored stockings sent knots running up his jaw, and his fists clenched.

In a perfect world, he and Della would go to Atlanta and fetch Claire, then they would settle in California and live happily ever after as the family he'd believed he would never have.

It was goddamned unfair.

"Jesus, mister." The driver's eyes darted away. "All I said was, we'll be at the station in about ten minutes."

Cameron hadn't realized he was staring. He shifted his gaze to the first snowflakes spinning out of the darkening sky.

Ten days, possibly a few more, and then it was over.

*   *   *

They were late reaching the station. Full darkness had descended and snow was beginning to accumulate on the platform. Clouds of hissing steam blew back from the engine and the firebox glowed like a sunken eye through the curtain of snowflakes.

The conductor waved everyone from the stage to the train, and men scurried to whisk their luggage to the baggage car. Since the dining car had closed, a porter stood beside the conductor pushing box suppers into the passenger's hands.

"This is hard to believe, isn't it?" After the interior of the stage, the cold, crisp air smelled like nectar, and Della loved the feathery touch of snow against her cheeks. "Remember how hot it was the day you rode up my driveway?"

That day might have happened years ago since it seemed as if Della had known James Cameron forever. Right now she knew that he was hungry and feeling out of sorts because the stage driver had controlled the stage and horses, not Cameron. And it would irritate him to ride on a train as a passenger. He didn't like to be in someone else's control. Smiling, she took his arm and tugged him toward the light spilling from the train onto the platform. "We don't want them to leave without us."

There was only one passenger car in use on the eastbound trip, and only the passengers from the Santa Fe stage had boarded. The other cars were designated for freight or closed off to be used during subsequent legs of the journey. Della and Cameron could have taken one of the bench seats for themselves and stretched out their legs, but without discussing it, they slid into the same seat.

"It looks like a good supper." Inside Della's box were two pieces of fried chicken, soft rolls, a hard-boiled egg, an apple, and a piece of frosted spice cake wrapped in newspaper. Finger food that didn't need utensils. This seemed like a good idea to Della. She placed her gloved hand on Cameron's sleeve. "I haven't been on a train in ten years. It's exciting."

"I don't guess the trains came this far west back then."

"They didn't. I took a stage most of the way."

Naturally they sat in the back row. The only items behind them were a latrine and a potbellied stove tended by a sleepy-eyed boy. Ahead, the stage passengers had spread out widely, separated by empty seats.

The whistle blew, a long blast of sound that made Della smile beneath sparkling eyes. The train lurched and couplings ground together. They lurched again and she felt a building vibration beneath her boots. Leaning to the window, she watched the platform slip away, disappearing behind a veil of snow.

"It hasn't felt real until now," she whispered, responding to the power of the wheels turning beneath them. "We're really going home." Her eyes widened and she swallowed back a surge of panic. Her fingers tightened on the box supper. "I wonder if my cousin still lives in Atlanta. We didn't keep in touch after the war."

The conductor came down the aisle to take their tickets and inform them they wouldn't pick up a sleeper car until tomorrow. After checking on the boy dozing beside the stove, he returned to the front of the car, dimming the lights as he went.

Della set aside her box supper and turned her face to the cold, dark window. Everything would be different. She had left behind a city in ruins. By now, buildings and homes were rebuilt. Atlanta would be like the landscape in dreams, partly familiar and also strangely unfamiliar.

Should she try to locate old friends? Biting her lips, she stared at the snowflakes streaming past the window and let her mind turn backward. Names and faces flickered through her memory, people she hadn't thought of in years.

It would have been nice to see some of them, but she couldn't bear knowing their conversation would center around losses and memories of a world that no longer existed.

"I don't think we should stay long," she decided slowly, thinking about it. There was no one she really wanted to see. Just Claire. "Perhaps a week."

Cameron propped his boot on the seat back in front of them and bit into his apple. "This is your trip. We'll do it however you like."

A sudden thought occurred to her and she turned stricken eyes to him. "Oh, Cameron. I've been so thoughtless and selfish. Are there people you want to see? Places you want to visit?" He lowered the apple and fixed his gaze on a point toward the front of the car. "Good heavens. I owe you an apology. I don't believe I ever asked where you were from . . ." It seemed a glaring omission now that she noticed, and one that embarrassed her greatly.

"My father was the third generation of Camerons to live in Winthrop."

"Winthrop." Frowning, Della tried to recall if she'd

heard the name. "What direction is Winthrop from Atlanta?"

"It's north."

She touched his sleeve and examined his profile. "We could take a few days and go there if you like. I'd enjoy seeing where you grew up."

"No."

The unadorned answer raised a half smile of annoyance and affection. If the stage ride hadn't worn her to a frazzle, Della would have pried out a more complete response. But the heat from the stove behind them and the gentle sway of the rocking car lulled her toward sleep.

"I think I'll eat the egg and the cake, then doze a bit."

The emotional ups and downs of the last few days, followed by the discomfort of the stage, and now the jumble of confusion and anxiety caused by finally boarding the train, had worn her out.

She attempted to doze sitting erect, her hands tidily folded in her lap, but her head fell forward and woke her. Then she tried resting her head against the window, but the cold on her cheek made it impossible to sleep.

"Come here." His voice was gruff and amused.

After a token hesitation, Della moved into his arms and found a perfect place to rest her head between his shoulder and throat. It occurred to her that if anyone looked back or passed them on the way to the latrine, they would look like lovers. She didn't care. This was the safest place on earth, here in James Cameron's arms. Pressed to his side and chest, enclosed by the solid warmth of his body, Della went to sleep with his heartbeat in her ear and his apple-scented breath warming her cheek.

Cameron held her as the train rushed through the snowy night. His arm grew tingly and then numb but he didn't move or disturb her. He wished that he could freeze time, wished the dawn would never come. He would have been happy to spend forever riding a train with Della Ward in his arms.

There were folks who claimed it wasn't healthy to ride faster than a horse could run, who claimed that train travel twisted a person's innards.

"No, I don't believe that," Cameron said, smiling.

"The *Two Creeks Gazette* sparked a heated debate by stating that trains are against nature and an abomination in God's eyes."

"Would it be fair to guess that the editor of the *Two Creeks Gazette* hadn't ridden a train?"

"That was my thought, too." Della nodded when a waiter clad in spotless white offered more coffee before whisking away their breakfast plates.

After three days her initial excitement had waned considerably. She'd been wearing the same clothing since they boarded and her traveling suit was beginning to look the worst for wear. Then it was either too hot or too cold. The boy who tended the stove kept it cherry red and roaring or he let the flames die to ash and didn't seem to notice the cold until frost laced the inside of the windows.

At each stop across the Great Plains, the train took on more passengers. There were few empty seats now. Babies cried, children ran up and down the aisles, the smell of crowded humanity filled the coach. Sleeping cars had been added, but there were few amenities. Della slept in the ladies' coach atop a thin mattress rolled out on a board.

The times she liked best were meals in the dining car, and when they stopped to take on fuel and the passengers pushed outside to stroll the platform and inhale great gulps of fresh air.

The difficult times were sitting hour after hour on the bench seat, feeling Cameron's solid shoulder against hers, and sometimes leaning into his body to doze a bit during the long afternoons.

Sometimes the physical contact between them felt sensual and arousing and where their bodies touched became the only thing she could think about. Those few inches of shoulder or thigh or hip became the only part of her body that seemed alive, that she could actually feel. When the electric tingling became more than her nerves could bear, she shifted on the wooden seat and turned her cheek toward the cold air at the window, seeking to cool thoughts as heated as the potbellied stove.

Other times, like now, she sat primly erect, eyes forward, and told herself that the rush of sensation emanating from the point where the sleeve of her jacket pressed Cameron's sleeve was nothing more than gratitude and the recognition that, for the moment, she was not alone or lonely.

Della told herself that a woman could daydream about being with a man without it meaning something like love or commitment. She had pondered this issue during the long hours and had concluded that maidens earnestly believed love and commitment must precede being with a man, and that was undoubtedly a prudent attitude. But a mature woman, like herself, say, could be with a man for the pleasure of it without tying either partner to an emotional commitment.

This meant that love was not necessary to justify following one's desires. That was excellent because she did not want to love James Cameron. Unless he loved her back and was willing to move away from his legend, that is.

As the train moved across Kansas she began to see that he'd been correct. A few military passengers wore side arms, and here and there a cowboy type sported a gun belt. But most of the passengers appeared to be farmers or businessmen who traveled unarmed.

"Ladies and gents, may I have your attention, please." The conductor shattered her reverie. "We'll be stopping in St. Joseph, Missouri, for three hours. There's a café and several good restaurants in town. You'll find many pleasing views of the Missouri River, and some might enjoy a stroll along the docks. You can buy current newspapers in the lobby of the Saratoga Hotel and there's a novelty shop next door to the hotel." He removed a brass watch from his vest pocket. "Be back on the platform at four o'clock."

"Are you hungry?" Cameron asked. Today his eyes were the piercing blue of a morning sky, and he was so handsome that Della's breath caught in her throat.

During a short stopover in Dodge City, Kansas, Cameron had ordered his trunk from the baggage car. When Della saw him again, he'd packed away his duster and Stetson, his riding pants and shirt. Now he wore a three-piece black suit and narrow-brimmed hat, and would have looked like a businessman, except for his boots.

And she doubted many businessmen carried a pistol in a shoulder holster.

"Unless you're starving, I'd like to walk for a while. Stretch our legs and enjoy the fresh air." Della pulled on her gloves and straightened her hat. "This is a treat." Ordinarily the train didn't stop for much longer than thirty or forty minutes.

She took Cameron's arm and they turned downhill toward the river. Immediately Della's heart lifted. It was lovely to be in the fresh cold air and free to speak without the people around them overhearing. They were almost to the docks before it dawned on her that the folks they passed paid them no attention.

"No one recognizes you," she said, looking up at Cameron. By now she knew the signs. That sudden surprise of recognition, followed by an effort not to be obvious, which was usually overwhelmed by the urge to speak to Cameron and shake his hand. But sometimes the look of recognition was followed by a measured study, and she could almost see the man calculating his chances if he drew his gun. "I also don't see many guns."

Cameron led her to a bench overlooking the activity swarming around the wharf and a good-sized cargo steamer. "There aren't as many pistols worn here as in the West. But there are probably more than you think. Still, a man can relax a little." He went to a vendor and returned with steaming cups of hot chocolate. "You've been quiet. Are you thinking about your daughter?"

"Actually I've been trying not to." When she thought about Claire, her stomach lurched and she felt sick. What could she possibly say to the child she'd left behind? *Hello, I'm the mother who abandoned you and*

left you with a vile-tempered grandmother and a control-
ling, sickly grandfather. Della lowered her face over the
hot chocolate and closed her eyes.

Increasingly the dread came over her in waves, knocking the strength out of her spine and knees and making
her hands shake. She had terrible visions of being unable
to stop herself from revealing her identity to Claire. And
Claire would spit her contempt. All the accusations and
hurtful words that Della had said to herself for ten years
would come out of Claire's mouth, carrying a hundred
times the power to wound.

Cameron stood slightly before her, drinking his chocolate, his gaze on the river.

"Cameron?" Her voice was hardly more than a whisper. "Do you think less of me for leaving my baby with
the Wards?"

"No."

"Mrs. Ward is a poisonous woman. If Claire reminds
her of me—maybe the Wards have treated her badly.
Mrs. Ward has a tongue like a razor, and Mr. Ward never
stood up to her. He wouldn't interfere if she mistreated
Claire. I knew that, but I left my baby, anyway."

"Don't do this, Della. You had no choice."

"I had a choice about what I wrote in that last letter to
Clarence. I wasn't a good and loving wife."

He turned with a frown. "You were seventeen, pregnant, forced to live with people who didn't like you or
welcome you. You were frightened and alone and struggling with responsibilities you weren't prepared for."

Cameron understood.

With blinding clarity Della realized that if she had
written that last terrible letter to James Cameron, he

would have understood the reasons and the impulse behind it. He would not have surrendered to her pleas for him to come home any more than Clarence had, but he wouldn't have been angry at her for wanting his help and protection. He would have known she didn't mean half the words written in that letter, because Cameron knew her better than Clarence ever had. Cameron knew her heart.

And Della would have understood that. There would have been no blame and no need for forgiveness. No letter, no flash of pique could have changed their belief in each other.

Concentrating on what she was discovering, she fixed her gaze on the stevedores loading the river steamer, but she didn't see them.

Cameron should have blamed her for writing that bitter letter and for leaving Claire with the Wards. He should have, but instead somehow he understood.

She blinked back tears of gratitude. Thank heaven Cameron did not see her demons in the same monstrous way that she did.

Was she testing him? Honestly, she didn't know. She preferred to think that she was checking the truth of the assumptions she'd made.

As a general rule, men did not excel at picking up hints, and Cameron seemed worse than most in this regard. Della understood this meant that she would have to speak frankly, but not so frankly as to embarrass either of them. Unfortunately she was out of practice at this sort of thing.

She wet her lips, glanced at Cameron, then back at the river. "You know, since we visited the gypsy camp, I've been asking myself what Clarence would think if I were ever to . . ."

She almost said "remarry," but stopped when she realized that might alarm him.

". . . were ever to start seeing another man." A glance revealed that Cameron was paying close attention. "I've concluded that Clarence probably wouldn't mind if the man were someone he approved of. Like a close friend."

There. She'd said it and demolished Cameron's reticence to pursue a courtship of his friend's widow. Had she spoken the truth? She had no idea. Probably not. As recently as a few days ago she'd dreamed about the hearse and, as crazy as it sounded, she had attributed the dream to Clarence and interpreted it to mean that she'd done wrong by kissing Cameron in the hotel corridor.

When Cameron didn't comment, she sighed. "What do you think?" she asked, speaking to his stiff back.

"I think we should walk to town, find a good restaurant, and have an early supper."

That wasn't what she wanted him to say.

Embarrassment flamed on her face. She had all but begged Cameron to court her and he was changing the subject. And the change was abrupt, even for a man who didn't easily discuss personal matters.

Della didn't speak a word between the docks and the dining room at the Saratoga Hotel. Neither did Cameron. By the time they were seated and considering menus, they were both in a bad mood.

"I'll have a whisky," Cameron said to the waiter.

Della looked at him. "It's early for whisky, isn't it?"

"No."

"I'll have a glass of Madeira." Wines had never appealed to her, especially Madeira, but it was the only wine she could remember on the spur of the moment.

"A friend once told me that women can put you in a corner where, no matter what a man says or how he says it, he'll cause pain where he didn't intend to."

Della lifted her chin. "I apologize for placing you in a corner." Why didn't he drop this topic and spare them both? She had asked him to court her and he had said no thank you by abruptly changing the subject. The issue was closed.

"I want you to know that I respect you and hold you in the highest esteem." Cameron spoke quietly and earnestly, but his face was flushed and clearly each word emerged with great effort. "It must be evident that I'm powerfully drawn to you. If I could, I'd . . ." He waved a hand. "But I can't. There are reasons that you don't understand."

Her shoulders moved with a tiny motion of relief. She hadn't misjudged him after all, and she hadn't made a fool of herself.

"Maybe I do understand," she said, hoping the softness in her eyes apologized for her sharpness. "I'd like to hear your reasons. Perhaps they aren't as insurmountable as you think."

She watched his eyes narrow and felt his gaze like a caress on her lips. Something moved deep inside and she marveled that one special man's gaze could fill her with such longing.

"You'll hear the reasons. But not now."

Knowing him made her forget sometimes that he was dangerous. Plus, she'd never considered him dangerous to her. But now she looked into his cool eyes, heard the warning in his voice, and felt a sudden shiver go down her spine.

Tilting her head, she tried to see him as others did. Hard. Coldly handsome. Ruthless. A legendary man who left death and destruction in his wake. Solitary and untouchable.

"Cameron . . ." Her voice sank to a whisper. "What is it that you want to tell me?" Something had been there from the beginning. Whatever it was hadn't diminished but had grown in power and importance. "Tell me now."

He shook his head. "Soon. But not yet."

The expression in the depth of his eyes frightened her. She saw hopelessness, sadness, and fury gathering force like a storm.

Later that evening, Della leaned her forehead against the cold window glass and peered outside, half expecting to see lightning flash ahead of the train. The feeling of dread returned, depressing her thoughts and making her wish that she could turn around and go no further.

Reaching blindly, she felt for Cameron's hand and released a breath when his fingers twined through hers.

He had admitted that he was powerfully drawn to her, and heaven knew that she went weak inside when he looked at her. Whatever he had to tell her, whatever lay ahead, they could work it out.

Chapter 16

The ride across Missouri to the depot at St. Louis seemed endless. Cameron didn't have much to say and neither did Della. He assumed her thoughts had turned toward seeing her daughter. Maybe she pondered what she could say to Mr. and Mrs. Ward, or perhaps she wondered if it was possible to see Claire without having to speak to the Wards.

His thoughts turned backward, stuck near the docks in St. Joseph. In all the years that he'd carried her photograph and dreamed and pretended, he'd never dared imagine that Della would seize the initiative and invite him to court her.

If the past had been different, and he wished to God that it were, he would have seized the opportunity to live his fantasy. Instead, knowing that Della favored him and would welcome his attentions was like a bayonet in the gut.

It shouldn't have gone this far. Because he was weak and wanted her, he'd let things get out of hand. Folding his arms across his chest, he stared toward the front of the train and mentally flogged himself. He'd behaved badly in Santa Fe when he'd lost control and kissed her in the hotel corridor. He succumbed to weakness every time he fed his spirit with her smiles or shining eyes or the electric touch of her fingertips on his sleeve.

Because he was a lonely man stockpiling memories, he'd let her assume that he kept his distance because she'd been the wife of a friend. Since he'd done nothing to correct that impression, he'd hurt her there on the docks in St. Joe.

Tomorrow the train would roll into the station at St. Louis. The next morning, they would head south toward Atlanta on one of the new fast trains that didn't make many stops.

"Cameron?"

He looked down into her upturned face.

"Are you all right?"

"Why would you ask?"

"I don't think I've heard you sigh before."

He'd sighed? That surprised him as much as it seemed to surprise Della. "You must be mistaken."

She arched an eyebrow then turned her face to the neat farms slipping past the train windows. Cameron tugged at his collar and wondered why the boy who tended the stove still had the job. Inside the car it felt like an August afternoon, not conducive to rehearsing the most important and the most devastating speech of his life.

Once he'd been articulate and nimble with words, a natural-born attorney according to his father, the judge. Then came the war. Long before he'd encountered Clarence Ward, the words had begun to dry up in his throat. After Clarence Ward and after he went west, there wasn't much that seemed worth saying. A man got out of the habit of conversation.

I've deceived you. I was not your husband's friend. I'm the Yankee who killed Clarence, then went through his pockets and stole his personal effects.

Once, he'd believed there wasn't a jury that he could not persuade to his way of thinking. Arrogant, yes. But ten years ago words had come easily and convincingly.

Everything you think you know about me is a lie. I didn't know Clarence Ward, didn't serve beside him, was not his friend.

There was no easy way to say it. No way to soften the death of a loved one, even ten years later. And no hope for forgiveness for having killed her husband and having caused the loss of her daughter and home. How could she forgive him when he'd never been able to forgive himself?

When the conductor came down the aisle announcing that the dining car was open, Cameron shook his head and pulled out his watch. The day had passed with little conversation between himself and Della. Both were wandering in an unforgiven past.

The train yard at St. Louis swarmed with tracks, sidecars, and men clad in sooty uniforms from half a dozen lines. The depot was large, ornate, crowded, and confusing. Della clung to Cameron's arm, struggling to keep their porter in sight as people flowed past them, rushing toward boarding platforms or hurrying toward the street. She didn't recall ever seeing so many people in one place.

Most were well dressed in fashions that made Della realize how provincial she and Cameron appeared. The thought made her smile. The traveling suit that had been the height of fashion in Two Creeks, Texas, was hopelessly dated in St. Louis, and her winter hat was simply deplorable. She decided that Cameron fared better than she since styles for men changed slowly, but his boots and the width of his lapels set him outside the present mode.

The absence of side arms impressed her, both at the depot and an hour later at the hotel. She'd observed a few hard-eyed men exchange glances of recognition with Cameron, but it wasn't personal. It was more the recognition of kindred types and a knowledge of weapons concealed in a boot or beneath a jacket. Della hadn't seen anyone wearing a gun belt.

"Can you relax here?" she asked curiously when Cameron crossed the lobby to where he had left her beside one of the large hotel ferns. "Or are you still worried that someone will pull a gun and shout a challenge?"

He gave her a smile that didn't warm his eyes. "I don't worry." Placing a hand in the center of her back, he led Della toward a carpeted staircase where a bellman waited with their trunks. "We're on the third floor."

Of course he didn't worry. Living or dying made no never-mind to James Cameron. Della lifted her skirts. "I'm glad you could get rooms. There are so many people everywhere, I wondered if the hotel would be full."

They had decided on accommodations near the train depot, taking the carriage driver's recommendation to stop at The River Manse. When the bellman opened Della's door and she stepped into a high-ceilinged, commodious room with a pleasant view of streets and treetops, she silently thanked the driver.

"I'll see to the gentleman, ma'am, then return and

light your fire." The bellman gestured to logs laid in a tile-faced hearth.

"Thank you." A fire would be welcome against the damp chill in the air.

But it seemed silly for him to return when Della could have lit the fire herself. However, that wasn't how things were done. It seemed the farther east they traveled, the more helpless women were expected to be. While she awaited the bellman's return, she discovered a water closet and then bounced on the bed with a sigh of pleasure. The train berths were short, narrow, and hard, and Della had decided she'd rather sleep on the ground than in a sleeping car. At this point, a real bed felt like a luxury.

The last door she explored revealed the back of another door. At first she didn't grasp what she was seeing. Then the second door swung open and her eyes widened on Cameron. For a long moment they regarded each other in silence, then Cameron turned abruptly to the bellman.

"The desk clerk said these were the last available rooms. I want you to return to the lobby and find out if that is correct. We would prefer accommodations that do not connect. Inform the desk clerk that price is not a concern."

"Yes, sir." The bellman's gaze strayed to Della before he hurried out Cameron's hallway door.

"The clerk didn't mention that the rooms connected. If we can't be moved, naturally I'll respect your—"

"I know," Della said hastily, feeling her cheeks color. "It isn't a difficulty. Really." She stepped backward. "I'll just keep my door closed and you keep your door closed."

She shut the door, leaned against it and drew a deep

breath. Well. It didn't matter that their rooms connected. If anything could be construed as improper, it would be camping together. Sleeping with their bedrolls only a few feet apart. This arrangement offered more privacy and propriety.

A knock sounded on the other side of her connecting door. "Della?" Cameron frowned as she opened the door. "The bellman says these are definitely the last available rooms. We could try another hotel."

Until she thought about checking out of this hotel, finding a carriage for hire, searching out another hotel, checking in again . . . Della hadn't realized how tired she was.

"That seems silly, doesn't it? Cameron, we're mature adults. This isn't a problem." Glancing over her shoulder, she looked toward the hallway door. "That must be the bellman coming to light the fire." She closed the door on Cameron before she opened the hallway door to admit the bellman, then she pressed her fingertips to her forehead and smiled. For a mature adult who didn't care about connecting rooms, she'd been quick to close her door rather than have the bellman see her talking to Cameron again.

When the bellman departed, leaving her with a cheery fire, she squared her shoulders and rapped on Cameron's door. He opened his side at once.

"What are our plans now?" Della asked. She spoke in a bright voice as if it were the most natural thing in the world to have a room that connected privately with his. And she had to concede the arrangement was convenient.

Cameron consulted his pocket watch. "Our train leaves early, at seven o'clock tomorrow morning."

"Then we'd be wise to make it an early night." Behind him, she saw flames in a fireplace that matched the one in her room. "I'm not very hungry. A light supper that we don't have to dress for would be welcome."

"I was thinking the same." He returned his watch to his waistcoat pocket. "Let's say in an hour and a half? Will that give you time to rest and freshen up a bit?"

"That's perfect."

"Good." He made no move to step back but stood in his doorway, looking down at her with that hard-eyed expression that made her stomach feel strange and tight.

"Well, then." Della wet her lips. She didn't feel right about shutting her door in his face. "Until later." She eased her door toward shut, wishing he would do the same. When there was only an inch of space left, she peeked and discovered he had closed his side. Good. Really, there was no need to open the doors again. Except . . .

She opened her door and rapped on his. Immediately it opened, startling her. He'd removed his jacket and stood before her in his shirt and waistcoat. "I just . . . I thought I'd take a little nap. Would you knock on this door in an hour? I'd appreciate it. I don't want to oversleep."

Cameron cleared his throat. "I'd be happy to."

"Thank you." She gave him a bright, false smile and closed the door before she could think about who closed whose door first.

Standing before the bureau mirror, she removed her hat and glanced at the connecting door in the glass. Should she lock her side? But that would imply a lack of trust. But if her trust was well placed, then he would never discover that she had locked her side. But if she truly trusted him to act as a gentleman, then there was no need to even consider locking the door.

"Sometimes you are a very silly woman," she murmured as she stripped off her traveling clothes and climbed into bed with a deep sigh of comfort and pleasure.

If James Cameron could not be trusted, then no man on earth could be trusted. Della's eyes popped open, and she sat up in bed to stare at the connecting door.

Cameron would never walk through that door.

He was a man of honor and integrity. Nothing could induce him to walk through the connecting door with impropriety on his mind. Secretly disappointed, Della fell asleep thinking about lost opportunities.

It was the damnedest thing. There might as well have been nothing in the room except the connecting door.

Cameron tried taking care of some correspondence, but every few minutes he paused with the pen in his hand, raised his head and looked at the door, half expecting, hoping, that Della would knock again. Next, he plumped the pillows and laid on top of the bed and tried to read. But he'd read a few paragraphs, glance up at the door, wait, then read the same paragraphs again before he looked up again. Eventually he made a disgusted sound and tossed the book aside.

It was a mystery why the connecting door had assumed such importance and why it seemed such a source of temptation.

There weren't many things that Della could be doing behind that door that he hadn't seen her do at dozens of campsites. He knew she went to sleep with her face planted in the pillow, then turned on her side as she drifted into deeper sleep. He'd heard the soft, gentle sound of her sleeping breath, almost a ladylike snore.

He knew the erotic sight of her lifted arms, brushing out her hair at the end of the day. The sight of long, nimble fingers plaiting a braid.

He'd watched her wash her face and throat, had tried not to stare at laundered unmentionables hanging on low brush to dry.

He had seen her kick off her boots at the end of the day and wiggle her toes with a sigh of pleasure.

He knew the lines of her body in every stance and posture.

After a long moment of scowling at the connecting door, he thrust his arms into his jacket and pushed his hat on his head. He'd wait in the bar downstairs until it was time to wake her. And he would try like hell not to think about what a long night it was going to be, lying here in the dark staring at the connecting door and thinking about miracles.

Swearing under his breath, he went out the hallway door.

Cameron's knock woke her. But when she opened the door on her side, his door was already closed again. That was fine. It was probably best not to be seen flushed with sleep and awkwardly positioned so he wouldn't see her shimmy and drawers.

After yawning and stretching, Della went through her trunk and laid out what she would wear to supper, a winter suit in gray wool trimmed with blue-and-gray paisley. In Two Creeks, she would have worn this suit to a potluck supper in the church basement if she'd been of a mind to attend such a function, which she seldom was.

She'd eaten out more often in the weeks with Cameron than she had in the ten years preceding his arrival.

"My life has changed completely since you came riding up my driveway," she said once they were seated in a modest restaurant a block from the River Manse. "Sometimes I pinch myself to make sure I'm awake and not dreaming all this."

Cameron smiled and buttered a roll. "It's interesting that you'd say that. Earlier today I was remembering you washing out your stockings in a muddy water hole no larger than a dishpan. There were some times out there on the plains when I imagine you wished you were dreaming."

"Once or twice," she conceded. "But not often. Back on the farm, I used to wake and just lie there in bed trying to think of a reason to get up." She straightened her silverware. "That's why I kept animals. So I'd have to get out of bed and feed them."

Since Cameron had come into her life, she'd been eager to jump up and discover what the new day would bring. It was like she was a different person. Because of him.

She raised her head and looked at a stubborn chin she well knew. And a mouth she dreamed about. Gazed into eyes that could turn as cold as a winter lake, or move across her cheek and throat as gently as a caress.

"This journey is almost over, isn't it?" she whispered.

"It has been a privilege to be your escort."

Sudden, unexplainable tears stung her eyes, and she lowered her head, not speaking again until they had eaten and the waiter placed coffee and pie before them.

"After I've seen Claire, and maybe I've spoken to her . . . when it's time to leave her again . . ."

"Then you'll return to Santa Fe." He pushed the pie and coffee away. "I'll hire someone to take you back to Two Creeks if that's what you want."

"I don't have a choice. Where else would I go?" She cleared her throat. "You won't take me back to the farm?"

"No."

"I know," she said with a faint smile. "You don't explain yourself. But I wish you would." She couldn't imagine making a campsite with anyone but Cameron. They had a routine, they worked well together. They knew when to talk and when to enjoy the silence. Knew when to offer each other company or solitude. She didn't want to make the long ride with a stranger.

"Cameron?" She swallowed the tears that had receded only as far as her tight throat. "When this is over—will I ever see you again?"

He turned his head and looked out the window at the conveyances passing in the street, and Della knew the answer was no. There were things she didn't understand, she thought, frustrated.

She closed her eyes and rubbed her temples. "I think I've had a headache since we left Santa Fe."

And dreams. There was the hearse dream, and anxiety dreams where something terrible was about to befall her if she didn't run or swim or fly faster. Dreams set on the Wards' plantation, dreams where she wandered on a battlefield or among rows and rows of gravestones, nightmares about the pumpkins and baby blossoms.

"You said that I'll return to Santa Fe. What about you? What are your plans?"

A veil dropped over his gaze and she knew this was another question he would evade, but she didn't understand why.

"We'll talk about it when the time comes," he said when she refused to say another word until he answered. When she still didn't speak, he frowned. "If something happens that prevents me from accompanying you back to Santa Fe, surely you know that I'll arrange an escort to see you safely home."

"What could happen that would prevent you from accompanying me?" She leveled a steady gaze on his growing discomfort.

"All in good time," he said finally.

"This is a good time."

"No, Della."

The finality in his voice underscored the cold, hard expression that she'd seen him wear when they encountered strangers. Most people stared and then backed away.

Since she didn't view Cameron as icy, hard, or unapproachable, she tended to forget that was how the rest of the world saw him and that was how he wanted it. This magnificent male animal treated her with care and gentleness, but he could be quick and deadly.

When she realized their eyes had locked across the table and the air had shifted, her mouth went dry. Usually she attributed the tension between them to irritation or frustration at a situation. That was easier to accept than to give the tension its true name. But she felt her breath quicken and knew what she experienced was wanton longing. She had felt it and fought it for a long time.

"I'm impulsive and bad tempered," she whispered, feeling the need to build a wall.

"I don't give a damn." He stared at her lips.

"I carry grudges. Look how long I've blamed and hated the Wards." She looked at the knots rising and falling along his jaw.

"It doesn't matter."

Oh Lord, she was falling into an abyss, spinning, tumbling, dizzy with wanting him. No wall would keep them apart.

Cameron swore softly and she wondered if she had spoken aloud. He stared at her through narrowed eyes. "I'm going to take you back to the hotel," he said softly, speaking between his teeth. "Then I'm going to the gentlemen's-club room to smoke and drink."

She didn't understand. A minute ago she would have wagered everything she owned that he felt the same raw needs that she did. She would have bet the earth that he ached with wanting her as she ached with needing him.

"Cameron." Her voice was a whisper. "What is it?" She couldn't have been wrong. She saw his desire in his hard, intent gaze, read it in the clenched fists resting on the tablecloth. "This thing, this secret, has been between us too long. In the name of heaven, tell me and let's be done with it. Cameron, I beg you."

Pain thinned his lips and tightened his expression, hurting her to witness it. Della drew a breath and held it, knowing she was seeing something that few people, if any, had seen. Impulsively she reached across the table and placed her palm over his balled fist. "Oh, Cameron, I'm sorry. Whatever it is—I'm sorry."

A sound close to despair grew out of his throat. "Don't say another word. Not a word." He moved his fist away from her hand and stood abruptly. "I should have told you long ago. It's a blot on my honor that I didn't." Briefly he closed his eyes, then stared at her. "I swear to you. I'll tell you everything after you've seen your daughter."

Della looked up in astonishment. His pain and the tone of his voice almost frightened her. She would have said that James Cameron couldn't feel that level of pain or despair, that he had left such emotions far behind him. In fact, no one watching Cameron now would guess what Della was seeing because she knew him and she loved him and she read him with her heart.

Silently she stood and took his arm. And for the first time fear vanquished her curiosity. She no longer wanted to know his secret.

Chapter 17

An hour ago Della had turned out the lamps, leaving the fire burning for warmth and light. Sitting in the center of her bed, she brushed her hair with long, even strokes and listened for any sound from the adjoining room.

Cameron had returned about thirty minutes ago, she'd heard his hallway door close then movement followed by silence. A few minutes later she'd caught the fragrant scent of one of his thin cigars and pictured him sitting in bed, smoking in the dark. He wouldn't sleep tonight, either.

Lowering her brush, she stared unseeing into the low flames flickering in the hearth. Would it be so wrong for two lonely people to reach out to each other? Just this one time? Would it harm anyone? Offend anyone?

She and Cameron were mature adults who understood that sex was not commitment. There would be no misunderstandings. And they would respect each other no less for having shared themselves. She knew this because she knew herself and she knew him. There would be awkwardness tomorrow, but it would melt like morning mist. And sex would complicate an association that already felt tangled, but they would manage those complications.

He wanted her. Despite his pulling back, Cameron needed her. Della knew that, sensed it with every cell in her body.

But he would never walk through that door and come to her. It would never happen. He would not betray his friendship with Clarence, nor would he betray the role he'd assumed of being her protector.

If they were ever to find comfort in each other's arms, Della would have to go to him. She swallowed hard and stared at the connecting doors. Could she be that brazen? Was she really that emancipated from the constricted woman she once had been? Did she need him that much?

Slowly she lowered the hairbrush to her lap. Her hands trembled. Don't think about it, just do it, she ordered herself. This was destined from the first. It's right, it's so right. But you must go to him.

Slipping from the bed, she moved on bare feet to the door, and opened her side. Then, heart pounding, she drew a deep breath and eased his door open.

A fire burned low in Cameron's fireplace, but it was the light from her hearth that fell through the doors and onto the bed. He lay against the pillows, one hand on an upraised knee, the other holding a cigar.

Della wet her lips, wishing to heaven that he would say something. She couldn't read his expression. "James," she said in a low, uncertain voice. "If you send me back to my room, I will die of humiliation."

Without taking his eyes off her, Cameron stubbed out the cigar in an ashtray on the side table. She couldn't know that the light behind her turned her nightgown transparent and he could see the curve of her waist and the shapely length of her legs. His throat dried and his arousal was instant.

Cameron knew what was right and honorable, knew what he had to do. But he also knew what it had cost her to open the doors and come to him. He knew he would damage her if he rejected her. First, he had to accept her, and then he had to tell her the whole truth. Heaven knew this was not the moment he would have chosen, and he cursed beneath his breath.

He opened his arms. "Come here."

The air ran out of her in a rush of relief, and she ran across the space that separated them, hesitated, then climbed onto his bed. "Thank God. I was afraid you might not . . ."

He framed her face between his hands and stroked his thumbs along the contours of her lips, stopping her nervous words. Her cheeks were soft beneath his palms, and her lips were wide and smooth. She was in his bed.

Gently he guided her into his arms and held her, feeling the warmth of her breasts against his shirt front, her breath on his neck.

"We have to talk," he said hoarsely.

He'd wanted to bury his hands in her loose hair almost from the first moment he'd seen her, and he did so now, letting the silken weight spill through his fingers. Her hair was thicker, heavier than he'd imagined, but as wonderful and erotic as he had fantasized it would be. Della was in his bed. The wonder of it awed him.

Bowing his head, he inhaled the scent of her skin, and a sound emerged from deep in his throat. He should send her away. Now. He absolutely knew it. Right now. But he had loved her for so long. He had needed someone—this someone—all of his life. At this moment he saw his life for what it was and what it would always be, lonely and alone. No one had gotten as close to him as the woman in his arms. How could he send her away? Miraculously she was in his bed, in his arms.

"James, kiss me."

He brought his mouth down hard on hers, letting his passion punish her for bringing him something he could not have. He plundered and invaded, took what she offered and more. When they leaned apart, their breathing was hot and ragged, and he had never wanted a woman more in his life.

"Good Lord," she whispered, her eyes wide, her face lit by firelight. "Never in my life have I been kissed like that! I didn't even know . . ."

"Della, listen to me." He tried to clear the hoarseness from his throat. He was a selfish bastard, kissing her when he had no right. Wanting her so much that his hands shook. "Stop. I have to talk to you."

"Now?" She kissed his throat, let her tongue touch his skin.

"Oh God." Smothering a groan, he caught her hands before she touched him again, demonstrating a depth of control that he hadn't known he possessed. "Now."

Her head fell back and she gazed at him from eyes smoky with desire. Her lips parted. "There's nothing you have to say that won't wait for thirty minutes."

She kissed him again and this time it was her tongue that tasted and explored while she opened the buttons down his shirt, leaving a trail of tingling heat where her fingertips brushed his skin.

He cursed, hating himself for wavering. Needing her like a drowning man needs air. While he could still think, he tried one last time. "Della, we cannot do this. When you hear what I have to tell you—"

"Shhh." She pushed his shirt down, her hands electric and arousing on his shoulders. "Your secret has waited this long, it can wait a little longer."

Cameron watched his trembling fingers pull the ribbon at her throat, and then the next ribbon, opening bows that revealed a deep V of creamy, firelit skin. And he couldn't fight it anymore. He wasn't that upstanding, wasn't that strong. He would take this one good thing in his life, this night that she offered, because he couldn't refuse her. It wasn't in him.

"Wait," he said against her lips. Sliding from the bed, he built up the fire so he could see her better. Then he pushed off his trousers and smiled at her sharp intake of breath. When she fumbled with her nightgown, he shook his head. "No." Taking her hand, he drew her off the bed and into his arms where he kissed her long and deep, savoring the length of her body pressed against his.

He wanted to remove her gown himself, revealing her by inches, watching the lace hem slide up her calves, her pale thighs, past a triangle of lustrous brown to the inner curve of her waist, where he paused to kiss her forehead, her eyelids, her temples before he drew the gown to her full, heavy breasts. She gazed into his eyes, her breathing rapid, then she raised her arms and he drew off the nightgown and let it flutter to the floor near their feet.

"No," he said when she would have covered herself from shyness or modesty. Gently he drew her arms away. "Let me look at you."

Gold and orange shadows played on the perfection of her form. She was all that he had imagined, everything wonderful and splendid that he had ever wanted a woman to be.

"You are so beautiful," he whispered, awed by her.

"So are you." Lifting a hand, she traced her fingertips along the scar on his shoulder, then touched a more recent scar on his chest. She flattened her palm over the scar that Luke Apple had left, then she closed her eyes and swayed.

He caught her and lifted her in his arms, felt her hair slide over his bare shoulder and arm before he placed her on the bed. She half sat up and reached for him, but he shook his head and gently pressed her back into the pillows.

For the first time that he could remember, he wanted to make love instead of having sex. Tonight meant much more than satisfying an urge. Seeing her with her head flung back and her throat arched, caressing her, loving her, was a dream he had carried for years, a dream that would never come true again.

He kissed her slowly, thoroughly, tasted her skin, made love to each breast, pressed his ear to her heart and listened to her pulse race as loud and fast as his own. He ran his tongue along the inside of her arm while his hands stroked her thighs preparing the way for his mouth.

When his fingers found her feathery center, she cried out his name and writhed beneath his hand, lifting to him, inflaming him with her desire. But for the first time in his life, a woman's pleasure was more important than his own.

He took his time, not hurrying, learning the taste and touch of her beneath his lips and hands, discovering tenderness. And finally, he brought his tongue to the hot liquid center where he teased until she was wild and thrashing and sobbing his name again and again. Only then did he rise above her and thrust forward. Her fingernails gripped his arms, his shoulders. Her hands flew over his chest, his face, his hair. And finally her eyes flew open, she gasped, then she arched up to him with a deep shudder. He dropped his head, kissed her, then let the tension build and build until he could contain it no longer, could only explode in helpless joy.

It was the worst thing he had ever done.

When his head cleared and he could breathe, he looked down into her softly shining gaze and detested himself. What he had just done was unforgivable.

"I had no idea," she whispered, touching his lips with her fingers. Wonder filled her eyes. "I thought I knew, but I didn't."

"Don't move." Easing away from her, he slipped out of bed and poured water into the basin on top of the bureau. After wetting a towel, he returned and sat beside her to blot the perspiration from her forehead and throat. He moved the wet towel toward her breasts, then stopped and pushed the cloth into her hand before turning away to gather her nightgown. "Are you thirsty? I have some whisky."

"Just water, please."

The fire had burned low, but he didn't build it up again. The wrong he had just done her tightened his chest with shame. It must show on his face, he thought, drawing on his trousers. And later, when he remembered every detail of tonight, he suspected his shame would deepen when he admitted that he could hate himself for what he'd done without regretting a single moment.

When she'd had her water and had done up the ribbons on her nightgown, Cameron plumped the pillows against the headboard and drew her into his arms. She rested her head on his shoulder and placed a hand on his chest. He loved the feel of her silky hair on his skin, and wished they could hold each other and whisper lovers' words. But the clock was ticking against them. Within mere minutes everything would change. He cleared his throat and felt her tense in his arms.

"Don't," she whispered. "Not tonight. Your secrets will keep until tomorrow. Please, James."

"By not telling you the truth long ago, I've done us both a great wrong." He closed his arms around her and bent his head to inhale the warm fragrance of her hair and skin. In minutes she would jerk away from him.

"I don't believe you've wronged anyone." She pressed her palm against his heart.

She would, and very quickly.

"I've told you about the war," he said, raising his head and looking into the darkness. He would rather have walked into a hail of bullets than say what had to be said. "But not everything."

"I've known from the first there was something else to tell," she said against his chest. In her voice he heard dread mixed with curiosity.

Speaking into the shadows above her head, he told her about that day in the forest when the war had ended for him. He told her about the man in the gray uniform appearing at the top of the ditch and both of them firing.

He felt her grow rigid in his arms. "Wait. You said a gray uniform, but you mean blue."

"I wore the blue uniform, Della."

She sat up and stared down at him with bewilderment and confusion. "But that can't be," she whispered, her voice barely audible. "That would make you a Yankee."

"We both fired." Looking into her face, he wondered if she could smell the burnt powder or hear the artillery in the distance. He could, and it seemed so real. "The Confederate soldier rolled into the ditch." Her eyes locked to his, wide and dark and not wanting to believe. "We were trapped together by the bombardment. Eventually I wanted to know who he was, so I went through his pockets."

"This was the man you told me about, the soldier who put a face on the enemy." He could hardly hear her words, but he heard the raw harshness, saw the rapid rise and fall of her breast. "This was the last man you killed, wasn't it? What was his name, James?" She asked the question, but she moved back on the bed and shook her head as if she didn't want to hear. A single tear spilled over her lashes and rolled down her cheek before she dashed it away with an angry gesture. "Say his name!"

He pulled a hand down his face. "You know who it was, Della. It was Clarence Ward."

Shaking hands covered her ears, then slid to her lips. Her eyes seemed huge and her face was white with shock. No sound emerged when her lips moved.

"I don't know why I kept your letter and his, and your wedding photograph." Reaching for her or touching her in any way would have been wrong, the worst thing he could do. But he wanted to hold and comfort her. "I regretted taking those items because I realized almost immediately that I'd have to find you and return what was yours."

Horror flattened her gaze. "I used to wonder how it had happened, and if Clarence had seen the face of the man who killed him. But when I had the chance to ask about the circumstances, I didn't." She blinked then shook her head. "Oh God. You said you were with him when he died, and I assumed . . ."

He couldn't bear to see her stunned expression so he swung his legs off the bed and bent forward, resting his elbows on his knees and rubbing hard at his jaw. There was nothing more to say. He stared at the flickering embers and listened.

"Everything that happened to me," she said in a raw voice, working it out, "happened because you fired a rifle that day. I lost my husband, my daughter lost her father. The Wards lost their son. I'm living on a dirt farm in Texas because you were trapped behind the lines. Because of you, I haven't seen my daughter in ten years. I'm alone with a tarnished reputation, thousands of miles from everything that was familiar . . . because you killed my husband. My whole life changed that day. Everything."

A long, rasping moan began in her chest and emerged from the back of her throat. If anguish had a voice, it would sound like this, too painful to bear hearing. "Oh my God! I slept with you!" She pushed herself to the far edge of the bed. "I gave myself to you!"

There was no defense. Nothing he could say. But he did turn to face her, that seemed the decent thing, and he saw the revulsion that twisted her expression.

"You son of a bitch. How could you! How could you bed the wife of a man you killed?"

She flew at him and Cameron saw her swing back her arm, but he didn't attempt to deflect the blow, didn't turn away. She hit him hard enough to snap his head to the side. When he faced her, she hit him again and a trickle of blood leaked from his nose. He didn't notice. Nothing physical could wound as deep as the revulsion and loathing burning in her eyes.

She glared down at her hand as if striking him had soiled her palm. Then she crawled off the bed and ran to her own room, slamming the door behind her. He heard the lock snap into place.

He didn't attempt to follow. Right now, she'd welcome the devil sooner than she would open her door to James Cameron. She needed time. He'd go to her in the morning, because he knew she'd have more questions.

But in the morning, she was gone.

After he broke down the connecting door, he discovered she had left behind the dinner dress and anything else that he'd bought her. Fragments of burned paper lay in the hearth ashes. Kneeling, he was able to make out a few words and realized that she'd burned the journal she'd been keeping.

Walking to the window, he leaned on the sill and gazed outside, wondering where she would go. He was a hunter, he'd find her. What worried him more was . . . then what?

She'd hailed a cab and directed the driver to take her to a hotel on the far side of town, something clean and respectable, but cheap. Fifty cents a night including breakfast didn't sound cheap to Della, but the cab driver swore that it was. For another nickel the driver carried her small trunk to the room she rented, then left her sitting awkwardly on the edge of the bed because there was no side chair. She had only a dim idea of where she was in relation to the train station. Not close to the River Manse, that was the important thing.

After the driver departed, Della locked the door, then emptied her drawstring purse and counted her money out on a plain white bedspread. She had left Two Creeks, Texas, with ten dollars. As Cameron had insisted on paying for everything, she'd spent only a dollar seventy-five during the journey. For the life of her she couldn't remember what she'd spent it on. Then she'd paid the driver fifteen cents to get her to this hotel and she'd given him a gratuity to cart her trunk upstairs since there were no bellmen. She had paid three nights in advance for the room, which left her with six dollars and fifty-five cents.

That was enough to carry her for a few days while she decided what to do next.

But first . . . she removed her hat and placed it atop a time-scarred bureau. Then she hung her traveling suit in the armoire and placed her shoes beneath her suit. Stockings, drawers, corset, and shimmy went into a bureau drawer, then she donned her oldest, faded flannel nightgown. The nightgown should have gone into the rag bin long ago, but when the world fell down around her ears, this was the item she reached for. She didn't know why she'd packed it, but she had and she was glad.

Della pulled down the window shade, shutting out the sight of a cold, dry day. Then she climbed into a bed almost as hard as the floor, slid beneath the covers, and pulled the pillow over her head.

And then she gave herself up to the damp-eyed confusion that battered her mind. The man she was beginning to love had killed her husband. And everything she thought she knew about Cameron was wrong. He wasn't a Southerner; he hadn't been Clarence's friend. He had deliberately deceived her.

Della did not emerge from her hotel room for twenty-four hours. She paced. She raged. And occasionally she fell into an exhausted sleep, only to waken with fury in her heart and wisps of bad dreams darkening her mind.

She had fed Cameron and washed and ironed his laundry. She had teased him and laughed with him. She had admired him. Once or twice she had let herself admit that she might love him. And the worst, the very worst: she had climbed into his bed and all but begged him to make love to her. The son of a bitch.

When she thought about making love to Clarence's killer, she felt wild and crazy inside, wanted to scream and tear her hair, wanted to smash furniture and claw down the walls. She wanted to buy a gun and shoot James Cameron straight through his black heart.

On the morning of her second day alone, she stood at the window and watched snow drifting past the window panes. It was a light snow that melted as soon as it reached the ground, not the raging blizzard that her heart longed to experience.

The intensity of her anger made her stomach cramp. An hour ago she had summoned a maid and requested tea and toast. Now she felt sick and wished she hadn't eaten.

But it wasn't the toast that made her ill. She should have pushed harder for the missing information. She had sensed it, had felt it, but she hadn't pressed. Something in her hadn't wanted to know.

Cameron had not lied outright, she gave him that. But he was guilty of the silent lie. Of letting her draw false conclusions and not correcting her when she assumed he was Clarence's friend. Or when she asked his opinion about Clarence. He was guilty of letting her iron his shirts when he knew she would not have if she'd known who he really was. He was guilty of letting her climb into his bed.

She glared at the snowflakes. There was no escaping the admission that she'd been a fool. If she had paid closer attention, she might have noticed Cameron's evasions. Sometimes he hadn't even needed to evade a direct question, because she refused to hear the truth.

Last night she had remembered asking him where he was from. He had answered, Winthrop. And what did she do? Instantly she had decided there must be a Winthrop, Georgia, instead of recalling the Winthrop outside of Boston, even though she had visited there as a child.

Turning from the window, she pressed the heels of her palms against her eyelids. He should have told her the truth at once.

Now she would never know for certain, but she believed she could have accepted the truth if he'd told her that first night. She might even have admired him for facing the widow of a man he had killed. It was even possible that she still would have invited him to sleep in her barn. Naturally she would be curious about him.

But Cameron had chosen to deceive her. He'd used her badly.

Needing to clear her mind, Della threw on some clothing and pulled a shawl over the shoulders of her traveling suit. There wasn't much traffic outside the hotel, thank heaven. The wagons and gigs that did pass splashed cold mud on the boards laid down as a walkway. When Della reached the wrought-iron gates of a small park, she turned inside to escape the mud and followed a brick path set beneath bare-branched elms.

The cold air and snowflakes melting on her cheeks were not enough to cool her anger. She had slept with Clarence's killer.

Cameron should have told her the truth before . . . to be fair, he had tried . . . but she had stopped him . . . she'd told him she would die of humiliation if he refused her . . . so he'd let her into his bed and then he had attempted to tell her the truth . . . but she wouldn't hear it . . .

Bending, she brushed a dusting of snow off the seat of a wooden bench, then sat heavily and rubbed her temples. Cameron had carried the letters and the photograph for ten long years. Why? Because he couldn't face her knowing he had devastated her life?

That couldn't be entirely correct. He'd found her in the saloon but had gone away without giving her the letters and the photo. If Cameron had done the right thing then, she wouldn't now be sitting in a snowy park in St. Louis.

On her way to see her daughter.

That was another deception. He wasn't doing a kind thing for the wife of a friend. Cameron acted out of guilt and shame. He felt responsible for Claire growing up with the Wards instead of with her parents, and he damn well should. Because of James Cameron, Claire's father was dead and her mother lived far away in a small Texas town no one had ever heard of.

No wonder he pressed her to reunite with her daughter. Cameron was trying to reassemble the pieces of lives he had broken.

That night she was almost asleep when she thought of something that brought her upright, clutching the sheet to her chest and blinking hard.

James Cameron had found her working in the saloon, they both recalled that brief meeting. But he had spoken to her, then he had gone away. And shortly afterward, her monthly allotment began to arrive.

"Oh my heavens," she whispered, squeezing her eyes shut.

Every instinct shouted that the money didn't come from Mr. Ward. It came from Cameron. That's why he hadn't given her the letters ten years ago. She would have noticed that he brought her the letters and then the money began to arrive. She would have guessed that he was easing his conscience by helping to support a woman he'd made a widow.

Lying back on the pillows, she stared up at the ceiling. All these years . . . it was Cameron's money that arrived at the bank every month. Cameron's money that had made it possible for her to quit working at the saloon. Cameron's money that kept her alive.

She remembered his comments about the farm. He

must have believed that he was supplementing an income she received from Clarence's father. He hadn't known that he was her sole source of support.

So if she telegraphed the bank in Two Creeks to wire her enough money to complete the journey to Atlanta, she would be requesting Cameron's money. James Cameron had been part of her life for ten years, she just hadn't known it.

For the next few days Della awoke at dawn, dressed, then wandered the streets of St. Louis. Sometimes she actually noticed the houses or shops she passed, but mostly she traveled in the past, thinking about everything, from the day she had arrived in Atlanta as a young girl up to the evening that she'd slept with the Yankee who killed her husband.

At midmorning of her fourth day alone, she returned to the small winter brown park and sat on the bench she had begun to think of as her own. It was time to consider finances and make decisions.

Food and additional days at the hotel were nibbling away her money. Like it or not, she would have to telegraph her banker in Two Creeks.

She had decided to finish the journey to Atlanta. She was almost there, and she hadn't changed her mind about wanting to fill an empty heart with the sight of her daughter.

Feeling overwhelmed by everything she had to do— wire her bank for money, get checked out of the hotel and get to the train station, buy her tickets—Della closed her eyes and rubbed her glove against her cheek. After a moment she felt the bench give slightly as someone sat beside her, then she inhaled the strong, rich aroma of coffee.

She slid a look toward the man seated beside her. "You!" Instantly her shoulders stiffened and her spine went rigid. "How did you find me?" That was a stupid question, and she knew it the minute the words fell out of her mouth.

Cameron set one of the coffee cups on the bench between them and kept the other. "Please, Della. Give me a minute and just listen."

Chapter 18

"I won't apologize for killing Clarence Ward." Not once had Cameron's rehearsed speech begun with words guaranteed to offend and make the situation worse. Damn it anyway.

"I want to throw this coffee in your face," she said, speaking between clenched teeth. "Give me one reason why I shouldn't."

"It was a war. If I hadn't killed Clarence, Clarence would have killed me. Only one soldier was going to walk out of those trees." He glanced at the steam hovering above the coffee and watched her reach for the cup. "I don't mind dying, but I'm not going to make it easy. The man who puts me down has to be faster, better, and luckier than I am. That wasn't Clarence, not that day in the woods."

"This is pointless." She touched the cup but didn't lift it. "I'm cold. I'm going back to the hotel."

"I've done three things in my life that I regret. I bought a commission and went to war. I waited ten years before I gave you what was rightfully yours. And I deceived you and took advantage, knowing you'd despise me after you learned the whole truth."

"Despise is too mild. You should have told me the truth immediately! Maybe nothing would have changed, or maybe everything would have changed and we wouldn't be sitting here now. But I should have been told who you were and offered a choice about whether I wanted to spend time with you given the circumstances." Her eyes burned and a nerve twitched in her cheek. But she stayed on the bench instead of rising.

"I can't change what I did, but maybe I can help you have a better life than you've had."

"It's terrible that it was you who killed Clarence."

"If it hadn't been me, it would have been some other Yankee soldier."

"But what's worse is that you took me to bed without telling me it was you who killed him."

"You're right," he said after a minute, staring straight ahead.

Della clenched her fists in her lap. "What makes this so unforgivable is the deceit. You came into my home and sat at my table. You let me believe that you were my husband's friend! What makes my stomach churn is that I was falling in love with you! I gave myself to the man who put a bullet into my husband's heart!"

He'd been imagining this confrontation for ten years. Her words and her expression shouldn't have sliced him into pieces. "I want to see this journey through to its end."

"I don't give a damn what you want."

"I think you want it, too, Della. You want to see Claire and talk to her and find out if the two of you can have a future together. I know." He raised his hand. "You say you only want to see her, and maybe that's where it ends.

But seeing her might be the beginning of something good for you both."

She stared at him as if he were something loathsome. "What are you proposing? That we continue the journey as if nothing happened? As if nothing has changed?"

"I said I'd take you to your daughter and that's what I mean to do. You don't have to sit beside me on the train, don't have to take your meals in my company. We'll continue on whatever terms you want."

She was silent long enough that his coffee started to ice over before she spoke again.

"It's you who sends the money every month, isn't it?" When he didn't answer, she sighed. "I thought so. Tell me something, Cameron."

It was Cameron again. The night she came to him, she had called him James. No one called him James.

"I'm curious. Does sending the money and taking me to Claire, do these things balance the scales in your mind? Once this journey ends, will you put the war away and let it go?"

"I killed a hundred men who had wives and parents and children and lives waiting for them," he said flatly. "If I knew the names of those people, I'd do something to try to make it right. I don't know what, but I'd try. But I only know the name and circumstances of one Confederate soldier."

"So you'll go on, hunting and killing outlaws whose names and circumstances you do know." She met his eyes. "Helping me won't alter one minute of what you remember or what you feel or what you think you owe."

"Do you want me to say that you're right? What the hell else can I do?"

"You said that the last man you killed put a face on the enemy, do you remember telling me that?"

Of course he did.

She stood up from the bench and looked down at him. "Now I have a face for the enemy, too."

"There's one more thing," he said, standing and moving close enough to inhale the scent of her, "then we won't talk about this again."

She stepped back, her gaze fixed.

"I didn't use you to scratch a momentary itch. I believe you know that or you wouldn't have come to me. I spent ten years looking at your photograph almost every day, Della. Sometimes it feels as if I've loved you all of my life." She sucked in a breath and her face went white. "That doesn't excuse letting you come into my bed. I should have stopped you and I should have told you the whole truth right then. No, that's wrong. I should have told you the truth the evening I rode down your driveway."

"You took advantage," she whispered. The accusation in her eyes was like a knife in his gut.

"The only thing I took from you was a memory. That's all I wanted." When she turned away from him, he cleared his throat, then pulled out his pocket watch and consulted the time. "We have three hours before the train leaves. Will you come, or do you want me to send you back to Texas?"

"I've already decided what I'll do." Her head came up and her eyes flashed. "You owe me this trip, Cameron!"

"That's how I figure it."

She moved past him, twitching her skirt aside so the

hem didn't touch his legs, and she refused his arm when he offered.

He watched a freight wagon rumble past the small park's gate, then smoothed the brim of his hat. "We'll take your trunk to the station, then we'll have time for a light supper. We should eat something because the line we're riding doesn't have dining cars."

She shook her head. "I don't want to sit in a restaurant with you. When we arrived, a man was selling hot potatoes on the platform. If he's still there, that's all I want. A potato."

They didn't speak again during the walk to her hotel, and he waited in a small, unadorned lobby while she packed.

He'd been watching her for two days, trying to decide when and how best to approach her. From the start he'd known there was nothing he could say to ease her pain or deflect her hatred. His goal had been to persuade her to continue on to Atlanta. Cameron could live with her hatred, that had been inevitable and he'd expected it. But he couldn't live with her not finding her daughter.

He sat on a horsehair chair with his hat on his knees and remembered the firelight glowing through her nightgown as she stood in the doorway. He remembered the sweetness of her mouth and the damp heat of her skin. No matter what happened in the years to come, he would always have that one perfect hour when she had looked up at him with shining eyes and called him James.

Della's preference was to ride in a separate car. Her second choice would have been to sit by herself. By now, however, she knew a traveler's manner of passing time was to speculate about fellow passengers. So she sat in silence beside Cameron, her arms folded across her chest, her head turned to the window. Observers would note silence and rigid postures and would conclude the existence of difficulties, but she and Cameron wouldn't be as interesting as they would have been if they had chosen separate seating.

"No, thank you," she said when the conductor came down the aisle passing out box lunches. Inside would be bread, butter, and cheese, two pieces of fried chicken, and cookies or a slab of frosted cake. It didn't matter if it was morning, noon, or night, the boxed meals were always the same.

Cameron also shook his head, but he did request coffee and assumed that she also wanted a cup. As recently as last week Della would have teased him about never missing an opportunity for coffee. Biting her lips, she turned her face back to the window.

Well-maintained farms appeared with increasing frequency as the train chuffed southeast. Since the train carried freight and mail, it stopped at almost every town, large or small, which explained why the journey to Atlanta would take eight seemingly endless days. They had missed the fast-moving express train.

"You should eat something," Cameron said. He paid the conductor, then passed her a cup of coffee. After a minute he decided she wasn't going to comment. "You haven't said a dozen words in the last three days."

They rolled past a field enclosing horses and cows, and Della wondered what it would be like to live with an animal the same general size and shape as yourself but whom you couldn't communicate with because he was a different species.

She slid a glance toward Cameron, then looked out the window again. "I have nothing to say." Having nothing to say hadn't stopped her from talking in the past. She waited, but Cameron was tactful enough not to say so.

In fact, there should have been a great deal to discuss and explore. That day sitting on the park bench had produced explosive declarations. Della had confessed to being on the brink of falling in love with him, and Cameron had admitted that he had fallen in love with a photograph he had carried for ten years. In different circumstances, they could have discussed these two wonders for weeks. At least Della could have. Cameron would have nodded and muttered and tugged at his collar, and she would have laughed watching his discomfort.

But Cameron had killed her husband. One act, committed in less than a minute, had put Clarence in the grave and had forever changed her life.

Closing her eyes, she dropped her head and rubbed her forehead. "I know it could have been any Yankee, you're absolutely right. It just happened to be you," she whispered. "From your point of view, it could have been any Confederate who appeared that day. It just happened to be Clarence." Cameron didn't speak. "For a while I blamed you that Clarence died with 'I hate you' in his ears. But that isn't true. It's my fault that he died believing I hated him."

Cameron faced forward and didn't glance at her, but she saw his hands tighten around his coffee cup.

"I know you were doing your duty as a soldier that day. I know you acted in self-defense. But in here," she touched her breast above her heart, "I feel betrayed. You killed my husband and you lied to me."

"I never lied to you."

"You lied by omission. You let me believe things you knew were untrue." She shifted on the seat to face his profile. "I believe that you are a man of integrity and honor. But if that's true, then how could you deceive me like you did?"

Finally he looked at her with tired eyes and an expressionless face. "I knew you would hate me when you learned the truth. And then I'd never get to know you or be with you for a while. I didn't plan to deceive you, Della. It just happened, and I was glad."

She blinked and her lips parted. It was that simple. He had deceived her because he'd fallen in love with a girl in a photograph, a girl who had not existed for years.

"Oh, Cameron." Her voice cracked and dropped to a scarcely audible tone. "Were you disappointed?"

He understood what she asked. "Never. You are everything I hoped you would become and more."

The back of her throat tightened and her eyes felt hot and scratchy. He wasn't the type of man to whisper sweet nothings into a woman's ear. He'd said all he could and probably more than he was comfortable with.

"I wish . . ." But wishes were foolish things, about as useful as a broken clock.

Della turned her head toward the window. She was sitting next to the man who had killed her husband. How was that possible? She had made love to him. Unthinkable, but it had happened. She could never forgive Cameron's deception or make sense out of being with him.

That hurt, too. When he'd told her the truth, she'd lost

a friend, a confidant, and a lover. No one had taken as
much from her, not even the Wards.

And the confusing worst of it was that right now, she
missed him and longed for him. She wished she could
bury herself in his arms and tell him that she had bad
dreams every night. She wanted to tell him that the
odd sense of dread and foreboding had not disappeared
as she had believed it would, once he told her everything.
She wanted to talk about Claire and the rising anxiety
that her courage would flag and she would have nothing
to say to her daughter. Or that Claire would dislike her.
And what of the Wards? She felt half sick when she
thought of seeing Clarence's parents again. Would it be
necessary?

"Della . . ."

"Don't," she said quietly. "There's nothing to talk
about."

With every click of the wheels on the rails, Della grew
more agitated. Until now there had been new expe-
riences to occupy her mind, and she had spent more
time than she cared to recall thinking about Cameron.
Clarence had faded from the front of her thoughts and
she didn't flog herself daily with guilt and remorse the
way she used to. And Claire . . . although Claire was the
entire reason for this journey, Della hadn't spent many
hours speculating about her daughter until now. Now
Claire seemed real. Tomorrow they would be in the same
town. She placed a hand on her stomach and felt ill.

"Are you all right?"

"I haven't been sleeping well. But I don't imagine you
have, either." The sleeping platforms on this train were

shorter, harder, and more uncomfortable than any so far. "Part of me wishes we'd arrive and find a hotel with decent beds, but another part of me wants to turn around and go back to Texas."

Cameron lowered a newspaper he'd purchased on the platform of the last station, where they had stopped long enough for passengers to seek fresh air. "I'd say it's natural to be a bit nervous."

"I've changed my mind," she stated abruptly. "I don't want to find Claire. It isn't right. I've been thinking about it, and I've decided it's easier not to know anything about her."

"That's nonsense," Cameron said, frowning.

"When I imagine her, she can be anything I want her to be. Short or tall, thin or rounded. I always think of her as smiling and laughing, and that's how I want to go on thinking of her."

"Della—"

"This was all a mistake." She gripped his arm and gave him a panicked look. "I'm sorry, Cameron. I've wasted your time and your money. I really don't want to do this. Truly." He didn't say anything, so she babbled on. "We'll stay overnight and sleep in decent beds, get some rest, then we'll go back to Santa Fe. Stop looking at me like that."

If she hadn't used up all of her tears, she might have burst into a fit of crying.

"What can I do to help you?" Cameron asked after a moment.

"Nothing." She pushed away from him and wrapped her arms around herself, looking out the window. The train wound through winter brown hills and when they stepped out for a breath of air, the temperature was cool and pleasant, but she felt cold. A chill had settled under her skin and she couldn't seem to shake it.

"You were with Sherman's army," she said that evening. She hadn't followed news about the war, hadn't wanted to. But everyone had known General Sherman's name. Sherman had brought the apocalypse upon them, and then the end. "We abandoned the plantation," Della said softly. "We took everything we could pack in a wagon and we drove to Atlanta. A week later Atlanta fell."

She looked at Cameron, then turned her gaze back to the dark window. "By then you were gone, walking north." Sherman's army had been accused of savagery. She was glad Cameron hadn't been part of that.

"Nothing out there looks familiar."

It was too dark to see anything, but she understood. Nothing looked familiar to her, either. "I remember the fires. So many people had fled that there weren't enough men to fight the fires or deliver water. There was a fire burning somewhere in the city for weeks and weeks. And you could buy food, but a piece of bad meat cost as much as a prime carriage horse once did."

It wasn't good to talk about these things; it was pointless. But these were Della's last memories of Atlanta. She had given birth to Claire while the air was thick with ash and smoke. The Yankees held Atlanta then, but most of the Union army had swept on, moving toward the coast.

Cameron's mouth thinned to a slash and his eyes were icy and hard. "For the first time, coming here feels like a bad idea."

"I know." Della bowed her head. "I feel shaky inside,

like nothing has changed. Tomorrow we'll wake up, look out the window, and the sky will be red with flames. Bricks will litter the streets, and the houses will be deserted." Toward the front of the car a baby cried. Della's heart skipped a beat and she thought she couldn't stand it. Claire was mere miles away.

That night she dreamed of following the hearse, walking close behind the creaking wheels. She could have looked inside the back window, past the curling gold vines, but guilt stopped her. Even in her dream, she understood that she had done Clarence a terrible wrong. She stumbled forward, listening to Mrs. Ward crying behind her.

She awoke in her cramped space, shaking and gasping. They were all here. Mr. and Mrs. Ward, Clarence, Claire. Even Cameron was part of a past that had never let her go.

Chapter 19

Midmorning sunlight sparkled across the water below the bridge spanning the Chattahoochee River. It seemed no more than an eyeblink later that the train whistled into the main station puffing dark soot and white clouds of steam.

The engine hissed to a stop, and the long journey was over.

"Della?"

Della blinked and discovered that she and Cameron were the last people in the car. Everyone else had rushed outside onto the platform where family and friends waited and porters rushed here and there pushing carts piled high with trunks and bags.

She didn't think her legs would support her weight. Her stomach rolled and churned as if she'd eaten something spoiled.

Cameron touched her arm and peered into her face. "You're pale. Are you all right?"

"I have a terrible headache." And she felt half sick and anxious. Had Claire heard the train's whistle? How close or far away was she?

Cameron slipped an arm around her waist and gently

tugged her upward. "Let's get you to a hotel and tuck you into bed. Some rest and a good night's sleep on a proper mattress, and you'll feel right as rain."

The air was different in the South, Della decided as they stepped onto the platform. Softer and moist without being damp. Locals would say that today was chilly, and the scent of woodsmoke suggested residents warmed their parlors with toasty fires. But to Della, now seasoned by living in the West, the temperature felt mild and pleasant. She glanced at the thick branches of tall pin oaks overhanging the platform and thought about snow back home. This was a different world.

And it was a world she didn't recognize. As they drove toward town in a hired carriage, Della silently peered out the side windows. Undoubtedly there were structures that had survived the war, but she didn't recognize any buildings or the names of the shops. Some street names sounded familiar, but others did not. Also, it seemed there were crowds of people about and more traffic to snarl the streets.

On the other hand, she hadn't known Atlanta well, and she hadn't lived here long. Moreover, during the time she had lived in town she'd spent most of her days confined, preparing for childbirth or recovering from childbirth. She had buried a husband here, had allowed her daughter to be stolen from her. There were no happy memories in Atlanta.

At the hotel, Cameron followed her upstairs and into the suite he'd engaged for her. Della halted by the foyer mirror to remove the pins from her hat, but the first thing she noticed was the absence of a connecting door. Relief and a tiny whiff of disappointment eased the tension in her shoulders.

Cameron didn't turn from the window until the bell-man and the maid had withdrawn, after they deposited Della's luggage and lit a fire in the hearth.

"I instructed the maid to bring you tea and toast."

"What will you do while I'm resting and dreading tomorrow?"

"Do you really dread seeing Claire?"

"Nothing has ever put me in such a state." Raising a hand, she touched the headache behind her forehead. "I feel like this is a terrible mistake. Like seeing Claire will only be a disaster."

In the park in St. Louis, she had sworn that she wouldn't confide in him, would not share her thoughts or feelings. She would treat James Cameron as an untrustworthy stranger. Now here she was, saying things she had sworn she wouldn't and fighting a powerful urge to run forward and throw herself into his arms. Cameron was the only person in the world who knew how she felt right now, or who might care, and he was the only person who could offer any comfort.

She drew a deep breath, straightened her shoulders, then deliberately turned her back to him and held her hands toward the warmth of the fire. Behind her, she heard the rustle of his jacket being pulled back, then the click of the lid to his pocket watch.

"Shall we have breakfast together tomorrow?" he asked, walking behind her on his way to the door. "Meet in the dining room at, say, eight o'clock?"

"That's fine. Cameron?" She turned her head and met his gaze as if she weren't thinking about the last time they had been together in a hotel. "There's something I've been curious about . . . Do you like not having to worry about some hothead pulling a gun on you?" It had been at least two weeks since Della had noticed anyone studying Cameron with that certain glint of recognition.

"It's not completely comfortable," he answered with a frown. "A man could get careless and let his guard down."

That would never happen with him, not entirely. The soldier was too much a part of James Cameron. He'd spent too many years being alert to his surroundings, being aware of every nuance. He was more relaxed than she'd seen him, but the term was relative. Cameron's idea of being relaxed would have been another man's notion of high alert.

"I'll see you in the morning," Della said, gazing into the flames, wishing she could have rested and sought comfort in the enemy's arms.

Mercator Ward was not an easy man to find. By mid-afternoon Cameron knew Ward was not in business, had done nothing to get his name in the newspapers, and had never been arrested. The Wards didn't live where they had ten years ago, and none of the neighbors there remembered them or could offer any information.

It was late afternoon before Cameron found a church secretary who remembered Mercator and Enid Ward.

"Standoffish people," the secretary said, his lips thinning with dislike. "Mrs. Ward in particular didn't take well to fellowship. A difficult woman, to put it kindly."

"Would you have a record of their current address?" Cameron asked. He followed the secretary through a side door and into the office of a small church that smelled of lemon polish and candle wax.

"Here it is." The secretary thumbed backward in a thick membership register. He read off an address, then explained that the street lay outside the city proper. "In a newer section that was built up after the war." It was impossible not to divide life into before-the-war and after-the-war.

Cameron hired a carriage to take him to the Wards' address and instructed the driver to park across the lane from the house. Sitting inside the carriage, he smoked a cigar and watched lights wink on inside the house as the sun sank below the horizon.

The house sat on a hilly acre of wooded land. Not surprisingly, it was constructed of fire-resistant red brick, trimmed with white shutters and porch pillars. Before the sunset faded, Cameron noted meticulously maintained grass, drifts of azaleas, and stone walkways. The house was larger than the place the Wards had rented after first coming to Atlanta, but smaller by far than the manor house Della had described.

He watched for an hour, during which time no one entered or left the house. There was nothing outside to indicate how many people lived within or if they were in residence, but instinct suggested a small household.

Eventually his mind wandered to Della's question. For most of his adult life, Cameron had stayed alive by being observant and wary of his surroundings and the people near him. That being the case, he knew he'd left his legend somewhere between Santa Fe and St. Louis.

It felt good to be anonymous. For the first time in years, he didn't experience the weight of other people's expectations, didn't feel he had to prove anything. Now when someone gazed at him for a beat too long, he looked into their eyes and understood he drew attention because he was tall and imposing, not because the observer wondered if he should pull a gun or get out of the way.

It wasn't going to be easy to return to a life where everything he did and said was noted and judged against someone's notion of how a legend was supposed to walk and talk and behave.

But that was the life he had chosen. As he'd told Della, he didn't know the names of the good men he'd killed during the war, but he did know the names and deeds of the outlaws he brought to justice. There lay his path to atonement.

He put the subject out of his mind the next morning when he met Della for breakfast. Della and Claire would be the focus of all he did or thought for the next few days. He told Della that he'd located the Wards.

"Did you see her?" Della asked, her voice breathless. She wet her lips and lowered her spoon.

"I didn't see anyone." He leaned back in the dining room chair and studied her. A decent bed didn't seem to have helped much. Dark circles smudged the area beneath her eyes, and her face was too pale. "Are you feeling any better?"

"It was a difficult night. Bad dreams and bad thoughts." Giving up on breakfast, she pushed a cereal bowl aside and frowned. "I keep wondering . . . what did they tell her about me?"

Cameron considered what he'd learned about the Wards from Della, their previous neighbors, and the church secretary. The Wards didn't strike him as people overburdened by kindness or generosity. He doubted they would have told Claire anything pleasant or flattering about a daughter-in-law they had not approved or liked.

"I have no idea."

"Well, guess, can't you?"

It was a flash of the temper he'd seen the first night he met her. And he couldn't help her now any more than he'd been able to help her then. "No," he said finally, keeping his voice level, "I'm not going to guess what people I don't know might have said to someone else I don't know."

She looked down and shook her head. "I'm sorry. Crazy things are spinning through my mind. My nerves are jumping around under my skin, and all I want to do is run away and forget about this."

Some of the foreboding she'd mentioned reached out to Cameron, and he wondered suddenly if coming to Atlanta had been the right thing to do. He hadn't expected Della to be as ambivalent, filled with dread one moment and excited the next. "Have you considered how you'll approach your daughter?"

She lifted her head. "Well, I don't plan to knock at their door and demand to see her."

"What do you intend to do?"

She raised a hand, started to say something, then watched her hand fall back to her lap. "I don't know. Every time I've tried to imagine today, my mind veers away." She bit her lips and twisted her hands. "In fact, I don't have to approach her. I only want to see her, that's all."

"I understand."

"There's no reason to actually talk to her, so I can remain at a distance. She doesn't need to learn that I'm alive—in case they've told her that I'm dead. I mean, it would probably be better for Claire if she went on believing that."

"If that's what you want."

"It is. So . . . I guess I'll go to the house and wait and hope Claire comes outside so I can see her."

"Do you want me to accompany you? Or is this something you need to do by yourself?"

It made his chest ache to witness her look of shock. "It never occurred to me that you wouldn't come! This was your idea." Impulsively she reached across the table and gripped his hand. "James Cameron, you can't bring me this far, then abandon me at the last minute!"

"I'll be there." The agitation in her voice and eyes alarmed him. He stroked her hand and tried to think of some way to help her. "Della . . . I know you detest me, and rightly so . . ."

She nodded, seeming to read his mind as she sometimes did. "But could we put all that aside for a day or two? I need a friend so badly, Cameron. I need you to catch me when I fall."

"You won't fall," he said softly. "You'll know what to do when the moment comes."

"I just want to see her, that's all," she said.

And she said it again when they were parked in a carriage across from the Wards' house. Crisp winter sunshine warmed the bricks and flashed off the window panes. In summer, tall water oaks would shade the side porch.

Della inhaled the steam from the coffee Cameron had

brought. "It's a nice house. A good place to grow up." She stared out the window. "I'm sure Claire has all the things that little girls need. Pretty dresses, and ribbons, and shoes for every ensemble and event. She probably has her own room."

Cameron would have bet on it. He had a feeling the house was too big for its residents. Not many people lived here. Servants and a very small family was his guess. His gaze shifted to the carriage house. He didn't sense emptiness, but he'd known last night there were no animals on the premises. Ward either boarded out his horses or rented carriage animals from the stable two blocks down the hill. In either case, the dusty windows on the carriage house suggested the Wards seldom required a carriage.

"Did you see the curtains twitch upstairs?" Della clutched his arm. "The third window from the right on the second story."

"I didn't notice anything."

"Oh. Then I probably imagined it." She drew a long breath. "Maybe Claire and Mrs. Ward went somewhere before we arrived. If they return while we're here, Mrs. Ward will recognize me." Her hands flew to pat the hair coiled on her neck, then she adjusted the angle of her hat, smoothed her lapels. "I've changed, but not that much. She might cause a scene. She might say, There's the mother who abandoned you!"

"I doubt it." He didn't know what else to say.

An hour later the front door opened, and a woman wearing an apron stepped outside and swept off the porch and front steps.

"I don't know who that is," Della whispered, both

hands pressed to her chest. She closed her eyes. "Suppose Claire went somewhere by herself, and she returns in the next few minutes. She'll see us sitting here and that will seem odd, I'd think. But I can't decide if I should identify myself or not. I hate this, but part of me wants to tell her that I'm her mother. But if I reveal who I am, it will be a terrible shock. I just know the encounter will end in disaster, and then I'll have ruined my one chance with her."

Cameron took both of her hands in his. "She's only nine years old. I doubt Claire is allowed to go anywhere by herself."

"Of course, you're right." Della pulled her hands away and rubbed her cheeks. "Wait. Maybe she went to school. No, the Wards would never send their granddaughter to public school. They would have tutors come to the house. But we haven't seen anyone."

Throwing out a hand, she gripped his wrist with surprising strength. "I can't do this. It isn't going to work out. Cameron, I really don't want to talk to Claire. I don't. If I talk to her, it won't go well, so let's leave. Right now. It's enough for me to know that she's living in this lovely house. That's all I need. She's safe, she's living in comfort, she's probably happy. Cameron, we have to go. Please."

He examined her face for less than a minute before he signaled the driver to take them back to town. As soon as the house was out of sight, Della's breathing slowed and she began to calm down.

"You're looking at me like you think I've lost my mind."

"I don't think that, but you're obviously upset. I'm

concerned about you." He held one of her gloved hands and she let him.

"I can't explain what happened back there," she said with a frown. "I don't know . . . I just felt a terrible pressure inside and knew that coming here was a mistake. All these years, I've pretended that Claire is in the next room. I see her in my mind, Cameron. I know what she looks like, I know her traits and her personality. But what if she's nothing like that?" Her eyes widened and she clutched his hand. "Or what if she guesses who I am? That would be terrible. Or worse, what if she doesn't see anything of herself in me? Wouldn't that be more terrible?"

Cameron didn't know the answer, but he knew it was good they were returning to the hotel.

When he had her upstairs, settled in the suite with biscuits and a fresh pot of chicory-flavored coffee, he cleared his throat, hoping to break into her long, silent reverie.

"I'm behaving badly," she said quietly. "I've never felt so confused in my life. I'm longing to hold my baby in my arms, but I'm afraid of her, too."

He sat beside her on the settee and took her hand in his. "May I make a suggestion?"

"Help me," she said simply.

"Maybe we're going about this wrong. Maybe we should send the Wards a note asking permission to call on them."

Della pulled her hand away. "They'll never agree to receive me."

"They'll guess what you want to discuss. So I'd anticipate that they'll agree to receive you rather than risk having you approach Claire on your own. From what you've told me, the Wards will want to control any meeting between you and Claire. And maybe that's best. They know Claire's temperament, they'll know if and when she should be told that you're here."

"They'll think I want to take Claire away from them."

"Maybe that's something to consider."

"You keep saying that, but you've seen where I live, and now you've seen where Claire lives." She turned her head. "She belongs here."

"Maybe you belong here, too, Della. Maybe that's the answer you're looking for." When he had observed the longing in her gaze as she watched the Wards' house, it had come to him that she should stay here. "You could get a place nearby . . ."

"I can't afford to live in Atlanta."

Cameron felt his eyes go as narrow and hard as his voice.

"That's one thing I intend to take care of for you. Mercator Ward has an obligation to his son's widow and his granddaughter's mother. Either he recognizes that after he and I talk about it, or I hire an attorney to explore what you should have inherited after Clarence's death. And while we're at it, we'll instruct the attorney to investigate if grandparents' rights supercede a parent's right. I doubt it. When Mr. Ward considers the extent of his possible legal difficulties, I suspect he'll provide an allowance generous enough that you can live wherever you damned well please—and do so in style."

A long sigh lifted her shoulders. "I'd love to stand on pride and say that I don't want Mr. Ward's money and wouldn't accept it." Her steady hazel eyes met his. "But the alternative is worse."

The alternative was that Cameron continued to send money each month for her support.

"Then we're agreed that I'll speak to Mr. Ward on this issue. Are we agreed that you'll send the Wards a note asking permission to call on them?"

Her shoulders stiffened. "It sticks in my throat that I have to ask their permission to see my daughter!"

"That's only the starting point, Della. And you aren't really asking to see Claire, you're requesting permission to call on the Wards to discuss Claire."

"At least we have a plan." She touched her forehead, and let her shoulders droop. "Oh, Cameron."

Fragile wasn't a description he would have applied to Della Ward. But at this moment he thought she might break and shatter if he said the wrong word.

The corners of her mouth trembled when she spoke again. "I have a strong feeling that everything should remain as it is now. That I should leave the real Claire with the Wards and be content with my imaginary Claire. By pursuing this, I feel like I may be opening a box that I don't want to see inside."

Cameron had gotten her to Atlanta, but he didn't feel he had a right to push further. "It's up to you," he said gruffly. "Stay, go . . . we'll do whatever you want."

Silently she moved to the window and stood looking outside for several minutes. "I don't know if it's wise to see her," she said finally. "I'll make that decision after speaking to the Wards. But I have to speak to them. You're right about that. I have to know that she's well and safe and happy." Nodding, she walked to the desk and removed a sheet of the hotel's stationery. "I'll write the request."

Cameron stood. "I'll make some preliminary inquiries about attorneys." He checked his pocket watch, then touched his tie and cleared his throat. "Shall we have supper together? Or does our truce only apply to the areas having to do with Claire?"

She tilted her head and considered, not answering immediately. "We could dine together," she said finally, sounding reluctant. "But make no mistake . . . you did me wrong and I can't forgive you."

"I understand." But his spirits soared.

She continued to stare at him. "I don't think we should tell the Wards exactly who you are. I'll just introduce you as a friend."

"That sounds like a wise decision."

"I hate to lie to them."

"I am your friend, Della."

She turned her back to him and leaned over the desk. "And, Cameron, if ever there was a whisky-drinking occasion, this is it. So pick a restaurant where it won't embarrass you when I have a whisky before supper and a liqueur afterward."

Mr. Ward's reply arrived as Della and Cameron were leaving her suite. Della accepted the envelope from the messenger, then pushed it into Cameron's hands. "You read it. I can't."

"Ward invites us for coffee at ten o'clock tomorrow morning." He glanced up at her. "You must have mentioned me."

"I did." A blush spread over her cheeks. "I mentioned

I was traveling with a family friend." She examined his
expression, then lifted her chin. "Well, in an odd way
you've been a friend to Clarence, too. You've supported
his wife when his own parents wouldn't. You're trying to
reunite his wife and daughter."

He had also killed Clarence and slept with Clarence's
wife, but Della didn't let herself think about that right
now. Gradually she was reaching an accommodation in
her mind. There was the Cameron who had committed
unforgivable acts. And there was the Cameron who had
let her get close, and whom she loved and missed. She
needed that Cameron now, needed his strength to lean
on, needed his clear head, needed his friendship.

Was she using him any less than he'd used her?

The question came back to her later that night as she
lay in the darkness, trying and failing to fall asleep. She
didn't know the answer.

But she did know that it was a blessing the suite did
not have a door that connected to Cameron's room. She
would have done the unthinkable and the unforgivable
by going to him tonight. Turning, she pushed her face
into the pillow and longed for him.

Chapter 20

"I attended a church social a few years ago and met a man there who had miraculously survived being caught in the midst of a cattle stampede." There was a chill in the air, or maybe she imagined it, but Della felt cold inside and out. "He said he felt the ground shake beneath his boots and heard the sounds of bawling and the animals' hooves long before he saw the cattle sweeping down on him." She looked out the carriage window at the homes of the Wards' neighbors. They were almost there. "I feel the ground shaking."

The carriage rolled to a stop before the stone walkway leading to the Wards' porch. "Are you afraid of seeing Claire? Or are you afraid of the Wards?" Cameron asked quietly.

Frowning, Della picked at the fingers of her gloves. "Mrs. Ward said awful things to me. When Clarence did come home, she tried to keep us apart. I know she complained about me in her letters to him. Sometimes Mr. Ward was sympathetic, but he'd shrug and say he had to live with her, so he didn't interfere in how she treated me. She opened and read my letters to Clarence, and she read his letters to me. Once she told me that my mother had sent me to stay with my cousin because my mother wanted to be rid of me so she could chase after men." Anger pulsed in the hollow of her throat. "She didn't even know my mother! Putting poisonous ideas in people's heads was her favorite amusement."

Drawing a deep breath, Della tamped down a burst of anger that felt as fresh as when she'd lived with the Wards. She hadn't expressed her resentment then. She hadn't stood up to her mother-in-law, had never raised her voice or responded rudely. She had wanted to, but from the day of her wedding, she had reminded herself that Enid Ward was her husband's mother. No matter how shrewish or hurtful she might be, she was also the woman who had raised the man that Della married. For that, she would respect Mrs. Ward and would always turn the other cheek.

But in doing so, she had made herself an easy victim and let herself be overpowered, overwhelmed, and ruthlessly bullied. She'd had no foundation of strength when the Wards stole Claire and forced Della to leave Atlanta.

"It's different now," Cameron said, his fingertips grazing her throat as he reached to tuck an errant strand of hair behind her ear. "You've grown up. You won't be manipulated or controlled."

"And I have you this time."

He nodded. "And you have me."

"Cameron?" She stared into his tanned face and piercing blue eyes and felt her heart turn over in her chest. From the moment she had first seen this man, she'd loved the lean, hard look of him. "Will it be awkward for you to meet the Wards?"

"Yes."

"Nothing is the way it's supposed to be, is it?" She was so glad he was here today, but she was supposed to hate him. And part of her did, she hastily reminded herself. If the Wards knew who Cameron was . . . Della pressed her lips together and shook her head. Sometimes the world was so confusing and unfair.

"Are you ready?"

"As ready as I'll ever be." Was anyone ever ready to walk into the unknown? Cameron jumped out of the carriage, put down the step, then handed her to the ground. She straightened the skirt and jacket of her traveling suit, recalling Mrs. Ward's interest in fashion. A decade had elapsed since Della had cared about fashion.

Frowning, her gaze on the house, she squared her shoulders and lifted her head. The Wards must have sent Claire away for the day. If Claire had been in the house, Della was positive that she would have sensed her daughter's presence.

Cameron extended his arm. Della hesitated, then wrapped her hand around his sleeve. She made herself place one foot in front of the other and then do it again, kicking at the hem of her skirt as if she were angry.

"They can't keep me away from my daughter," she said, sending Cameron a flashing glance and hoping bravado would squash a rising tide of apprehension and dread. "If I decide to see and talk to Claire, they can't stop me."

Cameron pressed her hand. "I have the name of an attorney. If necessary, we can go from here to his office."

After Cameron lifted a heavy brass knocker, Della narrowed her eyes. "I detest these people for taking my baby. They are not going to shove me aside again!"

The same dark woman who had swept the porch yesterday opened the door and studied Della with a curious glance. "The mister's expectin' ya'll. Come on inside."

It was so quiet in the foyer that Della heard her pulse thudding in her ears. She was unable to concentrate on anything but holding herself together; however, she caught a dim impression of expensive wall coverings and wood floors and bannisters polished to a high gloss.

The woman smoothed a spotless white apron, then led them down a wide corridor to the double doors of a parlor stuffed with chairs, settees, a dozen little tables, and every surface draped with something gauzy or fringed.

Della's gaze was drawn to the fire, and she didn't immediately see Mercator Ward sitting before the warmth in a high-winged chair. She jumped when he spoke.

"I apologize for not risin'." He gestured to a foot propped on a padded footstool. "A touch of the gout. Comes on me every year 'bout this time."

Shock dried Della's mouth. She would not have recognized this frail old man draped in an afghan that Mrs. Ward had made when Clarence was a boy. His hair had thinned and turned completely white. And while he was meticulously dressed, his clothing had been tailored for a man fifty pounds heavier and now hung on his sunken frame.

Della drew a breath and wet her lips. "Father Ward, this is James Cameron. Mr. Cameron was kind enough to escort me from Texas to Atlanta."

Cameron leaned to clasp Ward's hand and stared into his eyes. "I'm seeing to Mrs. Ward's interests. In that regard, there are some issues that you and I need to discuss. If tomorrow is convenient?"

"Well now, I can't think what we'd have to discuss, sir, but this visit is mighty puzzlin' to begin with. If you want to come again tomorrow to talk issues, I reckon we can do that. I sure never thought to see you again," he said to Della. "Sit down, sit down. Manda? I know you're out there in the hallway. Bring the coffee cart."

Della wondered if Mrs. Ward was also lurking in the hallway. She placed a hand over her heart and gave herself a moment to settle into the chair and will her racing pulse to slow.

"Will Mrs. Ward be joining us?" She ground her teeth together and told herself that she would stay in her chair and would not run out of the parlor.

Mr. Ward looked at her with an expression so like Clarence that she stared, then lowered her head and clasped her hands in her lap. How could she have forgotten that Clarence had a cleft in his chin?

"I guess you didn't hear. Mrs. Ward passed on about eight years ago." He tented his fingers beneath his chin and studied Della. "She was never right after the war. The war was hard on women. They gave their brothers and husbands and children. Gave their jewelry, money, heirlooms. Gave their homes. It was more than some could bear. The doctor said it was Mrs. Ward's heart that killed her, but it was the war."

If Della said the usual thing, that she was sorry, Mr. Ward would recognize the lie and the hypocrisy. She said the only truthful thing she could. "I'm sure you miss her."

"That's a fact."

Manda wheeled a cart into the parlor and positioned it before Della. She waited for Della's nod before she glanced at Mr. Ward, then withdrew.

The heavy silver coffee service had been sold during the early days of the war. This pot was painted china that matched the cups and the plates for raisin buns or triangles of toast and marmalade. Della couldn't have swallowed a bite. The coffee was difficult enough. She served the men, then took a sip from her saucer and set it aside.

Every now and then, she raised her eyes to the ceiling, listening for sounds from above. And she had covertly examined the parlor, searching for signs of a young lady.

"Well," Mr. Ward said after remarking on the chill in the air, "you said you came from Texas to Georgia. Is that where you live? Texas?"

"I live on the farm you gave me," she said, her tone cool.

"Is that right? I sure never figured you'd want to live there."

"What did you think I'd do?"

"Why, sell the place, of course. I figured you'd sell and then head for the nearest big city. Frankly, it's a puzzle that you didn't remarry, a handsome woman like you. I told Mrs. Ward, I said you'd be married within a year of leavin' here." He slid Cameron a long glance of speculation. "I bought that farm sight unseen. Never saw it myself."

"It's in damned sorry shape," Cameron commented, his tone suggesting that Ward was to blame.

Mr. Ward narrowed his eyes and gazed back and forth between them. "Why did you come here, Della?"

"She's here about Claire," Cameron said when Della couldn't speak.

Della's heart hammered against her ribs. A ringing began in her ears and got louder. The storm rushed forward and caught her up, thundering, flashing, howling in her mind. She thought her body was going to explode.

"Who?" Ward gripped his coffee cup and frowned.

"Claire . . . Della and your son's daughter."

Eyes fixed on Ward's dawning understanding, Della stood on shaking legs. She felt the blood drain from her face and she swayed on her feet. She shook her head and stepped backward. "No," she whispered. "No, don't say it."

"Claire died years ago," Mercator Ward said, looking surprised. "Don't you remember? She was just a bitty thing. Couldn't have been more than a week or two old."

"Oh God." She couldn't breathe, couldn't see. The room spun around her, picking up speed. She sank to the floor on her knees.

Ward raised an eyebrow at Cameron, then peered down at her. "Surely you remember. We followed the hearse to the old cemetery and buried the baby next to Clarence."

"No." Tears scalded her cheeks, choked her. The hearse. It was Claire's hearse she followed in the dream. Now she remembered the tiny white casket beyond the gold vines etched on the windows. "No, no, no, no, no." There was nothing more soul searing, nothing more brutally devastating than a tiny white casket.

"Please, please no." Pressing her hands against her empty belly, she doubled over until her forehead almost touched the wood floor. "My baby! My baby!"

Strong hands lifted her and held her. She gripped Cameron's lapels and looked up at him through streaming eyes. "My baby is dead! She died! Oh, Cameron. Help me. My baby died!"

"Lord a'mighty, girl. It was a long time ago. Is she touched in the head, Mr. Cameron?"

Even now her mind threw up a wall of resistence, not wanting to accept the unthinkable. Leaning past Cameron's shoulder, Della whispered in a harsh voice, "She's not dead. You've hidden her, haven't you?" She started to turn with the intention of running up to the second story. She had seen the curtains move yesterday. Claire was upstairs.

"Della." Cameron's large hands held her immobile. In his eyes she read sadness and pity, and her head jerked backward. More than anything else, his expression shocked her into facing what she had refused to see for ten years and didn't want to see now.

Her fingers dug into his sleeves. "I don't want it to be true."

"I know." His hands slid up her arms then framed her face. "I know."

"As long as Claire is alive, then I have a reason to be alive." She was empty, hollow inside. There was no substance to hold her upright. Her knees collapsed and she sagged against Cameron's chest.

He lifted her in his arms and carried her out of Mercator Ward's house.

It was only noon—too early for liquor, but Cameron ordered a bottle of whisky sent up to the suite. "Here. Sip this."

"I can't stop crying." But she sipped the whisky, then wiped a hand across her eyes and rested her head on the back of the sofa. "How could a mother *forget* that her baby died? How is that possible?"

Cameron sat beside her and pressed his handkerchief into her hand. There was nothing he could say, no words that could possibly comfort her or ease her pain. All he could do was be there and listen.

"I never doubted that she was alive. And while Claire was alive, I had someone to love even though she wasn't with me." Tears streamed down her cheeks. "So I pretended she was there on the farm. But I knew—damn it, I absolutely *knew* she was with the Wards. They stole her from me, but she was growing up happy and well cared for. I knew this beyond a shadow of a doubt. It was true!" She took another long swallow of whisky. "Except it wasn't true. Am I crazy, Cameron?"

"Maybe. In this one area."

"The truly crazy part is that the Wards said and did hurtful things, but the one thing I most blamed them and hated them for, they didn't do." Bitterness roughened her voice. "With every fiber of my being, I believed they stole Claire. I believed she was here, in Atlanta with the Wards. I believed it!"

She bent forward and mopped her eyes. "I'm sorry. I just can't stop crying. I keep thinking I've used up all my tears, but today the supply seems to be endless." She covered her face and her shoulders shook. "It's like losing her all over again. I've lost her twice."

Nothing made a man feel more helpless than a woman's tears. And particularly in this case. Della wept for the child she'd had with a man that Cameron had killed. After several minutes, he stood and walked out on the suite's terrace. A light haze hung over the Blue Ridge

Mountains reminding him of a time he didn't want to remember. After lighting a cigar, he watched a column of steam moving away from the train station. Before the war, Atlanta had been a railroad town. At least half a dozen lines had converged here. He didn't know if that was still true.

It was time to consider what came next.

When he looked at Della, he saw a soldier he'd killed, the last in a long line of good men. When she looked at him, Della saw the loss of everything she had loved and valued. Maybe now that she'd been forced to face and accept Claire's death, she could begin to recover and put the past behind her. But only if he walked away.

There was no reason for them to remain together. He could leave her enough money to go back to Texas if that's what she wanted to do. And he'd speak to Mercator Ward about providing her a stipend and an inheritance. And then . . .

She'd taken off her shoes, so he didn't hear her cross the terrace in her stockinged feet, didn't realize she was behind him until she slipped her arms around his waist and laid her head against his shoulder blades.

"Oh, James." Her voice was so low and anguished that he could hardly hear her. "My baby girl is dead. And it hurts so bad."

Now, finally, he was free to hold her and comfort her. Turning, he gathered her into his arms and placed his chin on top of her head. She fit in his arms like she'd been made to go there.

"Tell me how I can best help you," he said gruffly.

"Take me to bed and just hold me," she whispered after a minute. "Let me cry myself to sleep. I don't think I've slept in a week."

In the bedroom, he pulled the draperies shut, kicked off his boots, mounded the pillows against the headboard, then laid down and opened his arms. She hesitated, giving him a long, measuring look, then raised her skirt and placed her knee on the bed. In a moment, she'd stretched out beside him and nestled her head on his shoulder. He closed his arms around her.

She pressed her hand flat on his chest, then absently tugged at a button. "I said I believed Claire was with the Wards. But that can't be entirely true. I've had the dream for years, about following the hearse . . . and it was always hers, not Clarence's as I told myself it was. And there was the feeling of dread, of not wanting to know or to change anything."

The warmth of her ran down his right side. He stroked her arm and tried to rise above thinking about the soft fullness of her breasts pressed against the side of his chest. Today she'd worn her hair twisted into a bun on top of her head, and he could smell the scent of the lemon and vinegar that she used to rinse away any traces of shampoo. When she spoke, he caught a faint whiff of whisky.

It made him feel good to know that she mixed lemon and vinegar to rinse her hair, and that, unlike most women, she enjoyed a glass of whisky. He'd seen her small clothes hanging to dry on prairie bushes and knew her shimmies and petticoats and pantaloons were plain with only a narrow band of inexpensive lace trimming the hems. He'd tasted her cooking and ranked her biscuits among the best. He had seen her iron and he had heard her whistle. He'd watched her laugh with joy and weep in pain.

He would love her until the day he died. There could never be another woman for him.

He blinked and looked down at the top of her head. While he'd been indulging in reverie, Della had unbuttoned his shirt and slipped her hand inside. He felt her fingers on his skin. Instantly his chest and belly tightened into ridges of muscle.

She noticed. "James?" Her voice was a husky whisper. "I've been thinking . . ."

"Yes?" The word came out as a groan because her fingers had slid to his waist.

"I can't hate you any more for using me twice than for using me once."

Rising above her, he looked down into her damp hazel eyes. This close, he noticed green and gold flecks. "Are you sure?"

"Our truce is almost over." Her gaze dropped to his lips and his mouth suddenly dried. "We need to talk soon. But not now."

He reached for the small buttons running down her bodice then hesitated. "Della, this feels like taking advantage."

"If so, it's me taking advantage of you." She brushed his hand aside and opened the buttons herself. "I want the pain to go away for a while. I don't want to think about the past or the future. I just want to lose myself in the here and now, and I want you to help me do it."

Her bodice opened to the sight of soft mounded breasts, and Cameron's questions vanished along with any thought of hesitation. He took his time undressing her, not hurrying, learning the sight and touch and taste of her, kissing the various parts of her as he revealed them.

He kissed her shoulders and arms as he drew off her jacket, returned to her lips then ran his tongue down her throat to the deep cleft between her breasts. Here he encountered the powdery fragrance of rose water beneath the warm mix of musk and apple that was the scent of her skin.

Next, he removed her skirt and petticoats, then paused to admire the hourglass shape of her. Most women didn't like corsets, but Cameron appreciated the way a corset defined a woman's form, accenting breasts and hips. As this corset laced up the front, she faced him while he opened the laces, and she tugged at his shirt while he kissed the tops of her breasts, then the sides, and after he dropped the corset off the edge of the bed, he devoted himself to teasing her nipples into hard pink buds.

After pulling her to the side of the bed, he kicked off his trousers, then knelt on the floor, placed her foot on his naked thigh, then drew her garters off. He ran his hands up her leg, shaping the contours of ankle, calf, thigh beneath his palms, then teasing his fingers inside the top of her stockings. His mouth found the bare skin above her stockings and he licked the inside of her thighs as he rolled the stocking down on one leg and then the other.

"James." Reaching with suddenly urgent fingers, she drew him back to the bed and pressed him on his back. "It's my turn," she whispered against his lips. "I'm new at this . . ."

He'd made love to women, but being made love to was a new experience, and one he wasn't entirely comfortable with. It was difficult as hell to lay quietly while she slid down his body trailing hot kisses over his nakedness and doing things with her hands and fingers that made him feel crazy inside. The pins had come out of her hair, and a dark cloud of silken tresses spilled over his chest and belly.

When he felt her fingernails inside his thighs, he groaned her name. "Don't . . ."

"I want to."

The heat of her mouth on him was electric and more arousing than anything he could have imagined. He thought the top of his head would fly off if he couldn't have her beneath him now, now.

Pulling her up to him, he rolled her onto her back and rose above her, staring down into her radiant eyes and parted lips. He wanted to remember this moment always. Her hair wild on the pillow, her eyes shining with desire. He wanted the taste of her sweat on his lips, and the scent of their lovemaking permeating every breath.

"Della." He entered her gently, almost reverently.

He'd never had trouble arguing the law or debating issues or principles. But Cameron had never been a man to discuss feelings easily. Yet here, in bed, with no barrier between them, he could let his body speak to her of love and admiration and desire. His tenderness could share her loss. His caresses could comfort. And when their passion transcended gentleness and spiraled into the wild urgency of crescendo, he took what she offered and gave himself entirely.

After she had caught her breath, she leaned over him and kissed him, lingeringly and sweetly. "I can sleep now." Then she stretched out beside him and, in minutes, fell asleep.

Cameron woke her at seven for a supper he'd ordered delivered to the suite. Then he tucked her back into bed and lay beside her, smoking in the darkness, listening to her breathe, and thinking about the future.

She had said their truce would end soon. The message couldn't have been clearer.

Chapter 21

"I won't be long," Della said after the hired driver handed her out of the carriage. She spoke to Cameron through the window. "Perhaps twenty minutes."

He wore that hard-eyed, tight-lipped expression that made her think he'd have something to say if he were the type of man to speak of emotions.

"I'll be fine. Don't worry about me." Bending her head, she inhaled the fragrance of the flowers filling her arms.

"Do you know where to find the Wards' plot?"

She could have found it blindfolded. After reassuring him, she stepped away from the dust thrown up by the carriage wheels, turning toward an arched gate forged of scrolled wrought iron. For the third time she walked beneath the arch and onto the parklike grounds of the old Marshall Cemetery.

If this had been her first visit, Della might easily have gotten lost. Narrow, graveled roads meandered in all directions, curving through stands of tall pines or dividing acres of carved stones. In some places, hedges of winterbare lilac or verbena defined private areas; in other sections, low stone walls set off family plots.

Della turned right—by the tall, winged angel—and climbed a hill, passing beneath the branches of several thick old oaks, until she reached a stone bench protected from the chilly breeze by a stand of leafy azaleas. The bench faced a plot delineated by white stones forming a square around a handsome granite stone with the name Ward raised in the center.

Slowly Della walked around the square plot, examining the markers for Mr. Ward's parents and grandparents, reading the names of ancestors and Ward relatives. Eventually she came to a stone for Mercator Ward. His name and date of birth were already carved. There was even a Bible verse inscribed on the stone. Everything but the date of death. Beside his stone was that of Enid Ward. Beloved wife and mother. She'd been fifty-eight when she died.

Della stood before Mrs. Ward's grave for several minutes, not wanting to look at the next two gravestones.

First, she let herself notice the grass on the adjacent plots. Mr. Ward must have paid someone to maintain the family plot, as the grass was clipped close for the winter months and there were no weeds. A fresh coat of whitewash brightened the perimeter stones.

Finally she made herself read Clarence's stone; his name, his dates of birth and death, and a listing of his rank, the two medals he had been awarded, and the battle in which he died.

And then. Claire's small marker was embraced by a stone angel. She had lived eight days. The verse was simple. Now I lay me down to sleep, I pray the Lord my soul to keep . . .

Standing very tall and stiffly erect, Della blinked at the

heat behind her eyes. Then she divided her flowers and placed half at the base of Claire's stone and half at the base of Clarence's stone.

"Damn it." She could see Mrs. Ward's grave from the side of her eye. "Damn, damn!" Knowing she would feel small and mean spirited if she didn't do it, she took a few flowers from Claire and Clarence and placed them on Mrs. Ward's grave. She glared at the stone. "These flowers are not because you were a nice person, Enid Ward. You're getting them because I am a nice person."

For a long time, she stood looking at Claire and Clarence's markers and thinking about a life and family that was never meant to be. At length, she removed a spoon from her wrist bag. She'd taken it from the hotel. The soil was rich and loamy at the base of Clarence's headstone, and it was easy to dig a hole with the spoon. When the hole was deep enough, she rolled two letters and a photograph into a tube and pushed it into the hole before she replaced the dirt. Then she blinked hard and sat on the white stones at the foot of Clarence's grave. Della closed her eyes and lifted her face to the thin morning sunlight.

"I have to believe that you knew I didn't hate you. You had to know that," she said softly. "And I understand that you were hurt and angry and exhausted when you sat down to answer my last letter." She spoke to his stone, feeling the anger and guilt leave her. Letting it go. "If you had finished writing your letter, and then posted it, I think you would have regretted that letter as much as I regretted my last letter to you. If you had lived, Clarence, I believe you would have forgiven a young wife's self-pity and foolishness."

She heard Cameron's boots crunching the gravel as he walked up the hill, and she stood. "You were a good man, Clarence Ward. I'm glad I knew you for a little while."

She saw Cameron's hat first, then his face; and then his full, tall frame came into view, and she was surprised to see that he carried flowers. When he reached her, he removed his hat and held it against his chest, then he stepped forward and placed the flowers on Clarence's grave.

"Oh, James," Della whispered, taking his hands in hers. Suddenly she understood. "I've been so blind. You've been searching for the same thing I needed." She drew a breath and let it go. "I forgive you, James Cameron," she said softly, looking into his eyes. "You were doing your duty in a war that no one wanted. And so was Clarence. I forgive you."

"Christ." He grabbed her in his arms and buried his face in her hair, knocking her hat askew. "I've waited . . . and I didn't even know . . ."

When she sensed he wouldn't mind if she saw his eyes, Della pulled back and placed her hand on his cheek. "Can you forgive yourself?"

"Can you?" His hands tightened on her waist.

"I never thought I could . . . but yes. The war is over, James. It's finally over for us." They held each other, then she turned to the gravestones and the bright flowers beneath them. "It's time to say good-bye," she whispered. "I loved you both. I always will. But it's time to let go and say good-bye."

She let her gaze stray to Enid Ward's grave, then drew a deep breath and silently said what needed to be said.

"I'll never forget what you did and said. But I forgive you."

Before the hill blocked her view, she turned back for one last look, then she took Cameron's arm, and turned her gaze forward.

There was nothing further to hold them in Atlanta. Della persuaded Cameron to cancel his appointment with Mercator Ward, and they dashed to the station to catch the afternoon train bound for St. Louis.

"Ward owes you, Della," Cameron said when they were seated in the last row of seats in the last passenger car. "Plus, you're the only family he has left."

"You didn't see a stone waiting for me in the family plot," Della said wryly. They had brought their own box lunch from the hotel, and she peeked inside. Very nice. "I don't want his money."

Cameron didn't say anything, but she could see that he was considering her circumstances, wondering what she was thinking.

"That was interesting what Mr. Ward said about expecting me to sell the farm. Selling never occurred to me. I guess because I'm not a businesswoman, or maybe because I wasn't old enough or brave enough to think about starting a new life in a city. I should have. There would have been jobs in a city that didn't require wearing a skimpy costume."

"Are you thinking about selling now?"

She opened the box lunch again and slid him a thoughtful look. "I'm developing a plan."

"Would you like to tell me about it?"

"Actually, I would."

"Well . . ." he prompted after a minute.

She passed him a hard-boiled egg and a napkin. "I'm not ready yet. I have to decide just how selfish I can be and live with it. And there's something else I need to be sure about before I settle on a definite plan. I hope to have everything settled in my mind by the time we reach Santa Fe. How long do you think that will take?"

"Ten or eleven days."

"Good." She knocked her egg against the bench seat, then began to peel the shell into her napkin. "I imagine you'll start wearing your gun again when we reach St. Louis."

"More likely a day or so before."

Della nodded soberly. She had come to terms with James Cameron being the Yankee who had shot and killed her husband. And when she had watched him place his hat over his heart, then lay his flowers on Clarence's grave, she'd known she couldn't hate him. And she had found it in herself to forgive his deception.

But there were other obstacles between them.

Those problems began to surface the first day out of St. Louis. The train stopped around noon for a mail and freight pick up in a small town about fifty miles west of St. Louis. When Della suggested they use the occasion to stretch their legs and get some fresh air, Cameron followed her outside to the platform.

"There's such a difference in the weather between Georgia and Missouri," she said, adjusting a thick shawl around the shoulders of her traveling suit. "Do you think it's going to snow?"

"Looks like it could," Cameron answered, but he didn't

glance at the sky. The moment they stepped outside, he'd scanned the people on the platform, his gaze coming to rest on a man standing near the station house door.

The man studied Cameron with a slightly puzzled expression, as if trying to place why Cameron looked familiar. Eventually he would remember that Cameron had been the sheriff who arrested him for shooting up a saloon when Cameron had worn a badge for Ponca City, Oklahoma. The man had spent six days in jail and been ordered to pay the damages. It was a small item in Cameron's memory. Maybe not so insignificant for the man standing in the doorway. Cameron could recall the incident but not the man's name.

He touched the gun on his hip, glad that he'd changed out of his Eastern clothes in St. Louis. Carrying a weapon in his jacket or boot wasn't comfortable or efficient.

Della smiled expectantly, and Cameron realized she'd asked a question. "I'm sorry, what did you say?"

"I suggested we go inside and buy some fresh coffee. Can you smell it? The woman in the brown hat says there's a cart inside and the vendor brewed new coffee only an hour ago."

He considered passing the man standing in the station house doorway and all the possibilities for trouble. An accidental bump. The wrong expression. A misunderstood word. Cameron had seen it dozens of times—a hothead looking for a reason. There were too many bystanders on the platform to risk giving the man in the doorway a reason.

"You go ahead," he said to Della. "I'll stay here and have a cigar."

"You are passing up a cup of coffee? You?" She arched an eyebrow. "You can smoke inside."

"I know. But the air feels good."

She shrugged and went into the station house, passing the man in the doorway without a glance.

And in that moment, James Cameron knew he was finished as a bounty hunter and a gunfighter.

For the first time since he'd come west, he had stepped away from the possibility of a challenge. He'd spotted trouble and evaded instead of confronting it.

For the first time in more than a decade, he cared about dying. The realization shocked the hell out of him.

He loved a woman and, sooner or later, loving her was going to get him killed.

A man who didn't care if he lived or died always had the advantage. The man who cared was too careful, too slow. He hesitated. For one critical instant the man who cared thought about dying and those whom he'd never see again.

He brooded over his discovery as the train rolled across Kansas and then slowed as the rails rose toward the mountains. The man in the station house doorway had not boarded the train. He must have been seeing someone off. But others recognized him in the following days. Fortunately they were men looking for a hand-shake instead of trouble. But as sure as he was back in legend territory, trouble would come.

"You've been as quiet as a brick," Della said, lowering a newspaper to her lap. The potbellied stove behind them wasn't working and thin ice glazed the inside of the window. She was wrapped in a shawl and had dug out her heavy riding gloves to keep her fingers warm.

"I've been thinking about things." One of the things he'd thought about was missing her every night when she went to the ladies' sleeping car and he headed in the opposite direction to the gentlemens' sleeping car.

"What are you going to do, Cameron?"

"Do about what?"

"The conductor says we'll reach the terminus tomorrow. Then we'll take the stagecoach into Santa Fe. It will be supper time when we reach town, so we'll stay at a hotel." She looked down at her lap and a light blush flared on her cheeks. "The next day you'll find the man you mentioned and hire him to take me back to Two Creeks." She stared up at him. "And then, what will you do? What's next for James Cameron?"

He loved the sound of his name on her lips, but she only called him James in moments of high emotion.

"That's one of the items I'm considering. I'm wondering if prosecuting outlaws would be as satisfactory as catching them."

Her eyebrows soared in surprise. "You could walk away from bounty hunting and wearing a sheriff's badge?"

"It's just a thought." He narrowed his eyes, wondering if she had any idea that she had changed his life. "Hunting criminals and bringing them in to face justice has been my life for too long to stop entirely. But there are other ways to accomplish the same thing."

The trip to Atlanta, and everything that had happened there, had ended the war for Della. During the long days on the train, she had shared memories, speaking carefully and deliberately, testing to make certain the memories were real. She spoke calmly, sometimes fondly, sometimes with great sadness, but Cameron understood she was taking one last look at the past before she put it behind her forever.

He couldn't do that. Della's forgiveness had laid Clarence Ward's ghost to rest, and Cameron loved her for that and was grateful. He would not dream again of that day in the ditch when Clarence had appeared above him. Clarence's face and Clarence's death would not haunt him in the future. But there were dozens of other men in gray. Those good men who needed the score balanced.

That had not changed and never would. He would continue trying to even the score for the rest of his life. The question had become how to do it, now that it was too dangerous and too foolish to use his guns.

His father, the judge, would have been pleased to know the direction his thoughts were taking him. He wondered suddenly if Della was pleased.

"Do you still hate me?" he asked. By all rights she should. He had no argument to persuade her differently. But sometimes he thought about that moment in a St. Louis park when she'd admitted that she had been falling in love with him.

She didn't immediately answer. First, she folded the newspaper she'd been reading and tucked it away, then she turned her face to the icy window. Darkness was falling beyond the pane.

"No," she said so softly that he had to bend close to hear.

Relief and elation rushed through his body, then he caught himself. Not hating him wasn't the same as loving him.

As if she'd read his mind, the uncanny way she did

sometimes, she let her shoulder rest against his and said, "We have some things to talk about, James."

When she called him by name, a hot, liquid feeling spilled through his insides. But so far the only times she called him James were when she was nervous or about to make love. He didn't know what it meant that she'd called him James now.

"I suspect that conversation requires privacy," he said, glancing at the heads of passengers in the seats in front of them. "We'll talk over supper tomorrow night in Santa Fe."

"We could talk then." She kept her face turned toward the dark window. "Or . . . are you planning to rent a hotel suite?"

"I am."

She nodded. "I thought we could have supper, then order some whisky sent to the suite afterward. I'm thinking tomorrow night is definitely going to be a whisky-drinking occasion."

That could be good or bad. Usually it was bad. At least difficult.

He didn't sleep well in the narrow, short train berth. At four-thirty in the morning, he gave up, got dressed, and returned to the passenger car. He lit a cigar, put one boot up on the back of the seat in front of him, then scraped the ice off the window so he could see the stars winking in the cold morning blackness.

By now he knew better than to believe he could guess what she was thinking. But he had some thoughts of his own to talk about. Della Ward was not going back to Two Creeks, Texas. Not if he had anything to say about it. That's what he needed to find out. If he had anything to say about it.

Della took his arm as they came out of the restaurant and crossed Plaza Square. "I wasted a lot of food and your money," she said, tilting her head to look at the sky. It was a cold, dry night, spangled by a million stars. "I'd forgotten what an ordeal riding a stage is. My stomach is still rattling around."

"Are you tired?"

"It's been a long day." And she'd forgotten how nerve-racking it was to be in town with Cameron. Every diner in the restaurant might have been a shooter. Every shadow on the street could signal an ambush. Cameron's gaze constantly scanned his surroundings, and Della felt the tension in his muscles when she brushed against his body. This was no way to live.

"I'd suggest that we postpone any serious talk, but I think it has to be done now."

She nodded. Neither had wanted to talk about personal issues on the train within hearing of others. Consequently they had delayed addressing questions that now required immediate attention.

Once in the suite, Della hung up their jackets and hats and smoothed her hair while Cameron lit the lamps and poured them each a glass of good whisky. He put the bottle on the dining table and pulled out two chairs. That was where Della would also have chosen to talk. Many a problem had been thrashed out over a kitchen table. This wasn't a kitchen table, but it was close.

They sat down and silently studied each other. Lord, how she loved the look of this man. He seemed tall even when he was sitting. She liked the intense blue of his eyes and the way his brows slashed across his forehead. The straight, square set of his shoulders gave her that smoky feeling inside. And the way he held his mouth, with just a glimpse of white teeth showing.

He touched his glass to hers. "I know you have things to say. I have some things to say, too."

That was a bit of a surprise. "You can talk first, if you want." Suddenly, she was shy and unsure of the short speech she had rehearsed in her mind. If she had misunderstood what he'd said in the park in St. Louis, then she was about to make an enormous fool of herself.

"No, you go ahead. Ladies first."

"Really. I'd rather you spoke first."

They smiled, then both spoke at the same instant.

"I'm sorry, James, but you have to hang up your guns."

"I don't want you going back to Two Creeks, Texas."

They took a swallow of whisky, watching each other over the glass rims. Della let the heat of the whisky burn down the back of her throat and then she smiled. There were things to work out, but it was going to be all right. James knew it, too. He was giving her that half smile of speculation that made her knees go weak and turned her stomach to mush.

He stood up and started to slowly unbutton his waistcoat and shirt; his eyes narrowed down on her mouth. "I know if I'm going to have you, I have to put down my guns. I already figured that out. And if I don't, I'm going to get myself killed."

"We have to talk about that. If I'm staying with you, James, I can't be worrying that you're going to be shot dead every time you walk out the door." She tossed down the remainder of her whisky, then stood and put a foot on her chair. After unbuttoning her shoes, she kicked them off, then raised her skirt to her thigh and rolled down her garter. "I don't want to bury another husband."

"You're okay with . . . what happened in the past, and how we met?" He stared at her thigh, running his gaze up as high as he could then down to her ankle. He tossed his shirt and waistcoat aside and threw off his belt before he sat down to pull at his boots.

He meant Clarence. "I wish that part of you and me was different. I'll always be confused about that day. It was the worst day and the best day, because it brought you to me. But Cameron? It's finished. There's no need to ever talk about it again." She stepped out of her skirt, letting it puddle around her bare feet, then she tossed her shirtwaist over her shoulder and pulled open the laces on her corset, loving the intent look on his face as he watched her breasts spill out.

He stood again, then frowned with his fingers frozen on the waist of his trousers. "A minute ago . . . did you say husband?"

"I did. I'm imploring you to do the right thing by a poor widow whom you've taken sore advantage of, sir." He looked so horrified that she laughed. "That's a tease, James."

Stepping up to her, he took her by the waist and roughly pulled her against his body. He spoke, an inch from her lips. "You don't know the meaning of being taken advantage of."

She felt his heat flash through her, felt the hard thrust of his erection against her belly. Suddenly she was on fire and she couldn't breathe. "Show me," she whispered before his mouth crushed hers.

This was not gentle lovemaking. Tonight, neither of them wanted tenderness. They wanted heat and sweat and hard-punishing passion. He took her on the carpet, his kisses deep and demanding. At times Della rode him, at other moments she arched up to meet each hard thrust.

When they could take no more, could give no more, they sought release and then lay in each other's arms, panting and gasping. Della's mouth and breasts were swollen. Scratches covered Cameron's back. If she lived to be a hundred, Della would never forget tonight.

"You're right," she said drowsily when they'd donned dressing gowns and she was sitting on the sofa with her feet in his lap, drinking a fresh glass of whisky. "Now, *that* was being taken advantage of." She smiled at the surface of her glass. "You may have to show me again sometime."

Cameron laughed. "Do you know how beautiful you are? With your hair wild and fallen and your face glowing."

"I love you, James. Tell me you love me, too. I need to hear the words."

"I love you. I've loved you for ten years. I loved the fantasy of you. I love the reality of you." His voice sank to a gruff baritone. "I never once believed this could happen."

"You started thinking about hanging up your guns while we were on the train, didn't you?"

"Chasing across the West, searching for outlaws, is no life for a married man." A sudden grin lit his expression.

"My God. Me. Married." He poured more whisky into their glasses. "I'm thinking we should make our home in San Francisco. I doubt I'd experience any difficulty getting hired as a prosecutor. How does that sound to you?"

"From what I've heard about San Francisco, I think I'd like it there." She'd already decided to wire her banker in Two Creeks and instruct him to sell the farm. "I love you, James. I love you more than I have ever loved anyone or any thing." She even loved the possessive touch of his hand on her ankle. "I don't want to lose you. So, tell me this . . . will your fame follow us to San Francisco? Because it doesn't make sense for you to stop wearing your guns if all it means is that someone is going to shoot at you but you can't protect yourself."

"I don't want you to worry every time I leave our house."

Della nodded, examining his expression. "Do you think the legend and the fame will follow us?" she asked softly.

"I honestly don't know."

"That's not a comfortable way to live," she said uneasily. "It would always be there at the back of our minds. The worry that some idiot outlaw would track us to San Francisco and kill you so he could be the man who out-drew James Cameron."

"I've thought about that, too. I'm thinking about changing my name to Cameron James. But it isn't enough."

She smothered a yawn and decided the rest of her speech could wait another day or so. "Let's go to bed."

When she awoke near dawn, Cameron was propped against the pillows next to her. "Didn't you go to sleep?" Concerned, she sat up and peered at him in the pearly light.

"I know the answer," he said, taking her hand. "It will put an end to the damned legend, and no one will come looking for us."

"What's the answer?"

"I have to die."

Chapter 22

The arrangements were easier than Cameron had initially supposed. Sheriff Jed Rollins handled everything. Then it became a matter of waiting for the pieces to come together.

"We're ready," he said to Della after supper at what had become their favorite restaurant, The Brown Armadillo.

Startled, she put down her dessert spoon and glanced over her shoulder toward the door. "It won't happen in here, will it?"

"No."

"When?" Her eyes widened with fear.

"We decided it was better that you didn't know exactly when. Remember?"

Della wet her lips and lifted her chin. Candlelight glowed in her eyes, and he decided she had never looked lovelier.

"There's something I've been meaning to tell you since the first night we arrived in Santa Fe. I've been looking for the right moment. It sounds like I can't wait any longer."

"I think I know what you're going to say."

"You do?" Her eyebrows arched over sparkling eyes. "I doubt it."

"I'm guessing you wired your banker in Two Creeks and instructed him to sell your farm."

"That's true, I did. But that's not what I want to tell you." She waited, half smiling like she expected him to make another guess.

He hated this kind of thing. But he loved her. Reaching across the tablecloth, he took her hand and rubbed his thumb over the diamond ring he'd given her a couple of days ago. "You've made arrangements with a preacher? No, that couldn't be it. Not if you originally planned to tell me the night we arrived."

"And we decided to have the wedding in San Francisco." A charming pink tinted her cheeks at the mention of a wedding, and he wished they were alone so he could kiss her until they were both wild with wanting each other.

"I'm out of guesses," he said, signaling the waiter to bring their check.

"This isn't a good time to tell you this. But just in case things go terribly wrong and . . ." She wet her lips then reached across the table for his other hand. That surprised him. Ordinarily she would have pulled back as she didn't approve of public displays of affection any more than he did. He glanced up, scanned the restaurant, then clasped her hands and smiled at the light dancing in her eyes. She wore the eager expression of someone about to confide a secret that she wanted to share.

"James . . . I'm pregnant."

Shock narrowed his eyes. He felt paralyzed. He forgot to scan the restaurant for new arrivals, didn't notice the waiter place their check on the table. He almost forgot to breathe.

Laughing, she pulled her hands out of his grasp. "You're breaking my bones," she said, smiling and shaking her fingers.

"I don't know what to . . . are you sure?"

"I didn't want to tell you until I was absolutely certain." He must have looked as if he'd been struck by lightning, and that was exactly how he felt, because she gave him a tender smile and whispered, "Oh, James. I love you so much."

"But when . . . ?"

"The night I came to your room on our first trip through St. Louis."

"My God." He fell backward in his chair and stared at her across the candles. "You and me . . . we're going to have a baby."

Public displays be damned. Jumping to his feet, he moved around the table and pulled her to her feet and into his arms. Laughing and blushing, she smiled into his eyes, and he saw in her gaze everything he had ever dreamed of having. His hands slid up to gently frame her face. Her cheeks were as soft as rose petals against his palms.

"We're going to have a baby."

"Yes," she whispered. Then she put a hand on his chest. "People are staring."

"Let them, I don't give a damn. Della, good Lord. We're going to have a baby." It was miraculous. Unbelievable. The most astonishing and the most wonderful thing he had ever heard in his whole life. "Let's get out of here."

The instant they were outside and a few steps from the lights flanking the door of The Brown Armadillo, she came into his arms, warm and full bodied and fitting into him as if she were the missing piece that he had needed to be whole.

"I wanted you to know before—"

He cut off her words with a kiss that left them both breathing hard and staring at each other. Then he gripped her arms. "I love you, Della. Now and always."

"Why do you look so . . ." A gasp caught in her throat and her face paled. "Oh my God. James!"

"It's going to be all right." He tilted her face up to him. "I'm lucky, remember?"

"I love you. I love you, I love you, I love you."

A voice bellowed out of the darkness in the plaza. "James Cameron! Step away from that woman."

Another couple had emerged from The Brown Armadillo. Cameron hadn't noticed, but Luke Apple had. Luke chose his moment and stepped into the light near the restaurant door.

Della closed her eyes and he felt her shaking before he released her. She looked up at him, white-faced and eyes wide with love and fear. Then she moved backward toward the witnesses frozen near the restaurant door.

"I'm gonna kill you, James Cameron, gonna put you in a grave." Old Luke wore fresh-cleaned buckskins, and for once his hair didn't look matted and wild. "But you have to draw first."

Cameron had never drawn first, not once. But if Luke were to claim self-defense, Cameron had to be the first to fire.

"You think you can out-shoot me, old man?" He dropped his palm to the butt of his pistol.

"Oh yeah. Tonight your luck runs out."

However this ended, Cameron had wanted it to be Luke Apple who garnered the footnote in Western history.

From the corner of his eye, he saw Della standing under the light, wringing her hands. Her eyes seemed as big as saucers in her white face.

He had everything to live for. And that's why he hesitated to pull his gun. Luke Apple wouldn't hold back tonight any more than he had ever held back.

"Draw, Cameron! Let's get this over with once and for all."

He glanced at Della standing in the light, searing her image on his eyes, in his mind. Then he pulled his gun and fired.

Two bullets tore into his side. They felt like arrows dipped in lava. His pistol dropped from his fingers and he looked down at the wet stain growing on his jacket. The blood was already through his shirt and waistcoat and into his jacket. He was shot bad, then.

Yes. The light from the restaurant didn't seem as bright. And his knees were giving out; he was going to fall.

This is what it felt like to die, he thought, twisting as he fell so he could see her.

It seemed that he drifted on a warm gray sea for a very long time. Sometimes he was hungry, other times he felt a raging thirst, but mostly he was impatient, waiting for his father.

Eventually, without Cameron noticing how it happened, he was seated in a small boat, knee to knee with the judge.

"You're looking well, sir." This was true. His father appeared youthful and robust. "But you're late."

"Are you in a rush?" A smile curved his father's lips.

"Della's worrying." No one had ever been waiting for him before. He didn't want to prolong her anxiety. "I need to get back."

His father nodded the way he did in court, then he smiled again and patted Cameron on the knee. "I thought you might feel that way. Don't worry, son. This isn't your time."

Then he was floating again, and the boat moved away carrying his father into the mist hovering above the sea.

Every now and then he thought he heard her voice, believed he'd caught a glimpse of her. He tried to tell her not to worry, it wasn't his time. But he didn't know if he spoke aloud. And then one day he opened his eyes and she was real, standing beside his bed with a cool hand on his forehead.

"Della . . ."

"Oh, thank God!" Collapsing, she dropped to a chair and fell forward, pressing her forehead against the edge of the mattress. "Thank God." He reached to touch her hair, surprised to discover how weak he was. Raising his hand required more strength than he could summon. She sat up and wiped her eyes. "Rest. Don't try to talk, just rest. I think the worst is over now."

She fussed over him, wouldn't leave his bedside. She bathed him and fed him even when he insisted he could do it himself. She read to him, whistled tunes he liked, changed the dressings on his chest, and made him drink nasty-tasting tonics.

Finally she judged him fit enough to actually talk about something more important than the weather or his temperature.

"Your plan almost backfired," she said, turning back the sheet over his chest. "You damn near died. Doc Westwood gave you up for dead at least twice."

Moving gingerly, Cameron tested his body parts. He could raise his arms now. His chest ached still, but he was past the deep pain. "I would have sworn that Luke Apple wasn't any good with a gun. In all the time I've known him, I've never seen him use a gun. I did get him, didn't I?"

"You shot him in the fleshy part of the waist. The bullet went through. He was up and around before breakfast."

"Good."

Placing a hand on his forehead, she checked his temperature. "Luke came to your funeral. Caused a bit of a scandal, in fact. I had a word with him after the service. He said if you lived, I should thank you for giving him the credit for killing you. Said he hoped you lived and I should tell you that he'll miss you. At the time, I didn't know if you would live or not. He said he was proud that you trusted him with our secret."

"Quit fussing and sit next to me." She was beautiful today, wearing a plain everyday dress, her wonderful glossy hair wrapped in a bun on top of her head. "Did I have a nice funeral?"

"I thought so. The body the sheriff came up with looked enough like you that I almost fainted. Sheriff

Rollins started to tell me who he was, but I didn't want to know." She drew a breath. "There were lots of people."

"Now tell me about you. How are you feeling?"

"Tired." She slid down in bed beside him, rested her head on the pillow and gazed into his eyes. "As soon as you're able, we'll sneak out of town in a private stage. We'll go to Denver and catch a train to the coast from there."

He caught a loose tendril of her hair and rubbed it between his fingers. "I'm sorry we've had to delay the wedding."

She touched his lips. "It doesn't matter. Cameron? I love you. I thought I'd go insane when it looked like you might die. Don't you ever do this again, hear?"

He smiled, then kissed her palm and pressed her hand to his cheek. He'd never had anyone to love, had never had anyone who cared if he lived or died. Now this magnificent woman loved and wanted him, and there was a baby on the way. A baby who would be part of him and part of her. He had a family of his own, and a new life waiting in San Francisco.

He buried his face in her hair and blinked hard. "I love you, Della."

There were tears in the gunslinger's eyes.

Don't miss these marvelous novels
by Maggie Osborne

Three brides.
One groom.
The chase is on. . . .

I DO, I DO, I DO

A rich, proper spinster aching for a man's touch, Juliette March is an easy target for the seductive Jean Jacques Villette. When he disappears with her inheritance after their wedding, Juliette sets out to find the scoundrel. She never expects to meet Clara Klaus, who ran a boardinghouse until Jean Jacques swept her off her feet, then swept himself out of town.

While following the trail of their no-good husband, Clara and Juliette run into Zoe Wilder, another victim of the debonair Jean Jacques. Now Zoe's ready to put a bullet in his cheating heart. When these three vengeful ladies embark on a misbegotten quest to Alaska, things get downright dangerous—especially for the unsuspecting men they entice along the way.

Don't miss these marvelous novels
by Maggie Osborne

**Meet the irresistible Low Down,
who never had anything good happen to
her—until she asked for the one thing
that only a man could give her. . . .**

SILVER LINING

As scruffy and rootless as the other prospectors
searching for gold in the Rockies, Low Down
hadn't asked for anything in return for nursing
a raggedy bunch through the pox. But the men
insisted, so she spoke bluntly. A baby. Not a
husband, not a forced marriage, not the proud
man who drew the short straw and became
honor-bound to marry her and jilt his fiancée
back home. To be sure, Max McCord was easy
on the eyes, but he loved another woman and
dreamed of a different life. But they agreed to a
temporary marriage, never anticipating the havoc
good deeds gone awry would bring—or the
tempestuous love born of a strange twist of fate,
a gift they could share forever . . . if they dared
to risk their hearts.

*Subscribe to the new Pillow Talk
e-newsletter—and receive all these
fabulous online features directly in
your e-mail inbox:*

♥ Exclusive essays and other features by major romance
writers like Linda Howard, Kristin Hannah,
Julie Garwood, and Suzanne Brockmann

♥ Exciting behind-the-scenes news from
our romance editors

♥ Special offers, including contests to win signed
romance books and other prizes

♥ Author tour information, and monthly announce-
ments about the newest books on sale

♥ A Pillow Talk readers forum, featuring feedback
from romance fans...like you!

Two easy ways to subscribe:
Go to **www.ballantinebooks.com/PillowTalk**
or send a blank e-mail to
join-PillowTalk@list.randomhouse.com.

Pillow Talk—
the romance e-newsletter brought to you by
Ballantine Books